Popular Tales from the Norse

Sir George Webbe Dasent

Contents

POPULAR TALES
FROM THE NORSE

BY

Sir George Webbe Dasent

Notice to the Second Edition

The first edition of these Tales being exhausted, and a demand having arisen for a second, the Translator has thought it right to add thirteen tales, which complete the translation of Asbjoernsen and Moe's collection, and to strengthen the Introduction by working in some new matter, and by working out some points which were only slightly sketched in the first edition.

The favour with which the book was welcomed makes it almost a duty to say a word here on the many kind and able notices which have been written upon it. Duties are not always pleasant, but the fulfilment of this at least gives no pain; because, without one exception, every criticism which the Translator has seen has shown him that his prayer for 'gentle' readers has been fully heard. It will be forgiven him, he hopes, when he says that he has not seen good ground to change or even to modify any of the opinions as to the origin and diffusion of popular tales put forth in the first edition. Much indeed has been said by others *for* those views; what has been urged *against* them, with all kindness and good humour, in one or two cases, has not availed at all to weigh down mature convictions deliberately expressed after the studies of years, backed as they are by the researches and support of those who have given their lives to this branch of knowledge.

And now, before the Translator takes leave of his readers for the second time, he will follow the lead of the good godmother in one of these Tales, and forbid all good children to read the two which stand last in the book. There is this difference between him and the godmother. She found her foster-daughter out as soon as she came back. He will never know it, if any bad child has broken his behest. Still he hopes that all good children who read this book will bear in mind that there is just as much sin in breaking a commandment even though it be not found out, and so he bids them good-bye, and feels sure that no good child will dare to look into those two rooms. If, after this warning, they peep in, they may perhaps see something which will shock them.

'Why then print them at all?' some grown reader asks. Because this volume is meant for you as well as for children, and if you have gone ever so little into the world with open eyes, you must have seen, yes, every day, things much more shocking. Because there is nothing immoral in their spirit. Because they are intrinsically valuable, as illustrating manners and traditions, and so could not well be left out. Because they complete the number of the Norse originals, and leave none untranslated. And last, though not least, because the Translator hates family versions of anything, 'Family Bibles', 'Family Shakespeares'. Those who, with so large a choice of beauty before them, would pick out and gloat over this or that coarseness or freedom of expression, are like those who, in reading the Bible, should always turn to Leviticus, or those whose Shakespeare would open of itself at Pericles Prince of Tyre. Such readers the Translator does not wish to have.

Notice to the First Edition

These translations from the ***Norske Folkeeventyr***, collected with such freshness and faithfulness by MM. Asbjoernsen and Moe, have been made at various times and at long intervals during the last fifteen years; a fact which is mentioned only to account for any variations in style or tone--of which, however, the Translator is unconscious--that a critical eye may detect in this volume. One of them, ***The Master Thief***, has already appeared in Blackwood's Magazine for November 1851; from the columns of which periodical it is now re-printed, by the kind permission of the Proprietors.

The Translator is sorry that he has not been able to comply with the suggestion of some friends upon whose good-will he sets all store, who wished him to change and soften some features in these tales, which they thought likely to shock English feeling. He has, however, felt it to be out of his power to meet their wishes, for the merit of an undertaking of this kind rests entirely on its faithfulness and truth; and the man who, in such a work, wilfully changes or softens, is as guilty as he 'who puts bitter for sweet, and sweet for bitter'.

Of this guilt, at least, the Translator feels himself free; and, perhaps, if any, who may be inclined to be offended at first, will take the trouble to read the Introduction which precedes and explains the Tales, they may find, not only that the softening process would have spoilt these popular traditions for all except the most childish readers, but that the things which shocked them at the first blush, are, after all, not so very shocking.

For the rest, it ill becomes him to speak of the way in which his work has been done: but if the reader will only bear in mind that this, too, is an enchanted garden, in which whoever dares to pluck a flower, does it at the peril of his head; and if he will then read the book in a merciful and tender spirit, he will prove himself what the Translator most longs to find, 'a gentle reader', and both will part on the best terms.

INTRODUCTION

ORIGIN

The most careless reader can hardly fail to see that many of the Tales in this volume have the same groundwork as those with which he has been familiar from his earliest youth. They are Nursery Tales, in fact, of the days when there were tales in nurseries--old wives' fables, which have faded away before the light of gas and the power of steam. It is long, indeed, since English nurses told these tales to English children by force of memory and word of mouth. In a written shape, we have long had some of them, at least, in English versions of the *Contes de ma Mere l' Oye* of Perrault, and the *Contes de Fees* of Madame D'Aulnoy; those tight-laced, high- heeled tales of the 'teacup times' of Louis XIV and his successors, in which the popular tale appears to as much disadvantage as an artless country girl in the stifling atmosphere of a London theatre. From these foreign sources, after the voice of the English reciter was hushed--and it was hushed in England more than a century ago--our great-grandmothers learnt to tell of Cinderella and Beauty and the Beast, of Little Red Riding-hood and Blue Beard, mingled together in the *Cabinet des Fees* with Sinbad the Sailor and Aladdin's wondrous lamp; for that was an uncritical age, and its spirit breathed hot and cold, east and west, from all quarters of the globe at once, confusing the traditions and tales of all times and countries into one incongruous mass of fable, as much tangled and knotted as that famous pound of flax which the lassie in one of these Tales is expected to spin into an even wool within four-and-twenty hours. No poverty of invention or want of power on the part of translators could entirely destroy the innate beauty of those popular traditions; but here, in England at least, they had almost dwindled out, or at any rate had been lost sight of as home-growths. We had learnt to buy our own children back, disguised in foreign garb; and as for their being anything more than the mere pastime of an idle hour--as to their having any history or science of their own--such an absurdity was never once thought of. It had, indeed, been remarked, even in the eighteenth century--that dreary time of indifference and doubt--that some of the popular traditions of the nations north of the Alps contained striking resemblances and parallels to stories in the classical mythology. But those were the days when Greek and Latin lorded it over the other languages of the earth; and when any such resemblance or analogy was observed, it was commonly supposed that that base-born slave, the vulgar tongue, had dared to make a clumsy copy of something peculiarly belonging to the twin tyrants who ruled all the dialects of the world with a pedant's rod.

At last, just at the close of that great war which Western Europe waged against the genius and fortune of the first Napoleon; just as the eagle--Prometheus and the eagle in one shape--was fast fettered by sheer force and strength to his rock in the Atlantic, there arose a man in Central Germany, on the old Thuringian soil, to whom it was given to assert the dignity of vernacular literature, to throw off the yoke of classical tyranny, and to claim for all the dialects of Teutonic speech a right of ancient inheritance and perfect freedom before unsuspected and unknown. It is almost needless to mention this honoured name. For the furtherance of the good work which he began nearly fifty years ago, he still lives and still labours. There is no spot on which an accent of Teutonic speech is uttered where the name of Jacob Grimm is not a 'household word'. His General Grammar of all the Teutonic Dialects from Iceland to England has proved the equality of these tongues with their ancient classical oppressors. His Antiquities of Teutonic Law have shown that the codes of the Lombards, Franks, and Goths were not mere savage, brutal customaries, based, as had been supposed, on the absence of all law and right. His numerous treatises on early German authors have shown that the German poets of the Middle Age, Godfrey of Strasburg, Wolfram von Eschenbach, Hartman von der Aue, Walter von der Vogelweide, and the rest, can hold their own against any contemporary writers in other lands. And lastly, what rather concerns us here, his Teutonic Mythology, his Reynard the Fox, and the collection of German Popular Tales, which he and his brother William published, have thrown a flood of light on the early history of all the branches of our race, and have raised what had come to be looked on as mere nursery fictions and old wives' fables--to a study fit for the energies of grown men, and to all the dignity of a science.

In these pages, where we have to run over a vast tract of space, the reader who wishes to learn and not to cavil--and for such alone this introduction is intended--must be content with results rather than processes and steps. To use a homely likeness, he must be satisfied with the soup that is set before him, and not desire to see the bones of the ox out of which it has been boiled. When we say, therefore, that in these latter days the philology and mythology of the East and West have met and kissed each other; that they now go hand and hand; that they lend one another mutual support; that one cannot be understood without the other,--we look to be believed. We do not expect to be put to the proof, how the labours of Grimm and his disciples on this side were first rendered possible by the linguistic discoveries of Anquetil du Perron and others in India and France, at the end of the last century; then materially assisted and furthered by the researches of Sir William Jones, Colebrooke, and others, in India and England during the early part of this century, and finally have become identical with those of Wilson, Bopp, Lassen, and Max Mueller, at the present day. The affinity which exists in a mythological and philological point of view between the Aryan or Indo-European languages on the one hand, and the Sanscrit on the other, is now the first article of a literary creed, and the man who denies it puts himself as much beyond the pale of argument as he who, in a religious discussion, should meet a grave divine of the Church of England with the strict contradictory of her first article, and loudly declare his conviction, that there was no God. In a general way, then, we may be permitted to dogmatize, and to lay it down as a law which is always in force, that the first authentic history of a nation is the history of its tongue. We can form no notion of the literature of a country apart from its language, and the consideration of its language necessarily involves the consideration of its history. Here is England, for instance, with a language, and therefore a literature, composed of Celtic, Roman, Saxon, Norse, and Romance elements. Is not this simple fact suggestive of, nay, does it not challenge us to, an inquiry into the origin and history of the races who have passed over our island, and left their mark not only on the soil, but on our speech? Again, to take a wider view, and to rise from archaeology to science, what problem has interested the world in a greater degree than the origin of man, and what toil has not been spent in tracing all races back to their common stock? The science of comparative philology--the inquiry, not into one isolated language--for nowadays it may fairly be said of a man who knows only one language that he knows none--but into all the languages of one family, and thus to reduce them to one common centre, from which they spread like the rays of the sun--if it has not solved, is in a fair way of solving, this problem. When we have done for the various members of each family what has been done of late years for the Indo- European tongues, its solution will be complete. In such an inquiry the history of a race is, in fact, the history of its language, and can be nothing else; for we have to deal with times antecedent to all history, properly so called, and the stream which in later ages may be divided into many branches, now flows in a single channel.

From the East, then, came our ancestors, in days of immemorial antiquity, in that gray dawn of time of which all early songs and lays can tell, but of which it is as impossible as it is useless to attempt to fix the date. Impossible, because no means exist for ascertaining it; useless, because it is in reality a matter of utter indifference, when, as this tell-tale crust of earth informs us, we have an infinity of ages and periods to fall back on whether this great movement, this mighty lust to change their seats, seized on the Aryan race one hundred or one thousand years sooner or later. [1] But from the East we came, and from that central plain of Asia, now commonly called Iran. Iran, the habitation of the tillers and *earers* [2] of the earth, as opposed to Turan, the abode of restless horse-riding nomads; of Turks, in short, for in their name the root survives, and still distinguishes the great Turanian or Mongolian family, from the Aryan, Iranian, or Indo-European race. It is scarce worth while to inquire--even if inquiry could lead to any result--what cause set them in motion from their ancient seats. Whether impelled by famine or internal strife, starved out like other nationalities in recent times, or led on by adventurous chiefs, whose spirit chafed at the narrowness of home, certain it is that they left that home and began a wandering westwards, which only ceased when it reached the Atlantic and the Northern Ocean. Nor was the fate of those they left behind less strange. At some period almost as remote as, but after, that at which the wanderers for Europe started, the remaining portion of the stock, or a considerable offshoot from it, turned their faces east, and passing the Indian Caucasus, poured through the defiles of Affghanistan, crossed the plain of the Five Rivers, and descended on the fruitful plains of India. The different destiny of these stocks has been wonderful indeed. Of those who went west, we have only to enumerate the names under which they appear in history--Celts, Greeks, Romans, Teutons, Slavonians--to see and to know at once that the stream of this migration has borne on its waves all that has become most precious to man. To use the words of Max Mueller: 'They have been the prominent actors in the great drama of history, and have carried to their fullest growth all the elements of active life with which our nature is endowed. They have perfected society and morals, and we learn from their literature and works of art the elements of science, the laws of art, and the principles of philosophy. In continual struggle with each other and with Semitic and Mongolian races, these Aryan nations have become the rulers of history, and it seems to be their mission to link all parts of the world together by the chains of civilization, commerce, and religion.' We may add, that though by nature tough and enduring, they have not been obstinate and self-willed; they have been distinguished from all other nations, and particularly from their elder brothers whom they left behind, by their common sense, by their power of adapting themselves to all circumstances, and by making the best of their position; above all, they have been teachable, ready to receive impressions from without, and, when received, to develop them. To show the truth of this, we need only observe, that they adopted Christianity from another race, the most obstinate and stiff-necked the world has ever seen, who, trained under the Old Dispensation to preserve the worship of the one true God, were too proud to accept the further revelation of God under the New, and, rejecting their birth-right, suffered their inheritance to pass into other hands.

Such, then, has been the lot of the Western branch, of the younger brother, who, like the younger brother whom we shall meet so often in these Popular Tales, went out into the world, with nothing but his good heart and God's blessing to guide him; and now has come to all honour and fortune, and to be a king, ruling over the world. He went out and *did*. Let us see now what became of the elder brother, who stayed at home some time after his brother went out, and then only made a short journey. Having driven out the few aboriginal inhabitants of India with little effort, and following the course of the great rivers, the Eastern Aryans gradually established themselves all over the peninsula; and then, in calm possession of a world of their own, undisturbed by conquest from without, and accepting with apathy any change of dynasty among their rulers, ignorant of the past and careless of the future, they sat down once for all and ***thought***--thought not of what they had to do here, that stern lesson of every-day life which neither men nor nations can escape if they are to live with their fellows, but how they could abstract themselves entirely from their present existence, and immerse themselves wholly in dreamy speculations on the future. Whatever they may have been during their short migration and subsequent settlement, it is certain that they appear in the Vedas--perhaps the earliest collection which the world possesses--as a nation of philosophers. Well may Professor Mueller compare the Indian mind to a plant reared in a hot-house, gorgeous in colour, rich in perfume, precocious and abundant in fruit; it may be all this, 'but will never be like the oak, growing in wind and weather, striking its roots into real earth, and stretching its branches into real air, beneath the stars and sun of Heaven'; and well does he also remark, that a people of this peculiar stamp was never destined to act a prominent part in the history of the world; nay, the exhausting atmosphere of transcendental ideas could not but exercise a detrimental influence on the active and moral character of the Hindoos. [3]

In this passive, abstract, unprogressive state, they have remained ever since. Stiffened into castes, and tongue-tied and hand-tied by absurd rites and ceremonies, they were heard of in dim legends by Herodotus; they were seen by Alexander when that bold spirit pushed his phalanx beyond the limits of the known world; they trafficked with imperial Rome, and the later empire; they were again almost lost sight of, and became fabulous in the Middle Age; they were rediscovered by the Portuguese; they have been alternately peaceful subjects and desperate rebels to us English; but they have been still the same immovable and unprogressive philosophers, though akin to Europe all the while; and though the Highlander, who drives his bayonet through the heart of a high-caste Sepoy mutineer, little knows that his pale features and sandy hair, and that dusk face with its raven locks, both come from a common ancestor away in Central Asia, many, many centuries ago.

But here arises the question, what interest can we, the descendants of the practical brother, heirs to so much historical renown, possibly take in the records of a race so historically characterless, and so sunk in reveries and mysticism? The answer is easy. Those records are written in a language closely allied to the primaeval common tongue of those two branches before they parted, and descending from a period anterior to their separation. It may, or it may not, be the very tongue itself, but it certainly is not further removed than a few steps. The speech of the emigrants to the west rapidly changed with the changing circumstances and various fortune of each of its waves, and in their intercourse with the aboriginal population they often adopted foreign elements into their language. One of these waves, it is probable, passing by way of Persia and Asia Minor, crossed the Hellespont, and following the coast, threw off a mighty rill, known in after times as Greeks; while the main stream, striking through Macedonia, either crossed the Adriatic, or, still hugging the coast, came down on Italy, to be known as Latins. Another, passing between the Caspian and the Black Sea, filled the steppes round the Crimea, and; passing on over the Balkan and the Carpathians towards the west, became that great Teutonic nationality which, under various names, but all closely akin, filled, when we first hear of them in historical times, the space between the Black Sea and the Baltic, and was then slowly but surely driving before them the great wave of the Celts which had preceded them in their wandering, and which had probably followed the same line of march as the ancestors of the Greeks and Latins. A movement which lasted until all that was left of Celtic nationality was either absorbed by the intruders, or forced aside and driven to take refuge in mountain fastnesses and outlying islands. Besides all these, there was still another wave, which is supposed to have passed between the Sea of Aral and the Caspian, and, keeping still further to the north and east, to have passed between its kindred Teutons and the Mongolian tribes, and so to have lain in the background until we find them appearing as Slavonians on the scene of history. Into so many great stocks did the Western Aryans pass, each possessing strongly-marked nationalities and languages, and these seemingly so distinct that each often asserted that the other spoke a barbarous tongue. But, for all that, each of those tongues bears about with it still, and in earlier times no doubt bore still more plainly about with it, infallible evidence of common origin, so that each dialect can be traced up to that primaeval form of speech still in the main preserved in the Sanscrit by the Southern Aryan branch, who, careless of practical life, and immersed in speculation, have clung to their ancient traditions and tongue with wonderful tenacity. It is this which has given such value to Sanscrit, a tongue of which it may be said, that if it had perished the sun would never have risen on the science of comparative philology. Before the discoveries in Sanscrit of Sir William Jones, Wilkins, Wilson, and others, the world had striven to find the common ancestor of European languages, sometimes in the classical, and sometimes in the Semitic tongues. In the one case the result was a tyranny of Greek and Latin over the non- classical tongues, and in the other the most uncritical and unphilosophical waste of learning. No doubt some striking analogies exist between the Indo-European family and the Semitic stock, just as there are remarkable analogies between the Mongolian and Indo- European families; but the ravings of Vallancy, in his effort to connect the Erse with Phoenician, are an awful warning of what unscientific inquiry, based upon casual analogy, may bring itself to believe, and even to fancy it has proved.

These general observations, then, and this rapid bird's eye view, may suffice to show the common affinity which exists between the Eastern and Western Aryans; between the Hindoo on the one hand, and the nations of Western Europe on the other. That is the fact to keep steadily before our eyes. We all came, Greek, Latin, Celt, Teuton, Slavonian, from the East, as kith and kin, leaving kith and kin behind us; and after thousands of years the language and traditions of those who went East, and those who went West, bear such an affinity to each other, as to have established, beyond discussion or dispute, the fact of their descent from a common stock.

DIFFUSION

This general affinity established, we proceed to narrow our subject to its proper limits, and to confine it to the consideration, *first*, of Popular Tales in general, and *secondly*, of those Norse Tales in particular, which form the bulk of this volume.

In the first place, then, the fact which we remarked on setting out, that the groundwork or plot of many of these tales is common to all the nations of Europe, is more important, and of greater scientific interest, than might at first appear. They form, in fact, another link in the chain of evidence of a common origin between the East and West, and even the obstinate adherents of the old classical theory, according to which all resemblances were set down to sheer copying from Greek or Latin patterns, are now forced to confess, not only that there was no such wholesale copying at all, but that, in many cases, the despised vernacular tongues have preserved the common traditions far more faithfully than the writers of Greece and Rome. The sooner, in short, that this theory of copying, which some, even besides the classicists, have maintained, is abandoned, the better, not only for the truth, but for the literary reputation of those who put it forth. No one can, of course, imagine that during that long succession of ages when this mighty wedge of Aryan migration was driving its way through that prehistoric race, that nameless nationality, the traces of which we everywhere find underlying the intruders in their monuments and implements of bone and stone--a race akin, in all probability, to the Mongolian family, and whose miserable remnants we see pushed aside, and huddled up in the holes and corners of Europe, as Lapps, and Finns, and Basques-- No one, we say, can suppose for a moment, that in that long process of contact and absorption, some traditions of either race should not have been caught up and adopted by the other. We know it to be a fact with regard to their language, from the evidence of philology, which cannot lie; and the witness borne by such a word as the Gothic Atta for *father*, where a Mongolian has been adopted in preference to an Aryan word, is irresistible on this point; but that, apart from such natural assimilation, all the thousand shades of resemblance and affinity which gleam and flicker through the whole body of popular tradition in the Aryan race, as the Aurora plays and flashes in countless rays athwart the Northern heaven, should be the result of mere servile copying of one tribe's traditions by another, is a supposition as absurd as that of those good country-folk, who, when they see an Aurora, fancy it must be a great fire, the work of some incendiary, and send off the parish engine to put it out. No! when we find in such a story as the Master-thief traits, which are to be found in the Sanscrit *Hitopadesa* [4], and which reminds us at once of the story of Rhampsinitus in Herodotus; which are also to be found in German, Italian, and Flemish popular tales, but told in all with such variations of character and detail, and such adaptations to time and place, as evidently show the original working of the national consciousness upon a stock of tradition common to all the race, but belonging to no tribe of that race in particular; and when we find this occurring not in one tale but in twenty, we are forced to abandon the theory of such universal copying, for fear lest we should fall into a greater difficulty than that for which we were striving to account.

To set this question in a plainer light, let us take a well-known instance; let us take the story of William Tell and his daring shot, which is said to have been made in the year 1307. It is just possible that the feat might be historical, and, no doubt, thousands believe it for the sake of the Swiss patriot, as firmly as they believe in anything; but, unfortunately, this story of the bold archer who saves his life by shooting an apple from the head of his child at the command of a tyrant, is common to the whole Aryan race. It appears in Saxo Grammaticus, who flourished in the twelfth century, where it is told of Palnatoki, King Harold Gormson's thane and assassin. In the thirteenth century the *Wilkina Saga* relates it of Egill, Voelundr's--our Wayland Smith's--younger brother. So also in the Norse Saga of *Saint Olof*, king and martyr; the king, who died in 1030, eager for the conversion of one of his heathen chiefs Eindridi, competes with him in various athletic exercises, first in swimming and then in archery. After several famous shots on either side, the king challenges Eindridi to shoot a tablet off his son's head without hurting the child.

Eindridi is ready, but declares he will revenge himself if the child is hurt. The king has the first shot, and his arrow strikes close to the tablet. Then Eindridi is to shoot, but at the prayers of his mother and sister, refuses the shot, and has to yield and be converted [*Fornm. Sog.*, 2, 272]. So, also, King Harold Sigurdarson, who died 1066, backed himself against a famous marksman, Hemingr, and ordered him to shoot a hazel nut off the head of his brother Bjoern, and Hemingr performed the feat [Mueller's *Saga Bibl.*, 3, 359]. In the middle of the fourteenth century, the *Malleus Maleficarum* refers it to Puncher, a magician of the Upper Rhine. Here in England, we have it in the old English ballad of *Adam Bell, Clym of the Clough*, and *William of Cloudesly*, where William performs the feat [see the ballad in Percy's *Reliques*]. It is not at all of Tell in Switzerland before the year 1499, and the earlier Swiss chronicles omit it altogether. It is common to the Turks and Mongolians; and a legend of the wild Samoyeds, who never heard of Tell or saw a book in their lives, relates it, chapter and verse, of one of their famous marksmen. What shall we say then, but that the story of this bold master-shot was primaeval amongst many tribes and races, and that it only crystallized itself round the great name of Tell by that process of attraction which invariably leads a grateful people to throw such mythic wreaths, such garlands of bold deeds of precious memory, round the brow of its darling champion [5].

Nor let any pious Welshman be shocked if we venture to assert that Gellert, that famous hound upon whose last resting-place the traveller comes as he passes down the lovely vale of Gwynant, is a mythical dog, and never snuffed the fresh breeze in the forest of Snowdon, nor saved his master's child from ravening wolf. This, too, is a primaeval story, told with many variations. Sometimes the foe is a wolf, sometimes a bear, sometimes a snake. Sometimes the faithful guardian of the child is an otter, a weasel, or a dog. It, too, came from the East. It is found in the *Pantcha-Tantra*, in the *Hitopadesa*, in Bidpai's *Fables*, in the Arabic original of *The Seven Wise Masters*, that famous collection of stories which illustrate a stepdame's calumny and hate, and in many mediaeval versions of those originals [6]. Thence it passed into the Latin *Gesta Romanorum*, where, as well as in the Old English version published by Sir Frederick Madden, it may be read as a service rendered by a faithful hound against a snake. This, too, like Tell's master-shot, is as the lightning which shineth over the whole heaven at once, and can be claimed by no one tribe of the Aryan race, to the exclusion of the rest. 'The Dog of Montargis' is in like manner mythic, though perhaps not so widely spread. It first occurs in France, as told of Sybilla, a fabulous wife of Charlemagne; but it is at any rate as old as the time of Plutarch, who relates it as an anecdote of brute sagacity in the days of Pyrrhus.

There can be no doubt, with regard to the question of the origin of these tales, that they were common in germ at least to the Aryan tribes before their migration. We find those germs developed in the popular traditions of the Eastern Aryans, and we find them developed in a hundred forms and shapes in every one of the nations into which the Western Aryans have shaped themselves in the course of ages. We are led, therefore, irresistibly to the conclusion, that these traditions are as much a portion of the common inheritance of our ancestors, as their language unquestionably is; and that they form, along with that language, a double chain of evidence, which proves their Eastern origin. If we are to seek for a simile, or an analogy, as to the relative positions of these tales and traditions, and to the mutual resemblances which exist between them as the several branches of our race have developed them from the common stock, we may find it in one which will come home to every reader as he looks round the domestic hearth, if he should be so happy as to have one. They are like as sisters of one house are like. They have what would be called a strong family likeness; but besides this likeness, which they owe to father or mother, as the case may be, they have each their peculiarities of form, and eye, and face, and still more, their differences of intellect and mind. This may be dark, that fair; this may have gray eyes, that black; this may be open and graceful, that reserved and close; this you may love, that you can take no interest in. One may be bashful, another winning, a third worth knowing and yet hard to know. They are so like and so unlike. At first it may be, as an old English writer beautifully expresses it, 'their father hath writ them as his own little story', but as they grow up they throw off the copy, educate themselves for good or ill, and finally assume new forms of feeling and feature under an original development of their own.

Or shall we take another likeness, and say they are national dreams; that they are like the sleeping thoughts of many men upon one and the same thing. Suppose a hundred men to have been eye-witnesses of some event on the same day, and then to have slept and dreamt of it; we should have as many distinct representations of that event, all turning upon it and bound up with it in some way, but each preserving the personality of the sleeper, and working up the common stuff in a higher or lower degree, just as the fancy and the intellect of the sleeper was at a higher or lower level of perfection. There is, indeed, greater truth in this likeness than may at first sight appear. In the popular tale, properly so called, the national mind dreams all its history over again; in its half conscious state it takes this trait and that trait, this feature and that feature, of times and ages long past. It snatches up bits of its old beliefs, and fears, and griefs, and glory, and pieces them together with something that happened yesterday, and then holds up the distorted reflection in all its inconsequence, just as it has passed before that magic glass, as though it were genuine history, and matter for pure belief. And here it may be as well to say, that besides that old classical foe of vernacular tradition, there is another hardly less dangerous, which returns to the charge of copying, but changes what lawyers call the *venue* of the trial from classical to Eastern lands. According to this theory, which came up when its classical predecessor was no longer tenable, the traditions and tales of Western Europe came from the East, but they were still all copies. They were supposed to have proceeded entirely from two sources; one the ***Directorium Humanae Vitae*** of John of Capua, translated between 1262-78 from a Hebrew version, which again came from an Arabic version of the 8th century, which came from a Pehlvi version made by one Barzouyeh, at the command of Chosrou Noushirvan, King of Persia, in the 6th century, which again came from the ***Pantcha Tantra***, a Sanscrit original of unknown antiquity. This is that famous book of ***Calila and Dimna***, as the Persian version is called, attributed to Bidpai, and which was thus run to earth in India. The second source of Western tradition was held to be that still more famous collection of stories commonly known by the name of the 'Story of the Seven Sages,' but which, under many names--Kaiser Octavianus, Diocletianus, Dolopathos, Erastus, etc.--plays a most important part in mediaeval romance. This, too, by a similar process, has been traced to India, appearing first in Europe at the beginning of the thirteenth century in the Latin ***Historia Septem Sapientum Romae***, by Dame Jehans, monk in the Abbey of Haute Selve. Here, too, we have a Hebrew, an Arabic, and a Persian version; which last came avowedly from a Sanscrit original, though that original has not yet been discovered. From these two sources of fable and tradition, according to the new copying theory, our Western fables and tales had come by direct translation from the East. Now it will be at once evident that this theory hangs on what may be called a single thread. Let us say, then, that all that can be found in *Calila and Dimna*, or the later Persian version, made A.D. 1494, of Hossein Vaez, called the *Anvari Sohaili*, 'the Canopic Lights'--from which, when published in Paris by David Sahid of Ispahan, in the year 1644, La Fontaine drew the substance of many of his best fables.--Let us say, too, that all can be found in the *Life of the Seven Sages*, or the Book of Sendabad as it was called in Persia, after an apocryphal Indian sage--came by translation--that is to say, through the cells of Brahmins, Magians, and monks, and the labours of the learned--into the popular literature of the West. Let us give up all that, and then see where we stand. What are we to say of the many tales and fables which are to be found in neither of those famous collections, and not tales alone, but traits and features of old tradition, broken bits of fable, roots and germs of mighty growths of song and story, nay, even the very words, which exist in Western popular literature, and which modern philology has found obstinately sticking in Sanscrit, and of which fresh proofs and instances are discovered every day? What are we to say of such a remarkable resemblance as this?

The noble King Putraka fled into the Vindhya mountains in order to   live apart from his unkind kinsfolk; and as he wandered about there   he met two men who wrestled and fought with one another. 'Who are   you?' he asked. 'We are the sons of Mayasara, and here lie our   riches; this bowl, this staff, and these shoes; these are what we   are fighting for, and whichever is stronger is to have them for his   own.'

So when Putraka had heard that, he asked them with a laugh: 'Why,   what's the good of owning these things?' Then they answered   'Whoever puts on these shoes gets the power to fly; whatever is   pointed at with this staff rises up at once; and whatever food one   wishes for in this bowl, it comes at once.' So when Putraka had   heard that he said 'Why fight about it? Let this be the prize;   whoever beats the other in a race, let him have them all'.

'So be it', said the two fools, and set off running, but Putraka   put on the shoes at once, and flew away with the staff and bowl up   into the clouds'.

Well, this is a story neither in the *Pantcha Tantra* nor the *Hitopadesa*, the Sanscrit originals of *Calila and Dimna*. It is not in the *Directorium Humanae*

Vitae, and has not passed west by that way. Nor is it in the **Book of Sendabad**, and thence come west in the **History of the Seven Sages**. Both these paths are stopped. It comes from the **Katha Sarit Sagara**, the 'Sea of Streams of Story' of Somadeva Bhatta of Cashmere, who, in the middle of the twelfth century of our era, worked up the tales found in an earlier collection, called the **Vrihat Katha**, 'the lengthened story', in order to amuse his mistress, the Queen of Cashmere. Somadeva's collection has only been recently known and translated. But west the story certainly came long before, and in the extreme north-west we still find it in these Norse Tales in 'The Three Princesses of Whiteland', No. xxvi.

> 'Well!' said the man, 'as this is so, I'll give you a bit of advice. Hereabouts, on a moor, stand three brothers, and there they have stood these hundred years, fighting about a hat, a cloak, and a pair of boots. If any one has these three things, he can make himself invisible, and wish himself anywhere he pleases. You can tell them you wish to try the things, and after that, you'll pass judgment between them, whose they shall be'.

> Yes! the king thanked the man, and went and did as he told him.

> 'What's all this?' he said to the brothers. 'Why do you stand here fighting for ever and a day? Just let me try these things, and I'll give judgment whose they shall be.'

> They were very willing to do this; but as soon as he had got the hat; cloak, and boots, he said: 'When we meet next time I'll tell you my judgment'; and with these words he wished himself away.

Nor in the Norse tales alone. Other collections shew how thoroughly at home this story was in the East. In the Relations of **Ssidi Kur**, a Tartar tale, a Chan's son first gets possession of a cloak which two children stand and fight for, which has the gift of making the wearer invisible, and afterwards of a pair of boots, with which one can wish one's self to whatever place one chooses. Again, in a Wallachian tale, we read of three devils who fight for their inheritance--a club which turns every-thing to stone, a hat which makes the wearer invisible, and a cloak by help of which one can wish one's self whithersoever one pleases. Again, in a Mongolian tale, the Chan's son comes upon a group of children who fight for a hood which makes the wearer invisible; he is to be judge between them, makes them run a race for it, but meanwhile puts it on and vanishes from their sight. A little further on he meets an-other group, who are quarrelling for a pair of boots, the wearer of which can wish himself whithersoever he pleases, and gains possession of them in the same way.

Nor in one Norse tale alone, but in many, we find traces of these three won-derful things, or of things like them. They are very like the cloth, the ram, and the stick, which the lad got from the North Wind instead of his meal. Very like, too, the cloth, the scissors, and the tap, which will be found in No. xxxvi, 'The Best Wish'. If we drop the number three, we find the Boots again in 'Soria Moria Castle', No. lvi. [Moe, Introd., xxxii-iii] Leaving the Norse Tales, we see at once that they are the seven-leagued boots of Jack the Giant Killer. In the ***Nibelungen Lied***, when Sieg-fried finds Schilbung and Niblung, the wierd heirs of the famous 'Hoard', striving for the possession of that heap of red gold and gleaming stones; when they beg him to share it for them, promising him, as his meed, Balmung, best of swords; when he shares it, when they are discontent, and when in the struggle which ensues he gets possession of the 'Tarnhut', the 'cloak of darkness', which gave its wearer the strength of twelve men, and enabled him to go where he would be unseen, and which was the great prize among the treasures of the dwarfs[7]; who is there that does not see the broken fragments of that old Eastern story of the heirs struggling for their inheritance, and calling in the aid of some one of better wit or strength who ends by making the very prize for which they fight his own?

And now to return for a moment to ***Calila and Dimna*** and ***The Seven Sages***. Since we have seen that there are other stories, and many of them, for this is by no means the only resemblance to be found in Somadeva's book [8] which are common to the Eastern and Western Aryans, but which did not travel to Europe by transla-tion; let us go on to say that it is by no means certain, even when some Western story or fable is found in these Sanscrit originals and their translations, that that was the only way by which they came to Europe. A single question will prove this. How did the fables and apologues which are found in ***Aesop***, and which are also found in the *Pantcha Tantya* and the *Hitopadesa* come West? That they came from the East is certain; but by what way, certainly not by translations or copying, for they had travelled west long before translations were thought of. How was it that Themistius, a Greek orator of the fourth century [J. Grimm, *Reinhart Fuchs*, cclxiii, Intr.] had heard of that fable of the lion, fox, and bull, which is in substance the same as that of the lion, the bull, and the two jackals in the *Pantcha Tantya* and the *Hitopadesa*? How, but along the path of that primaeval Aryan migration, and by that deep-ground tone of tradition by which man speaks to man, nation to nation, and age to age; along which comparative philology has, in these last days, travelled back thither, listened to the accents spoken, and so found in the East the cradle of a common language and common belief.

And now, having, as we hope, finally established this Indian affinity, and disposed of mere Indian copying, let us lift our eyes and see if something more is not to be discerned on the wide horizon now open on our view. The most interesting problem for man to solve is the origin of his race. Of late years comparative philology, having accomplished her task in proving the affinity of language between Europe and the East, and so taken a mighty step towards fixing the first seat of the greatest--greatest in wit and wisdom, if not in actual numbers--portion of the human race, has pursued her inquiries into the languages of the Turanian, the Semitic, and the Chamitic or African races, with more or less successful results. In a few more years, when the African languages are better known, and the roots of Egyptian and Chinese words are more accurately detected, Science will be better able to speak as to the common affinity of all the tribes that throng the earth. In the meantime, let the testimony of tradition and popular tales be heard, which in this case have outstripped comparative philology, and lead instead of following her. It is beyond the scope of this essay, which aims at being popular and readable rather than learned and lengthy, to go over a prolonged scientific investigation step by step. We repeat it. The reader must have faith in the writer, and believe the words now written are the results of an inquiry, and not ask for the inquiry itself. In all mythologies and traditions, then, there are what may be called natural resemblances, parallelisms suggested to the senses of each race by natural objects and every-day events, and these might spring up spontaneously all over the earth as home growths, neither derived by imitation from other tribes, nor from seeds of common tradition shed from a common stock. Such resemblances have been well compared by William Grimm, [*Kinder and Hausmaerchen*, vol. 3, *3d* edition (Goettingen, 1856) a volume worthy of the utmost attention.] to those words which are found in all languages derived from the imitation of natural sounds, or, we may add, from the first lisping accents of infancy. But the case is very different when this or that object which strikes the senses is accounted for in a way so extraordinary and peculiar, as to stamp the tradition with a character of its own. Then arises a like impression on the mind, if we find the same tradition in two tribes at the opposite ends of the earth, as is produced by meeting twin brothers, one in Africa and the other in Asia; we say at once 'I know you are so and so's brother, you are so like him'. Take an instance: In these Norse Tales, No. xxiii, we are told how it was the bear came to have a stumpy tail, and in an African tale, [9] we find how it was the hyaena became tailless and earless. Now, the tailless condition both of the bear and the hyaena could scarcely fail to attract attention in a race of hunters, and we might expect that popular tradition would attempt to account for both, but how are we to explain the fact, that both Norseman and African account for it in the same way-- that both owe their loss to the superior cunning of another animal. In Europe the fox bears away the palm for wit from all other animals, so he it is that persuades the bear in the Norse Tales to sit with his tail in a hole in the ice till it is fast frozen in, and snaps short off when he tries to tug it out. In Bornou, in the heart of Africa, it is the weasel who is the wisest of beasts, and who, having got some meat in common with the hyaena, put it into a hole, and said:

'Behold two men came out of the forest, took the meat, and put it into a hole: stop, I will go into the hole, and then thou mayst   stretch out thy tail to me, and I will tie the meat to thy tail for   thee to draw it out'. So the weasel went into the hole, the hyaena   stretched its tail out to it, but the weasel took the hyaena's tail, fastened a stick, and tied the hyaena's tail to the stick,   and then said to the hyaena 'I have tied the meat to thy tail;   draw, and pull it out'. The hyaena was a fool, it did not know the   weasel surpassed it in subtlety; it thought the meat was tied; but when it tried to draw out its tail, it was fast. When the weasel said again to it 'Pull', it pulled, but could not draw it out; so   it became vexed, and on pulling with force, its tail broke. The   tail being torn out, the weasel was no more seen by the hyaena: the   weasel was hidden in the hole with its meat, and the hyaena saw it   not. [*Ka-*

nuri Proverbs, p. 167.]

Here we have a fact in natural history accounted for, but accounted for in such a peculiar way as shows that the races among which they are current must have derived them from some common tradition. The mode by which the tail is lost is different indeed; but the manner in which the common ground-work is suited in one case to the cold of the North, and the way in which fish are commonly caught at holes in the ice as they rise to breathe; and in the other to Africa and her pitfalls for wild beasts, is only another proof of the oldness of the tradition, and that it is not merely a copy.

Take another instance. Every one knows the story in the Arabian Nights, where the man who knows the speech of beasts laughs at something said by an ox to an ass. His wife wants to know why he laughs, and persists, though he tells her it will cost him his life if he tells her. As he doubts what to do, he hears the cock say to the house-dog 'Our master is not wise; I have fifty hens who obey me; if he followed my advice, he'd just take a good stick, shut up his wife in a room with him, and give her a good cudgelling.' The same story is told in Straparola [10] with so many variations as to show it is no copy; it is also told in a Servian popular tale, with variations of its own; and now here we find it in Bornou, as told by Koelle.

There was a servant of God who had one wife and one horse; but his wife was one-eyed, and they lived in their house. Now this servant of God understood the language of the beasts of the forest when they spoke, and of the birds of the air when they talked as they flew by. This servant of God also understood the cry of the hyaena when it arose at night in the forest, and came to the houses and cried near them; so, likewise, when his horse was hungry and neighed, he understood why it neighed, rose up, brought the horse grass, and then returned and sat down. It happened one day that birds had their talk as they were flying by above and the servant of God understood what they talked. This caused him to laugh, whereupon his wife said to him 'What dost thou hear that thou laughest?' He replied to his wife 'I shall not tell thee what I hear, and why I laugh'. The woman said to her husband 'I know why thou laughest; thou laughest at me because I am one-eyed'. The man then said to his wife 'I saw that thou wast one-eyed before I loved thee, and before we married and sat down in our house'. When the woman heard her husband's word she was quiet.

But once at night, as they were lying on their bed, and it was past midnight, it happened that a rat played with his wife on the top of the house and that both fell to the ground. Then the wife of the rat said to her husband 'Thy sport is bad; thou saidst to me that thou wouldst play, but when we came together we fell to the ground, so that I broke my back'.

When the servant of God heard the talk of the rat's wife, as he was lying on his bed, he laughed. Now, as soon as he laughed his wife arose, seized him, and said to him as she held him fast: 'Now this time I will not let thee go out of this house except thou tell me what thou hearest and why thou laughest'. The man begged the woman, saying 'Let me go'; but the woman would not listen to her husband's entreaty.

The husband then tells his wife that he knows the language of beasts and birds, and she is content; but when he wakes in the morning he finds he has lost his wonderful gift; and the moral of the tale is added most ungallantly: 'If a man shews and tells his thoughts to a woman, God will punish him for it'. Though, perhaps, it is better, for the sake of the gentler sex, that the tale should be pointed with this unfair moral, than that the African story should proceed like all the other variations, and save the husband's gift at the cost of the wife's skin.

Take other African instances. How is it that the wandering Bechuanas got their story of 'The Two Brothers', the ground-work of which is the same as 'The Machandelboom' and the 'Milk-white Doo', and where the incidents and even the words are almost the same? How is it that in some of its traits that Bechuana story embodies those of that earliest of all popular tales, recently published from an Egyptian Papyrus, coeval with the abode of the Israelites in Egypt? and how is it that that same Egyptian tale has other traits which reminds us of the Dun Bull in 'Katie Woodencloak', as well as incidents which are the germ of stories long since reduced to writing in Norse Sagas of the twelfth and thirteenth centuries? [11] How is it that we still find among the Negroes in the West Indies [12] a rich store of popular tales, and the Beast Epic in full bloom, brought with them from Africa to the islands of the West; and among those tales and traditions, how is it that we find a 'Wishing Tree', the counter-part of that in a German popular tale, and 'a little dirty scrub of a child', whom his sisters despise, but who is own brother to Boots in the Norse Tales, and like him outwits the Troll, spoils his substance, and saves his sisters? How is it that we find the good woman who washes the loathsome head rewarded, while the bad man who refuses to do that dirty work is punished for his pride; the very groundwork, nay the very words, that we meet in Bushy-bride, another Norse Tale? How is it that we find a Mongolian tale, which came confessedly from India, made up of two of our Norse tales, 'Rich Peter the Pedlar' and 'The Giant that had no heart in his body' [***The Deeds of Bogda Gesser Chan*** , by I. J. Schmidt (Petersburg and Leipzig, 1839).]? How should all these things be, and how could they possibly be, except on that theory which day by day becomes more and more a matter of fact; this, that the whole human race sprung from one stock, planted in the East, which has stretched out its boughs and branches laden with the fruit of language, and bright with the bloom of song and story, by successive offshoots to the utmost parts of the earth.

NORSE MYTHOLOGY

And now, in the second place, for that particular branch of the Aryan race, in which this peculiar development of the common tradition has arisen, which we are to consider as 'Norse Popular Tales'.

Whatever disputes may have existed as to the mythology of other branches of the Teutonic subdivision of the Aryan race--whatever discussions may have arisen as to the position of this or that divinity among the Franks, the Anglo-Saxons, or the Goths--about the Norsemen there can be no dispute or doubt. From a variety of circumstances, but two before all the rest--the one their settlement in Iceland, which preserved their language and its literary treasures incorrupt; the other their late conversion to Christianity--their cosmogony and mythology stands before us in full flower, and we have not, as elsewhere, to pick up and piece together the wretched fragments of a faith, the articles of which its own priests had forgotten to commit to writing, and which those of another creed had dashed to pieces and destroyed, wherever their zealous hands could reach. In the two Eddas, therefore, in the early Sagas, in Saxo's stilted Latin, which barely conceals the popular songs and legends from which the historian drew his materials, we are enabled to form a perfect conception of the creed of the heathen Norsemen. We are enabled to trace, as has been traced by the same hand in another place [*Oxford Essays for* 1898: 'The Norsemen in Iceland'.], the natural and rational development of that creed from a simple worship of nature and her powers, first to monotheism, and then to a polytheistic system. The tertiary system of Polytheism is the soil out of which the mythology of the Eddas sprang, though through it each of the older formations crops out in huge masses which admit of no mistake as to its origin. In the Eddas the natural powers have been partly subdued, partly thrust on one side, for a time, by Odin and the Aesir, by the Great Father and his children, by One Supreme and twelve subordinate gods, who rule for an appointed time, and over whom hangs an impending fate, which imparts a charm of melancholy to this creed, which has clung to the race who once believed in it long after the creed itself has vanished before the light of Christianity. According to this creed, the Aesir and Odin had their abode in Asgard, a lofty hill in the centre of the habitable earth, in the midst of Midgard, that *middle earth* which we hear of in early English poetry, the abode of gods and men. Round that earth, which was fenced in against the attacks of ancient and inveterate foes by a natural fortification of hills, flowed the great sea in a ring, and beyond that sea was Utgard, the outlying world, the abode of Frost Giants, and Monsters, those old-natural powers who had been dispossessed by Odin and the Aesir when the new order of the universe arose, and between whom and the new gods a feud as inveterate as that cherished by the Titans against Jupiter was necessarily kept alive. It is true indeed that this feud was broken by intervals of truce during which the Aesir and the Giants visit each other, and appear on more or less friendly terms, but the true relation between them was war; pretty much as the Norseman was at war with all the rest of the world. Nor was this struggle between two rival races or powers confined to the gods in Asgard alone. Just as their ancient foes were the Giants of Frost and Snow, so between the race of men and the race of Trolls was there a perpetual feud. As the gods were men magnified and exaggerated, so were the Trolls diminished Frost Giants; far superior to man in strength and stature, but inferior to man in wit and invention. Like the Frost Giants, they inhabit the rough and rugged places of the earth, and, historically speaking, in all probability represent the old aboriginal races who retired into the mountainous fastnesses of the land, and whose strength was exaggerated, because the intercourse between the races was small. In almost every respect they stand in the same relations to men as the Frost Giants stand to the Gods.

There is nothing, perhaps, more characteristic of a true, as compared with a false religion, than the restlessness of the one when brought face to face with the quiet dignity and majesty of the other. Under the Christian dispensation, our blessed Lord, his awful sacrifice once performed, 'ascended up on high', having 'led captivity captive', and expects the hour that shall make his foes 'his footstool'; but false gods, Jupiter, Vishnu, Odin, Thor, must constantly keep themselves, as it were, before the eyes of men, lest they should lose respect. Such gods being invariably what the philosophers call ***subjective***, that is to say, having no existence except in the minds of those who believe in them; having been created by man in his own image, with his own desires and passions, stand in constant need of being recreated. They change as the habits and temper of the race which adores them alter; they are ever bound to do something fresh, lest man should forget them, and new divinities usurp their place. Hence came endless avatars in Hindoo mythology, reproducing all the dreamy monstrosities of that passive Indian mind. Hence came Jove's adventures, tinged with all the lust and guile which the wickedness of the natural man planted on a hot-bed of iniquity is capable of conceiving. Hence bloody Moloch, and the foul abominations of Chemosh and Milcom. Hence, too, Odin's countless adventures, his journeys into all parts of the world, his constant trials of wit and strength, with his ancient foes the Frost Giants, his hair-breadth escapes. Hence Thor's labours and toils, his passages beyond the sea, girt with his strength-belt, wearing his iron gloves, and grasping his hammer which split the skulls of so many of the Giant's kith and kin. In the Norse gods, then, we see the Norseman himself, sublimed and elevated beyond man's nature, but bearing about with him all his bravery and endurance, all his dash and spirit of adventure, all his fortitude and resolution to struggle against a certainty of doom which, sooner or later, must overtake him on that dread day, the 'twilight of the gods', when the wolf was to break loose, when the great snake that lay coiled round the world should lash himself into wrath, and the whole race of the Aesirs and their antagonists were to perish in internecine strife.

Such were the gods in whom the Norseman believed--exaggerations of himself, of all his good and all his bad qualities. Their might and their adventures, their domestic quarrels and certain doom, were sung in venerable lays, now collected in what we call the Elder, or Poetic Edda; simple majestic songs, whose mellow accents go straight to the heart through the ear, and whose simple severity never suffers us to mistake their meaning. But, besides these gods, there were heroes of the race whose fame and glory were in every man's memory, and whose mighty deeds were in every minstrel's mouth. Helgi, Sigmund, Sinfjoetli, Sigurd, Signy, Brynhildr, Gudrun; champions and shield- maidens, henchmen and corse-choosers, now dead and gone, who sat round Odin's board in Valhalla. Women whose beauty, woes, and sufferings were beyond those of all women; men whose prowess had never found an equal. Between these, love and hate; all that can foster passion or beget revenge. Ill assorted marriages; the right man to the wrong woman, and the wrong man to the right woman; envyings, jealousies, hatred, murders, all the works of the natural man, combine together to form that marvellous story which begins with a curse--the curse of ill-gotten gold--and ends with a curse, a widow's curse, which drags down all on whom it falls, and even her own flesh and blood, to certain doom. Such was the theme of the wondrous Volsung Tale, the far older, simpler and grander original of that Nibelungen Need of the thirteenth century, a tale which begins with the slaughter of Fafnir by Sigurd, and ends with Hermanaric, 'that fierce faith-breaker', as the Anglo-Saxon minstrel calls him, when he is describing, in rapid touches, the mythic glories of the Teutonic race.

This was the story of the Volsungs. They traced themselves back, like all heroes, to Odin, the great father of gods and men. From him sprung Sigi, from him Rerir, from him Volsung, ripped from his mother's womb after a six years' bearing, to become the Eponymus of that famous race. In the centre of his hall grew an oak, the tall trunk of which passed through the roof, and its boughs spread far and wide in upper air. Into that hall, on a high feast day, when Signy, Volsung's daughter, was to be given away to Siggeir, King of Gothland, strode an old one-eyed guest. His feet were bare, his hose were of knitted linen, he wore a great striped cloak, and a broad flapping hat. In his hand he bore a sword, which, at one stroke, he drove up to the hilt in the oak trunk. 'There', said he, 'let him of all this company bear this sword who is man enough to pull it out. I give it him, and none shall say he ever bore a better blade.' With these words he passed out of the hall, and was seen no more. Many tried, for that sword was plainly a thing of price, but none could stir it, till Sigmund, the best and bravest of Volsung's sons, tried his hand, and, lo! the weapon yielded itself at once. This was that famous blade **Gram**, of which we shall hear again. Sigmund bore it in battle against his brother-in-law, who quarrelled with him about this very sword, when Volsung fell, and Sigmund and his ten brothers were taken and bound. All perished but Sigmund, who was saved by his sister Signy, and hidden in a wood till he could revenge his father and brethren. Here with Sinfjoetli, who was at once his son and nephew, he ran as a werewolf through the forest, and wrought many wild deeds. When Sinfjoetli was of age to help him, they proceed to vengeance, and burn the treacherous brother-in-law alive, with all his followers. Sigmund then regains his father's kingdom, and in extreme old age dies in battle against the sons of King Hunding. Just as he was about to turn the fight, a warrior of more than mortal might, a one-eyed man in a blue cloak, with a flapping hat, rose up against him spear in hand. At that outstretched spear Sigmund smites with his trusty sword. It snaps in twain. Then he knows that his luck is gone; he sees in his foe Odin the giver of the sword, sinks down on the gory battle-field, and dies in the arms of Hjordis, his young wife, refusing all leechcraft, and bowing his head to Odin's will. By the fortune of war, Hjordis, bearing a babe under her girdle, came into the hands of King Hialprek of Denmark, there she bore a son to Sigmund, Sigurd, the darling of Teutonic song and story. Regin, the king's smith, was his foster-father, and as the boy grew up the fairest and stoutest of all the Volsungs, Regin, who was of the dwarf race, urged him day by day to do a doughty deed, and slay Fafnir the Dragon. For Fafnir, Regin, and Otter had been brothers, sons of Reidmar. In one of their many wanderings, Odin, Loki, and Haenir came to a river and a forge. There, on the bank under the forge, they saw an otter with a salmon in its mouth, which it ate greedily with its eyes shut. Loki took a stone, threw it, and killed the beast, and boasted how he had got both fish and flesh at one throw. Then the Aesir passed on and came at night to Reidmar's house, asked a lodging, got it, and showed their spoil. 'Seize and bind them lads', cried Reidmar; 'for they have slain your brother Otter'. So they were seized and bound by Regin and Fafnir, and offered an atonement to buy off the feud, and Reidmar was to name the sum. Then Otter was flayed, and the Aesir were to fill the skin with red gold, and cover it without, that not a hair could be seen. To fetch the gold Odin sent Loki down to the abodes of the Black Elves; there in a stream he caught Andvari the Dwarf, and made him give up all the gold which he had hoarded up in the stony rock. In vain the Dwarf begged and prayed that he might keep one ring, for it was the source of all his wealth, and ring after ring dropped from it. 'No; not a penny should he have' said Loki. Then the dwarf laid a curse on the ring, and said it should be every man's bane who owned it. 'So much the better' said Loki; and when he got back, Odin saw the ring how fair it was, and kept it to himself, but gave the gold to Reidmar. So Reidmar filled the skin with gold as full as he could, and set it up on end, and Odin poured gold over it, and covered it up. But when Reidmar looked at it he saw still one grey hair, and bade them cover that too, else the atonement was at an end. Then

Odin drew forth the ring and laid it over the grey hair. So the Aesir was set free, but before they went, Loki repeated the curse which Andvari had laid upon the ring and gold. It soon began to work. First, Regin asked for some of the gold, but not a penny would Reidmar give. So the two brothers laid their heads together and slew their sire. Then Regin begged Fafnir to share the gold with him. But 'no', Fafnir was stronger, and said he should keep it all himself, and Regin had best be off, unless he wished to fare the same way as Reidmar. So Regin had to fly, but Fafnir took a dragon's shape; 'and there', said Regin, 'he lies on the "Glistening Heath", coiled round his store of gold and precious things, and that's why I wish you to kill him.' Sigurd, told Regin who was the best of smiths, to forge him a sword. Two are made, but both snap asunder at the first stroke. 'Untrue are they like you and all your race' cries Sigurd. Then he went to his mother and begged the broken bits of **Gram**, and out of them Regin forged a new blade, that clove the anvil in the smithy, and cut a lock of wool borne down upon it by a running stream. 'Now, slay me Fafnir', said Regin; but Sigurd must first find out King Hunding's sons, and avenge his father Sigmund's death. King Hialprek lends him force; by Odin's guidance he finds them out, routs their army, and slays all those brothers. On his return, his foster-father still eggs him on to slay the Dragon, and thus to shew that there was still a Volsung left. So, armed with Gram, and mounted on Gran, his good steed, whom Odin had taught him how to choose, Sigurd rode to the 'Glistening Heath', dug a pit in the Dragon's path, and slew him as he passed over him down to drink at the river. Then Regin came up, and the old feeling of vengeance for a brother's blood grew strong, and as an atonement, Sigurd was to roast Fafnir's heart, and carry it to Regin, who swilled his fill of the Dragon's blood, and lay down to sleep. But as Sigurd roasted the heart, and wondered if it would soon be done, he tried it with his finger to see if it were soft. The hot roast burned his finger, and he put it into his mouth, and tasted the life-blood of the Dragon. Then in a moment he understood the song of birds, and heard how the swallows over his head said one to the other, 'There thou sittest, Sigurd, roasting Fafnir's heart. Eat it thyself and become the wisest of men.' Then another said 'There lies Regin, and means to cheat him who trusts him.' Then a third said 'Let Sigurd cut off his head then, and so own all the gold himself.' Then Sigurd went to Regin and slew him, and ate the heart, and rode on Gran to Fafnir's lair, and took the spoil and loaded his good steed with it, and rode away.

And now Sigurd was the most famous of men. All the songs and stories of the North made him the darling of that age. They dwell on his soft hair, which fell in great locks of golden brown, on his bushy beard of auburn hue, his straight features, his ruddy cheeks, his broad brow, his bright and piercing eye, of which few dared to meet the gaze, his taper limbs and well knit joints, his broad shoulders, and towering height. 'So tall he was, that as he strode through the full- grown rye, girt with Gram, the tip of the scabbard just touched the ears of corn.' Ready of tongue too, and full of forethought. His great pleasure was to help other men, and to do daring deeds; to spoil his foes, and give largely to his friends. The bravest man alive, and one that never knew fear. On and on he rode, till on a lone fell he saw a flickering flame, and when he reached it, there it flamed and blazed all round a house. No horse but Gran could ride that flame; no man alive but Sigurd sit him while he leaped through it. Inside the house lay a fair maiden, armed from head to foot, in a deep sleep. Brynhildr, Atli's sister, was her name, a Valkyrie, a corse-chooser; but out of wilfulness she had given the victory to the wrong side, and Odin in his wrath had thrust the horn of sleep into her cloak, and laid her under a curse to slumber there till a man bold enough to ride through that flame came to set her free, and win her for his bride. So then she woke up, and taught him all runes and wisdom, and they swore to love each other with a mighty oath, and then Sigurd left her and rode on.

So on he rode to King Giuki's hall, Giuki the Niflung, King of Frankland, whose wife was Grimhildr, whose sons were Gunnar and Hogni, whose stepson was Guttorm, and whose daughter was the fair Gudrun. Here at first he was full of Brynhildr, and all for going back to fetch his lovely bride from the lone fell. But Grimhildr was given to dark arts; she longed for the brave Volsung for her own daughter, she brewed him the philtre of forgetfulness, he drained it off, forgot Brynhildr, swore a brother's friendship with Gunnar and Hogni, and wedded the fair Gudrun. But now Giuki wanted a wife for Gunnar, and so off set the brothers and their bosom friend to woo, but whom should they choose but Brynhildr, Atli's sister, who sat there still upon the fell, waiting for the man who was bold enough to ride through the flickering flame. She knew but one could do it, and waited for that one to come back. So she had given out whoever could ride that flame should have her to wife. So when Gunnar and Hogni reached it, Gunnar rode at it, but his horse, good though it was, swerved from the fierce flame. Then by Grimhild's magic arts, Sigurd and Gunnar changed shapes and arms, and Sigurd leapt up on Gran's back, and the good steed bore him bravely through the flame. So Brynhildr the proud maiden was won and forced to yield. That evening was their wedding; but when they lay down to rest, Sigurd unsheathed his keen sword **Gram**, and laid it naked between them. Next morning when he arose, he took the ring which Andvari had laid under the curse, and which was among Fafnir's treasures, and gave it to Brynhildr as a 'morning gift', and she gave him another ring as a pledge. Then Sigurd rode back to his companions and took his own shape again, and then Gunnar went and claimed Brynhildr, and carried her home as his bride. But no sooner was Gunnar wedded, than Sigurd's eyes were opened, and the power of the philtre passed away, he remembered all that had passed, and the oath he had sworn to Brynhildr. All this came back upon him when it was too late, but he was wise and said nothing about it. Well, so things went on, till one day Brynhildr and Gudrun went down to the river to wash their hair. Then Brynhildr waded out into the stream as far as she could, and said she wouldn't have on her head the water that streamed from Gudrun's; for hers was the braver husband. So Gudrun waded out after her, and said the water ought to come on her hair first, because her husband bore away the palm from Gunnar, and every other man alive, for he slew Fafnir and Regin and took their inheritance. 'Aye', said Brynhildr, 'but it was a worthier deed when Gunnar rode through the flame, but Sigurd dared not try!' Then Gudrun laughed, and said 'Thinkst thou that Gunnar really rode the flame? I trow **he** went to bed with thee that night, who gave me this gold ring. And as for that ring yonder which you have on your finger, and which you got as your "morning-gift"; its name is Andvari's-spoil, and **that** I don't think Gunnar sought on the "Glistening Heath"'. Then Brynhildr held her peace and went home, and her love for Sigurd came back, but it was turned to hate, for she felt herself betrayed. Then she egged on Gunnar to revenge her wrong. At last the brothers yielded to her entreaties, but they were sworn brothers to Sigurd, and to break that oath by deed was a thing unheard of. Still they broke it in spirit; by charms and prayers they set on Guttorm their half-brother, and so at dead of night, while Gudrun held the bravest man alive fast locked in her white arms, the murderer stole to the bedside and drove a sword through the hero. Then Sigurd turned and writhed, and as Guttorm fled he hurled Gram after him, and the keen blade took him asunder at the waist, and his head fell out of the room and his heels in, and that was the end of Guttorm. But with revenge Brynhildr's love returned, and when Sigurd was laid upon the pile her heart broke; she burst forth into a prophetic song of the woes that were still to come, made them lay her by his side with Gram between them, and so went to Valhalla with her old lover. Thus Andvari's curse was fulfilled.

Gudrun, the weary widow, wandered away. After a while, she accepts atonement from her brothers for her husband's loss, and marries Atli, the Hun King, Brynhildr's brother. He cherished a grudge against Giuki's sons for the guile they had practised against their brother- in-law, which had broken his sister's heart, and besides he claimed, in right of Gudrun, all the gold which Sigurd won from the Dragon, but which the Niflung Princes had seized when he was slain. It was in vain to attack them in fair fight, so he sent them a friendly message, and invited them to a banquet; they go, and are overpowered. Hogni's heart is cut out of him alive, but he still smiles; Gunnar is cast into a pit full of snakes, but even then charms them to sleep with his harp, all but one, that flies at his heart and stings him to death. With them perished the secret of the Dragon's hoard, which they had thrown into the Rhine as they crossed it on the way to Hunland. Now comes horror on horror. Revenge for her brothers now belongs to Gudrun; she slays with her own hand her two sons by Atli, makes him eat their flesh, and drink their blood out of their skulls, and, while the king slept sound, slew him in his bed by the help of her brother Hogni's son. Then she set the hall a-blaze, and burnt all that were in it. After that she went to the sea-shore, and threw herself in to drown. But the deep will not have her, the billows bear her over to King Jonakr's land. He marries her, and has three sons by her, Saurli, Hamdir, and Erp, black-haired as ravens, like all the Niflungs. Svanhild, her daughter by Sigurd, who had her father's bright and terrible eyes, she has still with her, now grown up to be the fairest of women. So when Hermanaric the mighty, the great Gothic king, heard of Svanhild's beauty, he sent his son Randver to woo her for him, but Bikki the False said to the youth: 'Better far were this maiden for thee than for thy old father'; and the maiden and the prince thought it good advice. Then Bikki went and told the king, and Hermanaric bade them take and hang Randver at once. So on his way to the gallows, the prince took his hawk and plucked off all its feathers, and sent it to his father. But when his sire saw it, he knew at once that, as the hawk was featherless and unable to fly, so was his realm defenceless under an old and sonless king. Too late he sent to stop the hanging; his son was already dead. So one day as he rode back from hunting, he saw fair Svanhild washing her golden locks, and it came into his heart how there she sat, the cause of all his woe; and he and his men rode at her and over her, and their steeds trampled her to death. But when Gudrun heard this, she set on her three Niflung sons to avenge their sister. Byrnies and helms she gave them so true that no sword would bite on them. They were to steal on Hermanaric as he slept; Saurli was to cut off his hands, Hamdir his feet, and Erp his head. So as the three went along, the two asked Erp what help he would give them when they got to Hermanaric. 'Such as hand lends to foot' he said. 'No help at all' they cried; and passing from words to blows, and because their mother loved Erp best, they slew him. A little further on Saurli stumbled and fell forward, but saved himself with one hand, and said 'Here hand helps foot: better were it that Erp lived.' So they came on Hermanaric as he slept, and Saurli hewed off his hands, and Hamdir his feet, but he awoke and called for his men. Then said Hamdir: 'Were Erp alive, the head would be off, and he couldn't call out.' Then Hermanaric's men arose and took the twain, and when they found that no steel would touch them, an old one-eyed man gave them advice to stone them to death. Thus fell Saurli and Hamdir, and soon after Gudrun died too, and with her ends the Volsung and the Niflung tale.

And here it is worth while to say, since some minds are so narrowly moulded as to be incapable of containing more than one idea, that because it has seemed a duty to describe in its true light the old faith of our forefathers, it by no means follows that the same eyes are blind to the glorious beauty of Greek Mythology. That had the rare advantage of running its course free and unfettered until it fell rather by natural decay than before the weapon of a new belief. The Greeks were Atheists before they became Christian. Their faith had passed through every stage. We can contemplate it as it springs out of the dim misshapen symbol, during that phase when men's eyes are fixed more on meaning and reality than on beauty and form, we can mark how it gradually looks more to symmetry and shape, how it is transfigured in the Arts, until, under that pure air and bright sky, the glowing radiant figures of Apollo and Aphrodite, of Zeus and Athene--of perfect man-worship and woman-worship, stand out clear and round in the foreground against the misty distance of ancient times. Out of that misty distance the Norseman's faith never emerged. What that early phase of faith might have become, had it been once wedded to the Muses, and learnt to cultivate the Arts, it is impossible to say. As it is, its career was cut short in mid-course. It carried about with it that melancholy presentiment of dissolution which has come to be so characteristic of modern life, but of which scarce a trace exists in ancient times, and this feeling would always have made it different from that cheerful carelessness which so attracts us in the Greeks; but even that downcast brooding heart was capable of conceiving great and heroic thoughts, which it might have clothed in noble shapes and forms, had not the axe of Providence cut down the stately sapling in the North before it grew to be a tree, while it spared the pines of Delphi and Dodona's sacred oaks, until they had attained a green old age. And so this faith remained rude and rough; but even rudeness has a simplicity of its own, and it is better to be rough and true-hearted than polished and false. In all the feelings of natural affection, that faith need fear no comparison with any other upon earth. In these respects it is firm and steadfast as a rock, and pure and bright as a living spring. The highest God is a father, who protects his children; who gives them glory and victory while they live, and when they die, takes them to himself; to those fatherly abodes Death was a happy return, a glorious going home. By the side of this great father stands a venerable goddess, dazzling with beauty, the great mother of gods and men. Hand in hand this divine pair traverse the land; he teaching the men the use of arms and all the arts of war,--for war was then as now a noble calling, and to handle arms an honourable, nay necessary, profession. To the women she teaches domestic duties and the arts of peace; from her they learn to weave, and sew, and spin; from her, too, the husbandman learns to till his fields. From him springs poetry and song; from her legend and tradition. Nor should it ever be forgotten that the footsteps of Providence are always onward, even when they seem taken in the dark, and that their rude faith was the first in which that veneration for woman arose, which the Western nations may well claim as the brightest jewel in their crown of civilization; that while she was a slave in the East, a toy to the Greeks, and a housewife to the Romans, she was a helpmeet to the Teuton, and that those stern warriors recognized something divine in her nature, and bowed before her clearer insight into heavenly mysteries. The worship of the Virgin Mary was gradually developed out of this conception of woman's character, and would have been a thing absurd and impossible, had Christianity clung for ever to Eastern soil. And now to proceed, after thus turning aside to compare the mythology of the Greek with the faith of the Norseman. The mistake is to favour one or the other exclusively instead of respecting and admiring both; but it is a mistake which those only can fall into, whose souls are narrow and confined, who would say this thing and this person you shall love, and none other; this form and feature you shall worship and adore, and this alone; when in fact the whole promised land of thought and life lies before us at our feet, our nature encourages us to go in and possess it, and every step we make in this new world of knowledge brings us to fresh prospects of beauty, and to new pastures of delight.

Such were the gods, and such the heroes of the Norseman; who, like his own gods, went smiling to death under the weight of an inevitable destiny. But that fate never fell on their gods. Before this subjective mythological dream of the Norsemen could be fulfilled, the religious mist in which they walked was scattered by the sunbeams of Christianity. A new state and condition of society arose, and the creed which had satisfied a race of heathen warriors, who externally were at war with all the world, became in time an object of horror and aversion to the converted Christian. This is not the place to describe the long struggle between the new and the old faith in the North; how kings and queens became the foster-fathers and nursing- mothers of the Church; how the great chiefs, each a little king in himself, scorned and derided the whole scheme as altogether weak and effeminate; how the bulk of the people were sullen and suspicious, and often broke out into heathen mutiny; how kings rose and kings fell, just as they took one or the other side; and how, finally, after a contest which had lasted altogether more than three centuries, Denmark, Norway, Iceland, and Sweden--we run them over in the order of conversion--became faithful to Christianity, as preached by the missionaries of the Church of Rome. One fact, however, we must insist on, which might be inferred, indeed, both from the nature of the struggle itself, and the character of Rome; and that is, that throughout there was something in the process of conversion of the nature of a compromise--of what we may call the great principle of 'give and take'. In all Christian churches, indeed, and in none so much as the Church of Rome, nothing is so austere, so elevating, and so grand, as the uncompromising tone in which the great dogmas of the Faith are enunciated and proclaimed. Nothing is more magnificent, in short, than the theory of Christianity; but nothing is more mean and miserable than the time-serving way in which those dogmas are dragged down to the dull level of daily life, and that sublime theory reduced to ordinary practice. At Rome, it was true that the Pope could congratulate the faithful that whole nations in the barbarous and frozen North had been added to the true fold, and that Odin's grim champions now universally believed in the gospel of peace and love. It is so easy to dispose of a doubtful struggle in a single sentence, and so tempting to believe it when once written. But in the North, the state of things, and the manner of proceeding, were entirely different. There the dogma was proclaimed, indeed; but the manner of preaching it was not in that mild spirit with which the Saviour rebuked the disciple when he said 'Put up again thy sword into his place: for all they that take the sword shall perish with the sword.' There the sword was used to bring converts to the font, and the baptism was often one rather of blood than of water. There the new converts perpetually relapsed, chased away the missionaries and the kings who sheltered them, and only yielded at last to the overwhelming weight of Christian opinion in the Western world. St Olof, king and martyr, martyred in pitched battle by his mutinous allodial freemen, because he tried to drive rather than to lead them to the cross; and another Olof, greater than he, Olof Tryggvason, who fell in battle against the heathen Swedes, were men of blood rather than peace; but to them the introduction of the new faith into Norway is mainly owing. So also Charlemagne, at an earlier period, had dealt with the Saxons at the Main Bridge, when his ultimatum was 'Christianity or death'. So also the first missionary to Iceland--who met, indeed, with a sorry reception--was followed about by a stout champion named Thangbrand, who, whenever there was what we should now call a missionary meeting, challenged any impugner of the new doctrines to mortal combat on the spot. No wonder that, after having killed several opponents in the little tour which he made with his missionary friend through the island, it became too hot to hold him, and he, and the missionary, and the new creed, were forced to take ship and sail back to Norway.

'Precept upon precept, line upon line, here a little and there a little', was the motto of Rome in her dealings with the heathen Norsemen, and if she suited herself at first rather to their habits and temper than to those of more enlightened nations, she had an excuse in St Paul's maxim of making herself 'all things to all men.' Thus, when a second attempt to Christianize Iceland proved more successful--for in the meantime, King Olof Tryggvason, a zealous Christian, had seized as hostages all the Icelanders of family and fame who happened to be in Norway, and thus worked on the feelings of the chiefs of those families at home, who in their turn bribed the lawman who presided over the Great Assembly to pronounce in favour of the new Faith--even then the adherents of the old religion were allowed to perform its rites in secret, and two old heathen practices only were expressly prohibited, the exposure of infants and the eating of horseflesh, for horses were sacred animals, and the heathen ate their flesh after they had been solemnly sacrificed to the gods. As a matter of fact, it is far easier to change a form of religion than to extirpate a faith. The first indeed is no easy matter, as those students of history well know who are acquainted with the tenacity with which a large proportion of the English nation clung to the Church of Rome, long after the State had declared for the Reformation. But to change the faith of a whole nation in block and bulk on the instant, was a thing contrary to the ordinary working of Providence and unknown even in the days of miracles, though the days of miracles had long ceased when Rome advanced against the North. There it was more politic to raise a cross in the grove where the Sacred Tree had once stood, and to point to the sacred emblem which had supplanted the old object of national adoration, when the populace came at certain seasons with songs and dances to perform their heathen rites. Near the cross soon rose a church; and both were girt by a cemetery, the soil of which was doubly sacred as a heathen fane and a Christian sanctuary, and where alone the bodies of the faithful could repose in peace. But the songs and dances, and processions in the church-yard round the cross, continued long after Christianity had become dominant. So also the worship of wells and springs was christianized when it was found impossible to prevent it. Great churches arose over or near them, as at Walsingham, where an abbey, the holiest place in England, after the shrine of St Thomas at Canterbury, threw its majestic shade over the heathen wishing-well, and the worshippers of Odin and the Nornir were gradually converted into votaries of the Virgin Mary. Such practices form a subject of constant remonstrance and reproof in the treatises and penitential epistles of medieval divines, and in some few places and churches, even in England, such rites are still yearly celebrated. [13]

So, too, again with the ancient gods. They were cast down from honour, but not from power. They lost their genial kindly influence as the protectors of men and the origin of all things good; but their existence was tolerated; they became powerful for ill, and degenerated into malignant demons. Thus the worshippers of Odin had supposed that at certain times and rare intervals the good powers shewed themselves in bodily shape to mortal eye, passing through the land in divine progress, bringing blessings in their train, and receiving in return the offerings and homage of their grateful votaries. But these were naturally only exceptional instances; on ordinary occasions the pious heathen recognized his gods sweeping through the air in cloud and storm, riding on the wings of the wind, and speaking in awful accents, as the tempest howled and roared, and the sea shook his white mane and crest. Nor did he fail to see them in the dust and din of battle, when Odin appeared with his terrible helm, succouring his own, striking fear into their foes, and turning the day in many a doubtful fight; or in the hurry and uproar of the chase, where the mighty huntsman on his swift steed, seen in glimpses among the trees, took up the hunt where weary mortals laid it down, outstripped them all, and brought the noble quarry to the ground. Looking up to the stars and heaven, they saw the footsteps of the gods marked out in the bright path of the Milky Way; and in the Bear they hailed the war-chariot of the warrior's god. The great goddesses, too, Frigga and Freyja, were thoroughly old-fashioned domestic divinities. They help women in their greatest need, they spin themselves, they teach the maids to spin, and punish them if the wool remains upon their spindle. They are kind, and good, and bright, for *Holda*, *Bertha*, are the epithets given to them. And so, too, this mythology which, in its aspect to the stranger and the external world, was so ruthless and terrible, when looked at from within and at home, was genial, and kindly, and hearty, and affords another proof that men, in all ages and climes, are not so bad as they seem; that after all, peace and not war is the proper state for man, and that a nation may make war on others and exist; but that unless it has peace within, and industry at home, it must perish from the face of the earth. But when Christianity came, the whole character of this goodly array of divinities was soured and spoilt. Instead of the stately procession of the God, which the intensely sensuous eye of man in that early time connected with all the phenomena of nature, the people were led to believe in a ghastly grisly band of ghosts, who followed an infernal warrior or huntsman in hideous tumult through the midnight air. No doubt, as Grimm rightly remarks [D. M., p. 900: *Wuetendes Heer*], the heathen had fondly fancied that the spirits of those who had gone to Odin followed him in his triumphant progress either visibly or invisibly; that they rode with him in the whirlwind, just as they followed him to battle, and feasted with him in Valhalla; but now the Christian belief, when it had degraded the mighty god into a demon huntsman, who pursued his nightly round in chase of human souls, saw in the train of the infernal master of the hunt only the spectres of suicides, drunkards, and ruffians; and, with all the uncharitableness of a dogmatic faith, the spirits of children who died unbaptized, whose hard fate had thrown them into such evil company. This was the way in which that wide-spread superstition arose, which sees in the phantoms of the clouds the shapes of the Wild Huntsman and his accursed crew, and hears, in spring and autumn nights, when sea-fowl take the wing to fly either south or north, the strange accents and uncouth yells with which the chase is pressed on in upper air. Thus, in Sweden it is still Odin who passes by; in Denmark it is King Waldemar's Hunt; in Norway it is *Aaskereida*, that is *Asgard's Car*; in Germany, it is Wode, Woden, or Hackel-berend, or Dieterich of Bern; in France it is Hellequin, or King Hugo, or Charles the Fifth, or, dropping a name altogether, it is *Le Grand Veneur* who ranges at night through the Forest of Fontainebleau. Nor was England without her Wild Hunts-man and his ghastly following. Gervase of Tilbury, in the twelfth century, could tell it of King Arthur, round whose mighty name the superstition settled itself, for he had heard from the foresters how, 'on alternate days, about the full of the moon, one day at noon, the next at midnight when the moon shone bright, a mighty train of hunters on horses was seen, with baying hounds and blast of horns; and when those hunters were asked of whose company and household they were, they replied "of Arthur's".' We hear of him again in *The Complaynt of Scotland*, that curious composition attributed by some to Sir David Lyndsay of the Mount in Fife, and of Gilmerton in East Lothian, pp. 97, 98, where he says:

> Arthur knycht, he raid on nycht,
> With gyldin spur and candil lycht.

Nor should we forget, when considering this legend, that story of Herne the Hunter, who

Sometime a keeper here in Windsor Forest,
Doth all the winter time, at still midnight,
Walk round about an oak, with great ragg'd horns;
And there he blasts the trees, and takes the cattle,
And makes milch-kine yield blood, and shakes a chain
In a most hideous and dreadful manner.

Merry Wives of Windsor, act. iv, sc. 4.

And even yet, in various parts of England, the story of some great man, generally a member of one of the county families, who drives about the country at night, is common. Thus, in Warwickshire, it is the 'One-handed Boughton', who drives about in his coach and six, and makes the benighted traveller hold gates open for him; or it is 'Lady Skipwith', who passes through the country at night in the same manner. This subject might be pursued to much greater length, for popular tradition is full of such stories; but enough has been said to show how the awful presence of a glorious God can be converted into a gloomy superstition; and, at the same time, how the majesty of the old belief strives to rescue itself by clinging, in the popular consciousness, to some king or hero, as Arthur or Waldemar, or, failing that, to some squire's family, as Hackelberend, or the 'one- handed Boughton', or even to the Keeper Herne.

Odin and the Aesir then were dispossessed and degraded by our Saviour and his Apostles, just as they had of old thrown out the Frost Giants, and the two are mingled together, in medieval Norse tradition, as Trolls and Giants, hostile alike to Christianity and man. Christianity had taken possession indeed, but it was beyond her power to kill. To this half-result the swift corruption of the Church of Rome lent no small aid. Her doctrines, as taught by Augustine and Boniface, by Anschar and Sigfrid, were comparatively mild and pure; but she had scarce swallowed the heathendom of the North, much in the same way as the Wolf was to swallow Odin at the 'Twilight of the Gods', than she fell into a deadly lethargy of faith, which put it out of her power to digest her meal. Gregory the Seventh, elected pope in 1073, tore the clergy from the ties of domestic life with a grasp that wounded every fibre of natural affection, and made it bleed to the very root. With the celibacy of the clergy he established the hierarchy of the church, but her labours as a missionary church were over. Henceforth she worked not by missionaries and apostles, but by crusades and bulls. Now she raised mighty armaments to recover the barren soil of the Holy Sepulchre, or to annihilate heretic Albigenses. Now she established great orders, Templars and Hospitallers, whose pride and luxury, and pomp, brought swift destruction on one at least of those fraternities. Now she became feudal,--she owned land instead of hearts, and forgot that the true patrimony of St Peter was the souls of men. No wonder that, with the barbarism of the times, she soon fulfilled the Apostle's words, 'She that liveth in luxury is dead while she liveth', and became filled with idle superstitions and vain beliefs. No wonder, then, that instead of completing her conquest over the heathen, and carrying out their conversion, she became half heathen herself; that she adopted the tales and traditions of the old mythology, which she had never been able to extirpate, and related them of our Lord and his Apostles. No wonder, then, that having abandoned her mission of being the first power of intelligence on earth, she fell like Lucifer when the mist of medieval feudalism rolled away, and the light of learning and education returned--fell before the indignation of enlightened men, working upon popular opinion. Since which day, though she has changed her plans, and remodelled her superstitions to suit the times, she has never regained the supremacy which, if she had been wise in a true sense, she seemed destined to hold for ever.

NORSE POPULAR TALES

The preceding observations will have given a sufficient account of the mythology of the Norsemen, and of the way in which it fell. They came from the East, and brought that common stock of tradition with them. Settled in the Scandinavian peninsula, they developed themselves through Heathenism, Romanism, and Lutheranism, in a locality little exposed to foreign influence, so that even now the Daleman in Norway or Sweden may be reckoned among the most primitive examples left of peasant life. We should expect, then, that these Popular Tales, which, for the sake of those ignorant in such matters, it may be remarked, had never been collected or reduced to writing till within the last few years, would present a faithful picture of the national consciousness, or, perhaps, to speak more correctly, of that half consciousness out of which the heart of any people speaks in its abundance. Besides those world-old affinities and primaeval parallelisms, besides those dreamy recollections of its old home in the East, which we have already pointed out, we should expect to find its later history, after the great migration, still more distinctly reflected; to discover heathen gods masked in the garb of Christian saints; and thus to see a proof of our assertion above, that a nation more easily changes the form than the essence of its faith, and clings with a toughness which endures for centuries to what it has once learned to believe.

In all mythologies, the trait of all others which most commonly occurs, is that of the descent of the Gods to earth, where, in human form, they mix among mortals, and occupy themselves with their affairs, either out of a spirit of adventure, or to try the hearts of men. Such a conception is shocking to the Christian notion of the omnipotence and omnipresence of God, but we question if there be not times when the most pious and perfect Christian may not find comfort and relief from a fallacy which was a matter of faith in less enlightened creeds, and over which the apostle, writing to the Hebrews, throws the sanction of his authority, so far as angels are concerned. [Heb., xiii, 1: 'Let brotherly love continue. Be not forgetful to entertain strangers: for thereby some have entertained angels unawares.']

Nor could he have forgotten those words of the men of Lystra, 'The Gods are come down to us in the likeness of men'; and how they called 'Barnabas Jupiter', and himself Mercury, 'because he was the chief speaker.' Classical mythology is full of such stories. These wanderings of the Gods are mentioned in the Odyssey, and the sanctity of the rites of hospitality, and the dread of turning a stranger from the door, took its origin from a fear lest the wayfaring man should be a Divinity in disguise. According to the Greek story, Orion owed his birth to the fact that the childless Hyrieus, his reputed father, had once received unawares Zeus, Poseidon, and Hermes, or, to call them by their Latin names, Jupiter, Neptune, and Mercury. In the beautiful story of Philemon and Baucis, Jupiter and Mercury reward the aged couple who had so hospitably received them by warning them of the approaching deluge. The fables of Phaedrus and Aesop represent Mercury and Demeter as wandering and enjoying the hospitality of men. In India it is Brahma and Vishnu who generally wander. In the Edda, Odin, Loki, and Hoenir thus roam about, or Thor, Thialfi, and Loki. Sometimes Odin appears alone as a horseman, who turns in at night to the smith's house, and gets him to shoe his horse, a legend which reminds us at once of the Master-smith. [14] Sometimes it is Thor with his great hammer who wanders thus alone.

Now, let us turn from heathen to Christian times, and look at some of these old legends of wandering gods in a new dress. Throughout the Middle Age, it is our blessed Lord and St Peter that thus wander, and here we see that half-digested heathendom to which we have alluded. Those who may be shocked at such tales in this collection as 'the Master-Smith' and 'Gertrude's Bird', must just remember that these are almost purely heathen traditions, in which the names alone are Christian; and if it be any consolation to any to know the fact, we may as well state at once that this adaptation of new names to old beliefs is not peculiar to the Norsemen, but is found in all the popular tales of Europe. Germany was full of them, and there St Peter often appears in a snappish ludicrous guise, which reminds the reader versed in Norse mythology of the tricks and pranks of the shifty Loki. In the Norse tales he thoroughly preserves his saintly character.

Nor was it only gods that walked among men. In the Norse mythology, Frigga, Odin's wife, who knew beforehand all that was to happen, and Freyja, the goddess of love and plenty, were prominent figures, and often trod the earth; the three Norns or Fates, who sway the wierds of men, and spin their destinies at Mimirs' well of knowledge, were awful venerable powers, to whom the heathen world looked up with love and adoration and awe. To that love and adoration and awe, throughout the middle age, one woman, transfigured into a divine shape, succeeded by a sort of natural right, and round the Virgin Mary's blessed head a halo of lovely tales of divine help, beams with soft radiance as a crown bequeathed to her by the ancient goddesses. She appears as divine mother, spinner, and helpful virgin (vierge secourable). Flowers and plants bear her name. In England one of our commonest and prettiest insects is still called after her, but which belonged to Freyja, the heathen 'Lady', long before the western nations had learned to adore the name of the mother of Jesus. [15] So also Orion's Belt was called by the Norsemen, Frigga's spindle or **rock, Friggjar rock**. In modern Swedish, **Friggerock**, where the old goddess holds her own; but in Danish, **Mariaerock**, Our Lady's rock or spindle. Thus, too, **Karlavagn**, the 'car of men', or heroes, who rode with Odin, which we call 'Charles' Wain', thus keeping something, at least, of the old name, though none of its meaning, became in Scotland 'Peter's-pleugh', from the Christian saint, just as Orion's sword became 'Peter's-staff'. But what do 'Lady Landers' and 'Lady Ellison' mean, as applied to the 'Lady-Bird' in Scotland?

The reader of these Tales will meet, in that of 'the Lassie and her Godmother', No. xxvii, with the Virgin Mary in a truly mythic character, as the majestic guardian of sun, moon and stars, combined with that of a helpful, kindly woman, who, while she knows how to punish a fault, knows also how to reconcile and forgive.

The Norseman's god was a god of battles, and victory his greatest gift to men; but this was not the only aspect under which the Great Father was revered. Not victory in the fight alone, but every other good gift came down from him and the Aesir. Odin's supreme will was that treasure-house of bounty towards which, in one shape or the other, all mortal desires turned, and out of its abundance showers of mercy and streams of divine favour constantly poured down to refresh the weary race of men. All these blessings and mercies, nay, their very source itself, the ancient language bound up in a single word, which, however expressive it may still be, has lost much of the fulness of its meaning in its descent to these later times. This word was 'Wish', which originally meant the perfect ideal, the actual fruition of all joy and desire, and not, as now, the empty longing for the object of our desires. From this original abstract meaning, it was but a step to pass to the concrete, to personify the idea, to make it an immortal essence, an attribute of the divinity, another name for the greatest of all Gods himself. And so we find a host of passages in early writers, [**D. M.**, p. 126 fol., where they are cited at length.] in every one of which 'God' or 'Odin' might be substituted for 'Wish' with perfect propriety. Here we read how 'The Wish' has hands, feet, power, sight, toil, and art. How he works and labours, shapes and masters, inclines his ear, thinks, swears, curses, and rejoices, adopts children, and takes men into his house; behaves, in short, as a being of boundless power and infinite free- will. Still more, he rejoices in his own works as in a child, and thus appears in a thoroughly patriarchal point of view, as the Lord of creation, glorying in his handiwork, as the father of a family in early times was glad at heart when he reckoned his children as arrows in his quiver, and beheld his house full of a long line of retainers and dependants. For this attribute of the Great Father, for Odin as the God of Wish, the Edda uses the word 'Oski' which literally expresses the masculine personification of 'Wish', and it passed on and added the **works** wish, as a prefix to a number of others, to signify that they stood in a peculiar relation to the great giver of all good. Thus we have **oska-steinn**, wishing-stone, i.e. a stone which plays the part of a divining rod, and reveals secrets and hidden treasure; **oska-byrr**, a fair wind, a wind as fair as man's heart could wish it; **osk-barn** and **oska-barn**, a child after one's own heart, an adopted child, as when the younger Edda tells us that all those who die in battle are Odin's **choice- bairns**, his adopted children, those on whom he has set his heart, an expression which, in their turn, was taken by the Icelandic Christian writers to express the relation existing between God and the baptized; and, though last, not least, **oska-maer**, wish- maidens, another name for the Valkyries--Odin's corse-choosers--who picked out the dead for him on the field of battle, and waited on the heroes in Valhalla. Again, the Edda is filled with 'choice things', possessing some mysterious power of their own, some 'virtue', as our older English would express it, which belong to this or that god, and are occasionally lent or lost. Thus, Odin himself had a spear which gave victory to those on whose side it was hurled; Thor, a hammer which destroyed the Giants, hallowed vows, and returned of itself to his hand. He had a strength-belt, too, which, when he girded it on, his god-strength waxed one-half; Freyr had a sword which wielded itself; Freyja a necklace which, like the cestus of Venus, inspired all hearts with love; Freyr, again, had a ship called ***Skithblathnir***.

> She is so great, that all the Aesir, with their weapons and war
> gear, may find room on board her; and as soon as the sail is set,
> she has a fair wind whither she shall go; and when there is no need
> of faring on the sea in her, she is made of so many things, and
> with so much craft, that Freyr may fold her together like a cloth,
> and keep her in his bag.
> [Snorro's ***Edda***, Stockholm, 1842, translated by the writer.]

Of this kind, too, was the ring 'Dropper' which Odin had, and from which twelve other rings dropped every night; the apples which Idun, one of the goddesses, had, and of which, so soon as the Aesir ate, they became young again; the helm which Oegir, the sea giant had, which struck terror into all antagonists like the Aegis of Athene; and that wonderful mill which the mythical Frodi owned, of which we shall shortly speak.

Now, let us see what traces of this great god 'Wish' and his choice- bairns and wishing-things we can find in these Tales, faint echoes of a mighty heathen voice, which once proclaimed the goodness of the great Father in the blessings which he bestowed on his chosen sons. We shall not have long to seek. In tale No. xx, when Shortshanks meets those three old crookbacked hags who have only one eye, which he snaps up, and gets first a sword 'that puts a whole army to flight, be it ever so great', we have the 'one-eyed Odin', degenerated into an old hag, or rather--by no uncommon process--we have an old witch fused by popular tradition into a mixture of Odin and the three Nornir. Again, when he gets that wondrous ship 'which can sail over fresh water and salt water, and over high hills and deep dales,' and which is so small that he can put it into his pocket, and yet, when he came to use it, could hold five hundred men, we have plainly the Skith-blathnir of the Edda to the very life. So also in the Best Wish, No. xxxvi, the whole groundwork of this story rests on this old belief; and when we meet that pair of old scissors which cuts all manner of fine clothes out of the air, that tablecloth which covers itself with the best dishes you could think of, as soon as it was spread out, and that tap which, as soon as it was turned, poured out the best of mead and wine, we have plainly another form of Frodi's wishing-quern--another recollection of those things of choice about which the old mythology has so much to tell. Of the same kind are the tablecloth, the ram, and the stick in 'the Lad who went to the North Wind', No. xxxiv, and the rings in 'the Three Princesses of Whiteland', No. xxvi, and in 'Soria Moria Castle', No. lvi. In the first of those stories, too, we find those 'three brothers' who have stood on a moor 'these hundred years fighting about a hat, a cloak, and a pair of boots', which had the virtue of making him who wore them invisible; choice things which will again remind the reader of the ***Nibelungen Lied***, of the way in which Siegfried became possessed of the famous hoard of gold, and how he got that 'cap of darkness' which was so useful to him in his remaining exploits. So again in 'the Blue Belt', No. xxii, what is that belt which, when the boy girded it on, 'he felt as strong as if he could lift the whole hill', but Thor's 'choice-belt'; and what is the daring boy himself, who overcomes the Troll, but Thor himself, as engaged in one of his adventures with the Giants? So, too, in 'Little Annie the Goose- girl', No. lix, the stone which tells the Prince all the secrets of his brides is plainly the old Oskastein, or 'wishing-stone'. These instances will suffice to show the prolonged faith in 'Wish', and his choice things; a belief which, though so deeply rooted in the North, we have already traced to its home in the East, whence it stretches itself from pole to pole, and reappears in every race. We recognize it in the wishing-cap of Fortunatus, which is a Celtic legend; in the cornucopia of the Romans; in the goat Amalthea among the Greeks; in the wishing-cow and wishing-tree of the Hindoos; in the pumpkin-tree of the West Indian Ananzi stories; in the cow of the Servian legends, who spins yarn out of her ear; in the Sampo of the Finns; and in all those stories of cups, and glasses, and horns, and rings, and swords, seized by some bold spirit in the midst of a fairy revel, or earned by some kind deed rendered by mortal hand to one of the 'good folk' in her hour of need, and with which the '***luck***' [See the well- known story of 'The Luck of Eden Hall'.] of that mortal's house was ever afterwards bound up; stories with which the local traditions of all lands are full, but which all pay unconscious homage to the worship of that great God, to whom so many heathen hearts so often turned as the divine realizer of their prayers, and the giver of all good things, until they come at last to make an idol out of their hopes and prayers, and to immortalize the very 'Wish' itself.

Again, of all beliefs, that in which man has, at all times of his history, been most prone to set faith, is that of a golden age of peace and plenty, which had passed away, but which might be expected to return. Such a period was looked for when Augustus closed the temple of Janus, and peace, though perhaps not plenty, reigned over what the proud Roman called the habitable world. Such a period the early Christian expected when the Saviour was born, in the reign of that very Augustus; and such a period some, whose thoughts are more set on earth than heaven, have hoped for ever since, with a hope which, though deferred for eighteen centuries, has not made their hearts sick. Such a period of peace and plenty, such a golden time, the Norseman could tell of in his mythic Frodi's reign, when gold or *Frodi's meal*, as it was called, was so plentiful that golden armlets lay untouched from year's end to year's end on the king's highway, and the fields bore crops unsown. Here, in England, the Anglo-Saxon Bede [Hist., ii, 16.] knew how to tell the same story of Edwin, the Northumbrian King, and when Alfred came to be mythic, the same legend was passed on from Edwin to the West Saxon monarch. The remembrance of 'the bountiful Frodi' echoed in the songs of German poets long after the story which made him so bountiful had been forgotten; but the Norse Skalds could tell not only the story of Frodi's wealth and bounty, but also of his downfall and ruin. In Frodi's house were two maidens of that old giant race, Fenja and Menja. These daughters of the giant he had bought as slaves, and he made them grind his quern or hand-mill, Grotti, out of which he used to grind peace and gold. Even in that golden age one sees there were slaves, and Frodi, however bountiful to his thanes and people, was a hard task-master to his giant hand-maidens. He kept them to the mill, nor gave them longer rest than the cuckoo's note lasted, or they could sing a song. But that quern was such that it ground anything that the grinder chose, though until then it had ground nothing but gold and peace. So the maidens ground and ground, and one sang their piteous tale in a strain worthy of Aeschylus as the other worked-- they prayed for rest and pity, but Frodi was deaf. Then they turned in giant mood, and ground no longer peace and plenty, but fire and war. Then the quern went fast and furious, and that very night came Mysing the Sea-rover, and slew Frodi and all his men, and carried off the quern; and so Frodi's peace ended. The maidens the sea-rover took with him, and when he got on the high seas he bade them grind salt. So they ground; and at midnight they asked if he had not salt enough, but he bade them still grind on. So they ground till the ship was full and sank, Mysing, maids, and mill, and all, and that's why the sea is salt [nor. ***Ed. Skaldsk.***, ch. 43.]. Perhaps of all the tales in this volume, none could be selected as better proving the toughness of a traditional belief than No. ii, which tells 'Why the Sea is Salt'.

The notion of the Arch-enemy of God and man, of a fallen angel, to whom power was permitted at certain times for an all-wise purpose by the Great Ruler of the universe, was as foreign to the heathendom of our ancestors as his name was outlandish and strange to their tongue. This notion Christianity brought with it from the East; and though it is a plant which has struck deep roots, grown distorted and awry, and borne a bitter crop of superstition, it required all the authority of the Church to prepare the soil at first for its reception. To the notion of good necessarily follows that of evil. The Eastern mind, with its Ormuzd and Ahriman, is full of such dualism, and from that hour, when a more than mortal eye saw Satan falling like lightning from heaven [St Luke, x, 18.], the kingdom of darkness, the abode of Satan and his bad spirits, was established in direct opposition to the kingdom of the Saviour and his angels. The North had its own notion on this point. Its mythology was not without its own dark powers; but though they too were ejected and dispossessed, they, according to that mythology, had rights of their own. To them belonged all the universe that had not been seized and reclaimed by the younger race of Odin and Aesir; and though this upstart dynasty, as the Frost Giants in Promethean phrase would have called it, well knew that Hel, one of this giant progeny, was fated to do them all mischief, and to outlive them, they took her and made her queen of Niflheim, and mistress over nine worlds. There, in a bitterly cold place, she received the souls of all who died of sickness or old age; care was her bed, hunger her dish, starvation her knife. Her walls were high and strong, and her bolts and bars huge; 'Half blue was her skin, and half the colour of human flesh. A goddess easy to know, and in all things very stern and grim.' [Snor. ***Edda,*** ch. 34, Engl. Transl.]

But though severe, she was not an evil spirit. She only received those who died as no Norseman wished to die. For those who fell on the gory battle-field, or sank beneath the waves, Valhalla was prepared, and endless mirth and bliss with Odin.

Those went to Hel, who were rather unfortunate than wicked, who died before they could be killed. But when Christianity came in and ejected Odin and his crew of false divinities, declaring them to be lying gods and demons, then Hel fell with the rest; but fulfilling her fate, outlived them. From a person she became a place, and all the Northern nations, from the Goth to the Norseman, agreed in believing Hell to be the abode of the devil and his wicked spirits, the place prepared from the beginning for the everlasting torments of the damned. One curious fact connected with this explanation of Hell's origin will not escape the reader's attention. The Christian notion of Hell is that of a place of heat, for in the East, whence Christianity came, heat is often an intolerable torment, and cold, on the other hand, everything that is pleasant and delightful. But to the dweller in the North, heat brings with it sensations of joy and comfort, and life without fire has a dreary outlook; so their Hel ruled in a cold region over those who were cowards by implication, while the mead-cup went round, and huge logs blazed and crackled in Valhalla, for the brave and beautiful who had dared to die on the field of battle. But under Christianity the extremes of heat and cold have met, and Hel, the cold uncomfortable goddess, is now our Hell, where flames and fire abound, and where the devils abide in everlasting flame.

Still, popular tradition is tough, and even after centuries of Christian teaching, the Norse peasant, in his popular tales, can still tell of Hell as a place where fire-wood is wanted at Christmas, and over which a certain air of comfort breathes, though, as in the goddess Hel's halls, meat is scarce. The following passage from 'Why the Sea is Salt', No. ii, will sufficiently prove this:

'Well, here is the flitch', said the rich brother, 'and now go
 straight to Hell.'

'What I have given my word to do, I must stick to' said the other;
so he took the flitch and set off. He walked the whole day, and at
dusk he came to a place where he saw a very bright light.

'Maybe this is the place' said the man to himself. So he turned
aside, and the first thing he saw was an old, old man, with a long

white beard, who stood in an outhouse, hewing wood for the Christmas fire.

'Good even,' said the man with the flitch.

'The same to you; whither are you going so late?' said the man.

'Oh! I'm going to Hell, if I only knew the right way,' answered the poor man.

'Well, you're not far wrong, for this is Hell,' said the old man; 'When you get inside they will be all for buying your flitch, for meat is scarce in Hell; but mind you don't sell it unless you get the hand-quern which stands behind the door for it. When you come out, I'll teach you how to handle the quern, for it's good to grind almost anything.'

This, too, is the proper place to explain the conclusion of that intensely heathen tale, 'the Master-Smith', No. xvi. We have already seen how the Saviour and St Peter supply, in its beginning, the place of Odin and some other heathen god. But when the Smith sets out with the feeling that he has done a silly thing in quarrelling with the Devil, having already lost his hope of heaven, this tale assumes a still more heathen shape. According to the old notion, those who were not Odin's guests went either to Thor's house, who had all the thralls, or to Freyja, who even claimed a third part of the slain on every battle-field with Odin, or to Hel, the cold comfortless goddess already mentioned, who was still no tormentor, though she ruled over nine worlds, and though her walls were high, and her bolts and bars huge; traits which come out in 'the Master-Smith', No. xvi, when the Devil, who here assumes Hel's place, orders the watch to go back and lock up ***all the nine locks on the gates of Hell***--a lock for each of the goddesses ***nine*** worlds--and to put a padlock on besides. In the twilight between heathendom and Christianity, in that half Christian half heathen consciousness, which this tale reveals, heaven is the preferable abode, as Valhalla was of yore, but rather than be without a house to one's head after death, Hell was not to be despised; though, having behaved ill to the ruler of one, and actually quarrelled with the master of the other, the Smith was naturally anxious on the matter. This notion of different abodes in another world, not necessarily places of torment, comes out too in 'Not a Pin to choose between them', No. xxiv, where Peter, the second husband of the silly Goody, goes about begging from house to house in Paradise.

For the rest, whenever the Devil appears in these tales, it is not at all as the Arch-enemy, as the subtle spirit of the Christian's faith, but rather as one of the old Giants, supernatural and hostile indeed to man, but simple and easily deceived by a cunning reprobate, whose superior intelligence he learns to dread, for whom he feels himself no match, and whom, finally, he will receive in Hell at no price. We shall have to notice some other characteristics of this race of giants a little further on, but certainly no greater proof can be given of the small hold which the Christian Devil has taken of the Norse mind, than the heathen aspect under which he constantly appears, and the ludicrous way in which he is always outwitted.

We have seen how our Lord and the saints succeeded to Odin and his children in the stories which told of their wanderings on earth, to warn the wicked, or to help the good; we have seen how the kindliness and helpfulness of the ancient goddesses fell like a royal mantle round the form of the Virgin Mary. We have seen, too, on the other hand, how the procession of the Almighty God degenerated into the infernal midnight hunt. We have now to see what became of the rest of the power of the goddesses, of all that might which was not absorbed into the glory of the blessed Virgin. We shall not have far to seek. No reader of early medieval chronicles and sermons, can fail to have been struck with many passages which ascribe majesty and power to beings of woman's sex. Now it is a heathen goddess as *Diana*; now some half-historical character as *Bertha*; now a mythical being as *Holda*; now *Herodias*; now *Satia*; now *Domina Abundia*, or *Dame Habonde* [16].

A very short investigation will serve to identify the two ancient goddesses Frigga and Freyja with all these leaders of a midnight host. Just as Odin was banished from day to darkness, so the two great heathen goddesses, fused into one 'uncanny' shape, were supposed to ride the air at night. Medieval chroniclers, writing in bastard Latin, and following the example of classical authors, when they had to find a name for this demon-goddess, chose, of course, *Diana* the heathen huntress, the moon-goddess, and the ruler of the night. In the same way, when they threw Odin's name into a Latin shape, he, the god of wit and will, as well as power and victory, became Mercury. As for Herodias--not the mother, but the daughter who danced--she must have made a deep impression on the mind of the early Middle Age, for she was supposed to have been cursed after the beheading of John the Baptist, and to have gone on dancing for ever. When heathendom fell, she became confounded with the ancient Goddesses, and thus we find her, sometimes among the crew of the Wild Huntsman, sometimes, as we see in the passages below, in company with, or in the place of *Diana, Holda, Satia*, and *Abundia*, at the head of a bevy of women, who met at certain places to celebrate unholy rites and mysteries. As for *Holda, Satia*, and *Abundia*, 'the kind', 'the satisfying', and 'the abundant', they are plainly names of good rather than evil powers; they are ancient epithets drawn from the bounty of the 'Good Lady', and attest the feeling of respect which still clung to them in the popular mind. As was the case whenever Christianity was brought in, the country folk, always averse to change, as compared with the more lively and intelligent dwellers in towns, still remained more or less heathen, [17] and to this day they preserve unconsciously many superstitions which can be traced up in lineal descent to their old belief. In many ways does the old divinity peep out under the new superstition--the long train, the midnight feast, 'the good lady' who presides, the bounty and abundance which her votaries fancied would follow in her footsteps, all belong to the ancient Goddess. Most curious of all is the way in which all these traditions from different countries insist on the third part of the earth, the third child born, the third soul as belonging to the 'good lady', who leads the revel; for this right of a third, or even of a half, was one which Freyja possessed. 'But Freyja is most famous of the Asynjor. She has that bower in heaven hight Folkvangr, and 'whithersoever she rideth to the battle, there hath she one half of the slain; but Odin the other half.' Again 'when she fares abroad, she drives two cats and sits in a car, and she lends an easy ear to the prayers of men.' [Snorro's *Edda*, Dasent's Translation, pp. 29 (Stockholm 1842).]

We have got then the ancient goddesses identified as evil influences, and as the leader of a midnight band of women, who practised secret and unholy rites. This leads us at once to witchcraft. In all ages and in all races this belief in sorcery has existed. Men and women practised it alike, but in all times female sorcerers have predominated. [18] This was natural enough. In those days women were priestesses; they collected drugs and simples; women alone knew the virtues of plants. Those soft hands spun linen, made lint, and bound wounds. Women in the earliest times with which we are acquainted with our forefathers, alone knew how to read and write, they only could carve the mystic runes, they only could chant the charms so potent to allay the wounded warrior's smart and pain. The men were busy out of doors with ploughing, hunting, barter, and war. In such an age the sex which possessed by natural right book-learning, physic, soothsaying, and incantation, even when they used these mysteries for good purposes, were but a step from sin. The same soft white hand that bound the wound and scraped the lint; the same gentle voice that sung the mystic rune, that helped the child-bearing woman, or drew the arrow-head from the dying champion's breast; the same bright eye that gazed up to heaven in ecstacy through the sacred grove and read the will of the Gods when the mystic tablets and rune-carved lots were cast--all these, if the will were bad, if the soothsayer passed into the false prophetess, the leech into a poisoner, and the priestess into a witch, were as potent and terrible for ill as they had once been powerful for good. In all the Indo-European tribes, therefore, women, and especially old women, have practised witchcraft from the earliest times, and Christianity found them wherever it advanced. But Christianity, as it placed mankind upon a higher platform of civilization, increased the evil which it found, and when it expelled the ancient goddesses, and confounded them as demons with Diana and Herodias, it added them and their votaries to the old class of malevolent sorcerers. There was but one step, but a simple act of the will, between the Norn and the hag, even before Christianity came in. As soon as it came, down went Goddess, Valkyrie, Norn, priestess, and soothsayer, into that unholy deep where the heathen hags and witches had their being; and, as Christianity gathered strength, developed its dogmas, and worked out its faith; fancy, tradition, leechcraft, poverty, and idleness, produced that unhappy class, the medieval witch, the persecution of which is one of the darkest pages in religious history.

It is curious indeed to trace the belief in witches through the Middle Age, and to mark how it increases in intensity and absurdity. At first, as we have seen in the passages quoted, the superstition seemed comparatively harmless, and though the witches themselves may have believed in their unholy power, there were not wanting divines who took a common-sense view of the matter, and put the absurdity of their pretensions to a practical proof. Such was that good parish priest who asked, when an old woman of his flock insisted that she had been in his house with the company of 'the Good Lady', and had seen him naked and covered him up, 'How, then, did you get in when all the doors were locked?' 'We can get in,' she said, 'even if the doors are locked.' Then the priest took her into the chancel of the church, locked the door, and gave her a sound thrashing with the pastoral staff, calling out 'Out with you, lady witch.' But as she could not, he sent her home, saying 'See now how foolish you are to believe in such empty dreams'. [19]

But as the Church increased in strength, as heresies arose, and consequent persecution, then the secret meetings of these sectarians, as we should now call them, were identified by the hierarchy with the rites of sorcery and magic, and with the relics of the worship of the old gods. By the time, too, that the hierarchy was established, that belief in the fallen angel, the Arch-Fiend, the Devil, originally so foreign to the nations of the West, had become thoroughly ingrafted on the popular mind, and a new element of wickedness and superstition was introduced at those unholy festivals. About the middle of the thirteenth century, we find the mania for persecuting heretics invading the tribes of Teutonic race from France and Italy, backed by all the power of the Pope. Like jealousy, persecution too often makes the meat it feeds on, and many silly, if not harmless, superstitions were rapidly put under the ban of the Church. Now the 'Good Lady' and her train begin to recede, they only fill up the background while the Prince of Darkness steps, dark and terrible, in front, and soon draws after him the following of the ancient goddess. Now we hear stories of demoniac possession; now the witches adore a demon of the other sex. With the male element, and its harsher, sterner nature, the sinfulness of these unholy assemblies is infinitely increased; folly becomes guilt, and guilt crime. [20]

From the middle of the fourteenth to the middle of the seventeenth century the history of Europe teems with processes against witches and sorcerers. Before the Reformation it reached its height, in the Catholic world, with the famous bull of Innocent the Eighth in 1484, the infamous **Malleus Maleficarum**, the first of the long list of witch-finding books, and the zeal with which the State lent all the terrors of the law to assist the ecclesiastical inquisitors. Before the tribunals of those inquisitors, in the fifteenth century, innumerable victims were arraigned on the double charge of heresy and sorcery--for the crimes ran in couples, both being children and sworn servants of the Devil. Would that the historian could say that with the era of the Reformation these abominations ceased. The Roman Hierarchy, with her bulls and inquisitors, had sown a bitter crop, which both she and the Protestant Churches were destined to reap; but in no part of the world were the labourers more eager and willing, when the fields were 'black' to harvest, than in those very reformed communities which had just shaken off the yoke of Rome, and which had sprung in many cases from the very heretics whom she had persecuted and burnt, accusing them at the same time, of the most malignant sorceries. [21]

Their excuse is, that no one is before his age. The intense personality given to the Devil in the Middle Age had possessed the whole mind of Europe. We must take them as we find them, with their bright fancy, their earnest faith, their stern fanaticism, their revolting superstition, just as when we look upon a picture we know that those brilliant hues and tones, that spirit which informs the whole, could never be, were it not for the vulgar earths and oil out of which the glorious work of art is mixed and made. Strangely monotonous are all the witch trials of which Europe has so many to show. At first the accused denies, then under torture she confesses, then relapses and denies; tortured again she confesses again, amplifies her story, and accuses others. When given to the stake, she not seldom asserts all her confessions to be false, which is ascribed to the power which the fiend still has over her. Then she is burnt and her ashes given to the winds. Those who wish to read one unexampled, perhaps for barbarity and superstition, and more curious than the rest from the prominence given in it to a man, may find it in the trial of Dr. Fian, the Scotch wizard, "which doctor was register to the Devil, that sundry times preached at North Baricke (North Berwick, in East Lothian) Kirke, to a number of notorious witches." [22] But we advise no one to venture on a perusal of this tract who is not prepared to meet with the most unutterable accusations and crimes, the most cruel tortures, and the most absurd confessions, followed as usual by the stoutest denial of all that had been confessed; when torture had done her worst on poor human nature, and the soul re-asserted at the last her supremacy over the body. [23] One characteristic of all these witch trials, is the fact, that in spite of their unholy connection and intrigues with the Evil One, no witch ever attained to wealth and station by the aid of the Prince of Darkness. The pleasure to do ill, is all the pleasure they feel. This fact alone might have opened the eyes of their persecutors, for if the Devil had the worldly power which they represented him to have, he might at least have raised some of his votaries to temporal rank, and to the pomps and the vanities of this world. An old German proverb expresses this notorious fact, by saying, that 'every seven years, a witch is three halfpence richer'; and so with all the unholy means of Hell at their command, they dragged out their lives, along with their black cats, in poverty and wretchedness. To this fate at last, came the worshippers of the great goddess Freyja, whom our forefathers adored as the goddess of love and plenty; and whose car was drawn by those animals which popular superstition has ever since assigned to the 'old witch' of our English villages.

The North was not free, any more than the rest of the Protestant world, from this direful superstition, which ran over Europe like a pestilence in the sixteenth century. In Sweden especially, the witches and their midnight ridings to ***Blokulla***, the black hill, gave occasion to processes as absurd and abominable as the trial of Dr. Fian and the witch-findings of Hopkins. In Denmark, the sorceresses were supposed to meet at Tromsoe high up in Finmark, or even on Heckla in Iceland. The Norse witches met at a Blokolle of their own, or on the Dovrefell, or at other places in Norway or Finmark. As might be expected, we find many traces of witchcraft in these Tales, but it may be doubted whether these may not be referred rather to the old heathen belief in such arts still lingering in the popular mind than to the processes of the fifteenth and sixteenth centuries, which were far more a craze and mania of the educated classes acting under a mistaken religious fanaticism against popular superstitions than a movement arising from the mass of the community. Still, in 'the Mastermaid', No. xi, the witch of a sister-in-law, who had rolled the apple over to the Prince, and so charmed him, was torn to pieces between twenty-four horses. The old queen in 'The Lassie and her Godmother', No. xxvii, tries to persuade her son to have the young queen burnt alive for a wicked witch, who was dumb, and had eaten her own babes. In 'East o' the Sun and West o' the Moon', No. iv, it is a wicked stepmother who has bewitched the prince. In 'Bushy Bride', No. xlv, the ugly bride charms the king to sleep, and is at last thrown, with her wicked mother, into a pit full of snakes. In the 'Twelve Wild Ducks', No. viii, the wicked stepmother persuades the king that Snow-white and Rosy-red is a witch, and almost persuades him to burn her alive. In 'Tatterhood', No. xlvii, a whole troop of witches come to keep their revels on Christmas eve in the Queen's Palace, and snap off the young Princess's head. It is hard, indeed, in tales where Trolls play so great a part, to keep witch and Troll separate; but the above instances will show that the belief in the one, as distinct from the other, exists in the popular superstitions of the North.

The frequent transformation of men into beasts, in these tales, is another striking feature. This power the gods of the Norseman possessed in common with those of all other mythologies. Europa and her Bull, Leda and her Swan, will occur at once to the reader's mind; and to come to closer resemblances, just as Athene appears in the Odyssey as an eagle or a swallow perched on the roof of the hall [Od., iii, 372; and xxii, 239], so Odin flies off as a falcon, and Loki takes the form of a horse or bird. This was only part of that omnipotence which all gods enjoy. But the belief that men, under certain conditions, could also take the shape of animals, is primaeval, and the traditions of every race can tell of such transformations. Herodotus had heard how the Neurians, a Slavonic race, passed for wizards amongst the Scythians and the Greeks settled round the Black Sea, because each of them, once in the year, became a wolf for a few days, and then returned to his natural shape. Pliny, Pomponius Mela, and St. Augustin, in his great treatise, **De Civitate Dei**, tell the same story, and Virgil, in his Eclogues, has sung the same belief [24]. The Latins called such a man, a **turnskin--versipellis**, an expression which exactly agrees with the Icelandic expression for the same thing, and which is probably the true original of our **turncoat**. In Petronius the superstition appears in its full shape, and is worth repeating. At the banquet of Trimalchion, Nicoros gives the following account of the turn-skins of Nero's time:

It happened that my master was gone to Capua to dispose of some second-hand goods. I took the opportunity and persuaded our guest to walk with me to the fifth milestone. He was a valiant soldier, and a sort of grim water-drinking Pluto. About cock-crow, when the moon was shining as bright as mid-day, we came among the monuments. My friend began addressing himself to the stars, but I was rather in a mood to sing or to count them; and when I turned to look at him, lo! he had already stripped himself and laid down his clothes near him. My heart was in my nostrils, and I stood like a dead man; but he '*circumminxit vestimenta*', and on a sudden became a wolf. Do not think I jest; I would not lie for any man's estate.

But to return to what I was saying. When he became a wolf, he began howling, and fled into the woods. At first I hardly knew where I was, and afterwards, when I went to take up his clothes, they were turned into stone. Who then died with fear but I? Yet I drew my sword, and went cutting the air right and left, till I reached the villa of my sweetheart. I entered the court-yard. I almost breathed my last, the sweat ran down my neck, my eyes were dim, and I thought I should never recover myself. My Melissa wondered why I was out so late, and said to me: 'Had you come sooner you might at least have helped us, for a wolf has entered the farm, and worried all our cattle; but he had not the best of the joke, for all he escaped, for our slave ran a lance through his neck.' When I heard this, I could not doubt how it was, and, as it was clear daylight, ran home as fast as a robbed innkeeper. When I came to the spot where the clothes had been turned into stone, I could find nothing except blood. But when I got home, I found my friend the soldier in bed, bleeding at the neck like an ox, and a doctor dressing his wound. I then knew he was a turn-skin, nor would I ever have broke bread with him again; No, not if you had killed me. [25]

A man who had such a gift or greed was also called lycanthropus, a man-wolf or wolf-man, which term the Anglo-Saxons translated literally in Canute's Laws *vere-vulf*, and the early English *werewolf*. In old French he was *loupgarou*, which means the same thing; except that *garou* means man-wolf in itself without the antecedent *loup*, so that, as Madden observes, the whole word is one of those reduplications of which we have an example in *lukewarm*. In Brittany he was *bleiz-garou* and *denvleiz*, formed respectively from *bleiz*, wolf, and *den*, man; *garou* is merely a distorted form of *wer* or *vere*, man and *loup*. In later French the word became *waroul*, whence the Scotch *wrout*, *wurl*, and *worlin*. [26]

It was not likely that a belief so widely spread should not have extended itself to the North; and the grave assertions of Olaus Magnus in the sixteenth century, in his Treatise *De Gentibus Septentrionalibus*, show how common the belief in were-wolves was in Sweden so late as the time of Gustavus Vasa. In mythical times the *Volsunga Saga* [*Fornald Sog*, i, 130, 131.] expressly states of Sigmund and Sinfjoetli that they became were-wolves--which, we may remark, were Odin's sacred beasts--just in the same way as Brynhildr and the Valkyries, or corse-choosers, who followed the god of battles to the field, and chose the dead for Valhalla when the fight was done, became swan-maidens, and took the shape of swans. In either case, the wolf's skin or the swan's feathery covering was assumed and laid aside at pleasure, though the *Voelundr Quidr*, in the *Edda*, and the stories of 'The Fair Melusina', and other medieval swan-maidens, show that any one who seized that shape while thus laid aside, had power over its wearer. In later times, when this old heroic belief degenerated into the notion of sorcery, it was supposed that a girdle of wolfskin thrown over the body, or even a slap on the face with a wolfskin glove, would transform the person upon whom the sorcerer practised into the shape of a ravening wolf, which fled at once to the woods, where he remained in that shape for a period which varied in popular belief for nine days, three, seven, or nine years. While in this state he was especially ravenous after young children, whom he carried off as the were-wolf carried off William in the old romance, though all were-wolves did not treat their prey with the same tenderness as that were-wolf treated William.

But the favourite beast for Norse transformations in historic times, if we may judge from the evidence afforded by the Sagas, was the bear, the king of all their beasts, whose strength and sagacity made him an object of great respect [See Land-nama in many places. *Egil's Sag., Hrolf Krak. Sag.*].

This old belief, then, might be expected to be found in these Norse Tales, and accordingly we find men transformed in them into various beasts. Of old these transformations, as we have already stated, were active, if we may use the expression, as well as passive. A man who possessed the gift, frequently assumed the shape of a beast at his own will and pleasure, like the soldier in Petronius. Even now in Norway, it is matter of popular belief that Finns and Lapps, who from time immemorial have passed for the most skilful witches and wizards in the world, can at will assume the shape of bears; and it is a common thing to say of one of those beasts, when he gets unusually savage and daring, 'that can be no Christian bear'. On such a bear, in the parish of Ofoeden, after he had worried to death more than sixty horses and six men, it is said that a girdle of bearskin, the infallible mark of a man thus transformed, was found when he was at last tracked and slain. The tale called 'Farmer Weathersky', No. xli in this collection, shows that the belief of these spontaneous transformations still exists in popular tradition, where it is easy to see that Farmer Weathersky is only one of the ancient gods degraded into a demon's shape. His sudden departure through the air, horse, sledge, and lad, and all, and his answer 'I'm at home, alike north, and south, and east, and west'; his name itself, and his distant abode, surrounded with the corpses of the slain, sufficiently betray the divinity in disguise. His transformation, too, into a hawk answers exactly to that of Odin when he flew away from the Frost Giant in the shape of that bird. But in these tales such transformations are for the most part passive; they occur not at the will of the person transformed, but through sorcery practised on them by some one else. Thus the White Bear in the beautiful story of 'East o' the Sun and West o' the Moon', No. iv, is a Prince transformed by his stepmother, just as it is the stepmother who plays the same part in the romance of William and the Were-wolf. So the horse in 'the Widow's Son', No. xliv, is a Prince over whom a king has cast that shape. [27] So also in 'Lord Peter', No. xlii, which is the full story of what we have only hitherto known in part as 'Puss in Boots', the cat is a princess bewitched by the Troll who had robbed her of her lands; so also in 'The Seven Foals', No. xliii, and 'The Twelve Wild Ducks', No. viii, the Foals and the Ducks are Princes over whom that fate has come by the power of a witch or a Troll, to whom an unwary promise had been given. Thoroughly mythic is the trait in 'The Twelve Wild Ducks', where the youngest brother reappears with a wild duck's wing instead of his left arm, because his sister had no time to finish that portion of the shirt, upon the completion of which his retransformation depended.

But we should ill understand the spirit of the Norsemen, if we supposed that these transformations into beasts were all that the national heart has to tell of beasts and their doings, or that, when they appear, they do so merely as men-beasts, without any power or virtue of their own. From the earliest times, side by side with those productions of the human mind which speak of the dealings of men with men, there has grown up a stock of traditions about animals and their relations with one another, which forms a true Beast Epic, and is full of the liveliest traits of nature. Here, too, it was reserved for Grimm to restore these traditions to their true place in the history of the human mind, and show that the poetry which treats of them is neither satirical nor didactic, though it may contain touches of both these artificial kinds of composition, but, on the contrary, purely and intensely natural. It is Epic, in short, springing out of that deep love of nature and close observation of the habits of animals which is only possible in an early and simple stage of society. It used to be the fashion, when these Beast traditions were noticed, to point to Aesop as their original, but Grimm has sufficiently proved [Reinhart Fuchs, Introduction] that what we see in Aesop is only the remains of a great world-old cycle of such traditions which had already, in Aesop's day, been subjected by the Greek mind to that critical process which a late state of society brings to bear on popular traditions; that they were then already worn and washed out and moralized. He had also shown how the same process went on till in Phaedrus nothing but the dry bones of the traditions, with a drier moral, are served up to the reader; and he has done justice on La Fontaine, who wrote with all the wanton licentiousness of his day, and frittered away the whole nature of his fables by the frivolity of his allusions to the artificial society of his time. Nor has he spared Lessing, who, though he saw through the poverty of Phaedrus as compared with Aesop, and was alive to the weakness of La Fontaine, still wandered about in the classical mist which hung heavy over the learning of the eighteenth century, and saw in the Greek form the perfection of all fable, when in Aesop it really appears in a state of degeneracy and decay. Here too, as in so many other things, we have a proof that the world is older than we think it. The Beast-Fables in the *Pantcha Tantra* and the *Hitopadesa*, the Indian parallels to Aesop, reveal, in the connection in which they occur, and in the moral use to which they are put, a state of society long past that simple early time in which such fictions arise. They must have sprung up in the East in the very dawn of time; and thence travelling in all directions, we find them after many centuries in various shapes, which admit of no mistake as to their first origin, at the very ends of the earth, in countries as opposite as the Poles to each other; in New Zealand and Norway, in Central Africa and Servia, in the West Indies and in Mongolia; all separated by immense tracts of land or sea from their common centre. To the earnest inquirer, to one who believes that many dark things may yet be solved, it is very satisfactory to see that even Grimm, in his *Reynard the Fox*, is at a loss to understand why the North, properly so called, had none of the traditions which the Middle Age moulded into that famous Beast-Epic. But since then the North, as the Great Master himself confesses in his later works, has amply avenged herself for the slight thus cast upon her by mistake. In the year 1834, when Grimm thus expressed his surprise on this point, the North had no such traditions to show in books indeed, but she kept them stored up in her heart in an abundance with which no other land perhaps can vie. This book at least shows how natural it seems to the Norse mind now, and how much more natural of course it seemed in earlier times, when sense went for as much and reflection for so little, that beasts should talk; and how truly and faithfully it has listened and looked for the accents and character of each. The Bear is still the King of Beasts, in which character he appears in 'True and Untrue', No. i, but here, as in Germany, he is no match for the Fox in wit. Thus Reynard plays him a trick which condemns him for ever to a stumpy tail in No. xxiii. He cheats him out of his share of a firkin of butter in No. lvii. He is preferred as Herdsman, in No. x, before either Bear or Wolf, by the old wife who wants some one to tend her flock. Yet all the while he professes immense respect for the Bear, and calls him 'Lord', even when in the very act of outwitting him. In the tale called 'Well Done and Ill Paid', No. xxxviii, the crafty fox puts a finish to his misbehaviour to his 'Lord Bruin', by handing him over, bound hand and foot, to the peasant, and by causing his death outright. Here, too, we have an example, which we shall see repeated in the case of the giants, that strength and stature are not always wise, and that wit and wisdom never fail to carry the day against mere brute force. Another tale, however, restores the bear to his true place as the king of beasts, endowed not only with strength, but with something divine and terrible about him which the Trolls cannot withstand. This is 'The Cat on the Dovrefell', No. xii. In connection with which, it should be remembered that the same tradition existed in the thirteenth century in Germany,[Grimm, *Irisch. Elfenm.*, 114-9, and *D. M.*, 447.] that the bear is called familiarly grandfather in the North, and that the Lapps reckon him rather as akin to men than beasts; that they say he has the strength of ten and the wit of twelve men. If they slay him, they formally beg his pardon, as do also the Ostjaks, a tribe akin to the Lapps, and bring him to their huts with great formalities and mystic songs. To the Wolf, whose nickname is 'Graylegs', [28] these tales are more complimentary. He is not the spiteful, stupid, greedy Isengrim of Germany and France. Not that Isengrim, of whom old English fables of the thirteenth century tell us that he became a monk, but when the brethren wished to teach him his letters that he might learn the paternoster, all they could get out of him was *lamb, lamb*; nor could they ever get him to look to the cross, for his eyes, with his thoughts, 'were ever to the woodward'. [Douce, *Illust. to Shakspeare*, ii, 33, 344, quoted in *Reinhart Fuchs*, ccxxi.] He appears, on the contrary, in 'The Giant who had no Heart in his body', No. ix, as a kindly grateful beast, who repays tenfold out of the hidden store of his supernatural sagacity the gift of the old jade, which Boots had made over to him.

The horse was a sacred animal among the Teutonic tribes from the first moment of their appearance in history, and Tacitus [*Germania*, 9, 10.] has related, how in the shade of those woods and groves which served them for temples, white horses were fed at the public cost, whose backs no mortal man crossed, whose neighings and snortings were carefully watched as auguries and omens, and who were thought to be conscious of divine mysteries. In Persia, too, the classical reader will remember how the neighing of a horse decided the choice for the crown. Here, in England, at any rate, we have only to think of Hengist and Horsa, the twin-heroes of the Anglo-Saxon migration, as the legend ran--heroes whose name meant 'horse'--and of the vale of the White Horse in Berks., where the sacred form still gleams along the down, to be reminded of the sacredness of the horse to our forefathers. The Eddas are filled with the names of famous horses, and the Sagas contain many stories of good steeds, in whom their owners trusted and believed as sacred to this or that particular god. Such a horse is Dapplegrim in No. xl, of these tales, who saves his master out of all his perils, and brings him to all fortune, and is another example of that mysterious connection with the higher powers which animals in all ages have been supposed to possess.

Such a friend, too, to the helpless lassie is the Dun Bull in 'Katie Woodencloak', No. 1, out of whose ear comes the 'Wishing Cloth', which serves up the choicest dishes. The story is probably imperfect, as we should expect to see him again in human shape after his head was cut off, and his skin flayed; but, after being the chief character up to that point, he remains from that time forth in the background, and we only see him darkly in the man who comes out of the face of the rock and supplies the lassie's wants when she knocks on it. Dun, or blue, or mouse-colour, is the favourite colour for fairy kine. Thus the cow which Guy of Warwick killed was *dun*. The *Huldror* in Norway have large flocks of blue kine. In Scotland runs the story of the mouse-coloured Elfin Bull. In Iceland the colour of such kine is *apalgrar*, dapple grey. This animal has been an object of adoration and respect from the earliest times, and we need only remind our readers of the sanctity of cows and bulls among the Indians and Egyptians, of 'the Golden Calf' in the Bible; of Io and her wanderings from land to land; and, though last, not least, of Audhumla, the Mythic Cow in the Edda, who had so large a part in the creation of the first Giant in human forms. [Snorro's **Edda**, ch. vi, English translation.]

The dog, to which, with all his sagacity and faithfulness something unclean and impure clings, as Grimm well observes, plays no very prominent part in these Tales. [29] We find him, however, in 'Not a Pin to choose between them', No. xxiv, where his sagacity fails to detect his mistress; and, as 'the foe of his own house', the half- bred foxy hound, who chases away the cunning Fox in 'Well Done and Ill Paid', No. xxxviii. Still he, too, in popular superstition, is gifted with a sense of the supernatural; he howls when death impends, and in 'Buttercup', No. xviii, it is Goldtooth, their dog, who warns Buttercup and his mother of the approach of the old hag. In 'Bushy Bride', No. xlv, he appears only as the lassie's lap-dog, is thrown away as one of her sacrifices, and at last goes to the wedding in her coach; yet in that tale he has something weird about him, and he is sent out by his mistress three times to see if the dawn is coming.

In one Tale, No. xxxvii, the Goat appears in full force, and dashes out the brains of the Troll, who lived under the bridge over the burn. In another, 'Tatterhood', No. xlviii, he helps the lassie in her onslaught on the witches. He, too, was sacred to Thor in the old mythology, and drew his thundering car. Here something of the divine nature of his former lord, who was the great foe of all Trolls, seems to have been passed on in popular tradition to the animal who had seen so many adventures with the great God who swayed the thunder. This feud between the Goat and the Trolls comes out curiously in 'The Old Dame and her Hen', No. iii, where a goat falls down the trapdoor to the Troll's house, 'Who sent for you, I should like to know, you long-bearded beast' said the Man o' the Hill, who was in an awful rage; and with that he whipped up the Goat, wrung his head off, and threw him down into the cellar. Still he belonged to one of the heathen gods, and so in later Middle-Age superstition he is assigned to the Devil, who even takes his shape when he presides at the Witches' Sabbath.

Nor in this list must the little birds be forgotten which taught the man's daughter, in the tale of 'The Two Stepsisters', No. xvii, how to act in her trials. So, too, in 'Katie Woodencloak', No. l, the little bird tells the Prince, 'who understood the song of birds very well,' that blood is gushing out of the golden shoe. The belief that some persons had the gift of understanding what the birds said, is primaeval. We pay homage to it in our proverbial expression, 'a little bird told me'. Popular traditions and rhymes protect their nests, as in the case of the wren, the robin, and the swallow. Occasionally this gift seems to have been acquired by eating or tasting the flesh of a snake or dragon, as Sigurd, in the Volsung tale, first became aware of Regin's designs against his life, when he accidentally tasted the heart-blood of Fafnir, whom he had slain in dragon shape, and then all at once the swallow's song, perched above him, became as intelligible as human speech.

We now come to a class of beings which plays a large part, and always for ill, in these Tales. These are the Giants or Trolls. In modern Norse tradition there is little difference between the names, but originally Troll was a more general expression for a supernatural being than Giant, [30] which was rather confined to a race more dull than wicked. In the Giants we have the wantonness of boundless bodily strength and size, which, trusting entirely to these qualities, falls at last by its own weight. At first, it is true that proverbial wisdom, all the stores of traditional lore, all that could be learnt by what may be called rule of thumb, was ascribed to them. One sympathises too with them, and almost pities them as the representatives of a simple primitive race, whose day is past and gone, but who still possessed something of the innocence and virtue of ancient times, together with a stock of old experience, which, however useful it might be as an example to others, was quite useless to help themselves. They are the old Tories of mythology, as opposed to the Aesir, the advanced liberals. They can look back and say what has been, but to look forward to say what will be and shall be, and to mould the future, is beyond their ken. True as gold to the traditional and received, and worthless as dross for the new and progressive. Such a nature, when unprovoked, is easy and simple; but rouse it, and its exuberant strength rises in a paroxysm of rage, though its clumsy awkward blows, guided by mere cunning, fail to strike the slight and lissom foe who waits for and eludes the stroke, until his reason gives him the mastery over sheer brute force which has wearied itself out by its own exertions.[31]

This race, and that of the upstart Aesir, though almost always at feud, still had their intervals of common intercourse, and even social enjoyment. Marriages take place between them, visits are paid, feasts are given, ale is breached, and mirth is fast and furious. Thor was the worst foe the giants ever had, and yet he met them sometimes on good terms. They were destined to meet once for all on that awful day, 'the twilight of the gods', but till then, they entertained for each other some sense of mutual respect.

The Trolls, on the other hand, with whom mankind had more to do, were supposed to be less easy tempered, and more systematically malignant, than the Giants, and with the term were bound up notions of sorcery and unholy power. But mythology is a woof of many colours, in which the hues are shot and blended, so that the various races of supernatural beings are shaded off, and fade away almost imperceptibly into each other; and thus, even in heathen times, it must have been hard to say exactly where the Giant ended and the Troll began. But when Christianity came in, and heathendom fell; when the godlike race of the Aesir became evil demons instead of good genial powers, then all the objects of the old popular belief, whether Aesir, Giants, or Trolls, were mingled together in one superstition, as 'no canny'. They were all Trolls, all malignant; and thus it is that, in these tales, the traditions about Odin and his underlings, about the Frost Giants, and about sorcerers and wizards, are confused and garbled; and all supernatural agency that plots man's ill is the work of Trolls, whether the agent be the arch enemy himself, or giant, or witch, or wizard.

In tales such as 'The Old Dame and her Hen', No. iii, 'The Giant who had no Heart in his Body', No. ix, 'Shortshanks', No. xx, 'Boots and the Troll', No. xxxii, 'Boots who ate a match with the Troll', No. v, the easy temper of the old Frost Giants predominates, and we almost pity them as we read. In another, 'The Big Bird Dan', No. lv, we have a Troll Prince, who appears as a generous benefactor to the young Prince, and lends him a sword by help of which he slays the King of the Trolls, just as we sometimes find in the Edda friendly meetings between the Aesir and this or the Frost Giant. In 'Tatterhood', No. xlviii, the Trolls are very near akin to the witches of the Middle Age. In other tales, as 'The Mastermaid', No. xi, 'The Blue Belt', No. xxii, 'Farmer Weathersky', No. xli, a sort of settled malignity against man appears as the direct working and result of a bad and evil spirit. In 'Buttercup', No. xviii, and 'The Cat on the Dovrefell', we have the Troll proper,--the supernatural dwellers of the woods and hills, who go to church, and eat men, and porridge, and sausages indifferently, not from malignity, but because they know no better, because it is their nature, and because they have always done so. In one point they all agree--in their place of abode. The wild pine forest that clothes the spurs of the fells, but more than all, the interior recesses of the rocky fell itself, is where the Trolls live. Thither they carry off the children of men, and to them belongs all the untold riches of the mineral world. There, in caves and clefts in the steep face of the rock, sits the Troll, as the representative of the old giants, among heaps of gold and silver and precious things. They stride off into the dark forest by day, whither no rays of the sun can pierce; they return home at nightfall, feast themselves full, and snore out the night. One thing was fatal to them--the sight of the sun. If they looked him full in the face, his glory was too great for them, and they burst, as in 'Lord Peter', No. xlii, and in 'The Old Dame and her Hen', No. iii. This, too, is a deeply mythic trait. The old religion of the North was a bright and lively faith; it lived in the light of joy and gladness; its gods were the 'blithe powers'; opposed to them were the dark powers of mist and gloom, who could not bear the glorious face of the Sun, of Baldr's beaming visage, or the bright flash of Thor's levin bolt.

In one aspect, the whole race of Giants and Trolls stands out in strong historical light. There can be little doubt that, in their continued existence amongst the woods, and rocks, and hills, we have a memory of the gradual suppression and extinction of some hostile race, who gradually retired into the natural fastnesses of the land, and speedily became mythic. Nor, if we bear in mind their natural position, and remember how constantly the infamy of sorcery has clung to the Finns and Lapps, shall we have far to go to seek this ancient race, even at the present day. Between this outcast nomad race, which wandered from forest to forest, and from fell to fell, without a fixed place of abode, and the old natural powers and Frost Giants, the minds of the race which adored Odin and the Aesir soon engendered a monstrous man-eating cross-breed of supernatural beings, who fled from contact with the intruders as soon as the first great struggle was over, abhorred the light of day, and looked upon agriculture and tillage as a dangerous innovation which destroyed their hunting fields, and was destined finally to root them out from off the face of the earth. This fact appears in countless stories all over the globe, for man is true to himself in all climes, and the savage in Africa or across the Rocky Mountains, dreads tillage and detests the plough as much as any Lapp or Samoyed. 'See what pretty playthings, mother!' cries the Giants' daughter as she unties her apron, and shows her a plough, and horses, and peasants. 'Back with them this instant', cries the mother in wrath, 'and put them down as carefully as you can, for these playthings can do our race great harm, and when these come we must budge.' 'What sort of an earthworm is this?' said one Giant to another, when they met a man as they walked. 'These are the earthworms that will one day eat us up, brother,' answered the other; and soon both Giants left that part of Germany. Nor does this trait appear less strongly in these Norse Tales. The Giants or Trolls can neither brew nor wash properly, as we see in Shortshanks, No. xx, where the Ogre has to get Shortshanks to brew his ale for him; and in 'East o' the Sun and West o' the Moon', No. iv, where none of the Trolls are able to wash out the spot of tallow. So also in the 'Two Step-sisters', No. xvii, the old witch is forced to get human maids to do her household-work; and, lastly, the best example of all, in 'Lord Peter', No. xlii, where agriculture is plainly a secret of mankind, which the Giants were eager to learn, but which was a branch of knowledge beyond their power to attain.

'Stop a bit', said the Cat, 'and I'll tell you how the farmer sets
to work to get in his winter rye.'

And so she told him such a long story about the winter rye.

'First of all, you see, he ploughs the field, and then he dungs it,
 and then he ploughs it again, and then he harrows it,' and so she
went on till the sun rose.

Before we leave these gigantic natural powers, let us linger a moment to point out how heartily the Winds are sketched in these Tales as four brothers; of whom, of course, the North wind is the oldest, and strongest, and roughest. But though rough in form and tongue, he is a genial, kind-hearted fellow after all. He carries the lassie to the castle, 'East o' the Sun and West o' the Moon', whither none of his brothers had strength to blow. All he asks is that she won't be afraid, and then he takes a good rest, and puffs himself up with as much breath as ever he can hold, begins to blow a storm, and off they go. So, too, in 'The Lad who went to the North Wind', No. xxxiv, though he can't restore the meal he carried off, he gives the lad three things which make his fortune, and amply repay him. He, too, like the Grecian Boreas, is divine, and lineally descended from Hraesvelgr, that great giant in the Edda, who sits 'at the end of the world in eagle's shape, and when he flaps his wings, all the winds come that blow upon men.'

Enough surely has now been said to shew that the old religion and mythology of the Norseman still lives disguised in these popular tales. Besides this internal evidence, we find here and there, in the written literature of earlier days, hints that the same stories were even then current, and current then as now, among the lower classes. Thus, in *King Sverri's Saga* we read: 'And so it was just like what is said to have happened in old stories of what the king's children suffered from their stepmother's ill-will.' And again, in *Olof Tryggvason's Saga* by the monk Odd: 'And better is it to hear such things with mirth than stepmother's stories which shepherds tell, where no one can tell whether anything is true, and where the king is always made the least in their narrative.' But, in truth, no such positive evidence is needed. Any one who has read the Volsung tale as we have given it, will be at no loss to see where the 'little birds' who speak to the Prince and the lassie, in these tales, come from; nor when they read in the 'Big Bird Dan', No. lv, about 'the naked sword' which the Princess lays by her side every night, will they fail to recognize Sigurd's sword *Gram*, which he laid between himself and Brynhildr when he rode through the flame and won her for Gunnar. These mythical deep-rooted groves, throwing out fresh shoots from age to age in the popular literature of the race, are far more convincing proofs of the early existence of these traditions than any mere external evidence'. [32]

CONCLUSION

We have now only to consider the men and women of these Tales, and then our task is done. It will be sooner done, because they may be left to speak for themselves, and must stand or fall by their own words and actions. The tales of all races have a character and manner of their own. Among the Hindoos the straight stem of the story is overhung with a network of imagery which reminds one of the parasitic growth of a tropical forest. Among the Arabs the tale is more elegant, pointed with a moral, and adorned with tropes and episodes. Among the Italians it is bright, light, dazzling, and swift. Among the French we have passed from the woods, and fields, and hills, to my lady's ***boudoir***--rose-pink is the prevailing colour, and the air is loaded with patchouli and ***mille fleurs***. We miss the song of birds, the modest odour of wildflowers, and the balmy fragrance of the pine forest. The Swedes are more stiff, and their style is more like that of a chronicle than a tale. The Germans are simple, hearty, and rather comic than humorous; and M. Moe [33] has well said, that as we read them it is as if we sat and listened to some elderly woman of the middle class, who recites them with a clear, full, deep voice. In Scotland the few that have been collected by Mr Robert Chambers [***Popular Rhymes of Scotland*** (Ed. 1847).] are as good in tone and keeping as anything of the kind in the whole range of such popular collections. [34] The wonderful likeness which is shown between such tales as the 'Red Bull of Norway' in Mr Chambers' collection, and Katie Woodencloak in these Norse Tales, is to be accounted for by no theory of the importation of this or that particular tale in later times from Norway, but by the fact that the Lowland Scots, among whom these tales were told, were lineal descendants of Norsemen, who had either seized the country in the Viking times, or had been driven into it across the Border after the Norman Conquest.

These Norse Tales we may characterize as bold, out-spoken, and humorous, in the true sense of humour. In the midst of every difficulty and danger arises that old Norse feeling of making the best of everything, and keeping a good face to the foe. The language and tone are perhaps rather lower than in some other collections, but it must be remembered that these are the tales of 'hempen homespuns', of Norse yeomen, of **Norske Bonder**, who call a spade a spade, and who burn tallow, not wax; and yet in no collection of tales is the general tone so chaste, are the great principles of morality better worked out, and right and wrong kept so steadily in sight. The general view of human nature is good and kindly. The happiness of married life was never more prettily told than in 'Gudbrand on the Hillside', No. xxi, where the tenderness of the wife for her husband weighs down all other considerations; and we all agree with M. Moe that it would be well if there were many wives like Gudbrand's. The balance too, is very evenly kept between the sexes; for if any wife should point with indignation at such a tale as 'Not a Pin to choose between them', No. xxiv, where wives suffer; she will be amply avenged when she reads 'The Husband who was to mind the House', No. xxxix, where the husband has decidedly the worst of the bargain, and is punished as he deserves.

Of particular characters, one occurs repeatedly. This is that which we have ventured, for want of a better word, to call 'Boots', from that widely-spread tradition in English families, that the youngest brother is bound to do all the hard work his brothers set him, and which has also dignified him with the term here used. In Norse he is called '**Askefis**', or '**Espen Askefis**'. By M. Moe he is called '**Askepot**',[35] a word which the Danes got from Germany, and which the readers of Grimm's Tales will see at once is own brother to **Aschenpuettel**. The meaning of the word is 'one who pokes about the ashes and blows up the fire'; one who does dirty work in short; and in Norway, according to M. Moe, the term is almost universally applied to the youngest son of the family. He is Cinderella's brother in fact; and just as she had all the dirty work put upon her by her sisters, he meets with the same fate from his brothers. He is generally the youngest of three, whose names are often Peter and Paul, as in No. xlii, and who despise, cry down, and mock him. But he has in him that deep strength of character and natural power upon which the good powers always smile. He is the man whom Heaven helps, because he can help himself; and so, after his brothers try and fail, he alone can watch in the barn, and tame the steed, and ride up the glass hill, and gain the Princess and half the kingdom. The Norse 'Boots' shares these qualities in common with the 'Pinkel' of the Swedes, and the *Dummling* of the Germans, as well as with our 'Jack the Giant Killer', but he starts lower than these--he starts from the dust-bin and the coal-hole. There he sits idle whilst all work; there he lies with that deep irony of conscious power, which knows its time must one day come, and meantime can afford to wait. When that time comes, he girds himself to the feat, amidst the scoffs and scorn of his flesh and blood; but even then, after he has done some great deed, he conceals it, returns to his ashes, and again sits idly by the kitchen-fire, dirty, lazy, and despised, until the time for final recognition comes, and then his dirt and rags fall off--he stands out in all the majesty of his royal robes, and is acknowledged once for all, a king. In this way does the consciousness of a nation, and the mirror of its thought, reflect the image and personification of a great moral truth, that modesty, endurance, and ability will sooner or later reap their reward, however much they maybe degraded, scoffed at, and despised by the proud, the worthless, and the overbearing [36]

As a general rule, the women are less strongly marked than the men; for these tales, as is well said, are uttered 'with a manly mouth';[Moe, *Introd. Norsk. Event.*] and none of the female characters, except perhaps 'The Mastermaid', and 'Tatterhood', can compare in strength with 'The Master-Smith', 'The Master-Thief,' 'Shortshanks' or 'Boots'. Still the true womanly type comes out in full play in such tales as 'The Two Step-Sisters', No. xvii; 'East o' the Sun and West o' the Moon', No. iv; 'Bushy Bride', No. xlv, and 'The Twelve Wild Ducks', No. viii. In all these the lassie is bright, and good, and helpful; she forgets herself in her eagerness to help others. When she goes down the well after the unequal match against her step-sister in spinning bristles against flax; she steps tenderly over the hedge, milks the cow, shears the sheep, relieves the boughs of the apple-tree--all out of the natural goodness of her heart. When she is sent to fetch water from the well, she washes and brushes, and even kisses, the loathsome head; she believes what her enemies say, even to her own wrong and injury; she sacrifices all that she holds most dear, and at last even herself, because she is made to believe that it is her brother's wish. And so on her, too, the good powers smile. She can understand and profit by what the little birds say; she knows how to choose the right casket. And at last, after many trials, all at once the scene changes, and she receives a glorious reward, while the wicked stepmother and her ugly daughter meet with a just fate. Nor is another female character less tenderly drawn in Hacon Grizzlebeard, No. vi, where we see the proud, haughty princess subdued and tamed by natural affection into a faithful, loving wife. We sympathise with her more than with the 'Patient Grizzel' of the poets, who is in reality too good, for her story has no relief; while in Hacon Grizzlebeard we begin by being angry at the princess's pride; we are glad at the retribution which overtakes her, but we are gradually melted at her sufferings and hardships when she gives up all for the Beggar and follows him; we burst into tears with her when she exclaims 'Oh! the Beggar, and the babe, and the cabin!'--and we rejoice with her when the Prince says 'Here is the Beggar, and there is the babe, and so let the cabin burn away.'

Nor is it unprofitable here to remark how the professions fare when they appear in these tales. The Church cannot be said to be treated with respect, for 'Father Lawrence' is ludicrously deceived and scurvily treated by the Master-Thief, No. xxxv; nor does the priest come off any better in Goosey Grizzel, No. xxxiii, where he is thrown by the Farmer into the wet moss. Indeed, it seems as if the popular mind were determined to revenge itself when left to itself, for the superstition of Rome on the one hand, and the severity of strict Lutheranism on the other. It has little to say of either of them, but when it does speak, its accents are not those of reverence and love. The Law, too, as represented by those awful personages the Constable, the Attorney, and the Sheriff in 'The Mastermaid', No. xi, is held up to ridicule, and treated with anything but tenderness. But there is one profession for which a good word is said, a single word, but enough to show the feeling of the people. In the 'Twelve Wild Ducks' No. viii, the king is 'as soft and kind' to Snow-white and Rosy-red 'as a doctor'--a doctor, alas! not of laws, but of medicine; and thus this profession, so often despised, but in reality the noblest, has homage paid to it in that single sentence, which neither the Church with all its dignity, nor the Law with all its cunning, have been able to extort from the popular mind. Yet even this profession has a hard word uttered against it in 'Katie Woodencloak', No. l, where the doctor takes a great fee from the wicked queen to say she will never be well unless she has some of the Dun Bull's flesh to eat.

And now it is time to bring this introduction to an end, lest it should play the Wolf's part to Odin, and swallow up the Tales themselves. Enough has been said, at least, to prove that even nursery tales may have a science of their own, and to show how the old Nornir and divine spinners can revenge themselves if their old wives' tales are insulted and attacked. The inquiry itself might be almost indefinitely prolonged, for this is a journey where each turn of the road brings out a new point of view, and the longer we linger on our path, the longer we find something fresh to see. Popular mythology is a virgin mine, and its ore, so far from being exhausted or worked out, has here, in England at least, been scarcely touched. It may, indeed, be dreaded lest the time for collecting such English traditions is not past and gone; whether the steam-engine and printing-press have not played their great work of enlightenment too well; and whether the popular tales, of which, no doubt, the land was once full, have not faded away before those great inventions, as the race of Giants waned before the might of Odin and the Aesir. Still the example of this very Norway, which at one time was thought, even by her own sons, to have few tales of her own, and now has been found to have them so fresh and full, may serve as a warning not to abandon a search, which, indeed, can scarcely be said to have been ever begun; and to suggest a doubt whether the ill success which may have attended this or that particular attempt, may not have been from the fault rather of the seekers after traditions, than from the want of the traditions themselves. In point of fact, it is a matter of the utmost difficulty to gather such tales in any country, as those who have collected them most successfully will be the first to confess. It is hard to make old and feeble women, who generally are the depositaries of these national treasures, believe that the inquirer can have any real interest in the matter. They fear that the question is only put to turn them into ridicule; for the popular mind is a sensitive plant; it becomes coy, and closes its leaves at the first rude touch; and when once shut, it is hard to make these aged lips reveal the secrets of the memory. There they remain, however, forming part of an under-current of tradition, of which the educated classes, through whose minds flows the bright upper-current of faith, are apt to forget the very existence. Things out of sight, and therefore out of mind. Now and then a wave of chance tosses them to the surface from those hidden depths, and all Her Majesty's inspectors of schools are shocked at the wild shapes which still haunt the minds of the great mass of the community. It cannot be said that the English are not a superstitious people. Here we have gone on for more than a hundred years proclaiming our opinion that the belief in witches, and wizards, and ghosts, and fetches, was extinct throughout the land. Ministers of all denominations have preached them down, and philosophers convinced all the world of the absurdity of such vain superstitions; and yet it has been reserved for another learned profession, the Law, to produce in one trial at the Staffordshire assizes, a year or two ago, such a host of witnesses, who firmly believed in witchcraft, and swore to their belief in spectre dogs and wizards, as to show that, in the Midland counties at least, such traditions are anything but extinct. If so much of the bad has been spared by steam, by natural philosophy, and by the Church, let us hope that some of the good may still linger along with it, and that an English Grimm may yet arise who may carry out what Mr. Chambers has so well begun in Scotland, and discover in the mouth of an Anglo- Saxon Gammer Grethel, some, at least, of those popular tales which England once had in common with all the Aryan race.

For these Norse Tales one may say that nothing can equal the tenderness and skill with which MM. Asbjoernsen and Moe have collected them. Some of that tenderness and beauty may, it is hoped, be found in this English translation; but to those who have never been in the country where they are current, and who are not familiar with that hearty simple people, no words can tell the freshness and truth of the originals. It is not that the idioms of the two languages are different, for they are more nearly allied, both in vocabulary and construction, than any other two tongues, but it is the face of nature herself, and the character of the race that looks up to her, that fail to the mind's eye. The West Coast of Scotland is something like that nature in a general way, except that it is infinitely smaller and less grand; but that constant, bright blue sky, those deeply-indented, sinuous, gleaming friths, those headstrong rivers and headlong falls, those steep hillsides, those long ridges of fells, those peaks and needles rising sharp above them, those hanging glaciers and wreaths of everlasting snow, those towering endless pine forests, relieved by slender stems of silver birch, those green spots in the midst of the forest, those winding dales and upland lakes, those various shapes of birds and beasts, the mighty crashing elk, the fleet reindeer, the fearless bear, the nimble lynx, the shy wolf, those eagles and swans, and seabirds, those many tones and notes of Nature's voice making distant music through the twilight summer night, those brilliant, flashing, northern lights when days grow short, those dazzling, blinding storms of autumn snow, that cheerful winter frost and cold, that joy of sledging over the smooth ice, when the sharp-shod horse careers at full speed with the light sledge, or rushes down the steep pitches over the crackling snow through the green spruce wood--all these form a Nature of their own. These particular features belong in their fulness and combination to no other land. When in the midst of all this natural scenery, we find an honest manly race, not the race of the towns and cities, but of the dales and fells, free and unsubdued, holding its own in a country where there are neither lords nor ladies, but simple men and women. Brave men and fair women, who cling to the traditions of their forefathers, and whose memory reflects as from the faithful mirror of their native steel the whole history and progress of their race--when all these natural features, and such a manly race meet; then we have the stuff out of which these tales are made, the living rocks out of which these sharp-cut national forms are hewn. Then, too, our task of introducing them is over, we may lay aside our pen, and leave the reader and the tales to themselves.

TALES FROM THE NORSE

TRUE AND UNTRUE

Once on a time there were two brothers; one was called True, and the other Untrue. True was always upright and good towards all, but Untrue was bad and full of lies, so that no one could believe what he said. Their mother was a widow, and hadn't much to live on; so when her sons had grown up, she was forced to send them away, that they might earn their bread in the world. Each got a little scrip with some food in it, and then they went their way.

Now, when they had walked till evening, they sat down on a windfall in the wood, and took out their scraps, for they were hungry after walking the whole day, and thought a morsel of food would be sweet enough.

'If you're of my mind', said Untrue, 'I think we had better eat out of your scrip, so long as there is anything in it, and after that we can take to mine.'

Yes! True was well pleased with this, so they fell to eating, but Untrue got all the best bits, and stuffed himself with them, while True got only the burnt crusts and scraps.

Next morning they broke their fast off True's food, and they dined off it too, and then there was nothing left in his scrip. So when they had walked till late at night, and were ready to eats again, True wanted to eat out of his brother's scrip, but Untrue said 'No', the food was his, and he had only enough for himself.

'Nay! but you know you ate out of my scrip so long as there was anything in it', said True.

'All very fine, I daresay', answered Untrue; 'but if you are such a fool as to let others eat up your food before your face, you must make the best of it; for now all you have to do is to sit here and starve.'

'Very well!' said True, 'you're Untrue by name and untrue by nature; so you have been, and so you will be all your life long.'

Now when Untrue heard this, he flew into a rage, and rushed at his brother, and plucked out both his eyes. 'Now, try if you can see whether folk are untrue or not, you blind buzzard!' and so saying, he ran away and left him.

Poor True! there he went walking along and feeling his way through the thick wood. Blind and alone, he scarce knew which way to turn, when all at once he caught hold of the trunk of a great bushy lime- tree, so he thought he would climb up into it, and sit there till the night was over for fear of the wild beasts.

'When the birds begin to sing', he said to himself, 'then I shall know it is day, and I can try to grope my way farther on.' So he climbed up into the lime-tree. After he had sat there a little time, he heard how some one came and began to make a stir and clatter under the tree, and soon after others came; and when they began to greet one another, he found out it was Bruin the bear, and Greylegs the wolf, and Slyboots the fox, and Longears the hare who had come to keep St. John's eve under the tree. So they began to eat and drink, and be merry; and when they had done eating, they fell to gossipping together. At last the Fox said:

'Shan't we, each of us, tell a little story while we sit here?' Well! the others had nothing against that. It would be good fun, they said, and the Bear began; for you may fancy he was king of the company.

'The king of England', said Bruin, 'has such bad eyesight, he can scarce see a yard before him; but if he only came to this lime-tree in the morning, while the dew is still on the leaves, and took and rubbed his eyes with the dew, he would get back his sight as good as ever.'

'Very true!' said Greylegs. 'The king of England has a deaf and dumb daughter too; but if he only knew what I know, he would soon cure her. Last year she went to the communion. She let a crumb of the bread fall out of her mouth, and a great toad came and swallowed it down; but if they only dug up the chancel floor, they would find the toad sitting right under the altar rails, with the bread still sticking in his throat. If they were to cut the toad open and take and give the bread to the princess, she would be like other folk again as to her speech and hearing.'

'That's all very well', said the Fox; 'but if the king of England knew what I know, he would not be so badly off for water in his palace; for under the great stone, in his palace-yard, is a spring of the clearest water one could wish for, if he only knew to dig for it there.'

'Ah!' said the Hare in a small voice; 'the king of England has the finest orchard in the whole land, but it does not bear so much as a crab, for there lies a heavy gold chain in three turns round the orchard. If he got that dug up, there would not be a garden like it for bearing in all his kingdom.'

'Very true, I dare say', said the Fox; 'but now it's getting very late, and we may as well go home.'

So they all went away together.

After they were gone, True fell asleep as he sat up in the tree; but when the birds began to sing at dawn, he woke up, and took the dew from the leaves, and rubbed his eyes with it, and so got his sight back as good as it was before Untrue plucked his eyes out.

Then he went straight to the king of England's palace, and begged for work, and got it on the spot. So one day the king came out into the palace-yard, and when he had walked about a bit, he wanted to drink out of his pump; for you must know the day was hot, and the king very thirsty; but when they poured him out a glass, it was so muddy, and nasty, and foul, that the king got quite vexed.

'I don't think there's ever a man in my whole kingdom who has such bad water in his yard as I, and yet I bring it in pipes from far, over hill and dale', cried out the king. 'Like enough, your Majesty', said True; 'but if you would let me have some men to help me to dig up this great stone which lies here in the middle of your yard, you would soon see good water, and plenty of it.'

Well! the king was willing enough; and they had scarcely got the stone well out, and dug under it a while, before a jet of water sprang out high up into the air, as clear and full as if it came out of a conduit, and clearer water was not to be found in all England.

A little while after the king was out in his palace-yard again, and there came a great hawk flying after his chicken, and all the king's men began to clap their hands and bawl out, 'There he flies!' 'There he flies!' The king caught up his gun and tried to shoot the hawk, but he couldn't see so far, so he fell into great grief.

'Would to Heaven', he said, 'there was any one who could tell me a cure for my eyes; for I think I shall soon go quite blind!'

'I can tell you one soon enough', said True; and then he told the king what he had done to cure his own eyes, and the king set off that very afternoon to the lime-tree, as you may fancy, and his eyes were quite cured as soon as he rubbed them with the dew which was on the leaves in the morning. From that time forth there was no one whom the king held so dear as True, and he had to be with him wherever he went, both at home and abroad.

So one day, as they were walking together in the orchard, the king said, 'I can't tell how it is *that* I can't! there isn't a, man in England who spends so much on his orchard as I, and yet I can't get one of the trees to bear so much as a crab.'

'Well! well!' said True; 'if I may have what lies three times twisted round your orchard, and men to dig it up, your orchard will bear well enough.'

Yes! the king was quite willing, so True got men and began to dig, and at last he dug up the whole gold chain. Now True was a rich man; far richer indeed than the king himself, but still the king was well pleased, for his orchard bore so that the boughs of the trees hung down to the ground, and such sweet apples and pears nobody had ever tasted.

Another day too the king and True were walking about, and talking together, when the princess passed them, and the king was quite downcast when he saw her.

'Isn't it a pity, now, that so lovely a princess as mine should want speech and hearing', he said to True.

'Ay, but there is a cure for that', said True.

When the king heard that, he was so glad that he promised him the princess to wife, and half his kingdom into the bargain, if he could get her right again. So True took a few men, and went into the church, and dug up the toad which sat under the altar-rails. Then he cut open the toad, and took out the bread and gave it to the king's daughter; and from that hour she got back her speech, and could talk like other people.

Now True was to have the princess, and they got ready for the bridal feast, and such a feast had never been seen before; it was the talk of the whole land. Just as they were in the midst of dancing the bridal-dance in came a beggar lad, and begged for a morsel of food, and he was so ragged and wretched that every one crossed themselves when they looked at him; but True knew him at once, and saw that it was Untrue, his brother.

'Do you know me again?' said True.

'Oh! where should such a one as I ever have seen so great a lord', said Untrue.

'Still you *have* seen me before', said True. 'It was I whose eyes you plucked out a year ago this very day. Untrue by name, and untrue by nature; so I said before, and so I say now; but you are still my brother, and so you shall have some food. After that, you may go to the lime-tree where I sat last year; if you hear anything that can do you good, you will be lucky.'

So Untrue did not wait to be told twice. 'If True has got so much good by sitting in the lime-tree, that in one year he has come to be king over half England, what good may not I get', he thought. So he set off and climbed up into the lime-tree. He had not sat there long, before all the beasts came as before, and ate and drank, and kept St. John's eve under the tree. When they had left off eating, the Fox wished that they should begin to tell stories, and Untrue got ready to listen with all his might, till his ears were almost fit to fall off. But Bruin the bear was surly, and growled and said:

'Some one has been chattering about what we said last year, and so now we will hold our tongues about what we know'; and with that the beasts bade one another 'Good-night', and parted, and Untrue was just as wise as he was before, and the reason was, that his name was Untrue, and his nature untrue too.

WHY THE SEA IS SALT

Once on a time, but it was a long, long time ago, there were two brothers, one rich and one poor. Now, one Christmas eve, the poor one hadn't so much as a crumb in the house, either of meat or bread, so he went to his brother to ask him for something to keep Christmas with, in God's name. It was not the first time his brother had been forced to help him, and you may fancy he wasn't very glad to see his face, but he said:

'If you will do what I ask you to do, I'll give you a whole flitch of bacon.'

So the poor brother said he would do anything, and was full of thanks.

'Well, here is the flitch', said the rich brother, 'and now go straight to Hell.'

'What I have given my word to do, I must stick to', said the other; so he took the flitch and set off. He walked the whole day, and at dusk he came to a place where he saw a very bright light.

'Maybe this is the place', said the man to himself. So he turned aside, and the first thing he saw was an old, old man, with a long white beard, who stood in an outhouse, hewing wood for the Christmas fire.

'Good even', said the man with the flitch.

'The same to you; whither are you going so late?' said the man.

'Oh! I'm going to Hell, if I only knew the right way', answered the poor man.

'Well, you're not far wrong, for this is Hell', said the old man; 'when you get inside they will be all for buying your flitch, for meat is scarce in Hell; but mind, you don't sell it unless you get the hand-quern which stands behind the door for it. When you come out, I'll teach you how to handle the quern, for it's good to grind almost anything.'

So the man with the flitch thanked the other for his good advice, and gave a great knock at the Devil's door.

When he got in, everything went just as the old man had said. All the devils, great and small, came swarming up to him like ants round an anthill, and each tried to outbid the other for the flitch.

'Well!' said the man, 'by rights my old dame and I ought to have this flitch for our Christmas dinner; but since you have all set your hearts on it, I suppose I must give it up to you; but if I sell it at all, I'll have for it that quern behind the door yonder.'

At first the Devil wouldn't hear of such a bargain, and chaffered and haggled with the man; but he stuck to what he said, and at last the Devil had to part with his quern. When the man got out into the yard, he asked the old woodcutter how he was to handle the quern; and after he had learned how to use it, he thanked the old man and went off home as fast as he could, but still the clock had struck twelve on Christmas eve before he reached his own door.

'Wherever in the world have you been?' said his old dame, 'here have I sat hour after hour waiting and watching, without so much as two sticks to lay together under the Christmas brose.'

'Oh!' said the man, 'I couldn't get back before, for I had to go a long way first for one thing, and then for another; but now you shall see what you shall see.'

So he put the quern on the table, and bade it first of all grind lights, then a table-cloth, then meat, then ale, and so on till they had got everything that was nice for Christmas fare. He had only to speak the word, and the quern ground out what he wanted. The old dame stood by blessing her stars, and kept on asking where he had got this wonderful quern, but he wouldn't tell her.

'It's all one where I got it from; you see the quern is a good one, and the mill-stream never freezes, that's enough.'

So he ground meat and drink and dainties enough to last out till Twelfth Day, and on the third day he asked all his friends and kin to his house, and gave a great feast. Now, when his rich brother saw all that was on the table, and all that was behind in the larder, he grew quite spiteful and wild, for he couldn't bear that his brother should have anything.

''Twas only on Christmas eve', he said to the rest, 'he was in such straits, that he came and asked for a morsel of food in God's name, and now he gives a feast as if he were count or king'; and he turned to his brother and said:

'But whence, in Hell's name, have you got all this wealth?'

'From behind the door', answered the owner of the quern, for he didn't care to let the cat out of the bag. But later on the evening, when he had got a drop too much, he could keep his secret no longer, and brought out the quern and said:

'There, you see what has gotten me all this wealth'; and so he made the quern grind all kind of things. When his brother saw it, he set his heart on having the quern, and, after a deal of coaxing, he got it; but he had to pay three hundred dollars for it, and his brother bargained to keep it till hay-harvest, for he thought, if I keep it till then, I can make it grind meat and drink that will last for years. So you may fancy the quern didn't grow rusty for want of work, and when hay-harvest came, the rich brother got it, but the other took care not to teach him how to handle it.

It was evening when the rich brother got the quern home, and next morning he told his wife to go out into the hay-field and toss, while the mowers cut the grass, and he would stay at home and get the dinner ready. So, when dinner-time drew near, he put the quern on the kitchen table and said:

'Grind herrings and broth, and grind them good and fast.'

So the quern began to grind herrings and broth; first of all, all the dishes full, then all the tubs full, and so on till the kitchen floor was quite covered. Then the man twisted and twirled at the quern to get it to stop, but for all his twisting and fingering the quern went on grinding, and in a little while the broth rose so high that the man was like to drown. So he threw open the kitchen door and ran into the parlour, but it wasn't long before the quern had ground the parlour full too, and it was only at the risk of his life that the man could get hold of the latch of the house door through the stream of broth. When he got the door open, he ran out and set off down the road, with the stream of herrings and broth at his heels, roaring like a waterfall over the whole farm. Now, his old dame, who was in the field tossing hay, thought it a long time to dinner, and at last she said:

'Well! though the master doesn't call us home, we may as well go. Maybe he finds it hard work to boil the broth, and will be glad of my help.'

The men were willing enough, so they sauntered homewards; but just as they had got a little way up the hill, what should they meet but herrings, and broth, and bread, all running and dashing, and splashing together in a stream, and the master himself running before them for his life, and as he passed them he bawled out:

'Would to heaven each of you had a hundred throats! but take care you're not drowned in the broth.'

Away he went, as though the Evil One were at his heels, to his brother's house, and begged him for God's sake to take back the quern that instant; for, said he:

'If it grinds only one hour more, the whole parish will be swallowed up by herrings and broth.'

But his brother wouldn't hear of taking it back till the other paid him down three hundred dollars more.

So the poor brother got both the money and the quern, and it wasn't long before he set up a farm-house far finer than the one in which his brother lived, and with the quern he ground so much gold that he covered it with plates of gold; and as the farm lay by the sea-side, the golden house gleamed and glistened far away over the sea. All who sailed by put ashore to see the rich man in the golden house, and to see the wonderful quern, the fame of which spread far and wide, till there was nobody who hadn't heard tell of it.

So one day there came a skipper who wanted to see the quern; and the first thing he asked was if it could grind salt.

'Grind salt!' said the owner; 'I should just think it could. It can grind anything.'

When the skipper heard that, he said he must have the quern, cost what it would; for if he only had it, he thought he should be rid of his long voyages across stormy seas for a lading of salt. Well, at first the man wouldn't hear of parting with the quern; but the skipper begged and prayed so hard, that at last he let him have it, but he had to pay many, many thousand dollars for it. Now, when the skipper had got the quern on his back, he soon made off with it, for he was afraid lest the man should change his mind; so he had no time to ask how to handle the quern, but got on board his ship as fast as he could, and set sail. When he had sailed a good way off, he brought the quern on deck and said:

'Grind salt, and grind both good and fast.'

Well, the quern began to grind salt so that it poured out like water; and when the skipper had got the ship full, he wished to stop the quern, but whichever way he turned it, and however much he tried, it was no good; the quern kept grinding on, and the heap of salt grew higher and higher, and at last down sank the ship.

There lies the quern at the bottom of the sea, and grinds away at this very day, and that's why the sea is salt.

THE OLD DAME AND HER HEN

Once on a time there was an old widow who lived far away from the rest of the world, up under a hillside, with her three daughters. She was so poor that she had no stock but one single hen, which she prized as the apple of her eye; in short, it was always cackling at her heels, and she was always running to look after it. Well! one day, all at once, the hen was missing. The old wife went out, and round and round the cottage, looking and calling for her hen, but it was gone, and there was no getting it back.

So the woman said to her eldest daughter, 'You must just go out and see if you can find our hen, for have it back we must, even if we have to fetch it out of the hill.'

Well! the daughter was ready enough to go, so she set off and walked up and down, and looked and called, but no hen could she find. But all at once, just as she was about to give up the hunt, she heard some one calling out in a cleft in the rock:

 Your hen trips inside the hill!   Your hen trips inside the hill!

So she went into the cleft to see what it was, but she had scarce set her foot inside the cleft, before she fell through a trap-door, deep, deep down, into a vault under ground. When she got to the bottom she went through many rooms, each finer than the other; but in the innermost room of all, a great ugly man of the hill-folk came up to her and asked, 'Will you be my sweetheart?'

'No! I will not', she said. She wouldn't have him at any price! not she; all she wanted was to get above ground again as fast as ever she could, and to look after her hen which was lost. Then the Man o' the Hill got so angry that he took her up and wrung her head off, and threw both head and trunk down into the cellar.

While this was going on, her mother sat at home waiting and waiting, but no daughter came. So after she had waited a bit longer, and neither heard nor saw anything of her daughter, she said to her midmost daughter, that she must go out and see after her sister, and she added:

'You can just give our hen a call at the same time.'

Well! the second sister had to get off, and the very same thing befell her; she went about looking and calling, and all at once she too heard a voice away in the cleft of the rock saying:

Your hen trips inside the hill!   Your hen trips inside the hill!

She thought this strange, and went to see what it could be; and so she too fell through the trap-door, deep, deep down, into the vault. There she went from room to room, and in the innermost one the Man o' the Hill came to her and asked if she would be his sweetheart? No! that she wouldn't; all she wanted was to get above ground again, and hunt for her hen which was lost. So the Man o' the Hill got angry, and took her up and wrung her head off, and threw both head and trunk down into the cellar.

Now, when the old dame had sat and waited seven lengths and seven breadths for her second daughter, and could neither see nor hear anything of her, she said to the youngest:

'Now, you really must set off and see after your sisters. 'Twas silly to lose the hen, but 'twill be sillier still if we lose both your sisters; and you can give the hen a call at the same time'--for the old dame's heart was still set on her hen.

Yes! the youngest was ready enough to go; so she walked up and down, Wanting for her sisters and calling the hen, but she could neither see nor hear anything of them. So at last she too came up to the cleft in the rock, and heard how something said:

Your hen trips inside the hill!   Your hen trips inside the hill!

She thought this strange, so she too went to see what it was, and fell through the trap-door too, deep, deep down, into a vault. When she reached the bottom she went from one room to another, each grander than the other; but she wasn't at all afraid, and took good time to look about her. So, as she was peeping into this and that, she cast her eye on the trap-door into the cellar, and looked down it, and what should she see there but her sisters, who lay dead. She had scarce time to slam to the trap-door before the Man o' the Hill came to her and asked:

'Will you be my sweetheart?'

'With all my heart', answered the girl, for she saw very well how it had gone with her sisters. So, when the Man o' the Hill heard that, he got her the finest clothes in the world; she had only to ask for them, or for anything else she had a mind to, and she got what she wanted, so glad was the Man o' the Hill that any one would be his sweetheart.

But when she had been there a little while, she was one day even more doleful and downcast than was her wont. So the Man o' the Hill asked her what was the matter, and why she was in such dumps.

'Ah!' said the girl, 'it's because I can't get home to my mother. She's hard pinched, I know, for meat and drink, and has no one with her.'

'Well!' said the Man o' the Hill, 'I can't let you go to see her; but just stuff some meat and drink into a sack, and I'll carry it to her.'

Yes! she would do so, she said, with many thanks; but at the bottom of the sack she stuffed a lot of gold and silver, and afterwards she laid a little food on the top of the gold and silver. Then she told the ogre the sack was ready, but he must be sure not to look into it. So he gave his word he wouldn't, and set off. Now, as the Man o' the Hill walked off, she peeped out after him through a chink in the trap-door; but when he had gone a bit on the way, he said:

'This sack is so heavy, I'll just see what there is inside it.'

And so he was about to untie the mouth of the sack, but the girl called out to him:

I see what you're at!   I see what you're at!

'The deuce you do!' said the Man o' the Hill; 'then you must have plaguy sharp eyes in your head, that's all!'

So he threw the sack over his shoulder, and dared not try to look into it again. When he reached the widow's cottage, he threw the sack in through the cottage door, and said:

'Here you have meat and drink from your daughter; she doesn't want for anything.'

So, when the girl had been in the hill a good bit longer, one day a billy-goat fell down the trap-door.

'Who sent for you, I should like to know? you long-bearded beast!' said the

Man o' the Hill, who was in an awful rage, and with that he whipped up the goat, and wrung his head off, and threw him down into the cellar.

'Oh!' said the girl, 'why did you do that? I might have had the goat to play with down here.'

'Well!' said the Man o' the Hill, 'you needn't be so down in the mouth about it, I should think, for I can soon put life into the billy-goat again.'

So saying, he took a flask which hung up against the wall, put the billy-goat's head on his body again, and smeared it with some ointment out of the flask, and he was as well and as lively as ever again.

'Ho! ho!' said the girl to herself; 'that flask is worth something-- that it is.'

So when she had been some time longer in the hill, she watched for a day when the Man o' the Hill was away, took her eldest sister, and putting her head on her shoulders, smeared her with some of the ointment out of the flask, just as she had seen the Man o' the Hill do with the billy-goat, and in a trice her sister came to life again. Then the girl stuffed her into a sack, laid a little food over her, and as soon as the Man o' the Hill came home, she said to him:

'Dear friend! Now do go home to my mother with a morsel of food again; poor thing! she's both hungry and thirsty, I'll be bound; and besides that, she's all alone in the world. But you must mind and not look into the sack.'

Well! he said he would carry the sack; and he said, too, that he would not look into it; but when he had gone a little way, he thought the sack got awfully heavy; and when he had gone a bit farther he said to himself:

'Come what will, I must see what's inside this sack, for however sharp her eyes may be, she can't see me all this way off'

But just as he was about to untie the sack, the girl who sat inside the sack called out:

  I see what you're at!   I see what you're at!

'The deuce you do!' said the ogre; 'then you must have plaguey sharp eyes'; for he thought all the while it was the girl inside the hill who was speaking. So he didn't care so much as to peep into the sack again, but carried it straight to her mother as fast as he could, and when he got to the cottage door he threw it in through the door, and bawled out:

'Here you have meat and drink from your daughter; she wants for nothing.'

Now, when the girl had been in the hill a while longer, she did the very same thing with her other sister. She put her head on her shoulders, smeared her with ointment out of the flask, brought her to life, and stuffed her into the sack; but this time she crammed in also as much gold and silver as the sack would hold, and over all laid a very little food.

'Dear friend', she said to the Man o' the Hill, 'you really must run home to my mother with a little food again; and mind you don't look into the sack.'

Yes! the Man o' the Hill was ready enough to do as she wished, and he gave his word too that he wouldn't look into the sack; but when he had gone a bit of the way he began to think the sack got awfully heavy, and when he had gone a bit further, he could scarce stagger along under it, so he set it down, and was just about to untie the string and look into it, when the girl inside the sack bawled out:

   I see what you're at!   I see what you're at!

'The deuce you do', said the Man o' the Hill, 'then you must have plaguey sharp eyes of your own.'

Well, he dared not try to look into the sack, but made all the haste he could, and carried the sack straight to the girl's mother. When he got to the cottage door he threw the sack in through the door, and roared out:

'Here you have food from your daughter; she wants for nothing.'

So when the girl had been there a good while longer, the Man o' the Hill made up his mind to go out for the day; then the girl shammed to be sick and sorry, and pouted and fretted.

'It's no use your coming home before twelve o'clock at night', she said, 'for I shan't be able to have supper ready before--I'm so sick and poorly.'

But when the Man o' the Hill was well out of the house, she stuffed some of her clothes with straw, and stuck up this lass of straw in the corner by the chimney, with a besom in her hand, so that it looked just as if she herself were standing there. After that she stole off home, and got a sharp-shooter to stay in the cottage with her mother.

So when the clock struck twelve, or just about it, home came the Man o' the Hill, and the first thing he said to the straw-girl was, 'Give me something to eat.'

But she answered him never a word.

'Give me something to eat, I say!' called out the Man o' the Hill, 'for I am almost starved.'

No! she hadn't a word to throw at him.

'Give me something to eat!' roared out the ogre the third time.' I think you'd better open your ears and hear what I say, or else I'll wake you up, that I will!'

No! the girl stood just as still as ever; so he flew into a rage, and gave her such a slap in the face, that the straw flew all about the room; but when he saw that, he knew he had been tricked, and began to hunt everywhere; and at last, when he came to the cellar, and found both the girl's sisters missing, he soon saw how the cat jumped, and ran off to the cottage, saying, 'I'll soon pay her off!'

But when he reached the cottage, the sharp-shooter fired off his piece, and then the Man o' the Hill dared not go into the house, for he thought it was thunder. So he set off home again as fast as he could lay legs to the ground; but what do you think, just as he got to the trap-door, the sun rose and the Man o' the Hill burst.

Oh! if one only knew where the trap-door was, I'll be bound there's a whole heap of gold and silver down there still!

EAST O' THE SUN AND WEST O' THE MOON

Once on a time there was a poor husbandman who had so many children that he hadn't much of either food or clothing to give them. Pretty children they all were, but the prettiest was the youngest daughter, who was so lovely there was no end to her loveliness.

So one day, 'twas on a Thursday evening late at the fall of the year, the weather was so wild and rough outside, and it was so cruelly dark, and rain fell and wind blew, till the walls of the cottage shook again. There they all sat round the fire busy with this thing and that. But just then, all at once something gave three taps on the window-pane. Then the father went out to see what was the matter; and, when he got out of doors, what should he see but a great big White Bear.

'Good evening to you!' said the White Bear.

'The same to you', said the man.

'Will you give me your youngest daughter? If you will, I'll make you as rich as you are now poor', said the Bear.

Well, the man would not be at all sorry to be so rich; but still he thought he must have a bit of a talk with his daughter first; so he went in and told them how there was a great White Bear waiting outside, who had given his word to make them so rich if he could only have the youngest daughter.

The lassie said 'No!' outright. Nothing could get her to say anything else; so the man went out and settled it with the White Bear, that he should come again the next Thursday evening and get an answer. Meantime he talked his daughter over, and kept on telling her of all the riches they would get, and how well off she would be herself; and so at last she thought better of it, and washed and mended her rags, made herself as smart as she could, and was ready to start. I can't say her packing gave her much trouble.

Next Thursday evening came the White Bear to fetch her, and she got upon his back with her bundle, and off they went. So, when they had gone a bit of the way, the White Bear said:

'Are you afraid?'

'No! she wasn't.'

'Well! mind and hold tight by my shaggy coat, and then there's nothing to fear', said the Bear.

So she rode a long, long way, till they came to a great steep hill. There, on the face of it, the White Bear gave a knock, and a door opened, and they came into a castle, where there were many rooms all lit up; rooms gleaming with silver and gold; and there too was a table ready laid, and it was all as grand as grand could be. Then the White Bear gave her a silver bell; and when she wanted anything, she was only to ring it, and she would get it at once.

Well, after she had eaten and drunk, and evening wore on, she got sleepy after her journey, and thought she would like to go to bed, so she rang the bell; and she had scarce taken hold of it before she came into a chamber, where there was a bed made, as fair and white as any one would wish to sleep in, with silken pillows and curtains, and gold fringe. All that was in the room was gold or silver; but when she had gone to bed, and put out the light, a man came and laid himself alongside her. That was the White Bear, who threw off his beast shape at night; but she never saw him, for he always came after she had put out the light, and before the day dawned he was up and off again. So things went on happily for a while, but at last she began to get silent and sorrowful; for there she went about all day alone, and she longed to go home to see her father and mother and brothers and sisters. So one day, when the White Bear asked what it was that she lacked, she said it was so dull and lonely there, and how she longed to go home to see her father and mother, and brothers and sisters, and that was why she was so sad and sorrowful, because she couldn't get to them.

'Well, well!' said the Bear, 'perhaps there's a cure for all this; but you must promise me one thing, not to talk alone with your mother, but only when the rest are by to hear; for she'll take you by the hand and try to lead you into a room alone to talk; but you must mind and not do that, else you'll bring bad luck on both of us.'

So one Sunday the White Bear came and said now they could set off to see her father and mother. Well, off they started, she sitting on his back; and they went far and long. At last they came to a grand house, and there her brothers and sisters were running about out of doors at play, and everything was so pretty, 'twas a joy to see.

'This is where your father and mother live now', said the White Bear; 'but don't forget what I told you, else you'll make us both unlucky.'

'No! bless her, she'd not forget'; and when she had reached the house, the White Bear turned right about and left her.

Then when she went in to see her father and mother, there was such joy, there was no end to it. None of them thought they could thank her enough for all she had done for them. Now, they had everything they wished, as good as good could be, and they all wanted to know how she got on where she lived.

Well, she said, it was very good to live where she did; she had all she wished. What she said beside I don't know; but I don't think any of them had the right end of the stick, or that they got much out of her. But so in the afternoon, after they had done dinner, all happened as the White Bear had said. Her mother wanted to talk with her alone in her bed-room; but she minded what the White Bear had said, and wouldn't go upstairs.

'Oh! what we have to talk about, will keep', she said, and put her mother off. But some how or other, her mother got round her at last, and she had to tell her the whole story. So she said, how every night, when she had gone to bed, a man came and lay down beside her as soon as she had put out the light, and how she never saw him, because he was always up and away before the morning dawned; and how she went about woeful and sorrowing, for she thought she should so like to see him, and how all day long she walked about there alone, and how dull, and dreary, and lonesome it was.

'My!' said her mother; 'it may well be a Troll you slept with! But now I'll teach you a lesson how to set eyes on him. I'll give you a bit of candle, which you can carry home in your bosom; just light that while he is asleep, but take care not to drop the tallow on him.'

Yes! she took the candle, and hid it in her bosom, and as night drew on, the White Bear came and fetched her away.

But when they had gone a bit of the way, the White Bear asked if all hadn't happened as he had said?

'Well, she couldn't say it hadn't.'

'Now, mind', said he, 'if you have listened to your mother's advice, you have brought bad luck on us both, and then, all that has passed between us will be as nothing.'

'No', she said, 'she hadn't listened to her mother's advice.'

So when she reached home, and had gone to bed, it was the old story over again. There came a man and lay down beside her; but at dead of night, when she heard he slept, she got up and struck a light, lit the candle, and let the light shine on him, and so she saw that he was the loveliest Prince one ever set eyes on, and she fell so deep in love with him on the spot, that she thought she couldn't live if she didn't give him a kiss there and then. And so she did, but as she kissed him, she dropped three hot drops of tallow on his shirt, and he woke up.

'What have you done?' he cried; 'now you have made us both unlucky, for had you held out only this one year, I had been freed. For I have a stepmother who has bewitched me, so that I am a White Bear by day, and a Man by night. But now all ties are snapt between us; now I must set off from you to her. She lives in a Castle which stands EAST O' THE SUN AND WEST O' THE MOON, and there, too, is a Princess, with a nose three ells long, and she's the wife I must have now.'

She wept and took it ill, but there was no help for it; go he must.

Then she asked if she mightn't go with him?

No, she mightn't.

'Tell me the way, then', she said, 'and I'll search you out; *that* surely I may get leave to do.'

'Yes, she might do that', he said; 'but there was no way to that place. It lay EAST O' THE SUN AND WEST O' THE MOON, and thither she'd never find her way.'

So next morning, when she woke up, both Prince and castle were gone, and then she lay on a little green patch, in the midst of the gloomy thick wood, and by her side lay the same bundle of rags she had brought with her from her old home.

So when she had rubbed the sleep out of her eyes, and wept till she was tired, she set out on her way, and walked many, many days, till she came to a lofty crag.

Under it sat an old hag, and played with a gold apple which she tossed about. Her the lassie asked if she knew the way to the Prince, who lived with his step-mother in the Castle, that lay EAST O' THE SUN AND WEST O' THE MOON, and who was to marry the Princess with a nose three ells long.

'How did you come to know about him?' asked the old hag; 'but maybe you are the lassie who ought to have had him?'

Yes, she was.

'So, so; it's you, is it?' said the old hag. 'Well, all I know about him is, that he lives in the castle that lies EAST O' THE SUN AND WEST O' THE MOON, and thither you'll come, late or never; but still you may have the loan of my horse, and on him you can ride to my next neighbour. Maybe she'll be able to tell you; and when you get there, just give the horse a switch under the left ear, and beg him to be off home; and, stay, this gold apple you may take with you.'

So she got upon the horse, and rode a long long time, till she came to another crag, under which sat another old hag, with a gold carding-comb. Her the lassie asked if she knew the way to the castle that lay EAST O' THE SUN AND WEST O' THE MOON, and she answered, like the first old hag, that she knew nothing about it, except it was east o' the sun and west o' the moon.

'And thither you'll come, late or never, but you shall have the loan of my horse to my next neighbour; maybe she'll tell you all about it; and when you get there, just switch the horse under the left ear, and beg him to be off home.'

And this old hag gave her the golden carding-comb; it might be she'd find some use for it, she said. So the lassie got up on the horse, and rode a far far way, and a weary time; and so at last she came to another great crag, under which sat another old hag, spinning with a golden spinning-wheel. Her, too, she asked if she knew the way to the Prince, and where the castle was that lay EAST O' THE SUN AND WEST O' THE MOON. So it was the same thing over again.

'Maybe it's you who ought to have had the Prince?' said the old hag.

Yes, it was.

But she, too, didn't know the way a bit better than the other two. 'East o' the sun and west o' the moon it was', she knew--that was all.

'And thither you'll come, late or never; but I'll lend you my horse, and then I think you'd best ride to the East Wind and ask him; maybe, he knows those parts, and can blow you thither. But when you get to him, you need only give the horse a switch under the left ear, and he'll trot home of himself.'

And so, too, she gave her the gold spinning-wheel. 'Maybe you'll find a use for it', said the old hag.

Then on she rode many many days, a weary time, before she got to the East Wind's house, but at last she did reach it, and then she asked the East Wind if he could tell her the way to the Prince who dwelt east o' the sun and west o' the moon. Yes, the East Wind had often heard tell of it, the Prince and the castle, but he couldn't tell the way, for he had never blown so far.

'But, if you will, I'll go with you to my brother the West Wind, maybe he knows, for he's much stronger. So, if you will just get on my back, I'll carry you thither.'

Yes, she got on his back, and I should just think they went briskly along.

So when they got there, they went into the West Wind's house, and the East Wind said the lassie he had brought was the one who ought to have had the Prince who lived in the castle EAST O' THE SUN AND WEST O' THE MOON; and so she had set out to seek him, and how he had come with her, and would be glad to know if the West Wind knew how to get to the castle.

'Nay', said the West Wind, 'so far I've never blown; but if you will, I'll go with you to our brother the South Wind, for he's much stronger than either of us, and he has flapped his wings far and wide. Maybe he'll tell you. You can get on my back, and I'll carry you to him.'

Yes! she got on his back, and so they travelled to the South Wind, and weren't so very long on the way, I should think.

When they got there, the West Wind asked him if he could tell her the way to the castle that lay EAST O' THE SUN AND WEST O' THE MOON, for it was she who ought to have had the prince who lived there.

'You don't say so! That's she, is it?' said the South Wind.

'Well, I have blustered about in most places in my time, but so far have I never blown; but if you will, I'll take you to my brother the North Wind; he is the oldest and strongest of the whole lot of us, and if he don't know where it is, you'll never find any one in the world to tell you. You can get on my back, and I'll carry you thither.'

Yes! she got on his back, and away he went from his house at a fine rate. And this time, too, she wasn't long on her way.

So when they got to the North Wind's house, he was so wild and cross, cold puffs came from him a long way off.

'BLAST YOU BOTH, WHAT DO YOU WANT?' he roared out to them ever so far off, so that it struck them with an icy shiver.

'Well', said the South Wind, 'you needn't be so foul-mouthed, for here I am, your brother, the South Wind, and here is the lassie who ought to have had the Prince who dwells in the castle that lies EAST O' THE SUN AND WEST O' THE MOON, and now she wants to ask you if you ever were there, and can tell her the way, for she would be so glad to find him again.'

'YES, I KNOW WELL ENOUGH WHERE IT IS', said the North Wind; 'once in my life I blew an aspen-leaf thither, but I was so tired I couldn't blow a puff for ever so many days after. But if you really wish to go thither, and aren't afraid to come along with me, I'll take you on my back and see if I can blow you thither.'

Yes! with all her heart; she must and would get thither if it were possible in any way; and as for fear, however madly he went, she wouldn't be at all afraid.

'Very well, then', said the North Wind, 'but you must sleep here to- night, for we must have the whole day before us, if we're to get thither at all.'

Early next morning the North Wind woke her, and puffed himself up, and blew himself out, and made himself so stout and big, 'twas gruesome to look at him; and so off they went high up through the air, as if they would never stop till they got to the world's end.

Down here below there was such a storm; it threw down long tracts of wood and many houses, and when it swept over the great sea, ships foundered by hundreds.

So they tore on and on--no one can believe how far they went--and all the while they still went over the sea, and the North Wind got more and more weary, and so out of breath he could scarce bring out a puff, and his wings drooped and drooped, till at last he sunk so low that the crests of the waves dashed over his heels.

'Are you afraid?' said the North Wind.

'No!' she wasn't.

But they weren't very far from land; and the North Wind had still so much strength left in him that he managed to throw her up on the shore under the windows of the castle which lay EAST O' THE SUN AND WEST O' THE MOON; but then he was so weak and worn out, he had to stay there and rest many days before he could get home again.

Next morning the lassie sat down under the castle window, and began to play with the gold apple; and the first person she saw was the Long-nose who was to have the Prince.

'What do you want for your gold apple, you lassie?' said the Long- nose, and threw up the window.

'It's not for sale, for gold or money', said the lassie.

'If it's not for sale for gold or money, what is it that you will sell it for? You may name your own price', said the Princess.

'Well! if I may get to the Prince, who lives here, and be with him to-night, you shall have it', said the lassie whom the North Wind had brought.

Yes! she might; that could be done. So the Princess got the gold apple; but when the lassie came up to the Prince's bed-room at night he was fast asleep; she called him and shook him, and between whiles she wept sore; but all she could do she couldn't wake him up. Next morning as soon as day broke, came the Princess with the long nose, and drove her out again.

So in the daytime she sat down under the castle windows and began to card with her carding-comb, and the same thing happened. The Princess asked what she wanted for it; and she said it wasn't for sale for gold or money, but if she might get leave to go up to the Prince and be with him that night, the Princess should have it. But when she went up she found him fast asleep again, and all she called, and all she shook, and wept, and prayed, she couldn't get life into him; and as soon as the first gray peep of day came, then came the Princess with the long nose, and chased her out again.

So, in the day time, the lassie sat down outside under the castle window, and began to spin with her golden spinning-wheel, and that, too, the Princess with the long nose wanted to have. So she threw up the window and asked what she wanted for it. The lassie said, as she had said twice before, it wasn't for sale for gold or money; but if she might go up to the Prince who was there, and be with him alone that night, she might have it.

Yes! she might do that and welcome. But now you must know there were some Christian folk who had been carried off thither, and as they sat in their room, which was next the Prince, they had heard how a woman had been in there, and wept and prayed, and called to him two nights running, and they told that to the Prince.

That evening, when the Princess came with her sleepy drink, the Prince made as if he drank, but threw it over his shoulder, for he could guess it was a sleepy drink. So, when the lassie came in, she found the Prince wide awake; and then she told him the whole story how she had come thither.

'Ah', said the Prince, 'you've just come in the very nick of time, for to-morrow is to be our wedding-day; but now I won't have the Long-nose, and you are the only woman in the world who can set me free. I'll say I want to see what my wife is fit for, and beg her to wash the shirt which has the three spots of tallow on it; she'll say yes, for she doesn't know 'tis you who put them there; but that's a work only for Christian folk, and not for such a pack of Trolls, and so I'll say that I won't have any other for my bride than the woman who can wash them out, and ask you to do it.'

So there was great joy and love between them all that night. But next day, when the wedding was to be, the Prince said:

'First of all, I'd like to see what my bride is fit for.'

'Yes!' said the step-mother, with all her heart.

'Well', said the Prince, 'I've got a fine shirt which I'd like for my wedding shirt, but some how or other it has got three spots of tallow on it, which I must have washed out; and I have sworn never to take any other bride than the woman who's able to do that. If she can't, she's not worth having.'

Well, that was no great thing they said, so they agreed, and she with the long-nose began to wash away as hard as she could, but the more she rubbed and scrubbed, the bigger the spots grew.

'Ah!' said the old hag, her mother, 'you can't wash; let me try.'

But she hadn't long taken the shirt in hand, before it got far worse than ever, and with all her rubbing, and wringing, and scrubbing, the spots grew bigger and blacker, and the darker and uglier was the shirt.

Then all the other Trolls began to wash, but the longer it lasted, the blacker and uglier the shirt grew, till at last it was as black all over as if it had been up the chimney.

'Ah!' said the Prince, 'you're none of you worth a straw you can't wash. Why there, outside, sits a beggar lassie, I'll be bound she knows how to wash better than the whole lot of you. COME IN LASSIE!' he shouted.

Well, in she came.

'Can you wash this shirt clean, lassie, you?' said he.

'I don't know', she said, 'but I think I can.'

And almost before she had taken it and dipped it in the water, it was as white as driven snow, and whiter still.

'Yes; you are the lassie for me', said the Prince.

At that the old hag flew into such a rage, she burst on the spot, and the Princess with the long nose after her, and the whole pack of Trolls after her--at least I've never heard a word about them since.

As for the Prince and Princess, they set free all the poor Christian folk who had been carried off and shut up there; and they took with them all the silver and gold, and flitted away as far as they could from the Castle that lay EAST O' THE SUN AND WEST O' THE MOON.

BOOTS WHO ATE A MATCH WITH THE TROLL

Once on a time there was a farmer who had three sons; his means were small, and he was old and weak, and his sons would take to nothing. A fine large wood belonged to the farm, and one day the father told his sons to go and hew wood, and try to pay off some of his debts.

Well, after a long talk he got them to set off, and the eldest was to go first. But when he had got well into the wood, and began to hew at a mossy old fir, what should he see coming up to him but a great sturdy Troll.

'If you hew in this wood of mine', said the Troll, 'I'll kill you!'

When the lad heard that, he threw the axe down, and ran off home as fast as he could lay legs to the ground; so he came in quite out of breath, and told them what had happened, but his father called him 'hare-heart'--no Troll would ever have scared him from hewing when he was young, he said.

Next day the second son's turn came, and he fared just the same. He had scarce hewn three strokes at the fir, before the Troll came to him too, and said:

'If you hew in this wood of mine, I'll kill you.'

The lad dared not so much as look at him, but threw down the axe, took to his heels, and came scampering home just like his brother. So when he got home, his father was angry again, and said no Troll had ever scared him when he was young.

The third day Boots wanted to set off.

'You, indeed!' said the two elder brothers; 'you'll do it bravely, no doubt! you, who have scarce ever set your foot out of the door.'

Boots said nothing to this, but only begged them to give him a good store of food. His mother had no cheese, so she set the pot on the fire to make him a little, and he put it into a scrip and set off. So when he had hewn a bit, the Troll came to him too, and said:

'If you hew in this wood of mine, I'll kill you.'

But the lad was not slow; he pulled his cheese out of the scrip in a trice, and squeezed it till the whey spurted out.

'Hold your tongue!' he cried to the Troll, 'or I'll squeeze you as I squeeze the water out of this white stone.'

'Nay, dear friend!' said the Troll, 'only spare me, and I'll help you to hew.'

Well, on those terms the lad was willing to spare him, and the Troll hewed so bravely, that they felled and cut up many, many fathoms in the day.

But when even drew near, the Troll said:

'Now you'd better come home with me, for my house is nearer than yours.'

So the lad was willing enough; and when they reached the Troll's house, the Troll was to make up the fire, while the lad went to fetch water for their porridge, and there stood two iron pails so big and heavy, that he couldn't so much as lift them from the ground.

'Pooh!' said the lad, 'it isn't worth while to touch these finer- basins: I'll just go and fetch the spring itself.'

'Nay, nay, dear friend!' said the Troll; 'I can't afford to lose my spring; just you make up the fire, and I'll go and fetch the water.'

So when he came back with the water, they set to and boiled up a great pot of porridge.

'It's all the same to me', said the lad; 'but if you're of my mind, we'll eat a match!'

'With all my heart', said the Troll, for he thought he could surely hold his own in eating. So they sat down; but the lad took his scrip unawares to the Troll, and hung it before him, and so he spooned more into the scrip than he ate himself; and when the scrip was full, he took up his knife and made a slit in the scrip. The Troll looked on all the while, but said never a word. So when they had eaten a good bit longer, the Troll laid down his spoon, saying, 'Nay! but I can't eat a morsel more.'

'But you shall eat', said the youth; 'I'm only half done; why don't you do as I did, and cut a hole in your paunch? You'll be able to eat then as much as you please.'

'But doesn't it hurt one cruelly?' asked the Troll.

'Oh', said the youth, 'nothing to speak of.'

So the Troll did as the lad said, and then you must know very well that he lost his life; but the lad took all the silver and gold that he found in the hill-side, and went home with it, and you may fancy it went a great way to pay off the debt.

HACON GRIZZLEBEARD

Once on a time there was a princess who was so proud and pert that no suitor was good enough for her. She made game of them all, and sent them about their business, one after the other; but though she was so proud, still new suitors kept on coming to the palace, for she was a beauty, the wicked hussey!

So one day there came a prince to woo her, and his name was Hacon Grizzlebeard; but the first night he was there, the Princess bade the king's fool cut off the ears of one of the prince's horses, and slit the jaws of the other up to the ears. When the prince went out to drive next day, the Princess stood in the porch and looked at him.

'Well!' she cried, 'I never saw the like of this in all my life; the keen north wind that blows here has taken the ears off one of your horses, and the other has stood by and gaped at what was going on till his jaws have split right up to his ears.'

And with that she burst out into a roar of laughter, ran in, slammed to the door, and let him drive off.

So he drove home; but as he went, he thought to himself that he would pay her off one day. After a bit, he put on a great beard of moss, threw a great fur cloak over his clothes, and dressed himself up just like any beggar. He went to a goldsmith and bought a golden spinning wheel, and sat down with it under the Princess' window, and began to file away at his spinning wheel, and to turn it this way and that, for it wasn't quite in order, and, besides, it wanted a stand.

So when the Princess rose up in the morning, she came to the window and threw it up, and called out to the beggar if he would sell his golden spinning-wheel?

'No; it isn't for sale', said Hacon Grizzlebeard; 'but if I may have leave to sleep outside your bedroom door to-night, I'll give it you.'

Well, the Princess thought it a good bargain; there could be no danger in letting him sleep outside her door.

So she got the wheel, and at night Hacon Grizzlebeard lay down outside her bedroom. But as the night wore on he began to freeze.

'Hutetutetutetu! it is *so* cold; do let me in', he cried.

'You've lost your wits outright, I think', said the Princess.

'Oh, hutetutetutetu! it is so bitter cold, pray do let me in', said Hacon Grizzlebeard again.

'Hush! hush! hold your tongue!' said the Princess; 'if my father were to know that there was a man in the house, I should be in a fine scrape.'

'Oh, hutetutetutetu! I'm almost frozen to death; only let me come inside and lie on the floor', said Hacon Grizzlebeard.

Yes! there was no help for it. She had to let him in, and when he was, he lay on the ground and slept like a top.

Some time after, Hacon came again with the stand to the spinning-wheel, and sat down under the Princess' window, and began to file at it, for it was not quite fit for use. When she heard him filing, she threw up the window and began to talk to him, and to ask what he had there.

'Oh! only the stand to that spinning-wheel which your royal highness bought; for I thought, as you had the wheel, you might like to have the stand too.'

'What do you want for it?' asked the Princess; but it was not for sale any more than the wheel, but she might have them if she would give him leave to sleep on the floor of her bedroom next night.

Well! she gave him leave, only he was to be sure to lie still, and not to shiver and call out 'hutetu', or any such stuff. Hacon Grizzlebeard promised fair enough, but as the night wore on he began to shiver and shake, and to ask whether he might not come nearer, and lie on the floor alongside the Princess' bed.

There was no help for it; she had to give him leave, lest the king should hear the noise he made. So Hacon Grizzlebeard lay alongside the Princess' bed, and slept like a top.

It was a long while before Hacon Grizzlebeard came again; but when he came he had with him a golden wool-winder, and he sat down and began to file away at it under the Princess' window. Then came the old story over again. When the

Princess heard what was going on, she came to the window, and asked him how he did, and whether he would sell the golden wool-winder?

'It is not to be had for money; but if you'll give me leave to sleep to-night in your bedroom, with my head on your bedstead, you shall have it for nothing', said Hacon Grizzlebeard.

Well! she would give him leave, if he only gave his word to be quiet, and make no noise. So he said he would do his best to be still; but as the night wore on, he began to shiver and shake so, that his teeth chattered again.

'Hutetutetutetu! it is so bitter cold! Oh, do let me get into bed and warm myself a little', said Hacon Grizzlebeard.

'Get into bed!' said the Princess; 'why, you must have lost your wits.'

'Hutetutetutetu!' said Hacon; 'do let me get into bed. Hutetutetutetu.'

'Hush! hush! be still for God's sake', said the Princess; 'if father knows there is a man in here, I shall be in a sad plight. I'm sure he'll kill me on the spot.'

'Hutetutetutetu! let me get into bed', said Hacon Grizzlebeard, who kept on shivering so that the whole room shook.

Well! there was no help for it; she had to let him get into bed, where he slept both sound and soft; but a little while after the Princess had a child, at which the king grew so wild with rage, that he was near making an end of both mother and babe. Just after this happened, came Hacon Grizzlebeard tramping that way once more, as if by chance, and took his seat down in the kitchen, like any other beggar.

So when the Princess came out and saw him, she cried, 'Ah, God have mercy on me, for the ill-luck you have brought on me; father is ready to burst with rage; do let me follow you to your home.'

'Oh! I'll be bound you're too well bred to follow me', said Hacon, 'for I have nothing but a log but to live in; and how I shall ever get food for you I can't tell, for it's just as much as I can do to get food for myself.'

'Oh yes! it's all the same to me how you get it, or whether you get it at all', she said; 'only let me be with you, for if I stay here any longer, my father will be sure to take my life.'

So she got leave to be with the beggar, as she called him, and they walked a long, long way, though she was but a poor hand at tramping. When she passed out of her father's land into another, she asked whose it was?

'Oh! this is Hacon Grizzlebeard's, if you must know', said he.

'Indeed!' said the Princess; 'I might have married him if I chose, and then I should not have had to walk about like a beggar's wife.'

So, whenever they came to grand castles, and woods, and parks, and she asked whose they were? the beggar's answer was still the same: 'Oh: they are Hacon Grizzlebeard's.' And the Princess was in a sad way that she had not chosen the man who had such broad lands. Last of all, they came to a palace, where he said he was known, and where he thought he could get her work, so that they might have something to live on; so he built up a cabin by the woodside for them to dwell in; and every day he went to the king's palace, as he said, to hew wood and draw water for the cook, and when he came back he brought a few scraps of meat; but they did not go very far. One day, when he came home from the palace, he said: 'To-morrow I will stay at home and look after the baby, but you must get ready to go to the palace, do you hear! for the Prince said you were to come and try your hand at baking.'

'I bake!' said the Princess; 'I can't bake, for I never did such a thing in my life.'

'Well, you must go', said Hacon, 'since the Prince has said it. If you can't bake, you can learn; you have only got to look how the rest bake; and mind, when you leave, you must steal me some bread.'

'I can't steal', said the Princess.

'You can learn that too', said Hacon; 'you know we live on short commons. But take care that the Prince doesn't see you, for he has eyes at the back of his head.'

So when she was well on her way, Hacon ran by a short cut and reached the palace long before her, and threw off his rags and beard, and put on his princely robes.

The Princess took her turn in the bakehouse, and did as Hacon bade her, for she stole bread till her pockets were crammed full. So when she was about to go home at even, the Prince said:

'We don't know much of this old wife of Hacon Grizzlebeard's, I think we'd best see if she has taken anything away with her.'

So he thrust his hand into all her pockets, and felt her all over, and when he found the bread, he was in a great rage, and led them all a sad life. She began to weep and bewail, and said:

'The beggar made me do it, and I couldn't help it.' 'Well', said the Prince at last, 'it ought to have gone hard with you; but all the same, for the sake of the beggar you shall be forgiven this once.'

When she was well on her way, he threw off his robes, put on his skin cloak, and his false beard, and reached the cabin before her. When she came home, he was busy nursing the baby.

'Well, you have made me do what it went against my heart to do. This is the first time I ever stole, and this shall be the last'; and with that she told him how it had gone with her, and what the Prince had said.

A few days after Hacon Grizzlebeard came home at even and said:

'To-morrow I must stay at home and mind the babe, for they are going to kill a pig at the palace, and you must help to make the sausages.'

'I make sausages!' said the Princess; 'I can't do any such thing. I have eaten sausages often enough; but as to making them, I never made one in my life.'

Well, there was no help for it; the Prince had said it, and go she must. As for not knowing how, she was only to do what the others did, and at the same time Hacon bade her steal some sausages for him.

'Nay, but I can't steal them', she said; 'you know how it went last time.'

'Well, you can learn to steal; who knows but you may have better luck next time', said Hacon Grizzlebeard.

When she was well on her way, Hacon ran by a short cut, reached the palace long before her, threw off his skin cloak and false beard, and stood in the kitchen with his royal robes before she came in. So the Princess stood by when the pig was killed, and made sausages with the rest, and did as Hacon bade her, and stuffed her pockets full of sausages. But when she was about to go home at even, the Prince said:

'This beggar's wife was long-fingered last time; we may as well just see if she hasn't carried anything off.'

So he began to thrust his hands into her pockets, and when he found the sausages he was in a great rage again, and made a great to do, threatening to send for the constable and put her into the cage.

'Oh, God bless your royal highness; do let me off! The beggar made me do it', she said, and wept bitterly.

'Well', said Hacon, 'you ought to smart for it; but for the beggar's sake you shall be forgiven.'

When she was gone, he changed his clothes again, ran by the short cut, and when she reached the cabin, there he was before her. Then she told him the whole story, and swore, through thick and thin, it should be the last time he got her to do such a thing.

Now, it fell out a little time after, when the man came back from the palace, he said:

'Our Prince is going to be married, but the bride is sick, so the tailor can't measure her for her wedding gown. And the Prince's will is, that you should go up to the palace and be measured instead of the bride; for he says you are just the same height and shape. But after you have been measured, mind you don't go away; you can stand about, you know, and when the tailor cuts out the gown, you can snap up the largest pieces, and bring them home for a waistcoat for me.'

'Nay, but I can't steal', she said; 'besides, you know how it went last time.'

'You can learn then', said Hacon, 'and you may have better luck, perhaps.'

She thought it bad, but still she went and did as she was told. She stood by while the tailor was cutting out the gown, and she swept down all the biggest scraps, and stuffed them into her pockets; and when she was going away, the Prince said:

'We may as well see if this old girl has not been long-fingered this time too.'

So he began to feel and search her pockets, and when he found the pieces he was in a rage, and began to stamp and scold at a great rate, while she wept and said:

'Ah, pray forgive me; the beggar bade me do it, and I couldn't help it.'

'Well, you ought to smart for it', said Hacon; 'but for the beggar's sake it shall be forgiven you.'

So it went now just as it had gone before, and when she got back to the cabin, the beggar was there before her.

'Oh, Heaven help me', she said; 'you will be the death of me at last, by making me nothing but what is wicked. The Prince was in such a towering rage that he threatened me both with the constable and cage.'

Sometime after, Hacon came home to the cabin at even and said:

'Now, the Prince's will is, that you should go up to the palace and stand for the bride, old lass! for the bride is still sick, and keeps her bed; but he won't put off the wedding; and he says, you are so like her, that no one could tell one from the other; so to-morrow you must get ready to go to the palace.'

'I think you've lost your wits, both the Prince and you', said she. 'Do you think I look fit to stand in the bride's place? look at me! Can any beggar's trull look worse than I?'

'Well, the Prince said you were to go, and so go you must', said Hacon Grizzlebeard.

There was no help for it, go she must; and when she reached the palace, they dressed her out so finely that no princess ever looked so smart.

The bridal train went to church, where she stood for the bride, and when they came back, there was dancing and merriment in the palace. But just as she was in the midst of dancing with the Prince, she saw a gleam of light through the window, and lo! the cabin by the wood- side was all one bright flame.

'Oh! the beggar, and the babe, and the cabin', she screamed out, and was just going to swoon away.

'Here is the beggar, and there is the babe, and so let the cabin burn away', said Hacon Grizzlebeard.

Then she knew him again, and after that the mirth and merriment began in right earnest; but since that I have never heard tell anything more about them.

BOOTS, WHO MADE THE PRINCESS SAY, 'THAT'S A STORY'

Once on a time there was a king who had a daughter, and she was such a dreadful story-teller that the like of her was not to be found far or near. So the king gave out, that if any one could tell such a string of lies, as would get her to say, 'That's a story', he should have her to wife, and half the kingdom besides. Well, many came, as you may fancy, to try their luck, for every one would have been very glad to have the Princess, to say nothing of the kingdom; but they all cut a sorry figure, for the Princess was so given to story- telling, that all their lies went in at one ear and out of the other. Among the rest came three brothers to try their luck, and the two elder went first, but they fared no better than those who had gone before them. Last of all the third, Boots, set off and found the Princess in the farm-yard.

'Good-morning', he said, 'and thank you for nothing.'

'Good-morning', said she, 'and the same to you.'

Then she went on:

'You haven't such a fine farm-yard as ours, I'll be bound; for when two shepherds stand, one at each end of it, and blow their ram's horns, the one can't hear the other.'

'Haven't we though!' answered Boots; 'ours is far bigger; for when a cow begins to go with calf at one end of it, she doesn't get to the other end before the time to drop her calf is come.'

'I dare say!' said the Princess. 'Well, but you haven't such a big ox, after all, as ours yonder; for when two men sit one on each horn, they can't touch each other with a twenty-foot rule.'

'Stuff!' said Boots; 'is that all? why, we have an ox who is so big, that when two men sit, one on each horn, and each blows his great mountain-trumpet, they can't hear one another.'

'I dare say!' said the Princess; 'but you haven't so much milk as we, I'll be bound; for we milk our kine into great pails, and carry them in-doors, and empty them into great tubs, and so we make great, great cheeses.'

'Oh! you do, do you?' said Boots. 'Well, we milk ours into great tubs, and then we put them in carts and drive them in-doors, and then we turn them out into great brewing vats, and so we make cheeses as big as a great house. We had, too a dun mare to tread the cheese well together when it was making; but once she tumbled down into the cheese, and we lost her; and after we had eaten at this cheese seven years, we came upon a great dun mare, alive and kicking. Well, once after that I was going to drive this mare to the mill, and her back- bone snapped in two; but I wasn't put out, not I, for I took a spruce sapling, and put it into her for a back-bone, and she had no other back-bone all the while we had her. But the sapling grew up into such a tall tree, that I climbed right up to heaven by it, and when I got there, I saw the Virgin Mary sitting and spinning the foam of the sea into pig's-bristle ropes; but just then the spruce-fir broke short off, and I couldn't get down again; so the Virgin Mary let me down by one of the ropes, and down I slipped straight into a fox's hole, and who should sit there but my mother and your father cobbling shoes; and just as I stepped in, my mother gave your father such a box on the ear, that it made his whiskers curl.'

'That's a story!' said the Princess; 'my father never did any such thing in all his born days!'

So Boots got the Princess to wife, and half the kingdom besides.

THE TWELVE WILD DUCKS

Once on a time there was a Queen who was out driving, when there had been a new fall of snow in the winter; but when she had gone a little way, she began to bleed at the nose, and had to get out of her sledge. And so, as she stood there, leaning against the fence, and saw the red blood on the white snow, she fell a-thinking how she had twelve sons and no daughter, and she said to herself:

'If I only had a daughter as white as snow and as red as blood, I shouldn't care what became of all my sons.'

But the words were scarce out of her mouth before an old witch of the Trolls came up to her.

'A daughter you shall have', she said, 'and she shall be as white as snow, and as red as blood; and your sons shall be mine, but you may keep them till the babe is christened.'

So when the time came the Queen had a daughter, and she was as white as snow, and as red as blood, just as the Troll had promised, and so they called her 'Snow-white and Rosy-red.' Well, there was great joy at the King's court, and the Queen was as glad as glad could be; but when what she had promised to the old witch came into her mind, she sent for a silversmith, and bade him make twelve silver spoons, one for each prince, and after that she bade him make one more, and that she gave to Snow-white and Rosy-red. But as soon as ever the Princess was christened, the Princes were turned into twelve wild ducks, and flew away. They never saw them again--away they went, and away they stayed.

So the Princess grew up, and she was both tall and fair, but she was often so strange and sorrowful, and no one could understand what it was that failed her. But one evening the Queen was also sorrowful, for she had many strange thoughts when she thought of her sons. She said to Snow-white and Rosy-red,

'Why are you so sorrowful, my daughter? Is there anything you want? if so, only say the word, and you shall have it.'

'Oh, it seems so dull and lonely here', said Snow-white and Rosy-red; 'every one else has brothers and sisters, but I am all alone; I have none; and that's why I'm so sorrowful.'

'But you *had* brothers, my daughter', said the Queen; 'I had twelve sons who were your brothers, but I gave them all away to get you'; and so she told her the whole story.

So when the Princess heard that, she had no rest; for, in spite of all the Queen could say or do, and all she wept and prayed, the lassie would set off to seek her brothers, for she thought it was all her fault; and at last she got leave to go away from the palace. On and on she walked into the wide world, so far, you would never have thought a young lady could have strength to walk so far.

So, once, when she was walking through a great, great wood, one day she felt tired, and sat down on a mossy tuft and fell asleep. Then she dreamt that she went deeper and deeper into the wood, till she came to a little wooden hut, and there she found her brothers; just then she woke, and straight before her she saw a worn path in the green moss, and this path went deeper into the wood; so she followed it, and after a long time she came to just such a little wooden house as that she had seen in her dream.

Now, when she went into the room there was no one at home, but there stood twelve beds, and twelve chairs, and twelve spoons--a dozen of everything, in short. So when she saw that she was so glad, she hadn't been so glad for many a long year, for she could guess at once that her brothers lived here, and that they owned the beds, and chairs, and spoons. So she began to make up the fire, and sweep the room, and make the beds, and cook the dinner, and to make the house as tidy as she could; and when she had done all the cooking and work, she ate her own dinner, and crept under her youngest brother's bed, and lay down there, but she forgot her spoon upon the table.

So she had scarcely laid herself down before she heard something flapping and whirring in the air, and so all the twelve wild ducks came sweeping in; but as soon as ever they crossed the threshold they became Princes.

'Oh, how nice and warm it is in here', they said. 'Heaven bless him who made up the fire, and cooked such a good dinner for us.'

And so each took up his silver spoon and was going to eat. But when each had taken his own, there was one still left lying on the table, and it was so like the rest that they couldn't tell it from them.

'This is our sister's spoon', they said; 'and if her spoon be here, she can't be very far off herself.'

'If this be our sister's spoon, and she be here', said the eldest, 'she shall be killed, for she is to blame for all the ill we suffer.'

And this she lay under the bed and listened to.

'No', said the youngest, ''twere a shame to kill her for that. She has nothing to do with our suffering ill; for if any one's to blame, it's our own mother.'

So they set to work hunting for her both high and low, and at last they looked under all the beds, and so when they came to the youngest Prince's bed, they found her, and dragged her out. Then the eldest Prince wished again to have her killed, but she begged and prayed so prettily for herself.

'Oh! gracious goodness! don't kill me, for I've gone about seeking you these three years, and if I could only set you free, I'd willingly lose my life.'

'Well!' said they, 'if you will set us free, you may keep your life; for you can if you choose.'

'Yes; only tell me', said the Princess, 'how it can be done, and I'll do it, whatever it be.'

'You must pick thistle-down', said the Princes, 'and you must card it, and spin it, and weave it; and after you have done that, you must cut out and make twelve coats, and twelve shirts, and twelve neckerchiefs, one for each of us, and while you do that, you must neither talk, nor laugh, nor weep. If you can do that, we are free.'

'But where shall I ever get thistle-down enough for so many neckerchiefs, and shirts, and coats?' asked Snow-white and Rosy-red.

'We'll soon show you', said the Princes; and so they took her with them to a great wide moor, where there stood such a crop of thistles, all nodding and nodding in the breeze, and the down all floating and glistening like gossamers through the air in the sunbeams. The Princess had never seen such a quantity of thistledown in her life, and she began to pluck and gather it as fast and as well as she could; and when she got home at night she set to work carding and spinning yarn from the down. So she went on a long long time, picking, and carding, and spinning, and all the while keeping the Princes' house, cooking, and making their beds. At evening home they came, flapping and whirring like wild ducks, and all night they were Princes, but in the morning off they flew again, and were wild ducks the whole day.

But now it happened once, when she was out on the moor to pick thistle-down--and if I don't mistake, it was the very last time she was to go thither--it happened that the young King who ruled that land was out hunting, and came riding across the moor, and saw her. So he stopped there and wondered who the lovely lady could be that walked along the moor picking thistle-down, and he asked her her name, and when he could get no answer, he was still more astonished; and at last he liked her so much, that nothing would do but he must take her home to his castle and marry her. So he ordered his servants to take her and put her up on his horse. Snow-white and Rosy-red, she wrung her hands, and made signs to them, and pointed to the bags in which her work was, and when the King saw she wished to have them with her, he told his men to take up the bags behind them. When they had done that the Princess came to herself, little by little, for the King was both a wise man and a handsome man too, and he was as soft and kind to her as a doctor. But when they got home to the palace, and the old Queen, who was his stepmother, set eyes on Snow-white and Rosy-red, she got so cross and jealous of her because she was so lovely, that she said to the king:

'Can't you see now, that this thing whom you have picked up, and whom you are going to marry, is a witch. Why? she can't either talk, or laugh, or weep!'

But the King didn't care a pin for what she said, but held on with the wedding, and married Snow-white and Rosy-red and they lived in great joy and glory; but she didn't forget to go on sewing at her shirts.

So when the year was almost out, Snow-white and Rosy-red brought a Prince into the world; and then the old Queen was more spiteful and jealous than ever, and at dead of night, she stole in to Snow-white and Rosy-red, while she slept, and took away her babe, and threw it into a pitful of snakes. After that she cut Snow-white and Rosy-red in her finger, and smeared the blood over her mouth, and went straight to the King.

'Now come and see', she said, 'what sort of a thing you have taken for your Queen; here she has eaten up her own babe.'

Then the King was so downcast, he almost burst into tears, and said:

'Yes, it must be true, since I see it with my own eyes; but she'll not do it again, I'm sure, and so this time I'll spare her life.'

So before the next year was out she had another son, and the same thing happened. The King's stepmother got more and more jealous and spiteful. She stole into the young Queen at night while she slept, took away the babe, and threw it into a pit full of snakes, cut the young Queen's finger, and smeared the blood over her mouth, and then went and told the King she had eaten up her own child. Then the King was so sorrowful, you can't think how sorry he was, and he said:

'Yes, it must be true, since I see it with my own eyes; but she'll not do it again, I'm sure, and so this time too I'll spare her life.'

Well, before the next year was out, Snow-white and Rosy-red brought a daughter into the world, and her, too, the old Queen took and threw into the pit full of snakes, while the young Queen slept. Then she cut her finger, smeared the blood over her mouth, and went again to the King and said,

'Now you may come and see if it isn't as I say; she's a wicked, wicked witch, for here she has gone and eaten up her third babe, too.'

Then the King was so sad, there was no end to it, for now he couldn't spare her any longer, but had to order her to be burnt alive on a pile of wood. But just when the pile was all a-blaze, and they were going to put her on it, she made signs to them to take twelve boards and lay them round the pile, and on these she laid the neckerchiefs, and the shirts, and the coats for her brothers, but the youngest brother's shirt wanted its left arm, for she hadn't had time to finish it. And as soon as ever she had done that, they heard such a flapping and whirring in the air, and down came twelve wild ducks flying over the forest, and each of them snapped up his clothes in his bill and flew off with them.

'See now!' said the old Queen to the King, 'wasn't I right when I told you she was a witch, but make haste and burn her before the pile burns low.'

'Oh!' said the King, 'we've wood enough and to spare, and so I'll wait a bit, for I have a mind to see what the end of all this will be.'

As he spoke, up came the twelve princes riding along, as handsome well-grown lads as you'd wish to see; but the youngest prince had a wild duck's wing instead of his left arm.

'What's all this about?' asked the Princes.

'My Queen is to be burnt,' said the King, 'because she's a witch, and because she has eaten up her own babes.'

'She hasn't eaten them at all', said the Princes. 'Speak now, sister; you have set us free and saved us, now save yourself.'

Then Snow-white and Rosy-red spoke, and told the whole story; how every time she was brought to bed, the old Queen, the King's stepmother, had stolen into her at night, had taken her babes away, and cut her little finger, and smeared the blood over her mouth; and then the Princes took the King, and shewed him the snake-pit where three babes lay playing with adders and toads, and lovelier children you never saw.

So the King had them taken out at once, and went to his stepmother, and asked her what punishment she thought that woman deserved who could find it in her heart to betray a guiltless Queen and three such blessed little babes.

'She deserves to be fast bound between twelve unbroken steeds, so that each may take his share of her', said the old Queen.

'You have spoken your own doom', said the King, 'and you shall suffer it at once.'

So the wicked old Queen was fast bound between twelve unbroken steeds, and each got his share of her. But the King took Snow-white and Rosy-red, and their three children, and the twelve Princes; and so they all went home to their father and mother, and told all that had befallen them, and there was joy and gladness over the whole kingdom, because the Princess was saved and set free, and because she had set free her twelve brothers.

THE GIANT WHO HAD NO HEART IN HIS BODY

Once on a time there was a king who had seven sons, and he loved them so much that he could never bear to be without them all at once, but one must always be with him. Now, when they were grown up, six were to set off to woo, but as for the youngest, his father kept him at home, and the others were to bring back a princess for him to the palace. So the king gave the six the finest clothes you ever set eyes on, so fine that the light gleamed from them a long way off, and each had his horse, which cost many, many hundred dollars, and so they set off. Now, when they had been to many palaces, and seen many princesses, at last they came to a king who had six daughters; such lovely king's daughters they had never seen, and so they fell to wooing them, each one, and when they had got them for sweethearts, they set off home again, but they quite forgot that they were to bring back with them a sweetheart for Boots, their brother, who stayed at home, for they were over head and ears in love with their own sweethearts.

But when they had gone a good bit on their way, they passed close by a steep hill-side, like a wall, where the giant's house was, and there the giant came out, and set his eyes upon them, and turned them all into stone, princes and princesses and all. Now the king waited and waited for his six sons, but the more he waited, the longer they stayed away; so he fell into great trouble, and said he should never know what it was to be glad again.

'And if I had not you left', he said to Boots, 'I would live no longer, so full of sorrow am I for the loss of your brothers.'

'Well, but now I've been thinking to ask your leave to set out and find them again; that's what I'm thinking of', said Boots.

'Nay, nay!' said his father; 'that leave you shall never get, for then you would stay away too.'

But Boots had set his heart upon it; go he would; and he begged and prayed so long that the king was forced to let him go. Now, you must know the king had no other horse to give Boots but an old broken-down jade, for his six other sons and their train had carried off all his horses; but Boots did not care a pin for that, he sprang up on his sorry-old-steed.

'Farewell, father', said he; 'I'll come back, never fear, and like enough I shall bring my six brothers back with me'; and with that he rode off.

So, when he had ridden a while, he came to a Raven, which lay in the road and flapped its wings, and was not able to get out of the way, it was so starved.

'Oh, dear friend', said the Raven, 'give me a little food, and I'll help you again at your utmost need.'

'I haven't much food', said the Prince, 'and I don't see how you'll ever be able to help me much; but still I can spare you a little. I see you want it.'

So he gave the raven some of the food he had brought with him.

Now, when he had gone a bit further, he came to a brook, and in the brook lay a great Salmon, which had got upon a dry place and dashed itself about, and could not get into the water again.

'Oh, dear friend', said the Salmon to the Prince; 'shove me out into the water again, and I'll help you again at your utmost need.'

'Well!' said the Prince, 'the help you'll give me will not be great, I daresay, but it's a pity you should lie there and choke'; and with that he shot the fish out into the stream again.

After that he went a long, long way, and there met him a Wolf, which was so famished that it lay and crawled along the road on its belly.

'Dear friend, do let me have your horse', said the Wolf; 'I'm so hungry the wind whistles through my ribs; I've had nothing to eat these two years.'

'No', said Boots, 'this will never do; 'first I came to a raven, and I was forced to give him my food; next I came to a salmon, and him I had to help into the water again; and now you will have my horse. It can't be done, that it can't, for then I should have nothing to ride on.'

'Nay, dear friend, but you can help me', said Graylegs the wolf; 'you can ride upon my back, and I'll help you again in your utmost need.'

'Well! the help I shall get from you will not be great, I'll be bound', said the

Prince; 'but you may take my horse, since you are in such need.'

So when the wolf had eaten the horse, Boots took the bit and put it into the wolf's jaw, and laid the saddle on his back; and now the wolf was so strong, after what he had got inside, that he set off with the Prince like nothing. So fast he had never ridden before.

'When we have gone a bit farther', said Graylegs; 'I'll show you the Giant's house.'

So after a while they came to it.

'See, here is the Giant's house', said the Wolf; 'and see, here are your six brothers, whom the Giant has turned into stone; and see here are their six brides, and away yonder is the door, and in at that door you must go.'

'Nay, but I daren't go in', said the Prince; 'he'll take my life.'

'No! no!' said the Wolf; 'when you get in you'll find a Princess, and she'll tell you what to do to make an end of the Giant. Only mind and do as she bids you.'

Well! Boots went in, but, truth to say, he was very much afraid. When he came in the Giant was away, but in one of the rooms sat the Princess, just as the wolf had said, and so lovely a princess Boots had never yet set eyes on.

'Oh! heaven help you! whence have you come?' said the Princess, as she saw him; 'it will surely be your death. No one can make an end of the Giant who lives here, for he has no heart in his body.'

'Well! well!' said Boots; 'but now that I am here, I may as well try what I can do with him; and I will see if I can't free my brothers, who are standing turned to stone out of doors; and you, too, I will try to save, that I will.'

'Well, if you must, you must', said the Princess; 'and so let us see if we can't hit on a plan. Just creep under the bed yonder, and mind and listen to what he and I talk about. But, pray, do lie as still as a mouse.'

So he crept under the bed, and he had scarce got well underneath it, before the Giant came.

'Ha!' roared the Giant, 'what a smell of Christian blood there is in the house!'

'Yes, I know there is', said the Princess, 'for there came a magpie flying with a man's bone, and let it fall down the chimney. I made all the haste I could to get it out, but all one can do, the smell doesn't go off so soon.'

So the Giant said no more about it, and when night came, they went to bed.

After they had lain awhile, the Princess said:

'There is one thing I'd be so glad to ask you about, if I only dared.'

'What thing is that?' asked the Giant.

'Only where it is you keep your heart, since you don't carry it about you', said the Princess.

'Ah! that's a thing you've no business to ask about; but if you must know, it lies under the door-sill', said the Giant.

'Ho! ho!' said Boots to himself under the bed, 'then we'll soon see if we can't find it.'

Next morning the Giant got up cruelly early, and strode off to the wood; but he was hardly out of the house before Boots and the Princess set to work to look under the door-sill for his heart; but the more they dug, and the more they hunted, the more they couldn't find it.

'He has baulked us this time', said the Princess, 'but we'll try him once more.'

So she picked all the prettiest flowers she could find, and strewed them over the door-sill, which they had laid in its right place again; and when the time came for the Giant to come home again, Boots crept under the bed. Just as he was well under, back came the Giant.

Snuff--snuff, went the Giant's nose. 'My eyes and limbs, what a smell of Christian blood there is in here', said he.

'I know there is', said the Princess, 'for there came a magpie flying with a man's bone in his bill, and let it fall down the chimney. I made as much haste as I could to get it out, but I daresay it's that you smell.'

So the Giant held his peace, and said no more about it. A little while after, he asked who it was that had strewed flowers about the door-sill.

'Oh, I, of course', said the Princess.

'And, pray, what's the meaning of all this?' said the Giant.

'Ah!' said the Princess, 'I'm so fond of you that I couldn't help strewing them, when I knew that your heart lay under there.'

'You don't say so', said the Giant; 'but after all it doesn't lie there at all.'

So when they went to bed again in the evening, the Princess asked the Giant again where his heart was, for she said she would so like to know.

'Well', said the Giant, 'if you must know, it lies away yonder in the cupboard against the wall.'

'So, so!' thought Boots and the Princess; 'then we'll soon try to find it.'

Next morning the Giant was away early, and strode off to the wood, and so soon as he was gone Boots and the Princess were in the cupboard hunting for his heart, but the more they sought for it, the less they found it.

'Well', said the Princess, 'we'll just try him once more.'

So she decked out the cupboard with flowers and garlands, and when the time came for the Giant to come home, Boots crept under the bed again.

Then back came the Giant.

Snuff-snuff! 'My eyes and limbs, what a smell of Christian blood there is in here!'

'I know there is', said the Princess; 'for a little while since there came a magpie flying with a man's bone in his bill, and let it fall down the chimney. I made all the haste I could to get it out of the house again; but after all my pains, I daresay it's that you smell.'

When the Giant heard that, he said no more about it; but a little while after, he saw how the cupboard was all decked about with flowers and garlands; so he asked who it was that had done that? Who could it be but the Princess.

'And, pray, what's the meaning of all this tom-foolery?' asked the Giant.

'Oh, I'm so fond of you, I couldn't help doing it when I knew that your heart lay there', said the Princess.

'How can you be so silly as to believe any such thing?' said the Giant.

'Oh yes; how can I help believing it, when you say it', said the Princess.

'You're a goose', said the Giant; 'where my heart is, you will never come.'

'Well', said the Princess;' but for all that, 'twould be such a pleasure to know where it really lies.'

Then the poor Giant could hold out no longer, but was forced to say:

'Far, far away in a lake lies an island; on that island stands a church; in that church is a well; in that well swims a duck; in that duck there is an egg, and in that egg there lies my heart,--you darling!'

In the morning early, while it was still grey dawn, the Giant strode off to the wood.

'Yes! now I must set off too', said Boots; 'if I only knew how to find the way.'

He took a long, long farewell of the Princess, and when he got out of the Giant's door, there stood the Wolf waiting for him. So Boots told him all that had happened inside the house, and said now he wished to ride to the well in the church, if he only knew the way. So the Wolf bade him jump on his back, he'd soon find the way; and away they went, till the wind whistled after them, over hedge and field, over hill and dale. After they had travelled many, many days, they came at last to the lake. Then the Prince did not know how to get over it, but the Wolf bade him only not be afraid, but stick on, and so he jumped into the lake with the Prince on his back, and swam over to the island. So they came to the church; but the church keys hung high, high up on the top of the tower, and at first the Prince did not know how to get them down.

'You must call on the raven', said the Wolf.

So the Prince called on the raven, and in a trice the raven came, and flew up and fetched the keys, and so the Prince got into the church. But when he came to the well, there lay the duck, and swam about backwards and forwards, just as the Giant had said. So the Prince stood and coaxed it and coaxed it, till it came to him, and he grasped it in his hand; but just as he lifted it up from the water the duck dropped the egg into the well, and then Boots was beside himself to know how to get it out again.

'Well, now you must call on the salmon to be sure', said the Wolf; and the king's son called on the salmon, and the salmon came and fetched up the egg from the bottom of the well.

Then the Wolf told him to squeeze the egg, and as soon as ever he squeezed it the Giant screamed out.

'Squeeze it again', said the Wolf; and when the Prince did so, the Giant screamed still more piteously, and begged and prayed so prettily to be spared, saying he would do all that the Prince wished if he would only not squeeze his heart in two.

'Tell him, if he will restore to life again your six brothers and their brides, whom he has turned to stone, you will spare his life', said the Wolf. Yes, the Giant was ready to do that, and he turned the six brothers into king's sons again, and their brides into king's daughters.

'Now, squeeze the egg in two', said the Wolf. So Boots squeezed the egg to pieces, and the Giant burst at once.

Now, when he had made an end of the Giant, Boots rode back again on the wolf to the Giant's house, and there stood all his six brothers alive and merry, with their brides. Then Boots went into the hill- side after his bride, and so they all set off home again to their father's house. And you may fancy how glad the old king was when he saw all his seven sons come back, each with his bride--'But the loveliest bride of all is the bride of Boots, after all', said the king, 'and he shall sit uppermost at the table, with her by his side.'

So he sent out, and called a great wedding-feast, and the mirth was both loud and long, and if they have not done feasting, why, they are still at it.

THE FOX AS HERDSMAN

Once on a time there was a woman who went out to hire a herdsman, and she met a bear.

'Whither away, Goody?' said Bruin.

'Oh, I'm going out to hire a herdsman', answered the woman.

'Why not have me for a herdsman?' said Bruin.

'Well, why not?' said the woman. 'If you only knew how to call the flock; just let me hear?'

'OW, OW!' growled the bear.

'No, no! I won't have you', said the woman, as soon as she heard him say that, and off she went on her way.

So, when she had gone a bit further, she met a wolf.

'Whither away, Goody?' asked the Wolf.

'Oh!' said she, 'I'm going out to hire a herdsman.'

'Why not have me for a herdsman?' said the Wolf.

'Well, why not? if you can only call the flock; let me hear?' said she.

'UH, UH!' said the Wolf.

'No, no!' said the woman; 'you'll never do for me.'

Well, after she had gone a while longer, she met a fox.

'Whither away, Goody?' asked the Fox.

'Oh, I'm just going out to hire a herdsman', said the woman.

'Why not have me for your herdsman?' asked the Fox.

'Well, why not?' said she; 'if you only knew how to call the flock; let me hear?'

'DIL-DAL-HOLOM', sung out the Fox, in such a fine clear voice.

'Yes; I'll have you for my herdsman', said the woman; and so she set the Fox to herd her flock.

The first day the Fox was herdsman he ate up all the woman's goats; the next day he made an end of all her sheep; and the third day he ate up all her kine. So, when he came home at even, the woman asked what he had done with all her flocks?

'Oh!' said the Fox, 'their skulls are in the stream, and their bodies in the holt.'

Now, the Goody stood and churned when the fox said this, but she thought she might as well step out and see after her flock; and while she was away the Fox crept into the churn and ate up the cream. So when the Goody came back and saw that, she fell into such a rage, that she snatched up the little morsel of the cream that was left, and threw it at the fox as he ran off, so that he got a dab of it on the end of his tail, and that's the reason why the fox has a white tip to his brush.

THE MASTERMAID

Once on a time there was a king who had several sons--I don't know how many there were--but the youngest had no rest at home, for nothing else would please him but to go out into the world and try his luck, and after a long time the king was forced to give him leave to go. Now, after he had travelled some days, he came one night to a Giant's house, and there he got a place in the Giant's service. In the morning the Giant went off to herd his goats, and as he left the yard, he told the Prince to clean out the stable; 'and after you have done that, you needn't do anything else to-day; for you must know it is an easy master you have come to. But what is set you to do you must do well, and you mustn't think of going into any of the rooms which are beyond that in which you slept, for if you do, I'll take your life.'

'Sure enough, it is an easy master I have got', said the Prince to himself, as he walked up and down the room, and carolled and sang, for he thought there was plenty of time to clean out the stable.

'But still it would be good fun just to peep into his other rooms, for there must be something in them which he is afraid lest I should see, since he won't give me leave to go in.'

So he went into the first room, and there was a pot boiling on a hook by the wall, but the Prince saw no fire underneath it. I wonder what is inside it, he thought; and then he dipped a lock of his hair into it, and the hair seemed as if it were all turned to copper.

'What a dainty broth,' he said; 'if one tasted it, he'd look grand inside his gullet'; and with that he went into the next room. There, too, was a pot hanging by a hook, which bubbled and boiled; but there was no fire under that either.

'I may as well try this too', said the Prince, as he put another lock into the pot, and it came out all silvered.

'They haven't such rich broth in my father's house', said the Prince; 'but it all depends on how it tastes', and with that he went on into the third room. There, too, hung a pot, and boiled just as he had seen in the two other rooms, and the Prince had a mind to try this too, so he dipped a lock of hair into it, and it came out gilded, so that the light gleamed from it.

'"Worse and worse", said the old wife; but I say better and better', said the Prince; 'but if he boils gold here, I wonder what he boils in yonder.'

He thought he might as well see; so he went through the door into the fourth room. Well, there was no pot in there, but there was a Princess, seated on a bench, so lovely, that the Prince had never seen anything like her in his born days.

'Oh! in Heaven's name', she said, 'what do you want here?'

'I got a place here yesterday', said the Prince.

'A place, indeed! Heaven help you out of it.'

'Well, after all, I think I've got an easy master; he hasn't set me much to do to-day, for after I have cleaned out the stable, my day's work is over.'

'Yes, but how will you do it', she said; 'for if you set to work to clean it like other folk, ten pitchforks full will come in for every one you toss out. But I will teach you how to set to work; you must turn the fork upside down, and toss with the handle, and then all the dung will fly out of itself.'

'Yes, he would be sure to do that', said the Prince; and so he sat there the whole day, for he and the Princess were soon great friends, and had made up their minds to have one another, and so the first day of his service with the Giant was not long, you may fancy. But when the evening drew on, she said 'twould be as well if he got the stable cleaned out before the Giant came home; and when he went to the stable, he thought he would just see if what she had said were true, and so he began to work like the grooms in his father's stable; but he soon had enough of that, for he hadn't worked a minute before the stable was so full of dung that he hadn't room to stand. Then he did as the Princess bade him, and turned up the fork and worked with the handle, and lo! in a trice the stable was as clean as if it had been scoured. And when he had done his work, he went back into the room where the Giant had given him leave to be, and began to walk up and down, and to carol and sing. So after a bit, home came the Giant with his goats.

'Have you cleaned the stable?' asked the Giant.

'Yes, now it's all right and tight, master', answered the Prince.

'I'll soon see if it is', growled the Giant, and strode off to the stable, where he found it just as the Prince had said.

'You've been talking to my Mastermaid, I can see', said the Giant; 'for you've not sucked this knowledge out of your own breast.'

'Mastermaid!' said the Prince, who looked as stupid as an owl, 'what sort of thing is that, master? I'd be very glad to see it.'

'Well, well!' said the Giant; 'you'll see her soon enough'.

Next day the Giant set off with his goats again, and before he went he told the Prince to fetch home his horse, which was out at grass on the hill-side, and when he had done that he might rest all the day.

'For you must know, it is an easy master you have come to', said the Giant; 'but if you go into any of the rooms I spoke of yesterday, I'll wring your head off.'

So off he went with his flock of goats.

'An easy master you are indeed', said the Prince; 'but for all that, I'll just go in and have a chat with your Mastermaid; may be she'll be as soon mine as yours.' So he went in to her, and she asked him what he had to do that day.

'Oh! nothing to be afraid of', said he; 'I've only to go up to the hill-side to fetch his horse.'

'Very well, and how will you set about it?'

'Well, for that matter, there's no great art in riding a horse home. I fancy I've ridden fresher horses before now', said the Prince.

'Ah, but this isn't so easy a task as you think; but I'll teach you how to do it. When you get near it, fire and flame will come out of its nostrils, as out of a tar barrel; but look out, and take the bit which hangs behind the door yonder, and throw it right into his jaws, and he will grow so tame that you may do what you like with him.'

Yes! the Prince would mind and do that; and so he sat in there the whole day, talking and chattering with the Mastermaid about one thing and another, but they always came back to how happy they would be if they could only have one another, and get well away from the Giant; and, to tell the truth, the Prince would have clean forgotten both the horse and the hill-side, if the Mastermaid hadn't put him in mind of them when evening drew on, telling him he had better set out to fetch the horse before the Giant came home. So he set off, and took the bit which hung in the corner, ran up the hill, and it wasn't long before he met the horse, with fire and flame streaming out of its nostrils. But he watched his time, and, as the horse came open-jawed up to him, he threw the bit into its mouth, and it stood as quiet as a lamb. After that, it was no great matter to ride it home and put it up, you may fancy; and then the Prince went into his room again, and began to carol and sing.

So the Giant came home again at even with his goats; and the first words he said were:

'Have you brought my horse down from the hill?'

'Yes, master, that I have', said the Prince; 'and a better horse I never bestrode; but for all that I rode him straight home, and put him up safe and sound.'

'I'll soon see to that', said the Giant, and ran out to the stable, and there stood the horse just as the Prince had said.

'You've talked to my Mastermaid, I'll be bound, for you haven't sucked this out of your own breast', said the Giant again.

'Yesterday master talked of this Mastermaid, and to-day it's the same story', said the Prince, who pretended to be silly and stupid. 'Bless you, master! why don't you show me the thing at once? I should so like to see it only once in my life.'

'Oh, if that's all', said the Giant, 'you'll see her soon enough.'

The third day, at dawn, the Giant went off to the wood again with his goats; but before he went he said to the Prince:

'To-day you must go to Hell and fetch my fire-tax. When you have done that you can rest yourself all day, for you must know it is an easy master you have come to'; and with that off he went.

'Easy master, indeed!' said the Prince. 'You may be easy, but you set me hard tasks all the same. But I may as well see if I can find your Mastermaid, as you call her. I daresay she'll tell me what to do'; and so in he went to her again.

So when the Mastermaid asked what the Giant had set him to do that day, he told her how he was to go to Hell and fetch the fire-tax.

'And how will you set about it?' asked the Mastermaid.

'Oh, that you must tell me', said the Prince. 'I have never been to Hell in my life; and even if I knew the way, I don't know how much I am to ask for.'

'Well, I'll soon tell you', said the Mastermaid; 'you must go to the steep rock away yonder, under the hill-side, and take the club that lies there, and knock on the face of the rock. Then there will come out one all glistening with fire; to him you must tell your errand; and when he asks you how much you will have, mind you say, "As much as I can carry."'

Yes; he would be sure to say that; so he sat in there with the Mastermaid all that day too; and though evening drew on, he would have sat there till now, had not the Mastermaid put him in mind that it was high time to be off to Hell to fetch the Giant's fire-tax before he came home. So he went on his way, and did just as the Mastermaid had told him; and when he reached the rock, he took up the club and gave a great thump. Then the rock opened, and out came one whose face glistened, and out of whose eyes and nostrils flew sparks of fire.

'What is your will?' said he.

'Oh! I'm only come from the Giant to fetch his fire-tax', said the Prince.

'How much will you have then?' said the other.

'I never wish for more than I am able to carry', said the Prince.

'Lucky for you that you did not ask for a whole horse-load', said he who came out of the rock; 'but come now into the rock with me, and you shall have it.'

So the Prince went in with him, and you may fancy what heaps and heaps of gold and silver he saw lying in there, just like stones in a gravel pit; and he got a load just as big as he was able to carry, and set off home with it. Now, when the Giant came home with his goats at even, the Prince went into his room, and began to carol and sing as he had done the evenings before.

'Have you been to Hell after my fire-tax?' roared the Giant.

'Oh yes; that I have, master', answered the Prince.

'Where have you put it?' said the Giant.

'There stands the sack on the bench yonder', said the Prince.

'I'll soon see to that', said the Giant, who strode off to the bench, and there he saw the sack so full that the gold and silver dropped out on the floor as soon as ever he untied the string.

'You've been talking to my Mastermaid, that I can see', said the Giant; 'but if you have, I'll wring your head off.'

'Mastermaid!' said the Prince; 'yesterday master talked of this Mastermaid, and to-day he talks of her again, and the day before yesterday it was the same story. I only wish I could see what sort of thing she is! that I do.'

'Well, well, wait till to-morrow', said the Giant, 'and then I'll take you in to her myself.'

'Thank you kindly, master', said the Prince; 'but it's only a joke of master's, I'll be bound.'

So next day the Giant took him in to the Mastermaid, and said to her:

'Now, you must cut his throat, and boil him in the great big pot you wot of; and when the broth is ready, just give me a call.'

After that, he laid him down on the bench to sleep, and began to snore so, that it sounded like thunder on the hills.

So the Mastermaid took a knife and cut the Prince in his little finger, and let three drops of blood fall on a three-legged stool; and after that she took all the old rags, and soles of shoes, and all the rubbish she could lay hands on, and put them into the pot; and then she filled a chest full of ground gold, and took a lump of salt, and a flask of water that hung behind the door, and she took, besides, a golden apple, and two golden chickens, and off she set with the Prince from the Giant's house as fast as they could; and when they had gone a little way, they came to the sea, and after that they sailed over the sea; but where they got the ship from, I have never heard tell.

So when the Giant had slumbered a good bit, he began to stretch himself as he lay on the bench and called out, 'Will it be soon done?'

'Only just begun', answered the first drop of blood on the stool.

So the Giant lay down to sleep again, and slumbered a long, long time. At last he began to toss about a little, and cried out:

'Do you hear what I say; will it be soon done?' but he did not look up this time, any more than the first, for he was still half asleep.

'Half done', said the second drop of blood.

Then the Giant thought again it was the Mastermaid, so he turned over on his other side, and fell asleep again; and when he had gone on sleeping for many hours, he began to stir and stretch his old bones, and to call out,--

'Isn't it done yet?'

'Done to a turn', said the third drop of blood.

Then the Giant rose up and began to rub his eyes, but he couldn't see who it was that was talking to him, so he searched and called for the Mastermaid, but no one answered.

'Ah, well! I dare say she's just run out of doors for a bit', he thought, and took up a spoon and went up to the pot to taste the broth; but he found nothing but shoe-soles, and rags, and such stuff; and it was all boiled up together, so that he couldn't tell which was thick and which was thin. As soon as he saw this, he could tell how things had gone, and he got so angry he scarce knew which leg to stand upon. Away he went after the Prince and the Mastermaid, till the wind whistled behind him; but before long, he came to the water and couldn't cross it.

'Never mind', he said; 'I know a cure for this. I've only got to call on my stream-sucker.'

So he called on his stream-sucker, and he came and stooped down, and took one, two, three gulps; and then the water fell so much in the sea, that the Giant could see the Mastermaid and the Prince sailing in their ship.

'Now, you must cast out the lump of salt', said the Mastermaid.

So the Prince threw it overboard, and it grew up into a mountain so high, right across the sea, that the Giant couldn't pass it, and the stream-sucker couldn't help him by swilling any more water.

'Never mind!' cried the Giant; 'there's a cure for this too.' So he called on his hill-borer to come and bore through the mountain, that the stream-sucker might creep through and take another swill; but just as they had made a hole through the hill, and the stream-sucker was about to drink, the Mastermaid told the Prince to throw overboard a drop or two out of the flask, and then the sea was just as full as ever, and before the stream-sucker could take another gulp, they reached the land and were saved from the Giant.

So they made up their minds to go home to the Prince's father, but the Prince would not hear of the Mastermaid's walking, for he thought it seemly neither for her nor for him.

'Just wait here ten minutes', he said, 'while I go home after the seven horses which stand in my father's stall. It's no great way off, and I shan't be long about it; but I will not hear of my sweetheart walking to my father's palace.'

'Ah!' said the Mastermaid, 'pray don't leave me, for if you once get home to the palace, you'll forget me outright; I know you will.'

'Oh!' said he, 'how can I forget you; you with whom I have gone through so much, and whom I love so dearly?'

There was no help for it, he must and would go home to fetch the coach and seven horses, and she was to wait for him by the seaside. So at last the Mastermaid was forced to let him have his way; she only said:

'Now, when you get home, don't stop so much as to say good day to any one, but go straight to the stable and put to the horses, and drive back as quick as you can; for they will all come about you; but do as though you did not see them; and above all things, mind you do not taste a morsel of food, for if you do, we shall both come to grief.'

All this the Prince promised; but he thought all the time there was little fear of his forgetting her.

Now, just as he came home to the palace, one of his brothers was thinking of holding his bridal feast, and the bride, and all her kith and kin, were just come to the palace. So they all thronged round him, and asked about this thing and that, and wanted him to go in with them; but he made as though he did not see them, and went straight to the stall and got out the horses, and began to put them to. And when they saw they could not get him to go in, they came out to him with meat and drink, and the best of everything they had got ready for the feast; but the Prince would not taste so much as a crumb, and put to as fast as he could. At last the bride's sister rolled an apple across the yard to him, saying:

'Well, if you won't eat anything else, you may as well take a bite of this, for you must be both hungry and thirsty after so long a journey.'

So he took up the apple and bit a piece out of it; but he had scarce done so, before he forgot the Mastermaid, and how he was to drive back for her.

'Well, I think I must be mad', he said; 'what am I to do with this coach and horses?' So he put the horses up again, and went along with the others into the palace, and it was soon settled that he should have the bride's sister, who had rolled the apple over to him.

There sat the Mastermaid by the seashore, and waited and waited for the Prince, but no Prince came; so at last she went up from the shore, and after she had gone a bit she came to a little hut which lay by itself in a copse close by the king's palace.

She went in and asked if she might lodge there. It was an old dame that owned the hut, and a cross-grained scolding hag she was as ever you saw. At first she would not hear of the Mastermaid's lodging in her house, but at last, for fair words and high rent, the Mastermaid got leave to be there. Now the but was as dark and dirty as a pigsty, so the Mastermaid said she would smarten it up a little, that their house might look inside like other people's. The old hag did not like this either, and showed her teeth, and was cross; but the Mastermaid did not mind her. She took her chest of gold, and threw a handful or so into the fire, and lo! the gold melted, and bubbled and boiled over out of the grate, and spread itself over the whole hut, till it was gilded both outside and in. But as soon as the gold began to bubble and boil, the old hag got so afraid that she tried to run out as if the Evil One were at her heels; and as she ran out at the door, she forgot to stoop, and gave her head such a knock against the lintel, that she broke her neck, and that was the end of her.

Next morning the Constable passed that way, and you may fancy he could scarce believe his eyes when he saw the golden hut shining and glistening away in the copse; but he was still more astonished when he went in and saw the lovely maiden who sat there. To make a long story short, he fell over head and ears in love with her, and begged and prayed her to become his wife.

'Well, but have you much money?' asked the Mastermaid.

Yes, for that matter, he said, he was not so badly off, and off he went home to fetch the money, and when he came back at even he brought a half-bushel sack, and set it down on the bench. So the Mastermaid said she would have him, since he was so rich; but they were scarce in bed before she said she must get up again:

'For I have forgotten to make up the fire.'

'Pray, don't stir out of bed', said the Constable; 'I'll see to it.'

So he jumped out of bed, and stood on the hearth in a trice.

'As soon as you have got hold of the shovel, just tell me', said the Mastermaid.

'Well, I am holding it now', said the Constable.

Then the Mastermaid said:

'God grant that you may hold the shovel, and the shovel you, and may you heap hot burning coals over yourself till morning breaks.'

So there stood the Constable all night long, shovelling hot burning coals over himself; and though he begged, and prayed, and wept, the coals were not a bit cold-er for that; but as soon as day broke, and he had power to cast away the shovel, he did not stay long, as you may fancy, but set off as if the Evil One or the bailiff were at his heels; and all who met him stared their eyes out at him, for he cut capers as though he were mad, and he could not have looked in worse plight if he had been flayed and tanned, and every one wondered what had befallen him, but he told no one where he had been, for shame's sake.

Next day the Attorney passed by the place where the Mastermaid lived, and he too saw how it shone and glistened in the copse; so he turned aside to find out who owned the hut; and when he came in and saw the lovely maiden, he fell more in love with her than the Constable, and began to woo her in hot haste.

Well, the Mastermaid asked him, as she had asked the Constable, if he had a good lot of money? and the Attorney said he wasn't so badly off; and as a proof he went home to fetch his money. So at even he came back with a great fat sack of money--I think it was a whole bushel sack--and set it down on the bench; and the long and the short of the matter was, that he was to have her, and they went to bed. But all at once the Mastermaid had forgotten to shut the door of the porch, and she must get up and make it fast for the night.

'What, you do that!' said the Attorney, 'while I lie here; that can never be; lie still, while I go and do it.'

So up he jumped, like a pea on a drum-head, and ran out into the porch.

'Tell me', said the Mastermaid, 'when you have hold of the door- latch.'

'I've got hold of it now', said the Attorney.

'God grant, then', said the Mastermaid, 'that you may hold the door, and the door you, and that you may go from wall to wall till day dawns.'

So you may fancy what a dance the Attorney had all night long; such a waltz he never had before, and I don't think he would much care if he never had such a waltz again. Now he pulled the door forward, and then the door pulled him back, and so he went on, now dashed into one corner of the porch, and now into the other, till he was almost battered to death. At first he began to curse and swear, and then to beg and pray, but the door cared for nothing but holding its own till break of day. As soon as it let go its hold, off set the Attorney, leaving behind him his money to pay for his night's lodging, and forgetting his courtship altogether, for to tell the truth, he was afraid lest the house-door should come dancing after him.

All who met him stared and gaped at him, for he too cut capers like a madman, and he could not have looked in worse plight if he had spent the whole night in butting against a flock of rams.

The third day the Sheriff passed that way, and he too saw the golden hut, and turned aside to find out who lived there; and he had scarce set eyes on the Mastermaid, before he began to woo her. So she answered him as she had answered the other two. If he had lots of money she would have him, if not, he might go about his business. Well, the Sheriff said he wasn't so badly off, and he would go home and fetch the money, and when he came again at even, he had a bigger sack even than the Attorney--it must have been at least a bushel and a half, and put it down on the bench. So it was soon settled that he was to have the Mastermaid, but they had scarce gone to bed before the Mastermaid said she had forgotten to bring home the calf from the meadow, so she must get up and drive him into the stall. Then the Sheriff swore by all the powers that should never be, and, stout and fat as he was, up he jumped as nimbly as a kitten.

'Well, only tell me when you've got hold of the calf's tail', said the Mastermaid.

'Now I have hold of it', said the Sheriff.

'God grant', said the Mastermaid, 'that you may hold the calf's tail, and the calf's tail you, and that you may make a tour of the world together till day dawns'.

Well you may just fancy how the Sheriff had to stretch his legs; away they went, the calf and he, over high and low, across hill and dale, and the more the Sheriff cursed and swore, the faster the calf ran and jumped. At dawn of day the poor Sheriff was well nigh broken- winded, and so glad was he to let go the calf's tail, that he forgot his sack of money and everything else. As he was a great man, he went a little slower than the Attorney and the Constable, but the slower he went the more time people had to gape and stare at him; and I must say they made good use of their time, for he was terribly tattered and torn, after his dance with the calf.

Next day was fixed for the wedding at the palace, and the eldest brother was to drive to church with his bride, and the younger, who had lived with the Giant, with the bride's sister. But when they had got into the coach, and were just going to drive off, one of the trace-pins snapped off; and though they made at least three in its place, they all broke, from whatever sort of wood they were made. So time went on and on, and they couldn't get to church, and every one grew very downcast. But all at once the Constable said, for he too was bidden to the wedding, that yonder away in the copse lived a maiden.

'And if you can only get her to lend you the handle of her shovel with which she makes up her fire, I know very well it will hold.'

Well! they sent a messenger on the spot, with such a pretty message to the maiden, to know if they couldn't get the loan of her shovel which the Constable had spoken of; and the maiden said 'yes', they might have it; so they got a trace-pin which wasn't likely to snap.

But all at once, just as they were driving off, the bottom of the coach tumbled to bits. So they set to work to make a new bottom as they best might; but it mattered not how many nails they put into it, nor of what wood they made it, for as soon as ever they got the bottom well into the coach and were driving off, snap it went in two again, and they were even worse off than when they lost the trace- pin. Just then the Attorney said--for if the Constable was there, you may fancy the Attorney was there too: 'Away yonder, in the copse, lives a maiden, and if you could only get her to lend you one-half of her porch-door, I know it can hold together.'

Well! they sent another message to the copse, and asked so prettily if they couldn't have the loan of the gilded porch-door which the Attorney had talked of; and they got it on the spot. So they were just setting out; but now the horses were not strong enough to draw the coach, though there were six of them; then they put on eight, and ten, and twelve, but the more they put on, and the more the coach-man whipped, the more the coach wouldn't stir an inch. By this time it was far on in the day, and every one about the palace was in doleful dumps; for to church they must go, and yet it looked as if they should never get there. So at last the Sheriff said, that yonder in the gilded hut, in the copse, lived a maiden, and if they could only get the loan of her calf:

'I know it can drag the coach, though it were as heavy as a mountain.'

Well they all thought it would look silly to be drawn to church by a calf, but there was no help for it, so they had to send a third time, and ask so prettily in the King's name, if he couldn't get the loan of the calf the Sheriff had spoken of, and the Mastermaid let them have it on the spot, for she was not going to say 'no' this time either. So they put the calf on before the horses, and waited to see if it would do any good, and away went the coach over high and low, and stock and stone, so that they could scarce draw their breath; sometimes they were on the ground, and sometimes up in the air, and when they reached the church, the calf began to run round and round it like a spinning jenny, so that they had hard work to get out of the coach, and into the church. When they went back, it was the same story, only they went faster, and they reached the palace almost before they knew they had set out.

Now when they sat down to dinner, the Prince who had served with the Giant said he thought they ought to ask the maiden who had lent them her shovel-handle and porch-door, and calf, to come up to the palace.

'For', said he, 'if we hadn't got these three things, we should have been sticking here still.'

Yes; the King thought that only fair and right, so he sent five of his best men down to the gilded but to greet the maiden from the King, and to ask her if she wouldn't be so good as to came up and dine at the palace.

'Greet the King from me', said the Mastermaid, 'and tell him, if he's too good to come to me, so am I too good to go to him.'

So the King had to go himself, and then the Mastermaid went up with him without more ado; and as the King thought she was more than she seemed to be, he sat her down in the highest seat by the side of the youngest bridegroom.

Now, when they had sat a little while at table, the Mastermaid took out her golden apple, and the golden cock and hen, which she had carried off from the Giant, and put them down on the table before her, and the cock and hen began at once to peck at one another, and to fight for the golden apple.

'Oh! only look', said the Prince; 'see how those two strive for the apple.'

'Yes!' said the Mastermaid; 'so we two strove to get away that time when we were together in the hillside.'

Then the spell was broken, and the Prince knew her again, and you may fancy how glad he was. But as for the witch who had rolled the apple over to him, he had her torn to pieces between twenty-four horses, so that there was not a bit of her left, and after that they held on with the wedding in real earnest; and though they were still stiff and footsore, the Constable, the Attorney, and the Sheriff, kept it up with the best of them.

THE CAT ON THE DOVREFELL

Once on a time there was a man up in Finnmark who had caught a great white bear, which he was going to take to the king of Denmark. Now, it so fell out, that he came to the Dovrefell just about Christmas Eve, and there he turned into a cottage where a man lived, whose name was Halvor, and asked the man if he could get house-room there, for his bear and himself.

'Heaven never help me, if what I say isn't true!' said the man; 'but we can't give any one house-room just now, for every Christmas Eve such a pack of Trolls come down upon us, that we are forced to flit, and haven't so much as a house over our own heads, to say nothing of lending one to any one else.'

'Oh?' said the man, 'if that's all, you can very well lend me your house; my bear can lie under the stove yonder, and I can sleep in the side-room.'

Well, he begged so hard, that at last he got leave to stay there; so the people of the house flitted out, and before they went, everything was got ready for the Trolls; the tables were laid, and there was rice porridge, and fish boiled in lye, and sausages, and all else that was good, just as for any other grand feast.

So, when everything was ready, down came the Trolls. Some were great, and some were small; some had long tails, and some had no tails at all; some, too, had long, long noses; and they ate and drank, and tasted everything. Just then one of the little Trolls caught sight of the white bear, who lay under the stove; so he took a piece of sausage and stuck it on a fork, and went and poked it up against the bear's nose, screaming out:

'Pussy, will you have some sausage?'

Then the white bear rose up and growled, and hunted the whole pack of them out of doors, both great and small.

Next year Halvor was out in the wood, on the afternoon of Christmas Eve, cutting wood before the holidays, for he thought the Trolls would come again; and just as he was hard at work, he heard a voice in the wood calling out:

'Halvor! Halvor!'

'Well', said Halvor, 'here I am.'

'Have you got your big cat with you still?'

'Yes, that I have', said Halvor; 'she's lying at home under the stove, and what's more, she has now got seven kittens, far bigger and fiercer than she is herself.'

'Oh, then, we'll never come to see you again', bawled out the Troll away in the wood, and he kept his word; for since that time the Trolls have never eaten their Christmas brose with Halvor on the Dovrefell.

PRINCESS ON THE GLASS HILL

Once on a time there was a man who had a meadow, which lay high up on the hill-side, and in the meadow was a barn, which he had built to keep his hay in. Now, I must tell you, there hadn't been much in the barn for the last year or two, for every St John's night, when the grass stood greenest and deepest, the meadow was eaten down to the very ground the next morning, just as if a whole drove of sheep had been there feeding on it over night. This happened once, and it happened twice; so at last the man grew weary of losing his crop of hay, and said to his sons--for he had three of them, and the youngest was nicknamed Boots, of course--that now one of them must just go and sleep in the barn in the outlying field when St John's night came, for it was too good a joke that his grass should be eaten, root and blade, this year, as it had been the last two years. So whichever of them went must keep a sharp look-out; that was what their father said.

Well, the eldest son was ready to go and watch the meadow; trust him for looking after the grass! It shouldn't be his fault if man or beast, or the fiend himself, got a blade of grass. So, when evening came, he set off to the barn, and lay down to sleep; but a little on in the night came such a clatter, and such an earthquake, that walls and roof shook, and groaned, and creaked; then up jumped the lad, and took to his heels as fast as ever he could; nor dared he once look round till he reached home; and as for the hay, why it was eaten up this year just as it had been twice before.

The next St John's night, the man said again, it would never do to lose all the grass in the outlying field year after year in this way, so one of his sons must just trudge off to watch it, and watch it well too. Well, the next oldest son was ready to try his luck, so he set off, and lay down to sleep in the barn as his brother had done before him; but as the night wore on, there came on a rumbling and quaking of the earth, worse even than on the last St John's night, and when the lad heard it, he got frightened, and took to his heels as though he were running a race.

Next year the turn came to Boots; but when he made ready to go, the other two began to laugh and to make game of him, saying,

'You're just the man to watch the hay, that you are; you, who have done nothing all your life but sit in the ashes and toast yourself by the fire.'

But Boots did not care a pin for their chattering, and stumped away as evening drew on, up the hill-side to the outlying field. There he went inside the barn and lay down; but in about an hour's time the barn began to groan and creak, so that it was dreadful to hear.

'Well', said Boots to himself, 'if it isn't worse than this, I can stand it well enough.'

A little while after came another creak and an earthquake, so that the litter in the barn flew about the lad's ears.

'Oh!' said Boots to himself, 'if it isn't worse than this, I daresay I can stand it out.'

But just then came a third rumbling, and a third earthquake, so that the lad thought walls and roof were coming down on his head; but it passed off, and all was still as death about him.

'It'll come again, I'll be bound', thought Boots; but no, it didn't come again; still it was, and still it stayed; but after he had lain a little while, he heard a noise as if a horse were standing just outside the barn-door, and cropping the grass. He stole to the door, and peeped through a chink, and there stood a horse feeding away. So big, and fat, and grand a horse, Boots had never set eyes on; by his side on the grass lay a saddle and bridle, and a full set of armour for a knight, all of brass, so bright that the light gleamed from it.

'Ho, ho!' thought the lad; 'it's you, is it, that eats up our hay? I'll soon put a spoke in your wheel, just see if I don't.'

So he lost no time, but took the steel out of his tinder-box, and threw it over the horse; then it had no power to stir from the spot, and became so tame that the lad could do what he liked with it. So he got on its back, and rode off with it to a place which no one knew of, and there he put up the horse. When he got home, his brothers laughed and asked how he had fared?

'You didn't lie long in the barn, even if you had the heart to go so far as the field.'

'Well', said Boots, 'all I can say is, I lay in the barn till the sun rose, and neither saw nor heard anything; I can't think what there was in the barn to make you both so afraid.'

'A pretty story', said his brothers; 'but we'll soon see how you have watched the meadow'; so they set off; but when they reached it, there stood the grass as deep and thick as it had been over night.

Well, the next St John's eve it was the same story over again; neither of the elder brothers dared to go out to the outlying field to watch the crop; but Boots, he had the heart to go, and everything happened just as it had happened the year before. First a clatter and an earthquake, then a greater clatter and another earth-quake, and so on a third time; only this year the earthquakes were far worse than the year before. Then all at once everything was as still as death, and the lad heard how something was cropping the grass outside the barn-door, so he stole to the door, and peeped through a chink; and what do you think he saw? why, another horse standing right up against the wall, and chewing and champing with might and main. It was far finer and fatter than that which came the year before, and it had a saddle on its back, and a bridle on its neck, and a full suit of mail for a knight lay by its side, all of silver, and as grand as you would wish to see.

'Ho ho!' said Boots to himself; 'it's you that gobbles up our hay, is it? I'll soon put a spoke in your wheel'; and with that he took the steel out of his tinder-box, and threw it over the horse's crest, which stood as still as a lamb. Well, the lad rode this horse, too, to the hiding-place where he kept the other one, and after that he went home.

'I suppose you'll tell us', said one of his brothers, 'there's a fine crop this year too, up in the hayfield.'

'Well, so there is', said Boots; and off ran the others to see, and there stood the grass thick and deep, as it was the year before; but they didn't give Boots softer words for all that.

Now, when the third St John's eve came, the two elder still hadn't the heart to lie out in the barn and watch the grass, for they had got so scared at heart the night they lay there before, that they couldn't get over the fright; but Boots, he dared to go; and, to make a long story short, the very same thing happened this time as had happened twice before. Three earthquakes came, one after the other, each worse than the one which went before, and when the last came, the lad danced about with the shock from one barn wall to the other; and after that, all at once, it was still as death. Now when he had lain a little while, he heard something tugging away at the grass outside the barn, so he stole again to the door-chink, and peeped out, and there stood a horse close outside--far, far bigger and fatter than the two he had taken before.

'Ho, ho!' said the lad to himself, 'it's you, is it, that comes here eating up our hay? I'll soon stop that--I'll soon put a spoke in your wheel.' So he caught up his steel and threw it over the horse's neck, and in a trice it stood as if it were nailed to the ground, and Boots could do as he pleased with it. Then he rode off with it to the hiding-place where he kept the other two, and then went home. When he got home, his two brothers made game of him as they had done before, saying, they could see he had watched the grass well, for he looked for all the world as if he were walking in his sleep, and many other spiteful things they said, but Boots gave no heed to them, only asking them to go and see for themselves; and when they went, there stood the grass as fine and deep this time as it had been twice before.

Now, you must know that the king of the country where Boots lived had a daughter, whom he would only give to the man who could ride up over the hill of glass, for there was a high, high hill, all of glass, as smooth and slippery as ice, close by the king's palace. Upon the tip top of the hill the king's daughter was to sit, with three golden apples in her lap, and the man who could ride up and carry off the three golden apples, was to have half the kingdom, and the Princess to wife. This the king had stuck up on all the church-doors in his realm, and had given it out in many other kingdoms besides. Now, this Princess was so lovely, that all who set eyes on her, fell over head and ears in love with her whether they would or no. So I needn't tell you how all the princes and knights who heard of her were eager to win her to wife, and half the kingdom beside; and how they came riding from all parts of the world on high prancing horses, and clad in the grandest clothes, for there wasn't one of them who hadn't made up his mind that he, and he alone, was to win the Princess.

So when the day of trial came, which the king had fixed, there was such a crowd of princes and knights under the glass hill, that it made one's head whirl to look at them; and every one in the country who could even crawl along was off to the hill, for they all were eager to see the man who was to win the Princess. So the two elder brothers set off with the rest; but as for Boots, they said outright he shouldn't go with them, for if they were seen with such a dirty, changeling, all begrimed with smut from cleaning their shoes and sifting cinders in the dust-hole, they said folk would make game of them.

'Very well', said Boots, 'it's all one to me. I can go alone, and stand or fall by myself.'

Now when the two brothers came to the hill of glass, the knights and princes were all hard at it, riding their horses till they were all in a foam; but it was no good, by my troth; for as soon as ever the horses set foot on the hill, down they slipped, and there wasn't one who could get a yard or two up; and no wonder, for the hill was as smooth as a sheet of glass, and as steep as a house-wall. But all were eager to have the Princess and half the kingdom. So they rode and slipped, and slipped and rode, and still it was the same story over again. At last all their horses were so weary that they could scarce lift a leg, and in such a sweat that the lather dripped from them, and so the knights had to give up trying any more. So the king was just thinking that he would proclaim a new trial for the next day, to see if they would have better luck, when all at once a knight came riding up on so brave a steed, that no one had ever seen the like of it in his born days, and the knight had mail of brass, and the horse a brass bit in his mouth, so bright that the sunbeams shone from it. Then all the others called out to him he might just as well spare himself the trouble of riding at the hill, for it would lead to no good; but he gave no heed to them, and put his horse at the hill, and went up it like nothing for a good way, about a third of the height; and when he had got so far, he turned his horse round and rode down again. So lovely a knight the Princess thought she had never yet seen; and while he was riding, she sat and thought to herself: 'Would to heaven he might only come up and down the other side.'

And when she saw him turning back, she threw down one of the golden apples after him, and it rolled down into his shoe. But when he got to the bottom of the hill he rode off so fast that no one could tell what had become of him. That evening all the knights and princes were to go before the king, that he who had ridden so

far up the hill might show the apple which the princess had thrown, but there was
no one who had anything to show. One after the other they all came, but not a man
of them could show the apple.

At even the brothers of Boots came home too, and had such a long story to tell
about the riding up the hill.

'First of all', they said, 'there was not one of the whole lot who could get so
much as a stride up; but at last came one who had a suit of brass mail, and a brass
bridle and saddle, all so bright that the sun shone from them a mile off. He was a
chap to ride, just! He rode a third of the way up the hill of glass, and he could easily
have ridden the whole way up, if he chose; but he turned round and rode down,
thinking, maybe, that was enough for once.'

'Oh! I should so like to have seen him, that I should', said Boots, who sat by the
fireside, and stuck his feet into the cinders, as was his wont.

'Oh!' said his brothers, 'you would, would you? You; look fit to keep company
with such high lords, nasty beast that you are, sitting there amongst the ashes.'

Next day the brothers were all for setting off again, and Boots begged them this
time, too, to let him go with them and see the riding; but no, they wouldn't have
him at any price, he was too ugly and nasty, they said.

'Well, well!' said Boots;' if I go at all, I must go by myself. I'm not afraid.'

So when the brothers got to the hill of glass, all the princes and knights began
to ride again, and you may fancy they had taken care to shoe their horses sharp; but
it was no good--they rode and slipped, and slipped and rode, just as they had done
the day before, and there was not one who could get so far as a yard up the hill. And
when they had worn out their horses, so that they could not stir a leg, they were
all forced to give it up as a bad job. So the king thought he might as well proclaim
that the riding should take place the day after for the last time, just to give them
one chance more; but all at once it came across his mind that he might as well wait
a little longer, to see if the knight in brass mail would come this day too. Well! they
saw nothing of him; but all at once came one riding on a steed, far, far, braver and
finer than that on which the knight in brass had ridden, and he had silver mail,
and a silver saddle and bridle, all so bright that the sun-beams gleamed and glanced
from them far away. Then the others shouted out to him again, saying, he might as
well hold hard, and not try to ride up the hill, for all his trouble would be thrown

away; but the knight paid no heed to them, and rode straight at the hill, and right up it, till he had gone two- thirds of the way, and then he wheeled his horse round and rode down again. To tell the truth, the Princess liked him still better than the knight in brass, and she sat and wished he might only be able to come right up to the top, and down the other side; but when she saw him turning back, she threw the second apple after him, and it rolled down and fell into his shoe. But, as soon as ever he had come down from the hill of glass, he rode off so fast that no one could see what became of him.

At even, when all were to go in before the king and the Princess, that he who had the golden apple might show it, in they went, one after the other, but there was no one who had any apple to show, and the two brothers, as they had done on the former day, went home and told how things had gone, and how all had ridden at the hill, and none got up.

'But, last of all', they said, 'came one in a silver suit, and his horse had a silver saddle and a silver bridle. He was just a chap to ride; and he got two-thirds up the hill, and then turned back. He was a fine fellow, and no mistake; and the Princess threw the second gold apple to him.'

'Oh!' said Boots, 'I should so like to have seen him too, that I should.'

'A pretty story', they said. 'Perhaps you think his coat of mail was as bright as the ashes you are always poking about, and sifting, you nasty dirty beast.'

The third day everything happened as it had happened the two days before. Boots begged to go and see the sight, but the two wouldn't hear of his going with them. When they got to the hill there was no one who could get so much as a yard up it; and now all waited for the knight in silver mail, but they neither saw nor heard of him. At last came one riding on a steed, so brave that no one had ever seen his match; and the knight had a suit of golden mail, and a golden saddle and bridle, so wondrous bright that the sunbeams gleamed from them a mile off. The other knights and princes could not find time to call out to him not to try his luck, for they were amazed to see how grand he was. So he rode right at the hill, and tore up it like nothing, so that the Princess hadn't even time to wish that he might get up the whole way. As soon as ever he reached the top, he took the third golden apple from the Princess' lap, and then turned his horse and rode down again. As soon as he got down, he rode off at full speed, and was out of sight in no time.

Now, when the brothers got home at even, you may fancy what long stories they told, how the riding had gone off that day; and amongst other things, they had a deal to say about the knight in golden mail.

'He just was a chap to ride!' they said; 'so grand a knight isn't to be found in the wide world.'

'Oh!' said Boots, 'I should so like to have seen him, that I should.'

'Ah! 'said his brothers, 'his mail shone a deal brighter than the glowing coals which you are always poking and digging at; nasty dirty beast that you are.'

Next day all the knights and princes were to pass before the king and the Princess--it was too late to do so the night before, I suppose-- hat he who had the gold apple might bring it forth; but one came after another, first the princes, and then the knights, and still no one could show the gold apple.

'Well', said the king, 'some one must have it, for it was something that we all saw with our own eyes, how a man came and rode up and bore it off.'

So he commanded that every one who was in the kingdom should come up to the palace and see if they could show the apple. Well, they all came one after another, but no one had the golden apple, and after a long time the two brothers of Boots came. They were the last of all, so the king asked them if there was no one else in the kingdom who hadn't come.

'Oh, yes', said they; 'we have a brother, but he never carried off the golden apple. He hasn't stirred out of the dusthole on any of the three days.'

'Never mind that', said the king; 'he may as well come up to the palace like the rest.'

So Boots had to go up to the palace.

'How, now', said the king; 'have you got the golden apple? Speak out!'

'Yes, I have', said Boots; 'here is the first, and here is the second, and here is the third too'; and with that he pulled all three golden apples out of his pocket, and at the same time threw off his sooty rags, and stood before them in his gleaming golden mail.

'Yes!' said the king; 'you shall have my daughter, and half my kingdom, for you well deserve both her and it.'

So they got ready for the wedding, and Boots got the Princess to wife, and there was great merry-making at the bridal-feast, you may fancy, for they could all be merry though they couldn't ride up the hill of glass; and all I can say is, if they haven't left off their merry-making yet, why, they're still at it.

THE COCK AND HEN

(In this tale the notes of the Cock and Hen must be imitated.)

Hen--You promise me shoes year after year, year after year, and yet I get no shoes!

Cock--You shall have them, never fear! Henny penny!

Hen--I lay egg after egg, egg after egg, and yet I go about barefoot!

Cock--Well, take your eggs, and be off to the tryst, and buy yourself shoes, and don't go any longer barefoot!

HOW ONE WENT OUT TO WOO

Once on a time there was a lad who went out to woo him a wife. Amongst other places, he came to a farm-house, where the household were little better than beggars; but when the wooer came in, they wanted to make out that they were well to do, as you may guess. Now the husband had got a new arm to his coat.

'Pray, take a seat', he said to the wooer; 'but there's a shocking dust in the house.'

So he went about rubbing and wiping all the benches and tables with his new arm, but he kept the other all the while behind his back.

The wife she had got one new shoe, and she went stamping and sliding with it up against the stools and chairs, saying, 'How untidy it is here! Everything is out of its place!'

Then they called out to their daughter to come down and put things to rights; but the daughter, she had got a new cap; so she put her head in at the door, and kept nodding and nodding, first to this side, and then to that.

'Well! for my part', she said, 'I can't be everywhere at once.'

Aye! aye! that was a well-to-do household the wooer had come to.

THE MASTER-SMITH

Once on a time, in the days when our Lord and St Peter used to wander on earth, they came to a smith's house. He had made a bargain with the Devil, that the fiend should have him after seven years, but during that time he was to be the master of all masters in his trade, and to this bargain both he and the Devil had signed their names. So he had stuck up in great letters over the door of his forge: *'Here dwells the Master over all Masters.'*

Now when our Lord passed by and saw that, he went in.

'Who are you?' he said to the Smith.

'Read what's written over the door', said the Smith; 'but maybe you can't read writing. If so, you must wait till some one comes to help you.'

Before our Lord had time to answer him, a man came with his horse, which he begged the Smith to shoe.

'Might I have leave to shoe it?' asked our Lord.

'You may try, if you like', said the Smith; 'you can't do it so badly that I shall not be able to make it right again.'

So our Lord went out and took one leg off the horse, and laid it in the furnace, and made the shoe red-hot; after that, he turned up the ends of the shoe, and filed down the heads of the nails, and clenched the points; and then he put back the leg safe and sound on the horse again. And when he was done with that leg, he took the other fore-leg and did the same with it; and when he was done with that, he took the hind-legs--first, the off, and then the near leg, and laid them in the furnace, making the shoes red-hot, turning up the ends; filing the heads of the nails, and clenching the points; and after all was done, putting the legs on the horse again. All the while, the Smith stood by and looked on.

'You're not so bad a smith after all', said he.

'Oh, you think so, do you?' said our Lord.

A little while after came the Smith's mother to the forge, and called him to come home and eat his dinner; she was an old, old woman with an ugly crook on her back, and wrinkles in her face, and it was as much as she could do to crawl along.

'Mark now, what you see', said our Lord.

Then he took the woman and laid her in the furnace, and smithied a lovely young maiden out of her.

'Well', said the Smith, 'I say now, as I said before, you are not such a bad smith after all. There it stands over my door. *Here dwells the Master over all Masters*; but for all that, I say right out, one learns as long as one lives'; and with that he walked off to his house and ate his dinner.

So after dinner, just after he had got back to his forge, a man came riding up to have his horse shod.

'It shall be done in the twinkling of an eye', said the Smith, 'for I have just learnt a new way to shoe; and a very good way it is when the days are short.'

So he began to cut and hack till he had got all the horse's legs off, for he said, I don't know why one should go pottering backwards and forwards--first, with one leg, and then with another.

Then he laid the legs in the furnace, just as he had seen our Lord lay them, and threw on a great heap of coal, and made his mates work the bellows bravely; but it went as one might suppose it would go. The legs were burnt to ashes, and the Smith had to pay for the horse.

Well, he didn't care much about that, but just then an old beggar- woman came along the road, and he thought to himself, 'better luck next time'; so he took the old dame and laid her in the furnace, and though she begged and prayed hard for her life, it was no good.

'You're so old, you don't know what is good for you', said the Smith; 'now you shall be a lovely young maiden in half no time, and for all that, I'll not charge you a penny for the job.'

But it went no better with the poor old woman than with the horse's legs.

'That was ill done, and I say it', said our Lord.

'Oh! for that matter', said the Smith, 'there's not many who'll ask after her, I'll be bound; but it's a shame of the Devil, if this is the way he holds to what is written up over the door.'

'If you might have three wishes from me', said our Lord, 'what would you wish for?'

'Only try me', said the Smith, 'and you'll soon know.'

So our Lord gave him three wishes.

'Well', said the Smith, 'first and foremost, I wish that any one whom I ask to climb up into the pear-tree that stands outside by the wall of my forge, may stay sitting there till I ask him to come down again. The second wish I wish is, that any one whom I ask to sit down in my easy chair which stands inside the workshop yonder, may stay sitting there till I ask him to get up. Last of all, I wish that any one whom I ask to creep into the steel purse which I have in my pocket, may stay in it till I give him leave to creep out again.'

'You have wished as a wicked man', said St Peter; 'first and foremost, you should have wished for God's grace and goodwill.'

'I durstn't look so high as that', said the Smith; and after that our Lord and St Peter bade him 'good-bye', and went on their way.

Well, the years went on and on, and when the time was up, the Devil came to fetch the Smith, as it was written in their bargain.

'Are you ready?' he said, as he stuck his nose in at the door of the forge.

'Oh', said the Smith, 'I must just hammer the head of this tenpenny nail first; meantime, you can just climb up into the pear-tree, and pluck yourself a pear to gnaw at; you must be, both hungry and thirsty after your journey.'

So the Devil thanked him for his kind offer, and climbed up into the pear-tree.

'Very good', said the Smith; 'but now, on thinking the matter over, I find I shall never be able to have done hammering the head of this nail till four years are out at least, this iron is so plaguey hard; down you can't come in all that time, but may sit up there and rest your bones.'

When the Devil heard this, he begged and prayed till his voice was as thin as a silver penny that he might have leave to come down; but there was no help for it. There he was, and there he must stay. At last he had to give his word of honour not to come again till the four years were out, which the Smith had spoken of, and then the Smith said, 'Very well, now you may come down.'

So when the time was up, the Devil came again to fetch the Smith.

'You're ready now, of course', said he; 'you've had time enough to hammer the head of that nail, I should think.'

'Yes, the head is right enough now', said the Smith; 'but still you have come a little tiny bit too soon, for I haven't quite done sharpening the point; such plaguey hard iron I never hammered in all my born days. So while I work at the point, you may just as well sit down in my easy chair and rest yourself; I'll be bound you're weary after coming so far.'

'Thank you kindly', said the Devil, and down he plumped into the easy chair; but just as he had made himself comfortable, the Smith said, on second thoughts, he found he couldn't get the point sharp till four years were out. First of all, the Devil begged so prettily to be let out of the chair, and afterwards, waxing wroth, he began to threaten and scold; but the Smith kept on, all the while excusing himself, and saying it was all the iron's fault, it was so plaguy hard, and telling the Devil he was not so badly off to have to sit quietly in an easy chair, and that he would let him out to the minute when the four years were over. Well, at last there was no help for it, and the Devil had to give his word of honour not to fetch the Smith till the four years were out; and then the Smith said:

'Well now, you may get up and be off about your business', and away went the Devil as fast as he could lay legs to the ground.

When the four years were over, the Devil came again to fetch the Smith, and he called out, as he stuck his nose in at the door of the forge:

'Now, I know you must be ready.'

'Ready, aye, ready', answered the Smith; 'we can go now as soon as you please; but hark ye, there is one thing I have stood here and thought, and thought, I would ask you to tell me. Is it true what people say, that the Devil can make himself as small as he pleases?'

'God knows, it is the very truth', said the Devil.

'Oh!' said the Smith; 'it *is* true, is it? then I wish you would just be so good as to creep into this steel purse of mine, and see whether it is sound at the bottom, for to tell you the truth, I'm afraid my travelling money will drop out.'

'With all my heart', said the Devil, who made himself small in a trice, and crept into the purse; but he was scarce in when the Smith snapped to the clasp.

'Yes', called out the Devil inside the purse; 'it's right and tight everywhere.'

'Very good', said the Smith; 'I'm glad to hear you say so, but "more haste the worse speed", says the old saw, and "forewarned is forearmed", says another; so I'll just weld these links a little together, just for safety's sake'; and with that he laid the purse in the furnace, and made it red-hot.

'AU! AU!' screamed the Devil, 'are you mad? don't you know I'm inside the purse?'

'Yes, I do!' said the Smith; 'but I can't help you, for another old saw says, "one must strike while the iron is hot"'; and as he said this, he took up his sledge-hammer, laid the purse on the anvil, and let fly at it as hard as he could.

'AU! AU! AU!' bellowed the Devil, inside the purse. 'Dear friend, do let me out, and I'll never come near you again.'

'Very well!' said the Smith; 'now, I think, the links are pretty well welded, and you may come out'; so he unclasped the purse, and away went the Devil in such a hurry that he didn't once look behind him.

Now, some time after, it came across the Smith's mind that he had done a silly thing in making the Devil his enemy, for, he said to himself:

'If, as is like enough, they won't have me in the kingdom of Heaven, I shall be in danger of being houseless, since I've fallen out with him who rules over Hell.'

So he made up his mind it would be best to try to get either into Hell or Heaven, and to try at once, rather than to put it off any longer, so that he might know how things really stood. Then he threw his sledge-hammer over his shoulder and set off; and when he had gone a good bit of the way, he came to a place where two roads met, and where the path to the kingdom of Heaven parts from the path that leads to Hell, and here he overtook a tailor, who was pelting along with his goose in his hand.

'Good day', said the Smith; 'whither are you off to?'

'To the kingdom of Heaven', said the Tailor, 'if I can only get into it'--'but whither are you going yourself?'

'Oh, our ways don't run together', said the Smith; 'for I have made up my mind to try first in Hell, as the Devil and I know something of one another, from old times.'

So they bade one another 'Good-bye', and each went his way; but the Smith was a stout, strong man, and got over the ground far faster than the tailor, and so it wasn't long before he stood at the gates of Hell. Then he called the watch, and bade him go and tell the Devil there was some one outside who wished to speak a word with him.

'Go out', said the Devil to the watch, 'and ask him who he is?' So that when the watch came and told him that, the Smith answered:

'Go and greet the Devil in my name, and say it is the Smith who owns the purse he wots of; and beg him prettily to let me in at once, for I worked at my forge till noon, and I have had a long walk since.'

But when the Devil heard who it was, he charged the watch to go back and lock up all the nine locks on the gates of Hell.

'And, besides', he said, 'you may as well put on a padlock, for if he only once gets in, he'll turn Hell topsy-turvy!'

'Well!' said the Smith to himself, when he saw them busy bolting up the gates, 'there's no lodging to be got here, that's plain; so I may as well try my luck in the kingdom of Heaven'; and with that he turned round and went back till he reached the cross-roads, and then he went along the path the tailor had taken. And now, as he was cross at having gone backwards and forwards so far for no good, he strode along with all his might, and reached the gate of Heaven just as St Peter was open-ing it a very little, just enough to let the half- starved tailor slip in. The Smith was still six or seven strides off the gate, so he thought to himself, 'Now there's no time to be lost'; and, grasping his sledge-hammer, he hurled it into the opening of the door just as the tailor slunk in; and if the Smith didn't get in then, when the door was ajar, why I don't know what has become of him.

THE TWO STEP-SISTERS

Once on a time there was a couple, and each of them had a daughter by a former marriage. The woman's daughter was dull and lazy, and could never turn her hand to anything, and the man's daughter was brisk and ready; but somehow or other she could never do anything to her step-mother's liking, and both the woman and her daughter would have been glad to be rid of her.

So it fell one day the two girls were to go out and spin by the side of the well, and the woman's daughter had flax to spin, but the man's daughter got nothing to spin but bristles.

'I don't know how it is', said the woman's daughter, 'you're always so quick and sharp, but still I'm not afraid to spin a match with you.'

Well, they agreed that she whose thread first snapped, should go down the well. So they span away; but just as they were hard at it, the man's daughter's thread broke, and she had to go down the well. But when she got to the bottom she saw far and wide around her a fair green mead, and she hadn't hurt herself at all.

So she walked on a bit, till she came to a hedge which she had to cross.

'Ah! don't tread hard on me, pray don't, and I'll help you another time, that I will', said the Hedge.

Then the lassie made herself as light as she could, and trode so carefully she scarce touched a twig.

So she went on a bit further, till she came to a brindled cow, which walked there with a milking-pail on her horns. 'Twas a large pretty cow, and her udder was so full and round.

'Ah! be so good as to milk me, pray', said the Cow; 'I'm so full of milk. Drink as much as you please, and throw the rest over my hoofs, and see if I don't help you some day.'

So the man's daughter did as the cow begged. As soon as she touched the teats, the milk spouted out into the pail. Then she drank till her thirst was slaked; and the rest she threw over the cow's hoofs, and the milking-pail she hung on her horns again.

So when she had gone a bit further, a big wether met her, which had such thick long wool, it hung down and draggled after him on the ground, and on one of his horns hung a great pair of shears.

'Ah, please clip off my wool', said the Sheep, 'for here I go about with all this wool, and catch up everything I meet, and besides, it's so warm, I'm almost choked. Take as much of the fleece as you please, and twist the rest round my neck, and see if I don't help you some day.'

Yes! she was willing enough, and the sheep lay down of himself on her lap, and kept quite still, and she clipped him so neatly, there wasn't a scratch on his skin. Then she took as much of the wool as she chose, and the rest she twisted round the neck of the sheep.

A little further on, she came to an apple tree, which was loaded with apples; all its branches were bowed to the ground, and leaning against the stem was a slender pole.

'Ah! do be so good as to pluck my apples off me', said the Tree, 'so that my branches may straighten themselves again, for it's bad work to stand so crooked; but when you beat them down, don't strike me too hard. Then eat as many as you please, lay the rest round my root, and see if I don't help you some day or other.'

Yes, she plucked all she could reach with her hands, and then she took the pole and knocked down the rest, and afterwards she ate her fill, and the rest she laid neatly round the root.

So she walked on a long, long way, and then she came to a great farm- house, where an old hag of the Trolls lived with her daughter. There she turned in to ask if she could get a place.

'Oh!' said the old hag; 'it's no use your trying. We've had ever so many maids, but none of them was worth her salt.'

But she begged so prettily that they would just take her on trial, that at last they let her stay. So the old hag gave her a sieve, and bade her go and fetch water in it.

She thought it strange to fetch water in a sieve, but still she went, and when she came to the well, the little birds began to sing,

Daub in clay,   Stuff in straw!   Daub in clay,   Stuff in straw.

Yes, she did so, and found she could carry water in a sieve well enough; but when she got home with the water, and the old witch saw the sieve, she cried out: 'THIS YOU HAVEN'T SUCKED OUT OF YOUR OWN BREAST.'

So the old witch said, now she might go into the byre to pitch out dung and milk kine; but when she got there, she found a pitchfork so long and heavy, she couldn't stir it, much less work with it. She didn't know at all what to do, or what to make of it; but the little birds sang again that she should take the broom-stick and toss out a little with that, and all the rest of the dung would fly after it. So she did that, and as soon as ever she began with the broom-stick, the byre was as clean as if it had been swept and washed.

Now she had to milk the kine, but they were so restless that they kicked and frisked; there was no getting near them to milk them.

But the little birds sang outside:

A little drop, a tiny sup,   For the little birds to drink it up.

Yes, she did that; she just milked a tiny drop, 'twas as much as she could, for the little birds outside; and then all the cows stood still and let her milk them. They neither kicked nor frisked; they didn't even lift a leg.

So when the old witch saw her coming in with the milk, she cried out: 'THIS YOU HAVEN'T SUCKED OUT OF YOUR OWN BREAST. BUT NOW JUST TAKE THIS BLACK WOOL AND WASH IT WHITE.'

This the lassie was at her wits' end to know how to do, for she had never seen or heard of any one who could wash black wool white. Still she said nothing, but took the wool and went down with it to the well. There the little birds sang again and told her to take the wool and dip it into the great butt that stood there; and she did so, and out it came as white as snow.

'Well! I never!' said the old witch, when she came in with the wool, 'it's no good keeping you. You can do everything, and at last you'll be the plague of my life. We'd best part, so take your wages and be off.'

Then the old hag drew out three caskets, one red, one green, and one blue, and of these the lassie was to choose one as wages for her service. Now she didn't know at all which to choose, but the little birds sang:

    Don't take the red, don't take the green,   But take the blue, where may be seen   Three little crosses all in a row;   We saw the marks, and so we know.

So she took the blue casket, as the birds sang.

'Bad luck to you, then', said the old witch; 'see if I don't make you pay for this!'

So when the man's daughter was just setting off, the old witch shot a red-hot bar of iron after her, but she sprang behind the door and hid herself, so that it missed her, for her friends, the little birds, had told her beforehand how to behave. Then she walked on and on as fast as ever she could; but when she got to the apple tree, she heard an awful clatter behind her on the road, and that was the old witch and her daughter coming after her.

So the lassie was so frightened and scared, she didn't know what to do.

'Come hither to me, lassie, do you hear', said the Apple tree, 'I'll help you; get under my branches and hide, for if they catch you, they'll tear you to death, and take the casket from you.'

Yes! she did so, and she had hardly hidden herself before up came the old witch and her daughter.

'Have you seen any lassie pass this way, you apple tree', said the old hag.

'Yes, yes', said the Apple tree; 'one ran by here an hour ago; but now she's got so far ahead, you'll never catch her up.'

So the old witch turned back and went home again. Then the lassie walked on a bit, but when she came just about where the sheep was, she heard an awful clatter beginning on the road behind her, and she didn't know what to do, she was so scared and frightened; for she knew well enough it was the old witch, who had thought better of it.

'Come hither to me, lassie', said the Wether, 'and I'll help you. Hide yourself under my fleece, and then they'll not see you; else they'll take away the casket, and tear you to death.'

Just then up came the old witch, tearing along.

'Have you seen any lassie pass here, you sheep?' she cried to the wether.

'Oh yes', said the Wether, 'I saw one an hour ago, but she ran so fast, you'll never catch her.'

So the old witch turned round and went home.

But when the lassie had come to where she met the cow, she heard another awful clatter behind her.

'Come hither to me, lassie', said the Cow, 'and I'll help you to hide yourself under my udder, else the old hag will come and take away your casket, and tear you to death.'

True enough, it wasn't long before she came up.

'Have you seen any lassie pass here, you cow?' said the old hag.

'Yes, I saw one an hour ago', said the Cow, 'but she's far away now, for she ran so fast I don't think you'll ever catch her up!'

So the old hag turned round, and went back home again.

When the lassie had walked a long, long way farther on, and was not far from the hedge, she heard again that awful clatter on the road behind her, and she got scared and frightened, for she knew well enough it was the old hag and her daughter, who had changed their minds.

'Come hither to me, lassie', said the Hedge, 'and I'll help you. Creep under my twigs, so that they can't see you; else they'll take the casket from you, and tear you to death.'

Yes! she made all the haste she could to get under the twigs of the hedge.

'Have you seen any lassie pass this way, you hedge?' said the old hag to the hedge.

'No, I haven't seen any lassie', answered the Hedge, and was as smooth-tongued as if he had got melted butter in his mouth; but all the while he spread himself out, and made himself so big and tall, one had to think twice before crossing him. And so the old witch had no help for it but to turn round and go home again.

So when the man's daughter got home, her step-mother and her step- sister were more spiteful against her than ever; for now she was much neater, and so smart, it was a joy to look at her. Still she couldn't get leave to live with them, but they drove her out into a pigsty. That was to be her house. So she scrubbed it out so neat and clean, and then she opened her casket, just to see what she had got for her wages. But as soon as ever she unlocked it, she saw inside so much gold and silver, and lovely things, which came streaming out till all the walls were hung with them, and at last the pigsty was far grander than the grandest king's palace. And when the step-mother and her daughter came to see this, they almost jumped out of their skin, and began to ask what kind of a place she had down there?

'Oh', said the lassie, 'can't you see, when I have got such good wages. 'Twas such a family, and such a mistress to serve, you couldn't find their like anywhere.'

Yes! the woman's daughter made up her mind to go out to serve too, that she might get just such another gold casket. So they sat down to spin again, and now the woman's daughter was to spin bristles, and the man's daughter flax, and she whose thread first snapped, was to go down the well. It wasn't long, as you may fancy, before the woman's daughter's thread snapped, and so they threw her down the well.

So the same thing happened. She fell to the bottom, but met with no harm, and found herself on a lovely green meadow. When she had walked a bit she came to the hedge. 'Don't tread hard on me, pray, lassie, and I'll help you again', said the Hedge.

'Oh!' said she, 'what should I care for a bundle of twigs?' and tramped and stamped over the hedge till it cracked and groaned again.

A little farther on she came to the cow, which walked about ready to burst for want of milking.

'Be so good as to milk me, lassie', said the Cow, 'and I'll help you again. Drink as much as you please, but throw the rest over my hoofs.'

Yes! she did that; she milked the cow, and drank till she could drink no more; but when she left off, there was none left to throw over the cow's hoofs, and as for the pail, she tossed it down the hill and walked on.

When she had gone a bit further, she came to the sheep which walked along with his wool dragging after him.

'Oh, be so good as to clip me, lassie', said the Sheep, 'and I'll serve you again. Take as much of the wool as you will, but twist the rest round my neck.'

Well! she did that; but she went so carelessly to work, that she cut great pieces out of the poor sheep, and as for the wool, she carried it all away with her.

A little while after she came to the apple tree, which stood there quite crooked with fruit again.

'Be so good as to pluck the apples off me, that my limbs may grow straight, for it's weary work to stand all awry', said the Apple tree. 'But please take care not to beat me too hard. Eat as many as you will, but lay the rest neatly round my root, and I'll help you again.'

Well, she plucked those nearest to her, and thrashed down those she couldn't reach with the pole, but she didn't care how she did it, and broke off and tore down great boughs, and ate till she was as full as full could be, and then she threw down the rest under the tree.

So when she had gone a good bit further, she came to the farm where the old witch lived. There she asked for a place, but the old hag said she wouldn't have any more maids, for they were either worth nothing, or were too clever, and cheated her out of her goods. But the woman's daughter was not to be put off, she **would** have a place, so the old witch said she'd give her a trial, if she was fit for anything.

The first thing she had to do was to fetch water in a sieve. Well, off she went to the well, and drew water in a sieve, but as fast as she got it in it ran out again. So the little birds sung:

Daub in clay,   Put in straw!   Daub in clay,   Put in straw!

But she didn't care to listen to the birds' song, and pelted them with clay, till they flew off far away. And so she had to go home with the empty sieve, and got well scolded by the old witch.

Then she was to go into the byre to clean it, and milk the kine. But she was too good for such dirty work, she thought. Still, she went out into the byre, but when she got there, she couldn't get on at all with the pitchfork, it was so big. The birds said the same to her as they had said to her step-sister, and told her to take the broomstick, and toss out a little dung, and then all the rest would fly after it; but all she did with the broomstick was to throw it at the birds. When she came to milk, the kine were so unruly, they kicked and pushed, and every time she got a little milk in the pail, over they kicked it. Then the birds sang again:

A little drop and a tiny sup   For the little birds to drink it up.

But she beat and banged the cows about, and threw and pelted at the birds everything she could lay hold of, and made such a to do, 'twas awful to see. So she didn't make much either of her pitching, or milking, and when she came indoors she got blows as well as hard words from the old witch, who sent her off to wash the black wool white; but that, too, she did no better.

Then the old witch thought this really too bad, so she set out the three caskets, one red, one green, and one blue, and said she'd no longer any need of her services, for she wasn't worth keeping, but for wages she should have leave to choose whichever casket she pleased.

Then sung the little birds:

Don't take the red, don't take the green,   But choose the blue, where may be seen   Three little crosses all in a row;   We saw the marks, and so we know.

She didn't care a pin for what the birds sang, but took the red, which caught her eye most. And so she set out on her road home, and she went along quietly and easily enough; there was no one who came after *her*.

So when she got home, her mother was ready to jump with joy, and the two went at once into the ingle, and put the casket up there, for they made up their minds there could be nothing in it but pure silver and gold, and they thought to have all the walls and roof gilded like the pigsty. But lo! when they opened the casket there came tumbling out nothing but toads, and frogs, and snakes; and worse than that, whenever the woman's daughter opened her mouth, out popped a toad or a snake, and all the vermin one ever thought of, so that at last there was no living in the house with her.

That was all the wages *she* got for going out to service with the old witch.

BUTTERCUP

Once on a time there was an old wife who sat and baked. Now, you must know that this old wife had a little son, who was so plump and fat, and so fond of good things, that they called him Buttercup; she had a dog, too, whose name was Goldtooth, and as she was baking, all at once Goldtooth began to bark.

'Run out, Buttercup, there's a dear!' said the old wife, 'and see what Goldtooth is barking at.'

So the boy ran out, and came back crying out:

'Oh, Heaven help us! here comes a great big witch, with her head under her arm, and a bag at her back.'

'Jump under the kneading-trough and hide yourself', said his mother.

So in came the old hag!

'Good day', said she!

'God bless you!' said Buttercup's mother.

'Isn't your Buttercup at home to-day?' asked the hag.

'No, that he isn't. He's out in the wood with his father, shooting ptarmigan.'

'Plague take it', said the hag, 'for I had such a nice little silver knife I wanted to give him.'

'Pip, pip! here I am', said Buttercup under the kneading-trough, and out he came.

'I'm so old, and stiff in the back', said the hag, 'you must creep into the bag and fetch it out for yourself.'

But when Buttercup was well into the bag, the hag threw it over her back and strode off, and when they had gone a good bit of the way, the old hag got tired, and asked:

'How far is it off to Snoring?'

'Half a mile', answered Buttercup.

So the hag put down the sack on the road, and went aside by herself into the wood, and lay down to sleep. Meantime Buttercup set to work and cut a hole in the sack with his knife; then he crept out and put a great root of a fir-tree into the sack, and ran home to his mother.

When the hag got home and saw what there was in the sack, you may fancy she was in a fine rage.

Next day the old wife sat and baked again, and her dog began to bark just as he did the day before.

'Run out, Buttercup, my boy', said she, 'and see what Goldtooth is barking at.'

'Well, I never!' cried Buttercup, as soon as he got out; 'if there isn't that ugly old beast coming again with her head under her arm, and a great sack at her back.'

'Under the kneading-trough with you and hide', said his mother.

'Good day!' said the hag, 'is your Buttercup at home to-day?'

'I'm sorry to say he isn't', said his mother; 'he's out in the wood with his father, shooting ptarmigan.'

'What a bore', said the hag; 'here I have a beautiful little silver spoon I want to give him.'

'Pip, pip! here I am', said Buttercup, and crept out.

'I'm so stiff in the back', said the old witch, 'you must creep into the sack and fetch it out for yourself.'

So when Buttercup was well into the sack, the hag swung it over her shoulders and set off home as fast as her legs could carry her. But when they had gone a good bit, she grew weary, and asked:

'How far is it off to Snoring?'

'A mile and a half', answered Buttercup.

So the hag set down the sack, and went aside into the wood to sleep a bit, but while she slept, Buttercup made a hole in the sack and got out, and put a great stone into it. Now, when the old witch got home, she made a great fire on the hearth, and put a big pot on it, and got everything ready to boil Buttercup; but when she took the sack, and thought she was going to turn out Buttercup into the pot, down plumped the stone and made a hole in the bottom of the pot, so that the water ran out and quenched the fire. Then the old hag was in a dreadful rage, and said, 'If he makes himself ever so heavy next time, he shan't take me in again.' The third day everything went just as it had gone twice before; Goldtooth began to bark, and Buttercup's mother said to him:

'Do run out and see what our dog is barking at.'

So out he went, but he soon came back crying out:

'Heaven save us! Here comes the old hag again with her head under her arm, and a sack at her back.'

'Jump under the kneading-trough and hide', said his mother.

'Good day!' said the hag, as she came in at the door; 'is your Buttercup at home to-day?'

'You're very kind to ask after him', said his mother; 'but he's out in the wood with his father, shooting ptarmigan.'

'What a bore now', said the old hag; 'here have I got such a beautiful little silver fork for him.'

'Pip, pip! here I am', said Buttercup, as he came out from under the kneading-trough.

'I'm so stiff in the back', said the hag, 'you must creep into the sack and fetch it out for yourself.'

But when Buttercup was well inside the sack, the old hag swung it across her shoulders, and set off as fast as she could. This time she did not turn aside to sleep by the way, but went straight home with Buttercup in the sack, and when she reached her house it was Sunday.

So the old hag said to her daughter:

'Now you must take Buttercup and kill him, and boil him nicely till I come back, for I'm off to church to bid my guests to dinner.'

So, when all in the house were gone to church the daughter was to take Buttercup and kill him, but then she didn't know how to set about it at all.

'Stop a bit', said Buttercup; 'I'll soon show you how to do it; just lay your head on the chopping-block, and you'll soon see.'

So the poor silly thing laid her head down, and Buttercup took an axe and chopped her head off, just as if she had been a chicken. Then he laid her head in the bed, and popped her body into the pot, and boiled it so nicely; and when he had done that, he climbed up on the roof, and dragged up with him the fir-tree root and the stone, and put the one over the door, and the other at the top of the chimney.

So when the household came back from church, and saw the head on the bed, they thought it was the daughter who lay there asleep; and then they thought they would just taste the broth.

Good, by my troth! Buttercup broth,

said the old hag.

Good, by my troth! Daughter broth,

said Buttercup down the chimney, but no one heeded him. So the old hag's husband, who was every bit as bad as she, took the spoon to have a taste.

Good, by my troth! Buttercup broth,

said he.

Good, by my troth! Daughter broth,

said Buttercup down the chimney pipe.

Then they all began to wonder who it could be that chattered so, and ran out to see. But when they came out at the door, Buttercup threw down on them the fir-tree root and the stone, and broke all their heads to bits. After that he took all the gold and silver that lay in the house, and went home to his mother, and became a rich man.

TAMING THE SHREW

Once on a time there was a king, and he had a daughter who was such a scold, and whose tongue went so fast, there was no stopping it. So he gave out that the man who could stop her tongue should have the Princess to wife, and half his kingdom into the bargain. Now, three brothers, who heard this, made up their minds to go and try their luck; and first of all the two elder went, for they thought they were the cleverest; but they couldn't cope with her at all, and got well thrashed besides.

Then Boots, the youngest, set off, and when he had gone a little way he found an ozier band lying on the road, and he picked it up. When he had gone a little farther he found a piece of a broken plate, and he picked that up too. A little farther on he found a dead magpie, and a little farther on still, a crooked ram's horn; so he went on a bit and found the fellow to the horn; and at last, just as he was crossing the fields by the king's palace, where they were pitching out dung, he found a worn-out shoe-sole. All these things he took with him into the palace, and went before the Princess.

'Good day', said he.

'Good day', said she, and made a wry face.

'Can I get my magpie cooked here?' he asked.

'I'm afraid it will burst', answered the Princess.

'Oh! never fear! for I'll just tie this ozier band round it', said the lad, as he pulled it out.

'The fat will run out of it', said the Princess.

'Then I'll hold this under it', said the lad, and showed her the piece of broken plate.

'You are so crooked in your words', said the Princess, 'there's no knowing where to have you.'

'No, I'm not crooked', said the lad; 'but this is', as he held up one of the horns.

'Well!' said the Princess, 'I never saw the match of this in all my days.'

'Why, here you see the match to it', said the lad, as he pulled out the other ram's horn.

'I think', said the Princess, 'you must have come here to wear out my tongue with your nonsense.'

'No, I have not', said the lad; 'but this is worn out', as he pulled out the shoe-sole.

To this the Princess hadn't a word to say, for she had fairly lost her voice with rage.

'Now you are mine', said the lad; and so he got the Princess to wife, and half the kingdom.

SHORTSHANKS

Once on a time, there was a poor couple who lived in a tumble-down hut, in which there was nothing but black want, so that they hadn't a morsel to eat, nor a stick to burn. But though they had next to nothing of other things, they had God's blessing in the way of children, and every year they had another babe. Now, when this story begins, they were just looking out for a new child; and, to tell the truth, the husband was rather cross, and he was always going about grumbling and growling, and saying, 'For his part, he thought one might have too many of these God's gifts.' So when the time came that the babe was to be born, he went off into the wood to fetch fuel, saying, 'he didn't care to stop and see the young squaller; he'd be sure to hear him soon enough, screaming for food.'

Now, when her husband was well out of the house, his wife gave birth to a beautiful boy, who began to look about the room as soon as ever he came into the world.

'Oh! dear mother', he said, 'give me some of my brother's cast-off clothes, and a few days' food, and I'll go out into the world and try my luck; you have children enough as it is, that I can see.'

'God help you, my son!' answered his mother; 'that can never be, you are far too young yet.'

But the tiny one stuck to what he said, and begged and prayed till his mother was forced to let him have a few old rags, and a little food tied up in a bundle, and off he went right merrily and manfully into the wide world. But he was scarce out of the house before his mother had another boy, and he too looked about him, and said:

'Oh, dear mother! give me some of my brother's old clothes and a few days' food, and I'll go out into the world to find my twin-brother; you have children enough already on your hands, that I can see.'

'God help you, my poor little fellow!' said his mother; 'you are far too little, this will never do.'

But it was no good; the tiny one begged and prayed so hard, till he got some old tattered rags and a bundle of food; and so he wandered out into the world like a man, to find his twin-brother. Now, when the younger had walked a while, he saw his brother a good bit on before him, so he called out to him to stop.

'Holloa! can't you stop? why, you lay legs to the ground as if you were running a race. But you might just as well have stayed to see your youngest, brother before you set off into the world in such a hurry.'

So the elder stopped and looked round; and when the younger had come up to him and told him the whole story, and how he was his brother, he went on to say:

'But let's sit down here and see what our mother has given us for food.' So they sat down together, and were soon great friends.

Now when they had gone a bit farther on their way, they came to a brook which ran through a green meadow, and the youngest said now the time was come to give one another names, 'Since we set off in such a hurry that we hadn't time to do it at home, we may as well do it here.'

'Well!' said the elder, 'and what shall your name be?'

'Oh!' said the younger, 'my name shall be Shortshanks; and yours, what shall it be?'

'I will be called King Sturdy', answered the eldest.

So they christened each other in the brook, and went on; but when they had walked a while they came to a cross road, and agreed they should part there, and each take his own road. So they parted, but they hadn't gone half a mile before their roads met again. So they parted the second time, and took each a road; but in a little while the same thing happened, and they met again, they scarce knew how; and the same thing happened a third time also. Then they agreed that they should each choose a quarter of the heavens, and one was to go east and the other west; but before they parted, the elder said:

'If you ever fall into misfortune or need, call three times on me, and I will come and help you; but mind you don't call on me till you are at the last pinch.'

'Well!' said Shortshanks, 'if that's to be the rule, I don't think we shall meet again very soon.'

After that they bade each other good-bye, and Shortshanks went east, and King Sturdy west.

Now, you must know, when Shortshanks had gone a good bit alone, he met an old, old crook-backed hag, who had only one eye, and Shortshanks snapped it up.

'Oh! oh!' screamed the hag, 'what has become of my eye?'

'What will you give me', asked Shortshanks, 'if you get your eye back?'

'I'll give you a sword, and such a sword! It will put a whole army to flight, be it ever so great', answered the old woman.

'Out with it, then!' said Shortshanks.

So the old hag gave him the sword, and got her eye back again. After that, Shortshanks wandered on a while, and another old, old crook- backed hag met him who had only one eye, which Shortshanks stole before she was aware of him.

'Oh, oh! whatever has become of my eye', screamed the hag.

'What will you give me to get your eye back?' asked Shortshanks.

'I'll give you a ship', said the woman, 'which can sail over fresh water and salt water, and over high hills and deep dales.'

'Well! out with it', said Shortshanks.

So the old woman gave him a little tiny ship, no bigger than he could put in his pocket, and she got her eye back again, and they each went their way. But when he had wandered on a long, long way, he met a third time an old, old crook-backed hag, with only one eye. This eye, too, Shortshanks stole; and when the hag screamed and made a great to-do, bawling out what had become of her eye, Shortshanks said:

'What will you give me to get back your eye?'

Then she answered:

'I'll give you the art how to brew a hundred lasts of malt at one strike.'

Well! for teaching that art the old hag got back her eye, and they each went their way.

But when Shortshanks had walked a little way, he thought it might be worth while to try his ship; so he took it out of his pocket, and put first one foot into it, and then the other; and as soon as ever he set one foot into it, it began to grow bigger and bigger, and by the time he set the other foot into it, it was as big as other ships that sail on the sea. Then Shortshanks said:

'Off and away, over fresh water and salt water, over high hills and deep dales, and don't stop till you come to the king's palace.'

And lo! away went the ship as swiftly as a bird through the air, till it came down a little below the king's palace, and there it stopped. From the palace windows people had stood and seen Shortshanks come sailing along, and they were all so amazed that they ran down to see who it could be that came sailing in a ship through the air. But while they were running down, Shortshanks had stepped out of his ship and put it into his pocket again; for as soon as he stepped out of it, it became as small as it was when he got it from the old woman. So those who had run down from the palace saw no one but a ragged little boy standing down there by the strand. Then the king asked whence he came, but the boy said he didn't know, nor could he tell them how he had got there. There he was, and that was all they could get out of him; but he begged and prayed so prettily to get a place in the king's palace; saying, if there was nothing else for him to do, he could carry in wood and water for the kitchen-maid, that their hearts were touched, and he got leave to stay there.

Now when Shortshanks came up to the palace, he saw how it was all hung with black, both outside and in, wall and roof; so he asked the kitchen-maid what all that mourning meant?

'Don't you know?' said the kitchen-maid; 'I'll soon tell you: the king's daughter was promised away a long time ago to three ogres, and next Thursday evening one of them is coming to fetch her. Ritter Red, it is true, has given out that he is man enough to set her free, but God knows if he can do it; and now you know why we are all in grief and sorrow.'

So when Thursday evening came, Ritter Red led the Princess down to the strand, for there it was she was to meet the Ogre, and he was to stay by her there and watch; but he wasn't likely to do the Ogre much harm, I reckon, for as soon as ever the Princess had sat down on the strand, Ritter Red climbed up into a great tree that stood there, and hid himself as well as he could among the boughs. The Princess begged and prayed him not to leave her, but Ritter Red turned a deaf ear to her, and all he said was:

'Tis better for one to lose life than for two.'

That was what Ritter Red said.

Meantime Shortshanks went to the kitchen-maid, and asked her so prettily if he mightn't go down to the strand for a bit?

'And what should take you down to the strand?' asked the kitchen- maid. 'You know you've no business there.'

'Oh, dear friend', said Shortshanks, 'do let me go? I should so like to run down there and play a while with the other children; that I should.'

'Well, well!' said the kitchen-maid, 'off with you; but don't let me catch you staying there a bit over the time when the brose for supper must be set on the fire, and the roast put on the spit; and let me see; when you come back, mind you bring a good armful of wood with you.'

Yes! Shortshanks would mind all that; so off he ran down to the strand.

But just as he reached the spot where the Princess sat, what should come but the Ogre tearing along in his ship, so that the wind roared and howled after him. He was so tall and stout it was awful to look on him, and he had five heads of his own.

'Fire and flame!' screamed the Ogre.

'Fire and flame yourself!' said Shortshanks.

'Can you fight?' roared the Ogre.

'If I can't, I can learn', said Shortshanks.

So the Ogre struck at him with a great thick iron club which he had in his fist, and the earth and stones flew up five yards into the air after the stroke.

'My!' said Shortshanks, 'that was something like a blow, but now you shall see a stroke of mine.'

Then he grasped the sword he had got from the old crook-backed hag, and cut at the Ogre; and away went all his five heads flying over the sand. So when the Princess saw she was saved, she was so glad that she scarce knew what to do, and she jumped and danced for joy. 'Come, lie down, and sleep a little in my lap', she said to Shortshanks, and as he slept she threw over him a tinsel robe.

Now you must know, it wasn't long before Ritter Red crept down from the tree, as soon as he saw there was nothing to fear in the way, and he went up to the Princess and threatened her until she promised to say it was he who had saved her life; for if she wouldn't say so, he said he would kill her on the spot. After that he cut out the Ogre's lungs and tongue, and wrapped them up in his handkerchief, and so led the Princess back to the palace, and whatever honours he had not before, he got then, for the king did not know how to find honour enough for him, and made him sit every day on his right hand at dinner.

As for Shortshanks, he went first of all on board the Ogre's ship, and took a whole heap of gold and silver rings, as large as hoops, and trotted off with them as hard as he could to the palace. When the kitchen-maid set her eyes on all that gold and silver, she was quite scared, and asked him:

'But dear, good, Shortshanks, wherever did you get all this from?' for she was rather afraid he hadn't come rightly by it.

'Oh!' answered Shortshanks, 'I went home for a bit, and there I found these hoops, which had fallen off some old pails of ours, so I laid hands on them for you, if you must know.'

Well! when the kitchen-maid heard they were for her, she said nothing more about the matter, but thanked Shortshanks, and they were good friends again.

The next Thursday evening it was the same story over again; all were in grief and trouble, but Ritter Red said, as he had saved the Princess from one Ogre, it was hard if he couldn't save her from another; and down he led her to the strand as brave as a lion. But he didn't do this Ogre much harm either, for when the time came that they looked for the Ogre, he said, as he had said before:

''Tis better one should lose life than two', and crept up into his tree again. But Shortshanks begged the kitchen-maid to let him go down to the strand for a little.

'Oh!' asked the kitchen-maid, 'and what business have you down there?'

'Dear friend', said Shortshanks. 'do pray let me go. I long so to run down and play a while with the other children.'

Well! the kitchen-maid gave him leave to go, but he must promise to be back by the time the roast was turned, and he was to mind and bring a big bundle of wood with him. So Shortshanks had scarce got down to the strand, when the Ogre came tearing along in his ship, so that the wind howled and roared around him; he was twice as big as the other Ogre, and he had ten heads on his shoulders.

'Fire and flame!' screamed the Ogre.

Fire and flame yourself!' answered Shortshanks.

'Can you fight?' roared the Ogre.

'If I can't, I can learn', said Shortshanks.

Then the Ogre struck at him with his iron club; it was even bigger than that which the first Ogre had, and the earth and stones flew up ten yards into the air.

My!' said Shortshanks, 'that was something like a blow now you shall see a stroke of mine.' Then he grasped his sword, and cut off all the Ogre's ten heads at one blow, and sent them dancing away over the sand.

Then the Princess said again to him, 'Lie down and sleep a little while on my lap'; and while Shortshanks lay there, she threw over him a silver robe. But as soon as Ritter Red marked that there was no more danger in the way, he crept down from the tree, and threatened the Princess, till she was forced to give her word, to say it was he who had set her free; after that, he cut the lungs and tongue out of the Ogre, and wrapped them in his handkerchief, and led the Princess back to the palace. Then you may fancy what mirth and joy there was, and the king was at his wits' end to know how to show Ritter Red honour and favour enough.

This time, too, Shortshanks took a whole armful of gold and silver rings from the Ogre's ship, and when he came back to the palace the kitchen-maid clapped her hands in wonder, asking wherever he got all that gold and silver from. But Short-shanks answered that he had been home a while, and that the hoops had fallen off some old pails, so he had laid his hands on them for his friend the kitchen-maid. So when the third Thursday evening came, everything happened as it had happened twice before; the whole palace was hung with black, and all went about mourning and weeping. But Ritter Red said he couldn't see what need they had to be so afraid; he had freed the Princess from two Ogres, and he could very well free her from a third; so he led her down to the strand, but when the time drew near for the Ogre to come up, he crept into his tree again, and hid himself. The Princess begged and prayed, but it was no good, for Ritter Red said again:

''Tis better that one should lose life than two.'

That evening, too, Shortshanks begged for leave to go down to the strand.

'Oh!' said the kitchen-maid, 'what should take you down there?'

But he begged and prayed so, that at last he got leave to go, only he had to promise to be back in the kitchen again when the roast was to be turned. So off he went, but he had scarce reached the strand when the Ogre came with the wind howling and roaring after him. He was much, much bigger than either of the other two, and he had fifteen heads on his shoulders.

'Fire and flame!' roared out the Ogre.

'Fire and flame yourself!' said Shortshanks.

'Can you fight?' screamed the Ogre.

'If I can't, I can learn', said Shortshanks.

'I'll soon teach you', screamed the Ogre, and struck at him with his iron club, so that the earth and stones flew up fifteen yards into the air.

'My!' said Shortshanks, 'that was something like a blow; but now you shall see a stroke of mine.'

As he said that, he grasped his sword, and cut off all the Ogre's fifteen heads at one blow, and sent them all dancing over the sand.

So the Princess was freed from all the Ogres, and she both blessed and thanked Shortshanks for saving her life.

'Sleep now a while on my lap', she said; and he laid his head on her lap, and while he slept, she threw over him a golden robe.

'But how shall we let it be known that it is you that have saved me?' she asked, when he awoke.

'Oh, I'll soon tell you', answered Shortshanks. 'When Ritter Red has led you home again, and given himself out as the man who has saved you, you know he is to have you to wife, and half the kingdom. Now, when they ask you, on your wedding-day, whom you will have to be your cup-bearer, you must say, "I will have the ragged boy who does odd jobs in the kitchen, and carries in wood and water for the kitchen- maid." So when I am filling your cups, I will spill a drop on his plate, but none on yours; then he will be wroth, and give me a blow, and the same thing will happen three times. But the third time you must mind and say, "Shame on you! to strike my heart's darling; he it is who set me free, and him will I have!"'

After that Shortshanks ran back to the palace, as he had done before; but he went first on board the Ogre's ship, and took a whole heap of gold, silver, and precious stones, and out of them he gave the kitchen-maid another great armful of gold and silver rings.

Well! as for Ritter Red, as soon as ever he saw that all risk was over, he crept down from his tree, and threatened the Princess till she was forced to promise she would say it was he who had saved her. After that, he led her back to the palace, and all the honour shown him before was nothing to what he got now, for the king thought of nothing else than how he might best honour the man who had saved his daughter from the three Ogres. As for his marrying her, and having half the king-dom, that was a settled thing, the king said. But when the wedding-day came, the Princess begged she might have the ragged boy who carried in wood and water for the cook to be her cup-bearer at the bridal-feast.

'I can't think why you should want to bring that filthy beggar boy in here', said Ritter Red; but the Princess had a will of her own, and said she would have him, and no one else, to pour out her wine; so she had her way at last. Now everything went as it had been agreed between Shortshanks and the Princess; he spilled a drop on Ritter Red's plate, but none on hers, and each time Ritter Red got wroth and struck him. At the first blow Shortshank's rags fell off which he had worn in the kitchen; at the second the tinsel robe fell off; and at the third the silver robe; and then he stood in his golden robe, all gleaming and glittering in the light. Then the Princess said:

'Shame on you! to strike my heart's darling! he has saved me, and him will I have!'

Ritter Red cursed and swore it was he who had set her free; but the king put in his word, and said:

'The man who saved my daughter must have some token to show for it.'

Yes! Ritter Red had something to show, and he ran off at once after his hand-kerchief with the lungs and tongues in it, and Shortshanks fetched all the gold and silver, and precious things, he had taken out of the Ogres' ships. So each laid his tokens before the king, and the king said:

'The man who has such precious stores of gold, and silver, and diamonds, must have slain the Ogre, and spoiled his goods, for such things are not to be had else-where.'

So Ritter Red was thrown into a pit full of snakes, and Shortshanks was to have the Princess and half the kingdom.

One day Shortshanks and the king were out walking, and Shortshanks asked the king if he hadn't any more children?

'Yes', said the king, 'I had another daughter; but the Ogre has taken her away, because there was no one who could save her. Now you are going to have one daughter, but if you can set the other free whom the Ogre has carried off, you shall have her too with all my heart, and the other half of my kingdom.'

'Well', said Shortshanks, 'I may as well try; but I must have an iron cable, five hundred fathoms long, and five hundred men, and food for them to last fifteen weeks, for I have a long voyage before me.'

Yes! the king said he should have them, but he was afraid there wasn't a ship in his kingdom big enough to carry such a freight.

'Oh! if that's all', said Shortshanks, 'I have a ship of my own.'

With that he whipped out of his pocket the ship he had got from the old hag.

The king laughed, and thought it was all a joke; but Shortshanks begged him only to give him what he asked, and he should soon see if it was a joke. So they got together what he wanted, and Shortshanks bade him put the cable on board the ship first of all; but there was no one man who could lift it, and there wasn't room for more than one at a time round the tiny ship. Then Shortshanks took hold of the cable by one end, and laid a link or two into the ship; and as he threw in the links, the ship grew bigger and bigger, till at last it got so big, that there was room enough and to spare in it for the cable, and the five hundred men, and their food, and Shortshanks, and all. Then he said to the ship:

'Off and away, over fresh water and salt water, over high hill and deep dale, and don't stop till you come to where the king's daughter is.' And away went the ship over land and sea, till the wind whistled after it.

So when they had sailed far, far away, the ship stood stock still in the middle of the sea.

'Ah!' said Shortshanks, 'now we have got so far; but how we are to get back is another story.'

Then he took the cable and tied one end of it round his waist, and said:

'Now, I must go to the bottom, but when I give the cable a good tug, and want to come up again, mind you all hoist away with a will, or your lives will be lost as well as mine'; and with these words overboard he leapt, and dived down, so that the yellow waves rose round him in an eddy.

Well, he sank and sank, and at last he came to the bottom, and there he saw a great rock rising up with a door in it, so he opened the door and went in. When he got inside, he saw another Princess, who sat and sewed, but when she saw Shortshanks, she clasped her hands together and cried out:

'Now, God be thanked! you are the first Christian man I've set eyes on since I came here.'

'Very good', said Shortshanks; 'but do you know I've come to fetch you?'

'Oh!' she cried, 'you'll never fetch me; you'll never have that luck, for if the Ogre sees you, he'll kill you on the spot.'

'I'm glad you spoke of the Ogre', said Shortshanks; ''twould be fine fun to see him; whereabouts is he?'

Then the Princess told him the Ogre was out looking for some one who could brew a hundred lasts of malt at one strike, for he was going to give a great feast, and less drink wouldn't do.

'Well! I can do that', said Shortshanks.

'Ah!' said the Princess, 'if only the Ogre wasn't so hasty, I might tell him about you; but he's so cross; I'm afraid he'll tear you to pieces as soon as he comes in, without waiting to hear my story. Let me see what is to be done. Oh! I have it; just hide yourself in the side-room yonder, and let us take our chance.'

Well! Shortshanks did as she told him, and he had scarce crept into the side-room before the Ogre came in.

'HUF!' said the Ogre; 'what a horrid smell of Christian man's blood!'

'Yes!' said the Princess, 'I know there is, for a bird flew over the house with a Christian man's bone in his bill, and let it fall down the chimney. I made all the haste I could to get it out again, but I dare say it's that you smell.'

'Ah!' said the Ogre, 'like enough.'

Then the Princess asked the Ogre if he had laid hold of any one who could brew a hundred lasts of malt at one strike?

'No', said the Ogre, 'I can't hear of any one who can do it.'

'Well', she said, 'a while ago, there was a chap in here who said he could do it.'

'Just like you, with your wisdom!' said the Ogre; 'why did you let him go away then, when you knew he was the very man I wanted?'

'Well then, I didn't let him go', said the Princess; 'but father's temper is a little hot, so I hid him away in the side-room yonder; but if father hasn't hit upon any one, here he is.'

'Well', said the Ogre, 'let him come in then.'

So Shortshanks came in, and the Ogre asked him if it were true that he could brew a hundred lasts of malt at a strike?

'Yes it is', said Shortshanks.

'Twas good luck then to lay hands on you', said the Ogre, 'and now fall to work this minute; but heaven help you if you don't brew the ale strong enough.'

'Oh', said Shortshanks, 'never fear, it shall be stinging stuff'; and with that he began to brew without more fuss, but all at once he cried out:

'I must have more of you Ogres to help in the brewing, for these I have got a'nt half strong enough.'

Well, he got more--so many, that there was a whole swarm of them, and then the brewing went on bravely. Now when the sweet-wort was ready, they were all eager to taste it, you may guess; first of all the Ogre, and then all his kith and kin. But Shortshanks had brewed the wort so strong that they all fell down dead, one after another, like so many flies, as soon as they had tasted it. At last there wasn't one of them left alive but one vile old hag, who lay bed-ridden in the chimney-corner.

'Oh you poor old wretch', said Shortshanks, 'you may just as well taste the wort along with the rest.'

So, he went and scooped up a little from the bottom of the copper in a scoop, and gave her a drink, and so he was rid of the whole pack of them.

As he stood there and looked about him, he cast his eye on a great chest, so he took it and filled it with gold and silver; then he tied the cable round himself and the Princess and the chest, and gave it a good tug, and his men pulled them all up, safe and sound. As soon as ever Shortshanks was well up, he said to the ship,

'Off and away, over fresh water and salt water, high hill and deep dale, and don't stop till you come to the king's palace'; and straightway the ship held on her course, so that the yellow billows foamed round her. When the people in the palace saw the ship sailing up, they were not slow in meeting them with songs and music, welcoming Shortshanks with great joy; but the gladdest of all was the king, who had now got his other daughter back again.

But now Shortshanks was rather down-hearted, for you must know that both the princesses wanted to have him, and he would have no other than the one he had first saved, and she was the youngest. So he walked up and down, and thought and thought what he should do to get her, and yet do something to please her sister. Well, one day as he was turning the thing over in his mind, it struck him if he only had his brother King Sturdy, who was so like him that no one could tell the one from the other, he would give up to him the other princess and half the kingdom, for he thought one-half was quite enough.

Well, as soon as ever this came into his mind, he went outside the palace and called on King Sturdy, but no one came. So he called a second time a little louder, but still no one came. Then he called out the third time 'King Sturdy' with all his might, and there stood his brother before him. 'Didn't I say!' he said to Shortshanks, 'didn't I say you were not to call me except in your utmost need? and here there is not so much as a gnat to do you any harm', and with that he gave him such a box on the ear that Shortshanks tumbled head over heels on the grass.

'Now shame on you to 'hit so hard!' said Shortshanks. 'First of all I won a princess and half the kingdom, and then I won another princess and the other half of the kingdom; and now I'm thinking to give you one of the princesses and half the kingdom. Is there any rhyme or reason in giving me such a box on the ear?'

When King Sturdy heard that, he begged his brother to forgive him, and they were soon as good friends as ever again.

'Now', said Shortshanks, 'you know, we are so much alike, that no one can tell the one from the other; so just change clothes with me and go into the palace; then the princesses will think it is I that am coming in, and the one that kisses you first you shall have for your wife, and I will have the other for mine.'

And he said this because he knew well enough that the elder king's daughter was the stronger, and so he could very well guess how things would go. As for King Sturdy, he was willing enough, so he changed clothes with his brother and went into the palace. But when he came into the Princesses' bower they thought it was Shortshanks, and both ran up to him to kiss him; but the elder, who was stronger and bigger, pushed her sister on one side, and threw her arms round King Sturdy's neck, and gave him a kiss; and so he got her for his wife, and Shortshanks got the younger Princess. Then they made ready for the wedding, and you may fancy what a grand one it was, when I tell you, that the fame of it was noised abroad over seven kingdoms.

GUDBRAND ON THE HILL-SIDE

Once on a time there was a man whose name was Gudbrand; he had a farm which lay far, far away upon a hill-side, and so they called him Gudbrand on the Hill-side.

Now, you must know this man and his goodwife lived so happily together, and understood one another so well, that all the husband did the wife thought so well done there was nothing like it in the world, and she was always glad whatever he turned his hand to. The farm was their own land, and they had a hundred dollars lying at the bottom of their chest, and two cows tethered up in a stall in their farm-yard.

So one day his wife said to Gudbrand:

'Do you know, dear, I think we ought to take one of our cows into town, and sell it; that's what I think; for then we shall have some money in hand, and such well-to-do people as we ought to have ready money like the rest of the world. As for the hundred dollars at the bottom of the chest yonder, we can't make a hole in them, and I'm sure I don't know what we want with more than one cow. Besides, we shall gain a little in another way, for then I shall get off with only looking after one cow, instead of having, as now, to feed and litter and water two.'

Well, Gudbrand thought his wife talked right good sense, so he set off at once with the cow on his way to town to sell her; but when he got to the town, there was no one who would buy his cow.

'Well! well! never mind', said Gudbrand, 'at the worst, I can only go back home again with my cow. I've both stable and tether for her, I should think, and the road is no farther out than in'; and with that he began to toddle home with his cow.

But when he had gone a bit of the way, a man met him who had a horse to sell, so Gudbrand thought 'twas better to have a horse than a cow, so he swopped with the man. A little farther on he met a man walking along and driving a fat pig before him, and he thought it better to have a fat pig than a horse, so he swopped with the man. After that he went a little farther, and a man met him with a goat; so he thought it better to have a goat than a pig, and he swopped with the man that owned the goat. Then he went on a good bit till he met a man who had a sheep, and he swopped with him too, for he thought it always better to have a sheep than a goat. After a while he met a man with a goose, and he swopped away the sheep for the goose; and when he had walked a long, long time, he met a man with a cock, and he swopped with him, for he thought in this wise, ''Tis surely better to have a cock than a goose.' Then he went on till the day was far spent, and he began to get very hungry, so he sold the cock for a shilling, and bought food with the money, for, thought Gudbrand on the Hill-side, ''Tis always better to save one's life than to have a cock.'

After that he went on home till he reached his nearest neighbour's house, where he turned in.

'Well', said the owner of the house, 'how did things go with you in town?'

'Rather so so', said Gudbrand, 'I can't praise my luck, nor do I blame it either', and with that he told the whole story from first to last.

'Ah!' said his friend, 'you'll get nicely called over the coals, that one can see, when you get home to your wife. Heaven help you, I wouldn't stand in your shoes for something.'

'Well!' said Gudbrand on the Hill-side, 'I think things might have gone much worse with me; but now, whether I have done wrong or not, I have so kind a good-wife, she never has a word to say against anything that I do.'

'Oh!' answered his neighbour, 'I hear what you say, but I don't believe it for all that.'

'Shall we lay a bet upon it?' asked Gudbrand on the Hill-side. 'I have a hundred dollars at the bottom of my chest at home; will you lay as many against them?'

Yes! the friend was ready to bet; so Gudbrand stayed there till evening, when it began to get dark, and then they went together to his house, and the neighbour was to stand outside the door and listen, while the man went in to see his wife.

'Good evening!' said Gudbrand on the Hill-side.

'Good evening!' said the goodwife. 'Oh! is that you? now God be praised.'

Yes! it was he. So the wife asked how things had gone with him in town?

'Oh! only so so', answered Gudbrand; 'not much to brag of. When I got to the town there was no one who would buy the cow, so you must know I swopped it away for a horse.'

'For a horse', said his wife; 'well that is good of you; thanks with all my heart. We are so well to do that we may drive to church, just as well as other people; and if we choose to keep a horse we have a right to get one, I should think. So run out, child, and put up the horse.'

'Ah!' said Gudbrand, 'but you see I've not got the horse after all; for when I got a bit farther on the road, I swopped it away for a pig.'

'Think of that, now!' said the wife; 'you did just as I should have done myself; a thousand thanks! Now I can have a bit of bacon in the house to set before people when they come to see me, that I can. What do we want with a horse? People would only say we had got so proud that we couldn't walk to church. Go out, child, and put up the pig in the sty.'

'But I've not got the pig either', said Gudbrand; 'for when I got a little farther on, I swopped it away for a milch goat.'

'Bless us!' cried his wife, 'how well you manage everything! Now I think it over, what should I do with a pig? People would only point at us and say, "Yonder they eat up all they have got." No! now I have got a goat, and I shall have milk and cheese, and keep the goat too. Run out, child, and put up the goat.'

'Nay, but I haven't got the goat either', said Gudbrand, 'for a little farther on I swopped it away, and got a fine sheep instead.'

'You don't say so!' cried his wife; 'why, you do everything to please me, just as if I had been with you; what do we want with a goat? If I had it I should lose half my time in climbing up the hills to get it down. No! if I have a sheep, I shall have both wool and clothing, and fresh meat in the house. Run out, child, and put up the sheep.'

'But I haven't got the sheep any more than the rest', said Gudbrand; 'for when I had gone a bit farther, I swopped it away for a goose.'

'Thank you! thank you! with all my heart', cried his wife; 'what should I do with a sheep? I have no spinning-wheel, nor carding-comb, nor should I care to worry myself with cutting, and shaping, and sewing clothes. We can buy clothes now, as we have always done; and now I shall have roast goose, which I have longed for so often; and, besides, down to stuff my little pillow with. Run out, child, and put up the goose.'

'Ah!' said Gudbrand, 'but I haven't the goose either; for when I had gone a bit farther I swopped it away for a cock.'

'Dear me!' cried his wife, 'how you think of everything! just as I should have done myself. A cock! think of that! why it's as good as an eight-day clock, for every morning the cock crows at four o'clock, and we shall be able to stir our stumps in good time. What should we do with a goose? I don't know how to cook it; and as for my pillow, I can stuff it with cotton-grass. Run out, child, and put up the cock.'

'But, after all, I haven't got the cock', said Gudbrand; 'for when I had gone a bit farther, I got as hungry as a hunter, so I was forced to sell the cock for a shilling, for fear I should starve.'

'Now, God be praised that you did so!' cried his wife; 'whatever you do, you do it always just after my own heart. What should we do with the cock? We are our own masters, I should think, and can lie a-bed in the morning as long as we like. Heaven be thanked that I have got you safe back again; you who do everything so well that I want neither cock nor goose; neither pigs nor kine.'

Then Gudbrand opened the door and said; 'Well, what do you say now? Have I won the hundred dollars?' and his neighbour was forced to allow that he had.

THE BLUE BELT

Once on a time there was an old beggar-woman, who had gone out to beg. She had a little lad with her, and when she had got her bag full, she struck across the hills towards her own home. So when they had gone a bit up the hill-side, they came upon a little blue belt, which lay where two paths met, and the lad asked his mother's leave to pick it up.

'No', said she, 'maybe there's witchcraft in it'; and so with threats she forced him to follow her. But when they had gone a bit further, the lad said he must turn aside a moment out of the road, and meanwhile his mother sat down on a tree-stump. But the lad was a long time gone, for as soon as he got so far into the wood, that the old dame could not see him, he ran off to where the belt lay, took it up, tied it round his waist, and lo! he felt as strong as if he could lift the whole hill. When he got back, the old dame was in a great rage, and wanted to know what he had been doing all that while. You don't care how much time you waste, and yet you know the night is drawing on, and we must cross the hill before it is dark!' So on they tramped; but when they had got about half-way, the old dame grew weary, and said she must rest under a bush.

'Dear mother', said the lad, 'mayn't I just go up to the top of this high crag while you rest, and try if I can't see some sign of folk hereabouts?'

Yes! he might do that; so when he had got to the top, he saw a light shining from the north. So he ran down and told his mother.

'We must get on, mother; we are near a house, for I see a bright light shining quite close to us in the north.' Then she rose and shouldered her bag, and set off to see; but they hadn't gone far, before there stood a steep spur of the hill, right across their path.

'Just as I thought!' said the old dame; 'now we can't go a step farther; a pretty bed we shall have here!'

But the lad took the bag under one arm, and his mother under the other, and ran straight up the steep crag with them.

'Now, don't you see! don't you see that we are close to a house! don't you see the bright light?'

But the old dame said those were no Christian folk, but Trolls, for she was at home in all that forest far and near, and knew there was not a living soul in it, until you were well over the ridge, and had come down on the other side. But they went on, and in a little while they came to a great house which was all painted red.

'What's the good?' said the old dame, 'we daren't go in, for here the Trolls live.'

'Don't say so; we must go in. There must be men where the lights shine so', said the lad. So in he went, and his mother after him, but he had scarce opened the door before she swooned away, for there she saw a great stout man, at least twenty feet high, sitting on the bench.

'Good evening, grandfather!' said the lad.

'Well, here I've sat three hundred years', said the man who sat on the bench, 'and no one has ever come and called me grandfather before.' Then the lad sat down by the man's side, and began to talk to him as if they had been old friends.

'But what's come over your mother?' said the man, after they had chattered a while. 'I think she swooned away; you had better look after her.'

So the lad went and took hold of the old dame; and dragged her up the hall along the floor. That brought her to herself, and she kicked, and scratched, and flung herself about, and at last sat down upon a heap of firewood in the corner; but she was so frightened that she scarce dared to look one in the face.

After a while, the lad asked if they could spend the night there.

'Yes, to be sure', said the man.

So they went on talking again, but the lad soon got hungry, and wanted to know if they could get food as well as lodging.

'Of course', said the man, 'that might be got too.' And after he had sat a while longer, he rose up and threw six loads of dry pitch-pine on the fire. This made the old hag still more afraid.

'Oh! now he's going to roast us alive', she said, in the corner where she sat.

And when the wood had burned down to glowing embers, up got the man and strode out of his house.

'Heaven bless and help us! what a stout heart you have got', said the old dame; 'don't you see we have got amongst Trolls?'

'Stuff and nonsense!' said the lad; 'no harm if we have.'

In a little while back came the man with an ox so fat and big, the lad had never seen its like, and he gave it one blow with his fist under the ear, and down it fell dead on the floor. When that was done, he took it up by all the four legs, and laid it on the glowing embers, and turned it and twisted it about till it was burnt brown outside. After that, he went to a cupboard and took out a great silver dish, and laid the ox on it; and the dish was so big that none of the ox hung over on any side. This he put on the table, and then he went down into the cellar, and fetched a cask of wine, knocked out the head, and put the cask on the table, together with two knives, which were each six feet long. When this was done, he bade them go and sit down to supper and eat. So they went, the lad first and the old dame after, but she began to whimper and wail, and to wonder how she should ever use such knives. But her son seized one, and began to cut slices out of the thigh of the ox, which he placed before his mother. And when they had eaten a bit, he took up the cask with both hands, and lifted it down to the floor; then he told his mother to come and drink, but it was still so high she couldn't reach up to it; so he caught her up, and held her up to the edge of the cask while she drank; as for himself, he clambered up and hung down like a cat inside the cask while he drank. So when he had quenched his thirst, he took up the cask and put it back on the table, and thanked the man for the good meal, and told his mother to come and thank him too, and a-feared though she was, she dared do nothing else but thank the man. Then the lad sat down again alongside the man and began to gossip, and after they had sat a while, the man said,

'Well! I must just go and get a bit of supper too'; and so he went to the table and ate up the whole ox--hoofs, and horns, and all--and drained the cask to the last drop, and then went back and sat on the bench.

As for beds', he said, 'I don't know what's to be done. I've only got one bed and a cradle; but we could get on pretty well if you would sleep in the cradle, and then your mother might lie in the bed yonder.'

'Thank you kindly, that'll do nicely', said the lad; and with that he pulled off his clothes and lay down in the cradle; but, to tell you the truth; it was quite as big as a four-poster. As for the old dame, she had to follow the man who showed her to bed, though she was out of her wits for fear.

'Well!' thought the lad to himself, ''twill never do to go to sleep yet. I'd best lie awake and listen how things go as the night wears on.'

So after a while the man began to talk to the old dame, and at last he said:

'We two might live here so happily together, could we only be rid of this son of yours.'

'But do you know how to settle him? Is that what you're thinking of?' said she.

'Nothing easier', said he; at any rate he would try. He would just say he wished the old dame would stay and keep house for him a day or two, and then he would take the lad out with him up the hill to quarry corner-stones, and roll down a great rock on him. All this the lad lay and listened to.

Next day the Troll--for it was a Troll as clear as day--asked if the old dame would stay and keep house for him a few days; and as the day went on he took a great iron crowbar, and asked the lad if he had a mind to go with him up the hill and quarry a few corner-stones. With all his heart, he said, and went with him; and so, after they had split a few stones, the Troll wanted him to go down below and look after cracks in the rock; and while he was doing this, the Troll worked away, and wearied himself with his crowbar till he moved a whole crag out of its bed, which came rolling right down on the place where the lad was; but he held it up till he could get on one side, and then let it roll on.

'Oh!' said the lad to the Troll, 'now I see what you mean to do with me. You want to crush me to death; so just go down yourself and look after the cracks and refts in the rock, and I'll stand up above.'

The Troll did not dare to do otherwise than the lad bade him, and the end of it was that the lad rolled down a great rock, which fell upon the Troll, and broke one of his thighs.

'Well! you are in a sad plight', said the lad, as he strode down, lifted up the rock, and set the man free. After that he had to put him on his back and carry him home; so he ran with him as fast as a horse, and shook him so that the Troll screamed and screeched as if a knife were run into him. And when he got home, they had to put the Troll to bed, and there he lay in a sad pickle.

When the night wore on the Troll began to talk to the old dame again, and to wonder how ever they could be rid of the lad.

'Well', said the old dame, 'if you can't hit on a plan to get rid of him, I'm sure I can't.'

'Let me see', said the Troll; 'I've got twelve lions in a garden; if they could only get hold of the lad they'd soon tear him to pieces.'

So the old dame said it would be easy enough to get him there. She would sham sick, and say she felt so poorly, nothing would do her any good but lion's milk. All that the lad lay and listened to; and when he got up in the morning his mother said she was worse than she looked, and she thought she should never be right again unless she could get some lion's milk.

'Then I'm afraid you'll be poorly a long time, mother', said the lad, 'for I'm sure I don't know where any is to be got.'

'Oh! if that be all', said the Troll, 'there's no lack of lion's milk, if we only had the man to fetch it'; and then he went on to say how his brother had a garden with twelve lions in it, and how the lad might have the key if he had a mind to milk the lions. So the lad took the key and a milking pail, and strode off; and when he unlocked the gate and got into the garden, there stood all the twelve lions on their hind-paws, rampant and roaring at him. But the lad laid hold of the biggest, and led him about by the fore-paws, and dashed him against stocks and stones, till there wasn't a bit of him left but the two paws. So when the rest saw that, they were so afraid that they crept up and lay at his feet like so many curs. After that they followed him about wherever he went, and when he got home, they lay down outside the house, with their fore-paws on the door sill.

'Now, mother, you'll soon be well', said the lad, when he went in, 'for here is the lion's milk.'

He had just milked a drop in the pail.

But the Troll, as he lay in bed, swore it was all a lie. He was sure the lad was not the man to milk lions.

When the lad heard that, he forced the Troll to get out of bed, threw open the door, and all the lions rose up and seized the Troll, and at last the lad had to make them leave their hold.

That night the Troll began to talk to the old dame again.

'I'm sure I can't tell how to put this lad out of the way--he is so awfully strong; can't you think of some way?

'No,' said the old dame, 'if you can't tell, I'm sure I can't.'

'Well!' said the Troll, 'I have two brothers in a castle; they are twelve times as strong as I am, and that's why I was turned out and had to put up with this farm. They hold that castle, and round it there is an orchard with apples in it, and who-ever eats those apples sleeps for three days and three nights. If we could only get the lad to go for the fruit, he wouldn't be able to keep from tasting the apples, and as soon as ever he fell asleep my brothers would tear him in pieces.'

The old dame said she would sham sick, and say she could never be herself again unless she tasted those apples; for she had set her heart on them.

All this the lad lay and listened to.

When the morning came the old dame was so poorly that she couldn't utter a word but groans and sighs. She was sure she should never be well again, unless she had some of those apples that grew in the orchard near the castle where the man's brothers lived; only she had no one to send for them.

Oh! the lad was ready to go that instant; but the eleven lions went with him. So when he came to the orchard, he climbed up into the apple tree and ate as many apples as he could, and he had scarce got down before he fell into a deep sleep; but the lions all lay round him in a ring. The third day came the Troll's brothers, but they did not come in man's shape. They came snorting like man-eating steeds, and wondered who it was that dared to be there, and said they would tear him to pieces, so small that there should not be a bit of him left. But up rose the lions and tore the Trolls into small pieces, so that the place looked as if a dung heap had been tossed about it; and when they had finished the Trolls they lay down again. The lad did not wake till late in the afternoon, and when he got on his knees and rubbed the sleep out of his eyes, he began to wonder what had been going on, when he saw the marks of hoofs. But when he went towards the castle, a maiden looked out of a window who had seen all that had happened, and she said:

'You may thank your stars you weren't in that tussle, else you must have lost your life.'

'What! I lose my life! No fear of that, I think,' said the lad.

So she begged him to come in, that she might talk with him, for she hadn't seen a Christian soul ever since she came there. But when she opened the door the lions wanted to go in too, but she got so frightened that she began to scream, and so the lad let them lie outside. Then the two talked and talked, and the lad asked how it came that she, who was so lovely, could put up with those ugly Trolls. She never wished it, she said; 'twas quite against her will. They had seized her by force, and she was the King of Arabia's daughter. So they talked on, and at last she asked him what he would do; whether she should go back home, or whether he would have her to wife. Of course he would have her, and she shouldn't go home.

After that they went round the castle, and at last they came to a great hall, where the Trolls' two great swords hung high up on the wall.

'I wonder if you are man enough to wield one of these,' said the Princess.

'Who?--I?' said the lad. ''Twould be a pretty thing if I couldn't wield one of these.'

With that he put two or three chairs one a-top of the other, jumped up, and touched the biggest sword with his finger tips, tossed it up in the air, and caught it again by the hilt; leapt down, and at the same time dealt such a blow with it on the floor that the whole hall shook. After he had thus got down, he thrust the sword under his arm and carried it about with him.

So, when they had lived a little while in the castle, the Princess thought she ought to go home to her parents, and let them know what had become of her; so they loaded a ship, and she set sail from the castle.

After she had gone, and the lad had wandered about a little, he called to mind that he had been sent on an errand thither, and had come to fetch something for his mother's health; and though he said to himself, 'After all, the old dame was not so bad but she's all right by this time'--still he thought he ought to go and just see how she was. So he went and found both the man and his mother quite fresh and hearty.

'What wretches you are to live in this beggarly hut', said the lad. 'Come with me up to my castle, and you shall see what a fine fellow I am.'

Well! they were both ready to go, and on the way his mother talked to him, and asked, 'How it was he had got so strong?'

'If you must know, it came of that blue belt which lay on the hill- side that time when you and I were out begging', said the lad.

'Have you got it still?' asked she.

'Yes'--he had. It was tied round his waist.

'Might she see it?'

'Yes, she might'; and with that he pulled open his waistcoat and shirt to show it her.

Then she seized it with both hands, tore it off, and twisted it round her fist.

'Now', she cried, 'what shall I do with such a wretch as you? I'll just give you one blow, and dash your brains out!'

'Far too good a death for such a scamp', said the Troll. 'No! let's first burn out his eyes, and then turn him adrift in a little boat.'

So they burned out his eyes and turned him adrift, in spite of his prayers and tears; but, as the boat drifted, the lions swam after, and at last they laid hold of it and dragged it ashore on an island, and placed the lad under a fir tree. They caught game for him, and they plucked the birds and made him a bed of down; but he was forced to eat his meat raw, and he was blind. At last, one day the biggest lion was chasing a hare which was blind, for it ran straight over stock and stone, and the end was, it ran right up against a fir-stump and tumbled head over heels across the field right into a spring; but lo! when it came out of the spring it saw its way quite plain, and so saved its life.

'So, so!' thought the lion, and went and dragged the lad to the spring, and dipped him over head and ears in it. So, when he had got his sight again, he went down to the shore and made signs to the lions that they should all lie close together like a raft; then he stood upon their backs while they swam with him to the mainland. When he had reached the shore he went up into a birchen copse, and made the lions lie quiet. Then he stole up to the castle, like a thief, to see if he couldn't lay hands on his belt; and when he got to the door, he peeped through the keyhole, and there he saw his belt hanging up over a door in the kitchen. So he crept softly in across the floor, for there was no one there; but as soon as he had got hold of the belt, he began to kick and stamp about as though he were mad. Just then his mother came rushing out.

'Dear heart, my darling little boy! do give me the belt again', she said.

'Thank you kindly', said he. 'Now you shall have the doom you passed on me', and he fulfilled it on the spot. When the old Troll heard that, he came in and begged and prayed so prettily that he might not be smitten to death.

'Well, you may live', said the lad, 'but you shall undergo the same punishment you gave me'; and so he burned out the Troll's eyes, and turned him adrift on the sea in a little boat, but he had no lions to follow him.

Now the lad was all alone, and he went about longing and longing for the Princess; at last he could bear it no longer; he must set out to seek her, his heart was so bent on having her. So he loaded four ships and set sail for Arabia. For some time they had fair wind and fine weather, but after that they lay wind-bound under a rocky island. So the sailors went ashore and strolled about to spend the time, and there they found a huge egg, almost as big as a little house. So they began to knock it about with large stones, but, after all, they couldn't crack the shell. Then the lad came up with his sword to see what all the noise was about, and when he saw the egg, he thought it a trifle to crack it; so he gave it one blow and the egg split, and out came a chicken as big as an elephant.

'Now we have done wrong', said the lad; 'this can cost us all our lives'; and then he asked his sailors if they were men enough to sail to Arabia in four-and-twenty hours if they got a fine breeze. Yes! they were good to do that, they said, so they set sail with a fine breeze, and got to Arabia in three-and-twenty hours. As soon as they landed, the lad ordered all the sailors to go and bury themselves up to the eyes in a sandhill, so that they could barely see the ships. The lad and the captains climbed a high crag and sate down under a fir.

In a little while came a great bird flying with an island in its claws, and let it fall down on the fleet, and sunk every ship. After it had done that, it flew up to the sandhill and flapped its wings, so that the wind nearly took off the heads of the sailors, and it flew past the fir with such force that it turned the lad right about, but he was ready with his sword, and gave the bird one blow and brought it down dead.

After that he went to the town, where every one was glad because the king had got his daughter back; but now the king had hidden her away somewhere himself, and promised her hand as a reward to any one who could find her, and this though she was betrothed before. Now as the lad went along he met a man who had white bear-skins for sale, so he bought one of the hides and put it on; and one of the captains was to take an iron chain and lead him about, and so he went into the town and began to play pranks. At last the news came to the king's ears, that there never had been such fun in the town before, for here was a white bear that danced and cut capers just as it was bid. So a messenger came to say the bear must come to the castle at once, for the king wanted to see its tricks. So when it got to the castle every one was afraid, for such a beast they had never seen before; but the captain said there was no danger unless they laughed at it. They mustn't do that, else it would tear them to pieces. When the king heard that, he warned all the court not to laugh. But while the fun was going on, in came one of the king's maids, and began to laugh and make game of the bear, and the bear flew at her and tore her, so that there was scarce a rag of her left. Then all the court began to bewail, and the captain most of all.

'Stuff and nonsense', said the king; 'she's only a maid, besides it's more my affair than yours.'

When the show was over, it was late at night. 'It's no good your going away, when it's so late', said the king. 'The bear had best sleep here.'

'Perhaps it might sleep in the ingle by the kitchen fire', said the captain.

'Nay', said the king, 'it shall sleep up here, and it shall have pillows and cushions to sleep on.' So a whole heap of pillows and cushions was brought, and the captain had a bed in a side-room.

But at midnight the king came with a lamp in his hand and a big bunch of keys, and carried off the white bear. He passed along gallery after gallery, through doors and rooms, up-stairs and down-stairs, till at last he came to a pier which ran out into the sea. Then the king began to pull and haul at posts and pins, this one up and that one down, till at last a little house floated up to the water's edge. There he kept his daughter, for she was so dear to him that he had hid her, so that no one could find her out. He left the white bear outside while he went in and told her how it had danced and played its pranks. She said she was afraid, and dared not look at it; but he talked her over, saying there was no danger, if she only wouldn't laugh. So they brought the bear in, and locked the door, and it danced and played its tricks; but just when the fun was at its height, the Princess's maid began to laugh. Then the lad flew at her and tore her to bits, and the Princess began to cry and sob.

'Stuff and nonsense', cried the king; 'all this fuss about a maid! I'll get you just as good a one again. But now I think the bear had best stay here till morning, for I don't care to have to go and lead it along all those galleries and stairs at this time of night.'

'Well!' said the Princess, 'if it sleeps here, I'm sure I won't.'

But just then the bear curled himself up and lay down by the stove; and it was settled at last that the Princess should sleep there too, with a light burning. But as soon as the king was well gone, the white bear came and begged her to undo his collar. The Princess was so scared she almost swooned away; but she felt about till she found the collar, and she had scarce undone it before the bear pulled his head off. Then she knew him again, and was so glad there was no end to her joy, and she wanted to tell her father at once that her deliverer was come. But the lad would not hear of it; he would earn her once more, he said. So in the morning when they heard the king rattling at the posts outside, the lad drew on the hide, and lay down by the stove.

'Well, has it lain still?' the king asked.

'I should think so', said the Princess; 'it hasn't so much as turned or stretched itself once.'

When they got up to the castle again, the captain took the bear and led it away, and then the lad threw off the hide, and went to a tailor and ordered clothes fit for a prince; and when they were fitted on he went to the king, and said he wanted to find the Princess.

'You're not the first who has wished the same thing', said the king, 'but they have all lost their lives; for if any one who tries can't find her in four-and-twenty hours his life is forfeited.'

Yes; the lad knew all that. Still he wished to try, and if he couldn't find her, 'twas his look-out. Now in the castle there was a band that played sweet tunes, and there were fair maids to dance with, and so the lad danced away. When twelve hours were gone, the king said:

'I pity you with all my heart. You're so poor a hand at seeking; you will surely lose your life.'

'Stuff!' said the lad; 'while there's life there's hope! So long as there's breath in the body there's no fear; we have lots of time'; and so he went on dancing till there was only one hour left.

Then he said he would begin to search.

'It's no use now', said the king; 'time's up.'

'Light your lamp; out with your big bunch of keys', said the lad, 'and follow me whither I wish to go. There is still a whole hour left.'

So the lad went the same way which the king had led him the night before, and he bade the king unlock door after door till they came down to the pier which ran out into the sea.

'It's all no use, I tell you', said the king; 'time's up, and this will only lead you right out into the sea.'

'Still five minutes more', said the lad, as he pulled and pushed at the posts and pins, and the house floated up.

'Now the time is up', bawled the king; 'come hither, headsman, and take off his head.'

'Nay, nay!' said the lad; 'stop a bit, there are still three minutes! Out with the key, and let me get into this house.'

But there stood the king and fumbled with his keys, to draw out the time. At last he said he hadn't any key.

'Well, if you haven't, I *have*', said the lad, as he gave the door such a kick that it flew to splinters inwards on the floor.

At the door the Princess met him, and told her father this was her deliverer, on whom her heart was set. So she had him; and this was how the beggar boy came to marry the king's daughter of Arabia.

WHY THE BEAR IS STUMPY-TAILED

One day the Bear met the Fox, who came slinking along with a string of fish he had stolen.

'Whence did you get those from?' asked the Bear.

'Oh! my Lord Bruin, I've been out fishing and caught them', said the Fox.

So the Bear had a mind to learn to fish too, and bade the Fox tell him how he was to set about it.

'Oh! it's an easy craft for you', answered the Fox, 'and soon learnt. You've only got to go upon the ice, and cut a hole and stick your tail down into it; and so you must go on holding it there as long as you can. You're not to mind if your tail smarts a little; that's when the fish bite. The longer you hold it there the more fish you'll get; and then all at once out with it, with a cross pull sideways, and with a strong pull too.'

Yes; the Bear did as the Fox had said, and held his tail a long, long time down in the hole, till it was fast frozen in. Then he pulled it out with a cross pull, and it snapped short off. That's why Bruin goes about with a stumpy tail this very day.

NOT A PIN TO CHOOSE BETWEEN THEM

Once on a time there was a man, and he had a wife. Now this couple wanted to sow their fields, but they had neither seed-corn nor money to buy it with. But they had a cow, and the man was to drive it into town and sell it, to get money to buy corn for seed. But when it came to the pinch, the wife dared not let her husband start for fear he should spend the money in drink, so she set off herself with the cow, and took besides a hen with her.

Close by the town she met a butcher, who asked:

'Will you sell that cow, Goody?'

'Yes, that I will', she answered.

'Well, what do you want for her?'

'Oh! I must have five shillings for the cow, but you shall have the hen for ten pounds.'

'Very good!' said the man; 'I don't want the hen, and you'll soon get it off your hands in the town, but I'll give you five shillings for the cow.'

Well, she sold her cow for five shillings, but there was no one in the town who would give ten pounds for a lean tough old hen, so she went back to the butcher, and said:

'Do all I can, I can't get rid of this hen, master! you must take it too, as you took the cow.'

'Well', said the butcher, 'come along and we'll see about it.' Then he treated her both with meat and drink, and gave her so much brandy that she lost her head, and didn't know what she was about, and fell fast asleep. But while she slept, the butcher took and dipped her into a tar-barrel, and then laid her down on a heap of feathers; and when she woke up, she was feathered all over, and began to wonder what had befallen her.

'Is it me, or is it not me? No, it can never be me; it must be some great strange bird. But what shall I do to find out whether it is me or not. Oh! I know how I shall be able to tell whether it is me; if the calves come and lick me, and our dog Tray doesn't bark at me when I get home, then it must be me, and no one else.'

Now, Tray, her dog, had scarce set his eyes on the strange monster which came through the gate, than he set up such a barking, one would have thought all the rogues and robbers in the world were in the yard.

'Ah, deary me', said she, 'I thought so; it can't be me surely.' So she went to the straw-yard, and the calves wouldn't lick her, when they snuffed in the strong smell of tar. 'No, no!' she said, 'it can't be me; it must be some strange outlandish bird.'

So she crept up on the roof of the safe and began to flap her arms, as if they had been wings, and was just going to fly off.

When her husband saw all this, out he came with his rifle, and began to take aim at her.

'Oh!' cried his wife, 'don't shoot, don't shoot! it is only me.'

'If it's you', said her husband, 'don't stand up there like a goat on a house-top, but come down and let me hear what you have to say for yourself.'

So she crawled down again, but she hadn't a shilling to shew, for the crown she had got from the butcher she had thrown away in her drunkenness. When her husband heard her story, he said, 'You're only twice as silly as you were before', and he got so angry that he made up his mind to go away from her altogether, and never to come back till he had found three other Goodies as silly as his own.

So he toddled off, and when he had walked a little way he saw a Goody, who was running in and out of a newly-built wooden cottage with an empty sieve, and every time she ran in, she threw her apron over the sieve just as if she had something in it, and when she got in she turned it upside down on the floor.

'Why, Goody!' he asked, 'what are you doing?'

'Oh', she answered, 'I'm only carrying in a little sun; but I don't know how it is, when I'm outside, I have the sun in my sieve, but when I get inside, somehow or other I've thrown it away. But in my old cottage I had plenty of sun, though I never carried in the least bit. I only wish I knew some one who would bring the sun inside; I'd give him three hundred dollars and welcome.'

'Have you got an axe?' asked the man. 'If you have, I'll soon bring the sun inside.'

So he got an axe and cut windows in the cottage, for the carpenters had forgotten them; then the sun shone in, and he got his three hundred dollars.

'That was one of them', said the man to himself, as he went on his way.

After a while he passed by a house, out of which came an awful screaming and bellowing; so he turned in and saw a Goody, who was hard at work banging her husband across the head with a beetle, and over his head she had drawn a shirt without any slit for the neck.

'Why, Goody!' he asked, 'will you beat your husband to death?'

'No', she said, 'I only must have a hole in this shirt for his neck to come through.'

All the while the husband kept on screaming and calling out:

'Heaven help and comfort all who try on new shirts. If anyone would teach my Goody another way of making a slit for the neck in my new shirts, I'd give him three hundred dollars down and welcome.'

'I'll do it in the twinkling of an eye', said the man, 'if you'll only give me a pair of scissors.'

So he got a pair of scissors, and snipped a hole in the neck, and went off with his three hundred dollars.

'That was another of them', he said to himself, as he walked along.

Last of all, he came to a farm, where he made up his mind to rest a bit. So when he went in, the mistress asked him:

'Whence do you come, master?'

'Oh!' said he, 'I come from Paradise Place', for that was the name of his farm.

'From Paradise Place!' she cried, 'you don't say so! Why, then, you must know my second husband Peter, who is dead and gone, God rest his soul.'

For you must know this Goody had been married three times, and as her first and last husbands had been bad, she had made up her mind that the second only was gone to heaven.

'Oh yes', said the man; 'I know him very well.'

'Well', asked the Goody, 'how do things go with him, poor dear soul?'

'Only middling', was the answer; 'he goes about begging from house to house, and has neither food nor a rag to his back. As for money, he hasn't a sixpence to bless himself with.'

'Mercy on me', cried out the Goody; 'he never ought to go about such a figure when he left so much behind him. Why, there's a whole cupboard full of old clothes up-stairs which belonged to him, besides a great chest full of money yonder. Now, if you will take them with you, you shall have a horse and cart to carry them. As for the horse, he can keep it, and sit on the cart, and drive about from house to house, and then he needn't trudge on foot.'

So the man got a whole cart-load of clothes, and a chest full of shining dollars, and as much meat and drink as he would; and when he had got all he wanted, he jumped into the cart and drove off.

'That was the third', he said to himself, as he went along. Now this Goody's third husband was a little way off in a field ploughing, and when he saw a strange man driving off from the farm with his horse and cart, he went home and asked his wife who that was that had just started with the black horse.

'Oh, do you mean him?' said the Goody; 'why, that was a man from Paradise, who said that Peter, my dear second husband, who is dead and gone, is in a sad plight, and that he goes from house to house begging, and has neither clothes nor money; so I just sent him all those old clothes he left behind him, and the old money box with the dollars in it.' The man saw how the land lay in a trice, so he saddled his horse and rode off from the farm at full gallop. It wasn't long before he was close behind the man who sat and drove the cart; but when the latter saw this he drove the cart into a thicket by the side of the road, pulled out a handful of hair from the horse's tail, jumped up on a little rise in the wood, where he tied the hair fast to a birch, and then lay down under it, and began to peer and stare up at the sky.

'Well, well, if I ever!' he said, as Peter the third came riding up. 'No! I never saw the like of this in all my born days!'

Then Peter stood and looked at him for some time, wondering what had come over him; but at last he asked:

'What do you lie there staring at?'

'No', kept on the man, 'I never did see anything like it!--here is a man going straight up to heaven on a black horse, and here you see his horse's tail still hanging in this birch; and yonder up in the sky you see the black horse.'

Peter looked first at the man, and then at the sky, and said:

'I see nothing but the horse hair in the birch; that's all I see!'

'Of course you can't where you stand', said the man; 'but just come and lie down here, and stare straight up, and mind you don't take your eyes off the sky; and then you shall see what you shall see.'

But while Peter the third lay and stared up at the sky till his eyes filled with tears, the man from Paradise Place took his horse and jumped on its back and rode off both with it and the cart and horse.

When the hoofs thundered along the road, Peter the third jumped up; but he was so taken aback when he found the man had gone off with his horse that he hadn't the sense to run after him till it was too late.

He was rather down in the mouth when he got home to his Goody; but when she asked him what he had done with the horse, he said,

'I gave it to the man too for Peter the second, for I thought it wasn't right he should sit in a cart, and scramble about from house to house; so now he can sell the cart and buy himself a coach to drive about in.'

'Thank you heartily!' said his wife; 'I never thought you could be so kind.'

Well, when the man reached home, who had got the six hundred dollars and the cart-load of clothes and money, he saw that all his fields were ploughed and sown, and the first thing he asked his wife was, where she had got the seed-corn from.

'Oh', she said, 'I have always heard that what a man sows he shall reap, so I sowed the salt which our friends the north-country men laid up here with us, and if we only have rain I fancy it will come up nicely.'

'Silly you are', said her husband, 'and silly you will be so long as you live; but that is all one now, for the rest are not a bit wiser than you. There is not a pin to choose between you.'

ONE'S OWN CHILDREN ARE ALWAYS PRETTIEST

A sportsman went out once into a wood to shoot, and he met a Snipe.
'Dear friend', said the Snipe, 'don't shoot my children!'
'How shall I know your children?' asked the Sportsman; 'what are they like?'
'Oh!' said the Snipe, 'mine are the prettiest children in all the wood.'
'Very well', said the Sportsman, 'I'll not shoot them; don't be afraid.'
But for all that, when he came back, there he had a whole string of young snipes in his hand which he had shot.
'Oh, oh!' said the Snipe, 'why did you shoot my children after all?'
'What! these your children!' said the Sportsman; 'why, I shot the ugliest I could find, that I did!'
'Woe is me!' said the Snipe; 'don't you know that each one thinks his own children the prettiest in the world?'

THE THREE PRINCESSES OF WHITELAND

Once on a time there was a fisherman who lived close by a palace, and fished for the king's table. One day when he was out fishing he just caught nothing. Do what he would--however he tried with bait and angle--there was never a sprat on his hook. But when the day was far spent a head bobbed up out of the water, and said:

'If I may have what your wife bears under her girdle, you shall catch fish enough.'

So the man answered boldly, 'Yes'; for he did not know that his wife was going to have a child. After that, as was like enough, he caught plenty of fish of all kinds. But when he got home at night and told his story, how he had got all that fish, his wife fell a-weeping and moaning, and was beside herself for the promise which her husband had made, for she said, 'I bear a babe under my girdle.'

Well, the story soon spread, and came up to the castle; and when the king heard the woman's grief and its cause, he sent down to say he would take care of the child, and see if he couldn't save it.

So the months went on and on, and when her time came the fisher's wife had a boy; so the king took it at once, and brought it up as his own son, until the lad grew up. Then he begged leave one day to go out fishing with his father; he had such a mind to go, he said. At first the king wouldn't hear of it, but at last the lad had his way, and went. So he and his father were out the whole day, and all went right and well till they landed at night. Then the lad remembered he had left his handkerchief, and went to look for it; but as soon as ever he got into the boat, it began to move off with him at such speed that the water roared under the bow, and all the lad could do in rowing against it with the oars was no use; so he went and went the whole night, and at last he came to a white strand, far far away.

There he went ashore, and when he had walked about a bit, an old, old man met him, with a long white beard.

'What's the name of this land?' asked the lad.

'Whiteland', said the man, who went on to ask the lad whence he came, and what he was going to do. So the lad told him all.

'Aye, aye!' said the man; 'now when you have walked a little farther along the strand here, you'll come to three Princesses, whom you will see standing in the earth up to their necks, with only their heads out. Then the first--she is the eldest--will call out and beg you so prettily to come and help her; and the second will do the same; to neither of these shall you go; make haste past them, as if you neither saw nor heard anything. But the third you shall go to, and do what she asks. If you do this, you'll have good luck--that's all.'

When the lad came to the first Princess, she called out to him, and begged him so prettily to come to her, but he passed on as though he saw her not. In the same way he passed by the second; but to the third he went straight up.

'If you'll do what I bid you', she said, 'you may have which of us you please.'

'Yes'; he was willing enough; so she told him how three Trolls had set them down in the earth there; but before they had lived in the castle up among the trees.

'Now', she said, 'you must go into that castle, and let the Trolls whip you each one night for each of us. If you can bear that, you'll set us free.'

Well, the lad said he was ready to try.

'When you go in', the Princess went on to say, 'you'll see two lions standing at the gate; but if you'll only go right in the middle between them they'll do you no harm. Then go straight on into a little dark room, and make your bed. Then the Troll will come to whip you; but if you take the flask which hangs on the wall, and rub yourself with the ointment that's in it, wherever his lash falls, you'll be as sound as ever. Then grasp the sword that hangs by the side of the flask and strike the Troll dead.'

Yes, he did as the Princess told him; he passed in the midst between the lions, as if he hadn't seen them, and went straight into the little room, and there he lay down to sleep. The first night there came a Troll with three heads and three rods, and whipped the lad soundly; but he stood it till the Troll was done; then he took the flask and rubbed himself, and grasped the sword and slew the Troll.

So, when he went out next morning, the Princesses stood out of the earth up to their waists.

The next night 'twas the same story over again, only this time the Troll had six heads and six rods, and he whipped him far worse than the first; but when he went out next morning, the Princesses stood out of the earth as far as the knee. The third night there came a Troll that had nine heads and nine rods, and he whipped and flogged the lad so long that he fainted away; then the Troll took him up and dashed him against the wall; but the shock brought down the flask, which fell on the lad, burst, and spilled the ointment all over him, and so he became as strong and sound as ever again. Then he wasn't slow; he grasped the sword and slew the Troll; and next morning when he went out of the castle the Princesses stood before him with all their bodies out of the earth. So he took the youngest for his Queen, and lived well and happily with her for some time.

At last he began to long to go home for a little to see his parents. His Queen did not like this; but at last his heart was so set on it, and he longed and longed so much, there was no holding him back, so she said,

'One thing you must promise me. This--Only to do what your father begs you to do, and not what your mother wishes'; and that he promised.

Then she gave him a ring, which was of that kind that any one who wore it might wish two wishes. So he wished himself home, and when he got home his parents could not wonder enough what a grand man their son had become.

Now, when he had been at home some days, his mother wished him to go up to the palace and show the king what a fine fellow he had come to be. But his father said:

'No! don't let him do that; if he does, we shan't have any more joy of him this time.'

But it was no good, the mother begged and prayed so long, that at last he went. So when he got up to the palace, he was far braver, both in clothes and array, than the other king, who didn't quite like this, and at last he said:

'All very fine; but here you can see my queen, what like she is, but I can't see yours, that I can't. Do you know, I scarce think she's so good-looking as mine.'

'Would to Heaven', said the young king, 'she were standing here, then you'd see what she was like.' And that instant there she stood before them.

But she was very woeful, and said to him:

'Why did you not mind what I told you; and why did you not listen to what your father said? Now, I must away home, and as for you, you have had both your wishes.'

With that she knitted a ring among his hair with her name on it, and wished herself home, and was off.

Then the young king was cut to the heart, and went, day out day in, thinking and thinking how he should get back to his queen. 'I'll just try', he thought, 'if I can't learn where Whiteland lies'; and so he went out into the world to ask. So when he had gone a good way, he came to a high hill, and there he met one who was lord over all the beasts of the wood, for they all came home to him when he blew his horn; so the king asked if he knew where Whiteland was?

'No, I don't', said he, 'but I'll ask my beasts.' Then he blew his horn and called them, and asked if any of them knew where Whiteland lay? but there was no beast that knew.

So the man gave him a pair of snow-shoes.

'When you get on these', he said, 'you'll come to my brother, who lives hundreds of miles off; he is lord over all the birds of the air. Ask him. When you reach his house, just turn the shoes, so that the toes point this way, and they'll come home of themselves.' So when the king reached the house, he turned the shoes as the lord of the beasts had said, and away they went home of themselves.

So he asked again after Whiteland, and the man called all the birds with a blast of his horn, and asked if any of them knew where Whiteland lay; but none of the birds knew. Now, long, long after the rest of the birds, came an old eagle, which had been away ten round years, but he couldn't tell any more than the rest.

'Well! well!' said the man, 'I'll lend you a pair of snow-shoes, and when you get them on, they'll carry you to my brother, who lives hundreds of miles off; he's lord of all the fish in the sea; you'd better ask him. But don't forget to turn the toes of the shoes this way.'

The king was full of thanks, got on the shoes, and when he came to the man who was lord over the fish of the sea, he turned the toes round, and so off they went home like the other pair. After that, he asked again after Whiteland.

So the man called the fish with a blast, but no fish could tell where it lay. At last came an old pike, which they had great work to call home, he was such a way off. So when they asked him he said:

'Know it! I should think I did. I've been cook there ten years, and to-morrow I'm going there again; for now, the queen of Whiteland, whose king is away, is going to wed another husband.'

'Well!' said the man, 'as this is so, I'll give you a bit of advice. Hereabouts, on a moor, stand three brothers, and here they have stood these hundred years, fighting about a hat, a cloak, and a pair of boots. If any one has these three things he can make himself invisible, and wish himself any where he pleases. You can tell them you wish to try the things, and after that, you'll pass judgment between them, whose they shall be.'

Yes! the king thanked the man, and went and did as he told him.

'What's all this?' he said to the brothers. 'Why do you stand here fighting for ever and a day? Just let me try these things, and I'll give judgment whose they shall be.'

They were very willing to do this; but as soon as he had got the hat, cloak, and boots, he said:

'When we meet next time, I'll tell you my judgment', and with these words he wished himself away.

So as he went along up in the air, he came up with the North Wind.

'Whither away?' roared the North Wind.

'To Whiteland', said the king; and then he told him all that had befallen him.

'Ah', said the North Wind, 'you go faster than I--you do; for you can go straight, while I have to puff and blow round every turn and corner. But when you get there, just place yourself on the stairs by the side of the door, and then I'll come storming in, as though I were going to blow down the whole castle. And then when the prince, who is to have your queen, comes out to see what's the matter, just you take him by the collar and pitch him out of doors; then I'll look after him, and see if I can't carry him off.'

Well--the king did as the North Wind said. He took his stand on the stairs, and when the North Wind came, storming and roaring, and took hold of the castle wall, so that it shook again, the prince came out to see what was the matter. But as soon as ever he came, the king caught him by the collar and pitched him out of doors, and then the North Wind caught him up and carried him off. So when there was an end of him, the king went into the castle, and at first his queen didn't know him, he was so wan and thin, through wandering so far and being so woeful; but when he shewed her the ring, she was as glad as glad could be; and so the rightful wedding was held, and the fame of it spread far and wide.

THE LASSIE AND HER GODMOTHER

Once on a time a poor couple lived far, far away in a great wood. The wife was brought to bed, and had a pretty girl, but they were so poor they did not know how to get the babe christened, for they had no money to pay the parson's fees. So one day the father went out to see if he could find any one who was willing to stand for the child and pay the fees; but though he walked about the whole day from one house to another, and though all said they were willing enough to stand, no one thought himself bound to pay the fees. Now, when he was going home again, a lovely lady met him, dressed so fine, and who looked so thoroughly good and kind; she offered to get the babe christened, but after that, she said, she must keep it for her own. The husband answered, he must first ask his wife what she wished to do; but when he got home and told his story, the wife said, right out, 'No!'

Next day the man went out again, but no one would stand if they had to pay the fees; and though he begged and prayed, he could get no help. And again as he went home, towards evening the same lovely lady met him, who looked so sweet and good, and she made him the same offer. So he told his wife again how he had fared, and this time she said, if he couldn't get any one to stand for his babe next day, they must just let the lady have her way, since she seemed so kind and good.

The third day, the man went about, but he couldn't get any one to stand; and so when, towards evening, he met the kind lady again, he gave his word she should have the babe if she would only get it christened at the font. So next morning she came to the place where the man lived, followed by two men to stand godfathers, took the babe and carried it to church, and there it was christened. After that she took it to her own house, and there the little girl lived with her several years, and her foster-mother was always kind and friendly to her.

Now, when the lassie had grown to be big enough to know right and wrong, her foster-mother got ready to go on a journey. 'You have my leave', she said, 'to go all over the house, except those rooms which I shew you'; and when she had said that, away she went.

But the lassie could not forbear just to open one of the doors a little bit, when--POP! out flew a Star.

When her foster-mother came back, she was very vexed to find that the star had flown out, and she got very angry with her foster-daughter, and threatened to send her away; but the child cried and begged so hard that she got leave to stay.

Now, after a while, the foster-mother had to go on another journey; and, before she went, she forbade the lassie to go into those two rooms into which she had never been. She promised to beware; but when she was left alone, she began to think and to wonder what there could be in the second room, and at last she could not help setting the door a little ajar, just to peep in, when--POP! out flew the Moon.

When her foster-mother came home and found the Moon let out, she was very downcast, and said to the lassie she must go away, she could not stay with her any longer. But the lassie wept so bitterly, and prayed so heartily for forgiveness, that this time, too, she got leave to stay.

Some time after, the foster-mother had to go away again, and she charged the lassie, who by this time was half grown up, most earnestly that she mustn't try to go into, or to peep into, the third room. But when her foster-mother had been gone some time, and the lassie was weary of walking about alone, all at once she thought, 'Dear me, what fun it would be just to peep a little into that third room.' Then she thought she mustn't do it for her foster-mother's sake; but when the bad thought came the second time she could hold out no longer; come what might, she must and would look into the room; so she just opened the door a tiny bit, when--POP! out flew the Sun.

But when her foster-mother came back and saw that the sun had flown away, she was cut to the heart, and said, 'Now, there was no help for it, the lassie must and should go away; she couldn't hear of her staying any longer.' Now the lassie cried her eyes out, and begged and prayed so prettily; but it was all no good.

'Nay! but I must punish you!' said her foster-mother; 'but you may have your choice, either to be the loveliest woman in the world, and not to be able to speak, or to keep your speech, and be the ugliest of all women; but away from me you must go.'

And the lassie said, 'I would sooner be lovely.' So she became all at once wondrous fair; but from that day forth she was dumb.

So, when she went away from her foster-mother, she walked and wandered through a great, great wood; but the farther she went, the farther off the end seemed to be. So, when the evening came on, she clomb up into a tall tree, which grew over a spring, and there she made herself up to sleep that night. Close by lay a castle, and from that castle came early every morning a maid to draw water to make the Prince's tea, from the spring over which the lassie was sitting. So the maid looked down into the spring, saw the lovely face in the water, and thought it was her own; then she flung away the pitcher, and ran home; and, when she got there, she tossed up her head and said, 'If I'm so pretty, I'm far too good to go and fetch water.'

So another maid had to go for the water, but the same thing happened to her; she went back and said she was far too pretty and too good to fetch water from the spring for the Prince. Then the Prince went himself, for he had a mind to see what all this could mean. So, when he reached the spring, he too saw the image in the water; but he looked up at once, and became aware of the lovely lassie who sate there up in the tree. Then he coaxed her down and took her home; and at last made up his mind to have her for his queen, because she was so lovely; but his mother, who was still alive, was against it.

'She can't speak', she said, 'and maybe she's a wicked witch.'

But the Prince could not be content till he got her. So after they had lived together a while, the lassie was to have a child, and when the child came to be born, the Prince set a strong watch round her; but at the birth one and all fell into a deep sleep, and her foster- mother came, cut the babe on its little finger, and smeared the queen's mouth with the blood; and said:

'Now you shall be as grieved as I was when you let out the star'; and with these words she carried off the babe.

But when those who were on the watch woke, they thought the queen had eaten her own child, and the old queen was all for burning her alive, but the Prince was so fond of her that at last he begged her off, but he had hard work to set her free.

So the next time the young queen was to have a child, twice as strong a watch was set as the first time, but the same thing happened over again, only this time her foster-mother said:

'Now you shall be as grieved as I was when you let the moon out.'

And the queen begged and prayed, and wept; for when her foster-mother was there, she could speak--but it was all no good.

And now the old queen said she must be burnt, but the Prince found means to beg her off. But when the third child was to be born, a watch was set three times as strong as the first, but just the same thing happened. Her foster-mother came while the watch slept, took the babe, and cut its little finger, and smeared the queen's mouth with the blood, telling her now she should be as grieved as she had been when the lassie let out the sun.

And now the Prince could not save her any longer. She must and should be burnt. But just as they were leading her to the stake, all at once they saw her foster-mother, who came with all three children--two she led by the hand, and the third she had on her arm; and so she went up to the young queen and said:

'Here are your children; now you shall have them again. I am the Virgin Mary, and so grieved as you have been, so grieved was I when you let out sun, and moon, and star. Now you have been punished for what you did, and henceforth you shall have your speech.'

How glad the Queen and Prince now were, all may easily think, but no one can tell. After that they were always happy; and from that day even the Prince's mother was very fond of the young queen.

THE THREE AUNTS

Once on a time there was a poor man who lived in a hut far away in the wood, and got his living by shooting. He had an only daughter who was very pretty, and as she had lost her mother when she was a child, and was now half grown up, she said she would go out into the world and earn her bread.

'Well, lassie!' said the father, 'true enough you have learnt nothing here but how to pluck birds and roast them, but still you may as well try to earn your bread.'

So the girl went off to seek a place, and when she had gone a little while, she came to a palace. There she stayed and got a place, and the queen liked her so well, that all the other maids got envious of her. So they made up their minds to tell the queen how the lassie said she was good to spin a pound of flax in four and twenty hours, for you must know the queen was a great housewife, and thought much of good work.

'Have you said this? then you shall do it', said the queen; 'but you may have a little longer time if you choose.'

Now, the poor lassie dared not say she had never spun in all her life, but she only begged for a room to herself. That she got, and the wheel and the flax were brought up to her. There she sat sad and weeping, and knew not how to help herself. She pulled the wheel this way and that, and twisted and turned it about, but she made a poor hand of it, for she had never even seen a spinning-wheel in her life.

But all at once, as she sat there, in came an old woman to her.

'What ails you, child?' she said.

'Ah!' said the lassie, with a deep sigh, 'it's no good to tell you, for you'll never be able to help me.'

'Who knows?' said the old wife. 'May be I know how to help you after all.'

Well, thought the lassie to herself, I may as well tell her, and so she told her how her fellow-servants had given out that she was good to spin a pound of flax in four and twenty hours.

'And here am I, wretch that I am, shut up to spin all that heap in a day and a night, when I have never even seen a spinning-wheel in all my born days.'

'Well, never mind, child', said the old woman. 'If you'll call me Aunt on the happiest day of your life, I'll spin this flax for you, and so you may just go away and lie down to sleep.'

Yes, the lassie was willing enough, and off she went and lay down to sleep.

Next morning when she awoke, there lay all the flax spun on the table, and that so clean and fine, no one had ever seen such even and pretty yarn. The queen was very glad to get such nice yarn, and she set greater store by the lassie than ever. But the rest were still more envious, and agreed to tell the queen how the lassie had said she was good to weave the yarn she had spun in four and twenty hours. So the queen said again, as she had said it she must do it; but if she couldn't quite finish it in four and twenty hours, she wouldn't be too hard upon her, she might have a little more time. This time, too, the lassie dared not say No, but begged for a room to herself, and then she would try. There she sat again, sobbing and crying, and not knowing which way to turn, when another old woman came in and asked:

'What ails you, child?'

At first the lassie wouldn't say, but at last she told her the whole story of her grief.

'Well, well!' said the old wife, 'never mind. If you'll call me Aunt on the happiest day of your life, I'll weave this yarn for you, and so you may just be off, and lie down to sleep.'

Yes, the lassie was willing enough; so she went away and lay down to sleep. When she awoke, there lay the piece of linen on the table, woven so neat and close, no woof could be better. So the lassie took the piece and ran down to the queen, who was very glad to get such beautiful linen, and set greater store than ever by the lassie. But as for the others, they grew still more bitter against her, and thought of nothing but how to find out something to tell about her.

At last they told the queen the lassie had said she was good to make up the piece of linen into shirts in four and twenty hours. Well, all happened as before; the lassie dared not say she couldn't sew; so she was shut up again in a room by herself, and there she sat in tears and grief. But then another old wife came, who said she would sew the shirts for her if she would call her Aunt on the happiest day of her life. The lassie was only too glad to do this, and then she did as the old wife told her, and went and lay down to sleep.

Next morning when she woke she found the piece of linen made up into shirts, which lay on the table--and such beautiful work no one had ever set eyes on; and more than that, the shirts were all marked and ready for wear. So, when the queen saw the work, she was so glad at the way in which it was sewn, that she clapped her hands, and said:

'Such sewing I never had, nor even saw in all my born days'; and after that she was as fond of the lassie as of her own children; and she said to her:

'Now, if you like to have the Prince for your husband, you shall have him; for you will never need to hire work-women. You can sew, and spin, and weave all yourself.'

So as the lassie was pretty, and the Prince was glad to have her, the wedding soon came on. But just as the Prince was going to sit down with the bride to the bridal feast, in came an ugly old hag with a long nose--I'm sure it was three ells long.

So up got the bride and made a curtsey, and said: 'Good-day, Auntie.'

' *That* Auntie to my bride?' said the Prince.

'Yes, she was!'

'Well, then, she'd better sit down with us to the feast', said the Prince; but, to tell you the truth, both he and the rest thought she was a loathsome woman to have next you.

But just then in came another ugly old hag. She had a back so humped and broad, she had hard work to get through the door. Up jumped the bride in a trice, and greeted her with 'Good-day, Auntie!'

And the Prince asked again if that were his bride's aunt. They both said Yes; so the Prince said, if that were so, she too had better sit down with them to the feast.

But they had scarce taken their seats before another ugly old hag came in, with eyes as large as saucers, and so red and bleared, 'twas gruesome to look at her. But up jumped the bride again, with her 'Good-day, Auntie', and her, too, the Prince asked to sit down; but I can't say he was very glad, for he thought to himself: 'Heaven shield me from such Aunties as my bride has!' So when he had sat awhile, he could not keep his thoughts to himself any longer, but asked,

'But how, in all the world, can my bride, who is such a lovely lassie, have such loathsome, misshapen Aunts?'

'I'll soon tell you how it is', said the first. 'I was just as good- looking when I was her age; but the reason why I've got this long nose is, because I was always kept sitting, and poking, and nodding over my spinning, and so my nose got stretched and stretched, until it got as long as you now see it.'

'And I', said the second, 'ever since I was young, I have sat and scuttled back-wards and forwards over my loom, and that's how my back has got so broad and humped as you now see it.'

'And I', said the third, 'ever since I was little, I have sat, and stared, and sewn, and sewn and stared, night and day; and that's why my eyes have got so ugly and red, and now there's no help for them.'

'So! so! 'said the Prince, ''twas lucky I came to know this; for if folk can get so ugly and loathsome by all this, then my bride shall neither spin, nor weave, nor sew all her life long.'

THE COCK, THE CUCKOO, AND THE BLACK-COCK

[This is another of those tales in which the birds' notes must be imitated.]

Once on a time the Cock, the Cuckoo, and the Black-cock bought a cow between them. But when they came to share it, and couldn't agree which should buy the others out, they settled that he who woke first in the morning should have the cow.

So the Cock woke first.

Now the cow's mine!   Now the cow's mine!   Hurrah! hurrah!

he crew, and as he crew, up awoke the Cuckoo.

Half cow!   Half cow!

sang the Cuckoo, and woke up the Black-cock.

A like share, a like share;   Dear friends, that's only fair!   Saw see! See saw!

That's what the Black-cock said.

And now, can you tell me which of them ought to have the cow?

RICH PETER THE PEDLAR

Once on a time there was a man whom they called Rich Peter the Pedlar, because he used to travel about with a pack, and got so much money, that he became quite rich. This Rich Peter had a daughter, whom he held so dear that all who came to woo her, were sent about their business, for no one was good enough for her, he thought. Well, this went on and on, and at last no one came to woo her, and as years rolled on, Peter began to be afraid that she would die an old maid.

'I wonder now', he said to his wife, 'why suitors no longer come to woo our lass, who is so rich. 'Twould be odd if no body cared to have her, for money she has, and more she shall have. I think I'd better just go off to the Stargazers, and ask them whom she shall have, for not a soul comes to us now.'

'But how', asked the wife, 'can the Stargazers answer that?'

'Can't they?' said Peter; 'why! they read all things in the stars.'

So he took with him a great bag of money, and set off to the Stargazers, and asked them to be so good as to look at the stars, and tell him the husband his daughter was to have. Well! the Stargazers looked and looked, but they said they could see nothing about it. But Peter begged them to look better, and to tell him the truth; he would pay them well for it. So the Stargazers looked better, and at last they said that his daughter's husband was to be the miller's son, who was only just born, down at the mill below Rich Peter's house. Then Peter gave the Stargazers a hundred dollars, and went home with the answer he had got. Now, he thought it too good a joke that his daughter should wed one so newly born, and of such poor estate. He said this to his wife, and added:

'I wonder now if they would sell me the boy; then I'd soon put him out of the way?'

'I daresay they would', said his wife; 'you know they're very poor.'

So Peter went down to the mill, and asked the miller's wife whether she would sell him her son; she should get a heap of money for him?

'No!' that she wouldn't.

'Well!' said Peter, 'I'm sure I can't see why you shouldn't; you've hard work enough as it is to keep hunger out of the house, and the boy won't make it easier, I think.'

But the mother was so proud of the boy, she couldn't part with him. So when the miller came home, Peter said the same thing to him, and gave his word to pay six hundred dollars for the boy, so that they might buy themselves a farm of their own, and not have to grind other folks' corn, and to starve when they ran short of water. The miller thought it was a good bargain, and he talked over his wife; and the end was, that Rich Peter got the boy. The mother cried and sobbed, but Peter comforted her by saying the boy should be well cared for; only they had to promise never to ask after him, for he said he meant to send him far away to other lands, so that he might learn foreign tongues.

So when Peter the Pedlar got home with the boy, he sent for a carpenter, and had a little chest made, which was so tidy and neat, 'twas a joy to see. This he made water-tight with pitch, put the miller's boy into it, locked it up, and threw it into the river, where the stream carried it away.

'Now, I'm rid of him', thought Peter the Pedlar.

But when the chest had floated ever so far down the stream, it came into the mill-head of another mill, and ran down and hampered the shaft of the wheel, and stopped it. Out came the miller to see what stopped the mill, found the chest and took it up. So when he came home to dinner to his wife, he said:

'I wonder now whatever there can be inside this chest which came floating down the mill-head, and stopped our mill to-day?'

'That we'll soon know', said his wife; 'see, there's the key in the lock, just turn it.'

So they turned the key and opened the chest, and lo! there lay the prettiest child you ever set eyes on. So they were both glad, and were ready to keep the child, for they had no children of their own, and were so old, they could now hope for none.

Now, after a little while, Peter the Pedlar began to wonder how it was no one came to woo his daughter, who was so rich in land, and had so much ready money. At last, when no one came, off he went again to the Stargazers, and offered them a heap of money if they could tell him whom his daughter was to have for a husband.

'Why! we have told you already, that she is to have the miller's son down yonder', said the Stargazers.

'All very true, I daresay', said Peter the Pedlar; 'but it so happens he's dead; but if you can tell me whom she's to have, I'll give you two hundred dollars, and welcome.' So the Stargazers looked at the stars again, but they got quite cross, and said,

'We told you before, and we tell you now, she is to have the miller's son, whom you threw into the river, and wished to make an end of; for he is alive, safe and sound, in such and such a mill, far down the stream.'

So Peter the Pedlar gave them two hundred dollars for this news, and thought how he could best be rid of the miller's son. The first thing Peter did when he got home, was to set off for the mill. By that time the boy was so big that he had been confirmed, and went about the mill and helped the miller. Such a pretty boy you never saw.

'Can't you spare me that lad yonder?' said Peter the Pedlar to the miller.

'No! that I can't', he answered; 'I've brought him up as my own son, and he has turned out so well, that now he's a great help and aid to me in the mill, for I'm getting old and past work.'

'It's just the same with me', said Peter the Pedlar; 'that's why I'd like to have some one to learn my trade. Now, if you'll give him up to me, I'll give you six hundred dollars, and then you can buy yourself a farm, and live in peace and quiet the rest of your days.'

Yes! when the miller heard that, he let Peter the Pedlar have the lad.

Then the two travelled about far and wide, with their packs and wares, till they came to an inn, which lay by the edge of a great wood. From this Peter the Pedlar sent the lad home with a letter to his wife, for the way was not so long if you took the short cut across the wood, and told him to tell her she was to be sure and do what was written in the letter as quickly as she could. But it was written in the letter, that she was to have a great pile made there and then, fire it, and cast the miller's son into it. If she didn't do that, he'd burn her alive himself when he came back. So the lad set off with the letter across the wood, and when evening came on he reached a house far, far away in the wood, into which he went; but inside he found no one. In one of the rooms was a bed ready made, so he threw himself across it and fell asleep. The letter he had stuck into his hat-band, and the hat he pulled over his face. So when the robbers came back--for in that house twelve robbers had their abode-- and saw the lad lying on the bed, they began to wonder who he could be, and one of them took the letter and broke it open, and read it.

'Ho! ho!' said he; 'this comes from Peter the Pedlar, does it? Now we'll play him a trick. It would be a pity if the old niggard made an end of such a pretty lad.'

So the robbers wrote another letter to Peter the Pedlar's wife, and fastened it under his hat-band while he slept; and in that they wrote, that as soon as ever she got it she was to make a wedding for her daughter and the miller's boy, and give them horses and cattle, and household stuff, and set them up for themselves in the farm which he had under the hill; and if he didn't find all this done by the time he came back, she'd smart for it--that was all.

Next day the robbers let the lad go, and when he came home and delivered the letter, he said he was to greet her kindly from Peter the Pedlar, and to say that she was to carry out what was written in the letter as soon as ever she could.

'You must have behaved very well then', said Peter, the Pedlar's wife to the miller's boy, 'if he can write so about you now, for when you set off, he was so mad against you, he didn't know how to put you out of the way.' So she married them on the spot, and set them up for themselves, with horses, and cattle, and household stuff, in the farm up under the hill.

No long time after Peter the Pedlar came home, and the first thing he asked was, if she had done what he had written in his letter.

'Aye! aye!' she said; 'I thought it rather odd, but I dared not do anything else'; and so Peter asked where his daughter was.

'Why, you know well enough where she is', said his wife. 'Where should she be but up at the farm under the hill, as you wrote in the letter.'

So when Peter the Pedlar came to hear the whole story, and came to see the letter, he got so angry he was ready to burst with rage, and off he ran up to the farm to the young couple.

'It's all very well, my son, to say you have got my daughter', he said to the miller's lad; 'but if you wish to keep her, you must go to the Dragon of Deepferry, and get me three feathers out of his tail; for he who has them may get anything he chooses.'

'But where shall I find him?' said his son-in-law.

'I'm sure I can't tell', said Peter the Pedlar; 'that's your look-out, not mine.'

So the lad set off with a stout heart, and after he had walked some way, he came to a king's palace.

'Here I'll just step in and ask', he said to himself; 'for such great folk know more about the world than others, and perhaps I may here learn the way to the Dragon.'

Then the King asked him whence he came, and whither he was going?

'Oh!' said the lad, 'I'm going to the Dragon of Deepferry to pluck three feathers out of his tail, if I only knew where to find him.'

'You must take luck with you, then', said the King, 'for I never heard of any one who came back from that search. But if you find him, just ask him from me why I can't get clear water in my well; for I've dug it out time after time, and still I can't get a drop of clear water.'

'Yes, I'll be sure to ask him', said the lad. So he lived on the fat of the land at the palace, and got money and food when he left it.

At even he came to another king's palace; and when he went into the kitchen, the King came out of the parlour, and asked whence he came, and on what errand he was bound?

'Oh!' said the lad, 'I'm going to the Dragon of Deepferry to pluck three feathers out of his tail.'

'Then you must take luck with you', said the King, 'for I never yet heard that any one came back who went to look for him. But if you find him, be so good as to ask him from me where my daughter is, who has been lost so many years. I have hunted for her, and had her name given out in every church in the country, but no one can tell me anything about her.'

'Yes, I'll mind and do that', said the lad; and in that palace too he lived on the best, and when he went away he got both money and food.

So when evening drew on again he came at last to another king's palace. Here who should come out into the kitchen but the Queen, and she asked him whence he came, and on what errand he was bound?

'I'm going to the Dragon of Deepferry to pluck three feathers out of his tail', said the lad.

'Then you'd better take a good piece of luck with you', said the Queen, 'for I never heard of any one that came back from him. But if you find him, just be good enough to ask him from me where I shall find my gold keys which I have lost.'

'Yes! I'll be sure to ask him', said the lad.

Well! when he left the palace he came to a great broad river; and while he stood there and wondered whether he should cross it, or go down along the bank, an old hunchbacked man came up, and asked whither he was going?

'Oh, I'm going to the Dragon of Deepferry, if I could only find any one to tell where I can find him.'

'I can tell you that', said the man; 'for here I go backwards and forwards, and carry those over who are going to see him. He lives just across, and when you climb the hill you'll see his castle; but mind, if you come to talk with him, to ask him from me how long I'm to stop here and carry folk over.'

'I'll be sure to ask him', said the lad.

So the man took him on his back and carried him over the river; and when he climbed the hill, he saw the castle, and went in.

He found there a Princess who lived with the Dragon all alone; and she said:

'But, dear friend, how can Christian folk dare to come hither? None have been here since I came, and you'd best be off as fast as you can; for as soon as the Dragon comes home, he'll smell you out, and gobble you up in a trice, and that'll make me so unhappy.'

'Nay! nay!' said the lad; 'I can't go before I've got three feathers out of his tail.'

'You'll never get them', said, the Princess; 'you'd best be off.'

But the lad wouldn't go; he would wait for the Dragon, and get the feathers, and an answer to all his questions.

'Well, since you're so steadfast I'll see what I can do to help you', said the Princess; 'just try to lift that sword that hangs on the wall yonder.'

No; the lad could not even stir it.

'I thought so', said the Princess; 'but just take a drink out of this flask.'

So when the lad had sat a while, he was to try again; and then he could just stir it.

'Well! you must take another drink', said the Princess, 'and then you may as well tell me your errand hither.'

So he took another drink, and then he told her how one king had begged him to ask the Dragon, how it was he couldn't get clean water in his well?--how another had bidden him ask, what had become of his daughter, who had been lost many years since?--and how a queen had begged him to ask the Dragon what had become of her gold keys?--and, last of all, how the ferryman had begged him to ask the Dragon, how long he was to stop there and carry folk over?? When he had done his story, and took hold of the sword, he could lift it; and when he had taken another drink, he could brandish it.

'Now', said the Princess, 'if you don't want the Dragon to make an end of you, you'd best creep under the bed, for night is drawing on, and he'll soon be home, and then you must lie as still as you can, lest he should find you out. And when we have gone to bed, I'll ask him, but you must keep your ears open, and snap up all that he says; and under the bed you must lie till all is still, and the Dragon falls asleep; then creep out softly and seize the sword, and as soon as he rises, look out to hew off his head at one stroke, and at the same time pluck out the three feathers, for else he'll tear them out himself, that no one may get any good by them.'

So the lad crept under the bed, and the Dragon came home.

'What a smell of Christian flesh', said the Dragon.

'Oh, yes', said the Princess, 'a raven came flying with a man's bone in his bill, and perched on the roof. No doubt it's that you smell.'

'So it is, I daresay', said the Dragon.

So the Princess served supper; and after they had eaten, they went to bed. But after they had lain a while, the Princess began to toss about, and all at once she started up and said:

'Ah! ah!'

'What's the matter?' said the Dragon.

'Oh', said the Princess, 'I can't rest at all, and I've had such a strange dream.'

'What did you dream about? Let's hear?' said the Dragon.

'I thought a king came here, and asked you what he must do to get clear water in his well.'

'Oh', said the Dragon, 'he might just as well have found that out for himself. If he dug the well out, and took out the old rotten stump which lies at the bottom, he'd get clean water, fast enough. But be still now, and don't dream any more.'

When the Princess had lain a while, she began to toss about, and at last she started up with her

'Ah! ah!'

'What's the matter now?' said the Dragon.

'Oh! I can't get any rest at all, and I've had such a strange dream', said the Princess.

'Why, you seem full of dreams to-night', said the Dragon what was your dream now?'

'I thought a king came here, and asked you what had become of his daughter who had been lost many years since', said the Princess.

'Why, you are she', said the Dragon; 'but he'll never set eyes on you again. But now, do pray be still, and let me get some rest, and don't let's have any more dreams, else I'll break your ribs.'

Well, the Princess hadn't lain much longer before she began to toss about again. At last she started up with her

'Ah! ah!'

'What! Are you at it again?' said the Dragon. 'What's the matter now?' for he was wild and sleep-surly, so that he was ready to fly to pieces.

'Oh, don't be angry', said the Princess; 'but I've had such a strange dream.'

'The deuce take your dreams', roared the Dragon; 'what did you dream this time?'

I thought a queen came here, who asked you to tell her where she would find her gold keys, which she has lost.'

'Oh', said the Dragon, 'she'll find them soon enough if she looks among the bushes where she lay that time she wots of. But do now let me have no more dreams, but sleep in peace.'

So they slept a while; but then the Princess was just as restless as ever, and at last she screamed out:

'Ah! ah!'

'You'll never behave till I break your neck', said the Dragon, who was now so wroth that sparks of fire flew out of his eyes. 'What's the matter now?'

'Oh, don't be so angry', said the Princess; 'I can't bear that; but I've had such a strange dream.'

'Bless me!' said the Dragon, 'if I ever heard the like of these dreams--there's no end to them. And pray, what did you dream now?'

'I thought the ferryman down at the ferry came and asked how long he was to stop there and carry folk over', said the Princess.

'The dull fool!' said the Dragon; 'he'd soon be free, if he chose. When any one comes who wants to go across, he has only to take and throw him into the river, and say, "Now, carry folk over yourself till someone sets you free." But now, pray let's have an end of these dreams, else I'll lead you a pretty dance.'

So the Princess let him sleep on. But as soon as all was still, and the miller's lad heard that the Dragon snored, he crept out. Before it was light the Dragon rose; but he had scarce set both his feet on the floor before the lad cut off his head, and plucked three feathers out of his tail. Then came great joy, and both the lad and the Princess took as much gold, and silver, and money, and precious things as they could carry; and when they came down to the ford, they so puzzled the ferryman with all they had to tell, that he quite forgot to ask what the Dragon had said about him till they had got across.

'Halloa, you sir', he said, as they were going off, 'did you ask the Dragon what I begged you to ask?'

'Yes I did', said the lad, 'and he said, "When any one comes and wants to go over, you must throw him into the midst of the river, and say, 'Now, carry folk over yourself till some one comes to set you free,'" and then you'll be free.'

'Ah, bad luck to you', said the ferryman; 'had you told me that before, you might have set me free yourself.'

So, when they got to the first palace, the Queen asked if he had spoken to the Dragon about her gold keys? 'Yes', said the lad, and whispered in the Queen's ear, 'he said you must look among the bushes where you lay the day you wot of.'

'Hush! hush! Don't say a word', said the Queen, and gave the lad a hundred dollars.

When they came to the second palace, the King asked if he had spoken to the

Dragon of what he begged him?

'Yes', said the lad, 'I did; and see, here is your daughter.'

At that the King was so glad, he would gladly have given the Princess to the miller's lad to wife, and half the kingdom beside; but as he was married already, he gave him two hundred dollars, and coaches and horses, and as much gold and silver as he could carry away.

When he came to the third King's palace, out came the King and asked if he had asked the Dragon of what he begged him?

'Yes', said the lad, 'and he said you must dig out the well, and take out the rotten old stump which lies at the bottom, and then you'll get plenty of clear water.'

Then the King gave him three hundred dollars, and he set out home; but he was so loaded with gold and silver, and so grandly clothed, that it gleamed and glistened from him, and he was now far richer than Peter the Pedlar.

When Peter got the feathers he hadn't a word more to say against the wedding; but when he saw all that wealth, he asked if there was much still left at the Dragon's castle.

'Yes, I should think so', said the lad; 'there was much more than I could carry with me--so much, that you might load many horses with it; and if you choose to go, you may be sure there'll be enough for you.'

So his son-in-law told him the way so clearly, that he hadn't to ask it of any one.

'But the horses', said the lad 'you'd best leave this side the river; for the old ferryman, he'll carry you over safe enough.'

So Peter set off, and took with him great store of food and many horses; but these he left behind him on the river's brink, as the lad had said. And the old ferryman took him upon his back; but when they had come a bit out into the stream, he cast him into the midst of the river, and said,

'Now you may go backwards and forwards here, and carry folk over till you are set free.'

And unless some one has set him free, there goes Rich Peter the Pedlar backwards and forwards, and carries folk across this very day.

GERTRUDE'S BIRD

In those days when our Lord and St Peter wandered upon earth, they came once to an old wife's house, who sat baking. Her name was Gertrude, and she had a red mutch on her head. They had walked a long way, and were both hungry, and our Lord begged hard for a bannock to stay their hunger. Yes, they should have it. So she took a little tiny piece of dough and rolled it out, but as she rolled it, it grew and grew till it covered the whole griddle.

Nay, that was too big; they couldn't have that. So she took a tinier bit still; but when that was rolled out, it covered the whole griddle just the same, and that bannock was too big, she said; they couldn't have that either.

The third time she took a still tinier bit--so tiny you could scarce see it; but it was the same story over again--the bannock was too big.

'Well', said Gertrude, 'I can't give you anything; you must just go without, for all these bannocks are too big.'

Then our Lord waxed wroth, and said:

'Since you loved me so little as to grudge me a morsel of food, you shall have this punishment: you shall become a bird, and seek your food between bark and bole; and never get a drop to drink save when it rains.'

He had scarce said the last word before she was turned into a great black woodpecker, or Gertrude's bird, and flew from her kneading- trough right up the chimney; and till this very day you may see her flying about, with her red mutch on her head, and her body all black, because of the soot in the chimney; and so she hacks and taps away at the trees for her food, and whistles when rain is coming, for she is ever athirst, and then she looks for a drop to cool her tongue.

BOOTS AND THE TROLL

Once on a time there was a poor man who had three sons. When he died, the two elder set off into the world to try their luck, but the youngest they wouldn't have with them at any price.

'As for you', they said, 'you're fit for nothing but to sit and poke about in the ashes.'

So the two went off and got places at a palace--the one under the coachman, and the other under the gardener. But Boots, he set off too, and took with him a great kneading-trough, which was the only thing his parents left behind them, but which the other two would not bother themselves with. It was heavy to carry, but he did not like to leave it behind, and so, after he had trudged a bit, he too came to the palace, and asked for a place. So they told him they did not want him, but he begged so prettily that at last he got leave to be in the kitchen, and carry in wood and water for the kitchen maid. He was quick and ready, and in a little while every one liked him; but the two others were dull, and so they got more kicks than halfpence, and grew quite envious of Boots, when they saw how much better he got on.

Just opposite the palace, across a lake, lived a Troll, who had seven silver ducks which swam on the lake, so that they could be seen from the palace. These the king had often longed for; and so the two elder brothers told the coachman:

'If our brother only chose, he has said he could easily get the king those seven silver ducks.'

You may fancy it wasn't long before the coachman told this to the king; and the king called Boots before him, and said:

'Your brothers say you can get me the silver ducks; so now go and fetch them.'

'I'm sure I never thought or said anything of the kind,' said the lad.

'You did say so, and you shall fetch them', said the king, who would hold his own.

'Well! well!' said the lad; 'needs must, I suppose; but give me a bushel of rye, and a bushel of wheat, and I'll try what I can do.'

So he got the rye and the wheat, and put them into the kneading- trough he had brought with him from home, got in, and rowed across the lake. When he reached the other side he began to walk along the shore, and to sprinkle and strew the grain, and at last he coaxed the ducks into his kneading-trough, and rowed back as fast as ever he could.

When he got half over, the Troll came out of his house, and set eyes on him.

'HALLOA!' roared out the Troll; 'is it you that has gone off with my seven silver ducks.'

'AYE! AYE!' said the lad.

'Shall you be back soon?' asked the Troll.

'Very likely', said the lad.

So when he got back to the king, with the seven silver ducks, he was more liked than ever, and even the king was pleased to say, 'Well done!' But at this his brothers grew more and more spiteful and envious; and so they went and told the coachman that their brother had said, if he chose, he was man enough to get the king the Troll's bed-quilt, which had a gold patch and a silver patch, and a silver patch and a gold patch; and this time, too, the coachman was not slow in telling all this to the king. So the king said to the lad, how his brothers had said he was good to steal the Troll's bed-quilt, with gold and silver patches; so now he must go and do it, or lose his life.

Boots answered, he had never thought or said any such thing; but when he found there was no help for it, he begged for three days to think over the matter.

So when the three days were gone, he rowed over in his kneading- trough, and went spying about. At last he saw those in the Troll's cave come out and hang the quilt out to air, and as soon as ever they had gone back into the face of the rock, Boots pulled the quilt down, and rowed away with it as fast as he could.

And when he was half across, out came the Troll and set eyes on him, and roared out:

'HALLOA! Is it you who took my seven silver ducks?'

'AYE! AYE!' said the lad.

'And now, have you taken my bed-quilt, with silver patches and gold patches, and gold patches and silver patches?'

'Aye! aye!' said the lad.

'Shall you come back again?'

'Very likely', said the lad.

But when he got back with the gold and silver patchwork quilt, every one was fonder of him than ever, and he was made the king's body- servant.

At this, the other two were still more vexed, and, to be revenged, they went and told the coachman:

'Now, our brother has said, he is man enough to get the king the gold harp which the Troll has, and that harp is of such a kind, that all who listen when it is played grow glad, however sad they may be.'

Yes! the coachman went and told the king, and he said to the lad:

'If you have said this, you shall do it. If you do it, you shall have the Princess and half the kingdom. If you don't, you shall lose your life.'

'I'm sure I never thought or said anything of the kind', said the lad; 'but if there's no help for it, I may as well try; but I must have six days to think about it.'

Yes! he might have six days, but when they were over, he must set out.

Then he took a tenpenny nail, a birch-pin, and a waxen taper-end in his pocket, and rowed across, and walked up and down before the Troll's cave, looking stealthily about him. So when the Troll came out, he saw him at once.

'HO, HO!' roared the Troll; 'is it you who took my seven silver ducks?'

'AYE! AYE!' said the lad.

'And it is you who took my bed-quilt, with the gold and silver patches?' asked the Troll.

'Aye! aye!' said the lad.

So the Troll caught hold of him at once, and took him off into the cave in the face of the rock.

'Now, daughter dear', said the Troll, 'I've caught the fellow who stole the silver ducks and my bed-quilt, with gold and silver patches; put him into the fattening coop, and when he's fat, we'll kill him, and make a feast for our friends.'

She was willing enough, and put him at once into the fattening coop, and there he stayed eight days, fed on the best, both in meat and drink, and as much as he could cram. So, when the eight days were over, the Troll said to his daughter to go down and cut him in his little finger, that they might see if he were fat. Down she came to the coop.

'Out with your little finger!' she said.

But Boots stuck out his tenpenny nail, and she cut at it.

'Nay! nay! he's as hard as iron still', said the Troll's daughter, when she got back to her father; 'we can't take him yet.'

After another eight days the same thing happened, and this time Boots stuck out his birchen pin.

'Well, he's a little better', she said, when she got back to the Troll; 'but still he'll be as hard as wood to chew.'

But when another eight days were gone, the Troll told his daughter to go down and see if he wasn't fat now.

'Out with your little finger', said the Troll's daughter, when she reached the coop, and this time Boots stuck out the taper end.

'Now he'll do nicely', she said.

'Will he?' said the Troll. 'Well, then, I'll just set off and ask the guests; meantime you must kill him, and roast half and boil half.'

So when the Troll had been gone a little while, the daughter began to sharpen a great long knife.

'Is that what you're going to kill me with?' asked the lad.

'Yes it is,' said she.

'But it isn't sharp', said the lad. 'Just let me sharpen it for you, and then you'll find it easier work to kill me.'

So she let him have the knife, and he began to rub and sharpen it on the whetstone.

'Just let me try it on one of your hair plaits; I think it's about right now.'

So he got leave to do that; but at the same time that he grasped the plait of hair, he pulled back her head, and at one gash, cut off the Troll's daughter's head; and half of her he roasted and half of her he boiled, and served it all up.

After that he dressed himself in her clothes, and sat away in the corner.

So when the Troll came home with his guests, he called out to his daughter--for he thought all the time it was his daughter--to come and take a snack.

'No, thank you', said the lad, 'I don't care for food, I'm so sad and downcast.'

'Oh!' said the Troll, 'if that's all, you know the cure; take the harp, and play a tune on it.'

'Yes!' said the lad; 'but where has it got to; I can't find it.'

'Why, you know well enough', said the Troll; 'you used it last; where should it be but over the door yonder?

The lad did not wait to be told twice; he took down the harp, and went in and out playing tunes; but, all at once he shoved off the kneading-trough, jumped into it, and rowed off, so that the foam flew around the trough.

After a while the Troll thought his daughter was a long while gone, and went out to see what ailed her; and then he saw the lad in the trough, far, far out on the lake.

'HALLOA! Is it you', he roared, 'that took my seven silver ducks?'

'AYE, AYE!' said the lad.

'Is it you that took my bed-quilt, with the gold and silver patches.'

'Yes!' said the lad.

'And now you have taken off my gold harp?' screamed the Troll.

'Yes!' said the lad; 'I've got it, sure enough.'

'And haven't I eaten you up after all, then?'

'No, no! 'twas your own daughter you ate', answered the lad.

But when the Troll heard that, he was so sorry, he burst; and then Boots rowed back, and took a whole heap of gold and silver with him, as much as the trough could carry. And so, when he came to the palace with the gold harp, he got the Princess and half the kingdom, as the king had promised him; and, as for his brothers, he treated them well, for he thought they had only wished his good when they said what they had said.

GOOSEY GRIZZEL

Once on a time there was a widower, who had a housekeeper named Grizzel, who set her mutch at him and teazed him early and late to marry her. At last the man got so weary of her, he was at his wits' end to know how to get rid of her. So it fell on a day, between hay time and harvest, the two went out to pull hemp. Grizzel's head was full of her good looks and her handiness, and she worked away at the hemp till she grew giddy from the strong smell of the ripe seed, and at last down she fell flat, fast asleep among the hemp. While she slept, her master got a pair of scissors and cut her skirts short all round, and then he rubbed her all over, face and all, first with tallow and then with soot, till she looked worse than the Deil himself. So, when Grizzel woke and saw how ugly she was, she didn't know herself.

'Can this be me now?' said Grizzel. 'Nay, nay! it can never be me. So ugly have I never been; it's surely the Deil himself?'

Well! that she might really know the truth, she went off and knocked at her master's door, and asked,

'Is your Girzie at home the day, father?'

'Aye, aye, our Girzie is at home safe enough', said the man, who wanted to be rid of her.

'Well, well!' she said to herself, 'then I can't be his Grizzel,' and stole away; and right glad the man was, I can tell you.

So, when she had walked a bit she came to a great wood, where she met two thieves. 'The very men for my money, thought Grizzel, 'since I am the Deil, thieves are just fit fellows for me.'

But the thieves were not of the same mind, not they. As soon as they set eyes on her, they took to their heels as fast as they could, for they thought the Evil One was come to catch them. But it was no good, for Grizzel was long-legged and swift-footed, and she came up with them before they knew where they were.

'If you're going out to steal, I'll go with you and help,' said Grizzel, 'for I know the whole country round.' So, when the thieves heard that, they thought they had found a good mate, and were no longer afraid.

Then they said they were off to steal a sheep, only they didn't know where to lay hold of one.

'Oh!' said Grizzel, 'that's a small matter, for I was maid with a farmer ever so long out in the wood yonder, and I could find the sheepfold, though the night were dark as pitch.'

The thieves thought that grand; and when they came to the place, Grizzel was to go into the fold and turn out the sheep, and they were to lay hold on it. Now, the sheepfold lay close to the wall of the room where the farmer slept, so Grizzel crept quite softly and carefully into the fold; but, as soon as she got in, she began to scream out to the thieves, 'Will you have a wether or a ewe? here are lots to choose from.'

'Hush, hush!' said the thieves, 'only take one that is fine and fat.'

'Yes, yes! but will you have a wether or a ewe? will you have a wether or a ewe? for here are lots to choose from,' screeched Grizzel.

'Hush, hush!' said the thieves again, 'only take one that's fine and fat; it's all the same to us whether it's a wether or a ewe.'

'Yes!' screeched Grizzel, who stuck to her own; 'but will you have a wether or a ewe--a wether or a ewe? here are lots to choose from.'

'Hold your jaw!' said the thieves, 'and take a fine fat one, wether or ewe, its all one to us.'

But just then out came the farmer in his shirt, who had been waked by all this clatter, and wanted to see what was going on. So the thieves took to their heels, and Grizzel after them, upsetting the farmer in her flight.

'Stop, boys! stop, boys!' she screamed; but the farmer, who had only seen the black monster, grew so afraid that he could scarce stand, for he thought it was the Deil himself that had been in his sheepfold. The only help he knew was, to go in-doors and wake up the whole house; and they all sat down to read and pray, for he had heard that was the way to send the Deil about his business.

Now the next night the thieves said they must go and steal a fat goose, and Grizzel was to shew them the way. So when they came to the goosepen, Grizzel was to go in and turn one out, for she knew the ways of the place, and the thieves were to stand outside and catch it. But as soon as ever she got in she began to scream,

'Will you have goose or gander? you may pick and choose here.'

'Hush hush! choose only a fine fat one', said the thieves. 'Yes, yes! but will you have goose or gander--goose or gander? you may pick and choose', screamed Grizzel.

'Hush, hush! only choose one that's fine and fat, and it's all one to us whether it's goose or gander; but do hold your jaw', said they.

But while Grizzel and the thieves were settling this, one of the geese began to cackle, and then another cackled, and then the whole flock cackled and hissed, and out came the farmer to see what all the noise could mean, and away went the thieves, and Grizzel after them, at full speed, and the farmer thought again it was the black Deil flying away; for long-legged she was, and she had no skirts to hamper her.

'Stop a bit, boys!' she kept on screaming, 'you might as well have said whether you would have goose or gander?'

But they had no time to stop, they thought; and, as for the farmer, he began to read and pray with all his house, small and great, for they thought it was the Deil, and no mistake.

Now, the third day, when night came, the thieves and Grizzel were so hungry they did not know what to do; so they made up their minds to go to the larder of a rich farmer, who lived by the wood's side, and steal some food. Well, off they went, but the thieves did not dare to venture themselves, so Grizzel was to go up the steps which led to the larder, and hand the food out, and the others were to stand below and take it from her. So when Grizzel got inside, she saw the larder was full of all sorts of things, fresh meat and salt, and sausages and oat-cake. The thieves begged her to be still, and just throw out something to eat, and to bear in mind how badly they had fated for two nights. But Grizzel stuck to her own, that she did.

'Will you have fresh meat, or salt, or sausages, or oat-cake? Just look, what a lovely oat-cake', she bawled out enough to split your head. 'You may have what you please, for here's plenty to choose from.'

But the farmer woke with all this noise, and ran out to see what it all meant. As for the thieves, off they ran as fast as they could; but while the farmer was looking after them, down came Grizzel so black and ugly.

'Stop a bit! stop a bit, boys!' she bellowed; 'you may have what you please, for there's plenty to choose from.'

And when the farmer saw that ugly monster, he, too, thought the Deil was loose, for he had heard what had happened to his neighbours the evenings before; so he began both to read and pray, and every one in the whole parish began to read and pray, for they knew that you could read the Deil away.

The next evening was Saturday evening, and the thieves wanted to steal a fat ram for their Sunday dinner; and well they might, for they had fasted many days. But they wouldn't have Grizzel with them at any price. She brought bad luck with her jaw, they said; so while Grizzel was walking about waiting for them on Sunday morning, she got so awfully hungry--for she had fasted for three days--that she went into a turnip-field and pulled up some turnips to eat. But when the farmer who owned the turnips rose, he felt uneasy in his mind, and thought he would just go and take a look at his turnips on the Sunday morning. So he pulled on his trousers and went across the moss which lay under the hill, where the turnip-field lay. But when he got to the bottom of the field, he saw something black walking about in the field and pulling up his turnips, and he soon made up his mind that it was the Deil. So away he ran home as fast as he could, and said the Deil was among the turnips. This frightened the whole house out of their wits, and they agreed they'd best send for the priest, and get him to bind the Deil.

'That won't do', said the goodwife, 'this is Sunday morning, you'll never get the priest to come; for either he'll be in bed; or if he's up, he'll be learning his sermon by heart.'

'Oh!' said the goodman, 'never fear; I'll promise him a fat loin of veal, and then he'll come fast enough.'

So off he went to the priest's house; but when he got there, sure enough, the priest was still in bed. The maid begged the farmer to walk into the parlour while she ran up to the priest, and said:

'Farmer So-and-So was downstairs, and wished to have a word with him.'

Well! when the priest heard that such a worthy man was downstairs, he got up at once, and came down just as he was, in his slippers and nightcap.

So the goodman told his errand; how the Deil was loose in his turnip- field; and if the priest would only come and bind him, he would send him a fat loin of veal. Yes! the priest was willing enough, and called out to his groom, to saddle his horse, while he dressed himself.

'Nay, nay, father!' said the man; 'the Deil won't wait for us long, and no one knows where we shall find him again if we miss him now. Your reverence must come at once, just as you are.'

So the priest followed him just as he was, with the clothes he stood in, and went off in his nightcap and slippers. But when they got to the moss, it was so moist the priest couldn't cross it in his slippers. So the goodman took him on his back to carry him over. On they went, the goodman picking his way from one clump to the other, till they got to the middle; then Grizzel caught sight of them, and thought it was the thieves bringing the ram.

'Is he fat?' she screamed; 'is he fat?' and made such a noise that the wood rang again.

'The Deil knows if he's fat or lean; I'm sure I don't', said the goodman, when he heard that; 'but, if you want to know, you had better come yourself and see.'

And then he got so afraid, he threw the priest head over heels into the soft wet moss, and took to his legs; and if the priest hasn't got out, why I dare say he's lying there still.

THE LAD WHO WENT TO THE NORTH WIND

Once on a time there was an old widow who had one son; and as she was poorly and weak, her son had to go up into the safe to fetch meal for cooking; but when he got outside the safe, and was just going down the steps, there came the North Wind, puffing and blowing, caught up the meal, and so away with it through the air. Then the lad went back into the safe for more; but when he came out again on the steps, if the North Wind didn't come again and carry off the meal with a puff; and, more than that, he did so the third time. At this the lad got very angry; and as he thought it hard that the North Wind should behave so, he thought he'd just look him up, and ask him to give up his meal.

So off he went, but the way was long, and he walked and walked; but at last he came to the North Wind's house.

'Good day!' said the lad, 'and thank you for coming to see us yesterday.'

'GOOD DAY!' answered the North Wind, for his voice was loud and gruff, 'AND THANKS FOR COMING TO SEE ME. WHAT DO YOU WANT?'

'Oh!' answered the lad, 'I only wished to ask you to be so good as to let me have back that meal you took from me on the safe steps, for we haven't much to live on; and if you're to go on snapping up the morsel we have, there'll be nothing for it but to starve.'

'I haven't got your meal', said the North Wind; 'but if you are in such need, I'll give you a cloth which will get you everything you want, if you only say, 'Cloth, spread yourself, and serve up all kind of good dishes!'

With this the lad was well content. But, as the way was so long he couldn't get home in one day, so he turned into an inn on the way; and when they were going to sit down to supper he laid the cloth on a table which stood in the corner, and said,

'Cloth, spread yourself, and serve up all kinds of good dishes.'

He had scarce said so before the cloth did as it was bid; and all who stood by thought it a fine thing, but most of all the landlady. So, when all were fast asleep at dead of night, she took the lad's cloth, and put another in its stead, just like the one he had got from the North Wind, but which couldn't so much as serve up a bit of dry bread.

So, when the lad woke, he took his cloth and went off with it, and that day he got home to his mother.

'Now', said he, 'I've been to the North Wind's house, and a good fellow he is, for he gave me this cloth, and when I only say to it, "Cloth, spread yourself, and serve up all kind of good dishes", I get any sort of food I please.'

'All very true, I daresay,' said his mother; 'but seeing is believing, and I shan't believe it till I see it.'

So the lad made haste, drew out a table, laid the cloth on it, and said:

'Cloth, spread yourself, and serve up all kind of good dishes.'

But never a bit of dry bread did the cloth serve up.

'Well', said the lad, 'there's no help for it but to go to the North Wind again'; and away he went.

So he came to where the North Wind lived late in the afternoon.

'Good evening!' said the lad.

'Good evening!' said the North Wind.

'I want my rights for that meal of ours which you took', said the lad; 'for, as for that cloth I got, it isn't worth a penny.'

'I've got no meal', said the North Wind; 'but yonder you have a ram which coins nothing but golden ducats as soon as you say to it:

"Rain, ram! make money!"

So the lad thought this a fine thing; but as it was too far to get home that day, he turned in for the night to the same inn where he had slept before.

Before he called for anything, he tried the truth of what the North Wind had said of the ram, and found it all right; but, when the landlord saw that, he thought it was a famous ram, and, when the lad had fallen asleep, he took another which couldn't coin gold ducats, and changed the two.

Next morning off went the lad; and when he got home to his mother, he said:

'After all, the North Wind is a jolly fellow; for now he has given me a ram which can coin golden ducats if I only say "Ram, ram! make money."'

'All very true, I daresay', said his mother; 'but I shan't believe any such stuff until I see the ducats made.'

'Ram, ram! make money!' said the lad; but if the Ram made anything, it wasn't money.

So the lad went back again to the North Wind, and blew him up, and said the ram was worth nothing, and he must have his rights for the meal.

'Well!' said the North Wind; 'I've nothing else to give you but that old stick in the corner yonder; but it's a stick of that kind that if you say:

'"Stick, stick! lay on!" it lays on till you say: "Stick, stick! now stop!"'

So, as the way was long, the lad turned in this night too to the landlord; but as he could pretty well guess how things stood as to the cloth and the ram, he lay down at once on the bench and began to snore, as if he were asleep.

Now the landlord, who easily saw that the stick must be worth something, hunted up one which was like it, and when he heard the lad snore, was going to change the two; but, just as the landlord was about to take it, the lad bawled out:

'Stick, stick! lay on!'

So the stick began to beat the landlord, till he jumped over chairs, and tables, and benches, and yelled and roared:

'Oh my! oh my! bid the stick be still, else it will beat me to death, and you shall have back both your cloth and our ram.'

When the lad thought the landlord had got enough, he said:

'Stick, stick! now stop!'

Then he took the cloth and put it into his pocket, and went home with his stick in his hand, leading the ram by a cord round its horns; and so he got his rights for the meal he had lost.

THE MASTER THIEF

Once upon a time there was a poor cottager who had three sons. He had nothing to leave them when he died, and no money with which to put them to any trade, so that he did not know what to make of them. At last he said he would give them leave to take to anything each liked best, and to go whithersoever they pleased, and he would go with them a bit of the way; and so he did. He went with them till they came to a place where three roads met, and there each of them chose a road, and their father bade them good-bye, and went back home. I have never heard tell what became of the two elder; but as for the youngest, he went both far and long, as you shall hear.

So it fell out one night as he was going through a great wood that such bad weather overtook him. It blew, and sleeted, and drove so that he could scarce keep his eyes open; and in a trice, before he knew how it was, he got bewildered, and could not find either road or path. But as he went on and on, at last he saw a glimmering of light far far off in the wood. So he thought he would try and get to the light; and after a time he did reach it. There it was in a large house, and the fire was blazing so brightly inside, that he could tell the folk had not yet gone to bed; so he went in and saw an old dame bustling about and minding the house.

'Good evening!' said the youth.

'Good evening!' said the old dame.

'Hutetu! it's such foul weather out of doors to-night', said he.

'So it is', said she.

'Can I get leave to have a bed and shelter here to-night?' asked the youth.

'You'll get no good by sleeping here', said the old dame; 'for if the folk come home and find you here, they'll kill both me and you.'

'What sort of folk, then, are they who live here?' asked the youth.

'Oh, robbers! And a bad lot of them too', said the old dame. 'They stole me away when I was little, and have kept me as their housekeeper ever since.'

'Well, for all that, I think I'll just go to bed', said the youth. 'Come what may, I'll not stir out at night in such weather.'

'Very well', said the old dame; 'but if you stay, it will be the worse for you.'

With that the youth got into a bed which stood there, but he dared not go to sleep, and very soon after in came the robbers; so the old dame told them how a stranger fellow had come in whom she had not been able to get out of the house again.

'Did you see if he had any money?' said the robbers.

'Such a one as he money!' said the old dame, 'the tramper! Why, if he had clothes to his back, it was as much as he had.'

Then the robbers began to talk among themselves what they should do with him; if they should kill him outright, or what else they should do. Meantime the youth got up and began to talk to them, and to ask if they didn't want a servant, for it might be that he would be glad to enter their service.

'Oh', said they, 'if you have a mind to follow the trade that we follow, you can very well get a place here.'

'It's all one to me what trade I follow', said the youth; 'for when I left home, father gave me leave to take to any trade I chose.'

'Well, have you a mind to steal?' asked the robbers.

'I don't care', said the youth, for he thought it would not take long to learn that trade.

Now there lived a man a little way off who had three oxen. One of these he was to take to the town to sell, and the robbers had heard what he was going to do, so they said to the youth, if he were good to steal the ox from the man by the way without his knowing it, and without doing him any harm, they would give him leave to be their serving-man.

Well! the youth set off, and took with him a pretty shoe, with a silver buckle on it, which lay about the house; and he put the shoe in the road along which the man was going with his ox; and when he had done that, he went into the wood and hid himself under a bush. So when the man came by he saw the shoe at once.

'That's a nice shoe', said he. 'If I only had the fellow to it, I'd take it home with me, and perhaps I'd put my old dame in a good humour for once.' For you must know he had an old wife, so cross and snappish, it was not long between each time that she boxed his ears. But then he bethought him that he could do nothing with the odd shoe unless he had the fellow to it; so he went on his way and let the shoe lie on the road.

Then the youth took up the shoe, and made all the haste he could to get before the man by a short cut through the wood, and laid it down before him in the road again. When the man came along with his ox, he got quite angry with himself for being so dull as to leave the fellow to the shoe lying in the road instead of taking it with him; so he tied the ox to the fence, and said to himself, 'I may just as well run back and pick up the other, and then I'll have a pair of good shoes for my old dame, and so, perhaps, I'll get a kind word from her for once.'

So he set off, and hunted and hunted up and down for the shoe, but no shoe did he find; and at length he had to go back with the one he had. But, meanwhile the youth had taken the ox and gone off with it; and when the man came and saw his ox gone, he began to cry and bewail, for he was afraid his old dame would kill him outright when she came to know that the ox was lost. But just then it came across his mind that he would go home and take the second ox, and drive it to the town, and not let his old dame know anything about the matter. So he did this, and went home and took the ox without his dame's knowing it, and set off with it to the town. But the robbers knew all about it, and they said to the youth, if he could get this ox too, without the man's knowing it, and without his doing him any harm, he should be as good as any one of them. If that were all, the youth said, he did not think it a very hard thing.

This time he took with him a rope, and hung himself up under the arm- pits to a tree right in the man's way. So the man came along with his ox, and when he saw such a sight hanging there he began to feel a little queer.

'Well', said he, 'whatever heavy thoughts you had who have hanged yourself up there, it can't be helped; you may hang for what I care! I can't breathe life into you again'; and with that he went on his way with his ox. Down slipped the youth from the tree, and ran by a footpath, and got before the man, and hung himself up right in his way again.

'Bless me!' said the man, 'were you really so heavy at heart that you hanged yourself up there--or is it only a piece of witchcraft that I see before me? Aye, aye! you may hang for all I care, whether you are a ghost or whatever you are.' So he passed on with his ox.

Now the youth did just as he had done twice before; he jumped down from the tree, ran through the wood by a footpath, and hung himself up right in the man's way again. But when the man saw this sight for the third time, he said to himself:

'Well! this is an ugly business! Is it likely now that they should have been so heavy at heart as to hang themselves, all these three? No! I cannot think it is any-thing else than a piece of witchcraft that I see. But now I'll soon know for certain; if the other two are still hanging there, it must be really so; but if they are not, then it can be nothing but witchcraft that I see.'

So he tied up his ox, and ran back to see if the others were still really hanging there. But while he went and peered up into all the trees, the youth jumped down and took his ox and ran off with it. When the man came back and found his ox gone, he was in a sad plight, and, as any one might know without being told, he began to cry and bemoan; but at last he came to take it easier, and so he thought:

'There's no other help for it than to go home and take the third ox without my dame's knowing it, and to try and drive a good bargain with it, so that I may get a good sum of money for it.'

So he went home and set off with the ox, and his old dame knew never a word about the matter. But the robbers, they knew all about it, and they said to the youth, that if he could steal this ox as he had stolen the other two, then he should be master over the whole band. Well, the youth set off, and ran into the wood; and as the man came by with his ox he set up a dreadful bellowing, just like a great ox in the wood. When the man heard that, you can't think how glad he was, for it seemed to him that he knew the voice of his big bullock, and he thought that now he should find both of them again; so he tied up the third ox, and ran off from the road to look for them in the wood; but meantime the youth went off with the third ox. Now, when the man came back and found he had lost this ox too, he was so wild that there was no end to his grief. He cried and roared and beat his breast, and, to tell the truth, it was many days before he dared go home; for he was afraid lest his old dame should kill him outright on the spot.

As for the robbers, they were not very well pleased either, when they had to own that the youth was master over the whole band. So one day they thought they would try their hands at something which he was not man enough to do; and they set off all together, every man Jack of them, and left him alone at home. Now, the first thing that he did when they were all well clear of the house, was to drive the oxen out to the road, so that they might run back to the man from whom he had stolen them; and right glad he was to see them, as you may fancy. Next he took all the horses which the robbers had, and loaded them with the best things he could lay his hands on-gold and silver, and clothes and other fine things; and then he bade the old dame to greet the robbers when they came back, and to thank them for him, and to say that now he was setting off on his travels, and they would have hard work to find him again; and with that, off he started.

After a good bit he came to the road along which he was going when he fell among the robbers, and when he got near home, and could see his father's cottage, he put on a uniform which he had found among the clothes he had taken from the robbers, and which was made just like a general's. So he drove up to the door as if he were any other great man. After that he went in and asked if he could have a lodging? No; that he couldn't at any price.

'How ever should I be able', said the man, 'to make room in my house for such a fine gentleman--I who scarce have a rag to lie upon, and miserable rags too?'

'You always were a stingy old hunks', said the youth, 'and so you are still, when you won't take your own son in.'

'What, you my son!' said the man.

'Don't you know me again?' said the youth. Well, after a little while he did know him again.

'But what have you been turning your hand to, that you have made yourself so great a man in such haste?' asked the man.

'Oh! I'll soon tell you', said the youth. 'You said I might take to any trade I chose, and so I bound myself apprentice to a pack of thieves and robbers, and now I've served my time out, and am become a Master Thief.'

Now there lived a Squire close by to his father's cottage, and he had such a great house, and such heaps of money, he could not tell how much he had. He had a daughter too, and a smart and pretty girl she was. So the Master Thief set his heart upon having her to wife, and he told his father to go to the Squire and ask for his daughter for him.

'If he asks by what trade I get my living, you can say I'm a Master Thief.'

'I think you've lost your wits', said the man, 'for you can't be in your right mind when you think of such stuff.'

No! he had not lost his wits, his father must and should go to the Squire, and ask for his daughter.

'Nay, but I tell you, I daren't go to the Squire and be your spokesman; he who is so rich, and has so much money', said the man.

Yes, there was no help for it, said the Master Thief; he should go whether he would or no; and if he did not go by fair means, he would soon make him go by foul. But the man was still loath to go; so he stepped after him, and rubbed him down with a good birch cudgel, and kept on till the man came crying and sobbing inside the Squire's door.

'How now, my man! what ails you?' said the Squire. So he told him the whole story; how he had three sons who set off one day, and how he had given them leave to go whithersoever they would, and to follow whatever calling they chose. 'And here now is the youngest come home, and has thrashed me till he has made me come to you and ask for your daughter for him to wife; and he bids me say, besides, that he's a Master Thief.' And so he fell to crying and sobbing again.

'Never mind, my man', said the Squire, laughing; 'just go back and tell him from me, he must prove his skill first. If he can steal the roast from the spit in the kitchen on Sunday, while all the household are looking after it, he shall have my daughter. Just go and tell him that.'

So he went back and told the youth, who thought it would be an easy job. So he set about and caught three hares alive, and put them into a bag, and dressed himself in some old rags, until he looked so poor and filthy that it made one's heart bleed to see; and then he stole into the passage at the back-door of the Squire's house on the Sunday forenoon, with his bag, just like any other beggar-boy. But the Squire himself and all his household were in the kitchen watching the roast. Just as they were doing this, the youth let one hare go, and it set off and ran round and round the yard in front of the house.

'Oh, just look at that hare!' said the folk in the kitchen, and were all for running out to catch it.

Yes, the Squire saw it running too. 'Oh, let it run', said he; 'there's no use in thinking to catch a hare on the spring.'

A little while after, the youth let the second hare go, and they saw it in the kitchen, and thought it was the same they had seen before, and still wanted to run out and catch it; but the Squire said again it was no use. It was not long before the youth let the third hare go, and it set off and ran round and round the yard as the others before it. Now, they saw it from the kitchen, and still thought it was the same hare that kept on running about, and were all eager to be out after it.

'Well, it is a fine hare', said the Squire; 'come let's see if we can't lay our hands on it.'

So out he ran, and the rest with him--away they all went, the hare before, and they after; so that it was rare fun to see. But meantime the youth took the roast and ran off with it; and where the Squire got a roast for his dinner that day I don't know; but one thing I know, and that is, that he had no roast hare, though he ran after it till he was both warm and weary.

Now it chanced that the Priest came to dinner that day, and when the Squire told him what a trick the Master Thief had played him, he made such game of him that there was no end of it.

'For my part', said the Priest, 'I can't think how it could ever happen to me to be made such a fool of by a fellow like that.'

'Very well--only keep a sharp look-out', said the Squire; 'maybe he'll come to see you before you know a word of it.' But the Priest stuck to his text--that he did, and made game of the Squire because he had been so taken in.

Later in the afternoon came the Master Thief, and wanted to have the Squire's daughter, as he had given his word. But the Squire began to talk him over, and said, 'Oh, you must first prove your skill a little more; for what you did to-day was no great thing, after all. Couldn't you now play off a good trick on the Priest, who is sitting in there, and making game of me for letting such a fellow as you twist me round his thumb.'

'Well, as for that, it wouldn't be hard', said the Master Thief. So he dressed himself up like a bird, threw a great white sheet over his body, took the wings of a goose and tied them to his back, and so climbed up into a great maple which stood in the Priest's garden. And when the Priest came home in the evening, the youth began to bawl out:

'Father Laurence! Father Laurence!'--for that was the Priest's name.

'Who is that calling me?' said the Priest.

'I am an angel', said the Master Thief, 'sent from God to let you know that you shall be taken up alive into heaven for your piety's sake. Next Monday night you must hold yourself ready for the journey, for I shall come then to fetch you in a sack; and all your gold and your silver, and all that you have of this world's goods, you must lay together in a heap in your dining-room.'

Well, Father Laurence fell on his knees before the angel, and thanked him; and the very next day he preached a farewell sermon, and gave it out how there had come down an angel unto the big maple in his garden, who had told him that he was to be taken up alive into heaven for his piety's sake; and he preached and made such a touching discourse, that all who were at church wept, both young and old.

So the next Monday night came the Master Thief like an angel again, and the Priest fell on his knees and thanked him before he was put into the sack; but when he had got him well in, the Master Thief drew and dragged him over stocks and stones.

'OW! OW!' groaned the Priest inside the sack, 'wherever are we going?'

'This is the narrow way which leadeth unto the kingdom of heaven', said the Master Thief, who went on dragging him along till he had nearly broken every bone in his body. At last he tumbled him into a goose-house that belonged to the Squire, and the geese began pecking and pinching him with their bills, so that he was more dead than alive.

'Now you are in the flames of purgatory, to be cleansed and purified for life everlasting', said the Master Thief; and with that he went his way, and took all the gold which the Priest had laid together in his dining-room. The next morning, when the goose-girl came to let the geese out, she heard how the Priest lay in the sack, and bemoaned himself in the goose-house.

'In heaven's name, who's there, and what ails you?' she cried.

'Oh!' said the Priest, 'if you are an angel from heaven, do let me out, and let me return again to earth, for it is worse here than in hell. The little fiends keep on pinching me with tongs.'

'Heaven help us, I am no angel at all', said the girl, as she helped the Priest out of the sack; 'I only look after the Squire's geese, and like enough they are the little fiends which have pinched your reverence.'

'Oh!' groaned the Priest, 'this is all that Master Thief's doing. Ah! my gold and my silver, and my fine clothes.' And he beat his breast, and hobbled home at such a rate that the girl thought he had lost his wits all at once.

Now when the Squire came to hear how it had gone with the Priest, and how he had been along the narrow way, and into purgatory, he laughed till he well-nigh split his sides. But when the Master Thief came and asked for his daughter as he had promised, the Squire put him off again, and said:

'You must do one masterpiece better still, that I may see plainly what you are fit for. Now, I have twelve horses in my stable, and on them I will put twelve grooms, one on each. If you are so good a thief as to steal the horses from under them, I'll see what I can do for you.'

'Very well, I daresay I can do it', said the Master Thief; 'but shall I really have your daughter if I can?'

'Yes, if you can, I'll do my best for you', said the Squire. So the Master Thief set off to a shop, and bought brandy enough to fill two pocket-flasks, and into one of them he put a sleepy drink, but into the other only brandy. After that he hired eleven men to lie in wait at night, behind the Squire's stable-yard; and last of all, for fair words and a good bit of money, he borrowed a ragged gown and cloak from an old woman; and so, with a staff in his hand, and a bundle at his back, he limped off, as evening drew on, towards the Squire's stable. Just as he got there they were watering the horses for the night, and had their hands full of work. 'What the devil do you want?' said one of the grooms to the old woman.

'Oh, oh! hutetu! it is so bitter cold', said she, and shivered and shook, and made wry faces. 'Hutetu! it is so cold, a poor wretch may easily freeze to death'; and with that she fell to shivering and shaking again.

'Oh! for the love of heaven, can I get leave to stay here a while, and sit inside the stable door?'

'To the devil with your leave', said one. 'Pack yourself off this minute, for if the Squire sets his eye on you, he'll lead us a pretty dance.'

'Oh! the poor old bag-of-bones', said another, whose heart took pity on her, 'the old hag may sit inside and welcome; such a one as she can do no harm.'

And the rest said, some she should stay, and some she shouldn't; but while they were quarrelling and minding the horses, she crept further and further into the stable, till at last she sat herself down behind the door; and when she had got so far, no one gave any more heed to her.

As the night wore on, the men found it rather cold work to sit so still and quiet on horseback.

'Hutetu! it is so devilish cold', said one, and beat his arms crosswise.

'That it is', said another; 'I freeze so, that my teeth chatter.'

'If one only had a quid to chew', said a third.

Well! there was one who had an ounce or two; so they shared it between them, though it wasn't much, after all, that each got; and so they chewed and spat, and spat and chewed. This helped them somewhat; but in a little while they were just as bad as ever.

'Hutetu!' said one, and shivered and shook.

'Hutetu!' said the old woman, and shivered so, that every tooth in her head chattered. Then she pulled out the flask with brandy in it, and her hand shook so that the spirit splashed about in the flask, and then she took such a gulp, that it went 'bop' in her throat.

'What's that you've got in your flask, old girl?' said one of the grooms.

'Oh! it's only a drop of brandy, old man', said she.

'Brandy! Well, I never! Do let me have a drop', screamed the whole twelve, one after another.

'Oh! but it is such a little drop', mumbled the old woman, 'it will not even wet your mouths round.' But they must and would have it; there was no help for it; and so she pulled out the flask with the sleepy drink in it, and put it to the first man's lips; then she shook no more, but guided the flask so that each of them got what he wanted, and the twelfth had not done drinking before the first sat and snored. Then the Master Thief threw off his beggar's rags, and took one groom after the other so softly off their horses, and set them astride on the beams between the stalls; and so he called his eleven men, and rode off with the Squire's twelve horses. But when the Squire got up in the morning, and went to look after his grooms, they had just begun to come to; and some of them fell to spurring the beams with their spurs, till the splinters flew again, and some fell off, and some still hung on and sat there looking like fools.

'Ho! ho!' said the Squire; 'I see very well who has been here; but as for you, a pretty set of blockheads you must be to sit here and let the Master Thief steal the horses from between your legs.'

So they all got a good leathering because they had not kept a sharper look-out.

Further on in the day came the Master Thief again, and told how he had managed the matter, and asked for the Squire's daughter, as he had promised; but the Squire gave him one hundred dollars down, and said he must do something better still.

'Do you think now', said he, 'you can steal the horse from under me while I am out riding on his back?' 'O, yes! I daresay I could', said the Master Thief, 'if I were really sure of getting your daughter.'

Well, well, the Squire would see what he could do; and he told the Master Thief a day when he would be taking a ride on a great common where they drilled the troops. So the Master Thief soon got hold of an old worn-out jade of a mare, and set to work, and made traces and collar of withies and broom-twigs, and bought an old beggarly cart and a great cask. After that he told an old beggar woman, he would give her ten dollars if she would get inside the cask, and keep her mouth agape over the taphole, into which he was going to stick his finger. No harm should happen to her; she should only be driven about a little; and if he took his finger out more than once, she was to have ten dollars more. Then he threw a few rags and tatters over himself, and stuffed himself out, and put on a wig and a great beard of goat's hair, so that no one could know him again, and set off for the common, where the Squire had already been riding about a good bit. When he reached the place, he went along so softly and slowly that he scarce made an inch of way. 'Gee up! Gee up!' and so he went on a little; then he stood stock still, and so on a little again; and altogether the pace was so poor it never once came into the Squire's head that this could be the Master Thief.

At last the Squire rode right up to him, and asked if he had seen any one lurking about in the wood thereabouts. 'No', said the man, 'I haven't seen a soul.'

'Harkye, now', said the Squire, 'if you have a mind to ride into the wood, and hunt about and see if you can fall upon any one lurking about there, you shall have the loan of my horse, and a shilling into the bargain, to drink my health, for your pains.'

'I don't see how I can go', said the man, 'for I am going to a wedding with this cask of mead, which I have been to town to fetch, and here the tap has fallen out by the way, and so I must go along, holding my finger in the taphole.'

'Ride off', said the Squire; 'I'll look after your horse and cask.'

Well, on these terms the man was willing to go; but he begged the Squire to be quick in putting his finger into the taphole when he took his own out, and to mind and keep it there till he came back. At last the Squire grew weary of standing there with his finger in the taphole, so he took it out.

'Now I shall have ten dollars more!' screamed the old woman inside the cask; and then the Squire saw at once how the land lay, and took himself off home; but he had not gone far before they met him with a fresh horse, for the Master Thief had already been to his house, and told them to send one. The day after, he came to the Squire and would have his daughter, as he had given his word; but the Squire put him off again with fine words, and gave him two hundred dollars, and said he must do one more masterpiece. If he could do that, he should have her. Well, well, the Master Thief thought he could do it, if he only knew what it was to be.

'Do you think, now', said the Squire, 'you can steal the sheet off our bed, and the shift off my wife's back. Do you think you could do that?'

'It shall be done', said the Master Thief. 'I only wish I was as sure of getting your daughter.'

So when night began to fall, the Master Thief went out and cut down a thief who hung on the gallows, and threw him across his shoulders, and carried him off. Then he got a long ladder and set it up against the Squire's bedroom window, and so climbed up, and kept bobbing the dead man up and down, just for all the world like one that was peeping in at the window.

'That's the Master Thief, old lass!' said the Squire, and gave his wife a nudge on the side. 'Now see if I don't shoot him, that's all.'

So saying he took up a rifle which he had laid at his bedside.

'No! no! pray don't shoot him after telling him he might come and try', said his wife.

'Don't talk to me, for shoot him I will', said he; and so he lay there and aimed and aimed; but as soon as the head came up before the window, and he saw a little of it, so soon was it down again. At last he thought he had a good aim; 'bang' went the gun, down fell the dead body to the ground with a heavy thump, and down went the Master Thief too as fast as he could.

'Well', said the Squire, 'it is quite true that I am the chief magistrate in these parts; but people are fond of talking, and it would be a bore if they came to see this dead man's body. I think the best thing to be done is that I should go down and bury him.'

'You must do as you think best, dear', said his wife. So the Squire got out of bed and went downstairs, and he had scarce put his foot out of the door before the Master Thief stole in, and went straight upstairs to his wife.

'Why, dear, back already!' said she, for she thought it was her husband.

'O yes, I only just put him into a hole, and threw a little earth over him. It is enough that he is out of sight, for it is such a bad night out of doors; by-and-by I'll do it better. But just let me have the sheet to wipe myself with--he was so bloody-- and I have made myself in such a mess with him.'

So he got the sheet.

After a while he said:

'Do you know I am afraid you must let me have your nightshift too, for the sheet won't do by itself; that I can see.'

So she gave him the shift also. But just then it came across his mind that he had forgotten to lock the house-door, so he must step down and look to that before he came back to bed, and away he went with both shift and sheet.

A little while after came the true Squire.

'Why! what a time you've taken to lock the door, dear!' said his wife; 'and what have you done with the sheet and shift?'

'What do you say?' said the Squire.

'Why, I am asking what you have done with the sheet and shift that you had to wipe off the blood', said she.

'What, in the Deil's name!' said the Squire, 'has he taken me in this time too?'

Next day came the Master Thief and asked for the Squire's daughter, as he had given his word; and then the Squire dared not do anything else than give her to him, and a good lump of money into the bargain; for, to tell the truth, he was afraid lest the Master Thief should steal the eyes out of his head, and that the people would begin to say spiteful things of him if he broke his word. So the Master Thief lived well and happily from that time forward. I don't know whether he stole any more; but if he did, I am quite sure it was only for the sake of a bit of fun.

THE BEST WISH

Once on a time there were three brothers; I don't quite know how it happened, but each of them had got the right to wish one thing, whatever he chose. So the two elder were not long a-thinking; they wished that every time they put their hands in their pockets they might pull out a piece of money; for, said they:

'The man who has as much money as he wishes for is always sure to get on in the world.'

But the youngest wished something better still. He wished that every woman he saw might fall in love with him as soon as she saw him; and you shall soon hear how far better this was than gold and goods.

So, when they had all wished their wishes, the two elder were for setting out to see the world; and Boots, their youngest brother, asked if he mightn't go along with them; but they wouldn't hear of such a thing.

'Wherever we go', they said, 'we shall be treated as counts and kings; but you, you starveling wretch, who haven't a penny, and never will have one, who do you think will care a bit about you?'

'Well, but in spite of that, I'd like to go with you', said Boots; 'perhaps a dainty bit may fall to my share too off the plates of such high and mighty lords.'

At last, after begging and praying, he got leave to go with them, if he would be their servant, else they wouldn't hear of it.

So, when they had gone a day or so, they came to an inn, where the two who had the money alighted, and called for fish and flesh, and fowl, and brandy and mead, and everything that was good; but Boots, poor fellow, had to look after their luggage and all that belonged to the two great people. Now, as he went to and fro outside, and loitered about in the inn-yard, the innkeeper's wife looked out of window and saw the servant of the gentlemen upstairs; and, all at once, she thought she had never set eyes on such a handsome chap. So she stared and stared, and the longer she looked the handsomer he seemed.

'Why what, by the Deil's skin and bones, is it that you are standing there gaping at out of the window?' said her husband. 'I think 'twould be better if you just looked how the sucking pig is getting on, instead of hanging out of window in that way. Don't you know what grand folk we have in the house to-day?'

'Oh!' said his old dame, 'I don't care a farthing about such a pack of rubbish; if they don't like it they may lump it, and be off; but just do come and look at this lad out in the yard; so handsome a fellow I never saw in all my born days; and, if you'll do as I wish, we'll ask him to step in and treat him a little, for, poor lad, he seems to have a hard fight of it.'

'Have you lost the little brains you had, Goody?' said the husband, whose eyes glistened with rage; 'into the kitchen with you, and mind the fire; but don't stand there glowering after strange men.'

So the wife had nothing left for it but to go into the kitchen, and look after the cooking; as for the lad outside, she couldn't get leave to ask him in, or to treat him either; but just as she was about spitting the pig in the kitchen, she made an excuse for running out into the yard, and then and there she gave Boots a pair of scissors, of such a kind that they cut of themselves out of the air the loveliest clothes any one ever saw, silk and satin, and all that was fine.

'This you shall have because you are so handsome,' said the innkeeper's wife.

So when the two elder brothers had crammed themselves with roast and boiled, they wished to be off again, and Boots had to stand behind their carriage, and be their servant; and so they travelled a good way, till they came to another inn. There the two brothers again alighted and went indoors, but Boots, who had no money, they wouldn't have inside with them; no, he must wait outside and watch the luggage. 'And mind', they said, 'if any one asks whose servant you are, say we are two foreign Princes.'

But the same thing happened now as happened before; while Boots stood hanging about out in the yard, the innkeeper's wife came to the window and saw him, and she too fell in love with him, just like the first innkeeper's wife; and there she stood and stared, for she thought she could never have her fill of looking at him.

Then her husband came running through the room with something the two Princes had ordered.

'Don't stand there staring like a cow at a barn-door, but take this into the kitchen, and look after your fish-kettle, Goody', said the man; 'don't you see what grand people we have in the house to-day?'

'I don't care a farthing for such a pack of rubbish', said the wife; 'if they don't like what they get they may lump it, and eat what they brought with them. But just do come here, and see what you shall see! Such a handsome fellow as walks here, out in the yard, I never saw in all my born days. Shan't we ask him in and treat him a little; he looks as if he needed it, poor chap?' and then she went on:

'Such a love! such a love!'

'You never had much wit, and the little you had is clean gone, I can see', said the man, who was much more angry than the first innkeeper, and chased his wife back, neck and crop, into the kitchen.

'Into the kitchen with you, and don't stand glowering after lads', he said.

So she had to go in and mind her fish-kettle, and she dared not treat Boots, for she was afraid of her old man; but as she stood there making up the fire, she made an excuse for running out into the yard, and then and there she gave Boots a tablecloth, which was such that it covered itself with the best dishes you could think of, as soon as it was spread out.

'This you shall have', she said, 'because you're so handsome.'

So when the two brothers had eaten and drank of all that was in the house, and had paid the bill in hard cash, they set off again, and Boots stood up behind their carriage. But when they had gone so far that they grew hungry again, they turned into a third inn, and called for the best and dearest they could think of.

'For', said they, 'we are two kings on our travels, and as for our money, it grows like grass.'

Well, when the innkeeper heard that, there was such a roasting, and baking, and boiling; why! you might smell the dinner at the next neighbour's house, though it wasn't so very near; and the innkeeper was at his wits' end to find all he wished to put before the two kings. But Boots, he had to stand outside here too, and look after the things in the carriage.

So it was the same story over again. The innkeeper's wife came to the window and peeped out, and there she saw the servant standing by the carriage. Such a handsome chap she had never set eyes on before; so she looked and looked, and the more she stared the handsomer he seemed to the innkeeper's wife. Then out came the innkeeper, scampering through the room, with some dainty which the travelling kings had ordered, and he wasn't very soft-tongued when he saw his old dame standing and glowering out of the window.

'Don't you know better than to stand gaping and staring there, when we have such great folk in the house', he said; 'back into the kitchen with you this minute, to your custards.'

'Well! well!' she said, 'as for them, I don't care a pin. If they can't wait till the custards are baked, they may go without--that's all. But do, pray, come here, and you'll see such a lovely lad standing out here in the yard. Why I never saw such a pretty fellow in my life. Shan't we ask him in now, and treat him a little, for he looks as if it would do him good. Oh! what a darling! What a darling!'

'A wanton gadabout you've been all your days, and so you are still', said her husband, who was in such a rage he scarce knew which leg to stand on; 'but if you don't be off to your custards this minute, I'll soon find out how to make you stir your stumps; see if I don't.'

So the wife had off to her custards as fast as she could, for she knew that her husband would stand no nonsense; but as she stood there over the fire she stole out into the yard, and gave Boots a tap.

'If you only turn this tap', she said; 'you'll get the finest drink of whatever kind you choose, both mead, and wine, and brandy; and this you shall have because you are so handsome.'

So when the two brothers had eaten and drunk all they could, they started from the inn, and Boots stood up behind again as their servant, and thus they drove far and wide, till they came to a king's palace. There the two elder gave themselves out for two emperor's sons, and as they had plenty of money, and were so fine that their clothes shone again ever so far off, they were well treated. They had rooms in the palace, and the king couldn't tell how to make enough of them. But Boots, who went about in the same rags he stood in when he left home, and who had never a penny in his pocket, he was taken up by the king's guard, and put across to an island, whither they used to row over all the beggars and rogues that came to the palace. This the king had ordered, because he wouldn't have the mirth at the palace spoilt by those dirty blackguards; and thither, too, only just as much food as would keep body and soul together was sent over everyday. Now Boots' brothers saw very well that the guard was rowing him over to the island, but they were glad to be rid of him, and didn't pay the least heed to him.

But when Boots got over there, he just pulled out his scissors and began to snip and cut in the air; so the scissors cut out the finest clothes any one would wish to see; silk and satin both, and all the beggars on the island were soon dressed far finer than the king and all his guests in the palace. After that, Boots pulled out his table-cloth, and spread it out, and so they got food too, the poor beggars. Such a feast had never been seen at the king's palace, as was served that day at the Beggars' Isle.

'Thirsty, too, I'll be bound you all are', said Boots, and out with his tap, gave it a turn, and so the beggars got all a drop to drink; and such ale and mead the king himself had never tasted in all his life.

So, next morning, when those who were to bring the beggars their food on the island, came rowing over with the scrapings of the porridge- pots and cheese-parings--that was what the poor wretches had--the beggars wouldn't so much as taste them, and the king's men fell to wondering what it could mean; but they wondered much more when they got a good look at the beggars, for they were so fine the guard thought they must be Emperors or Popes at least, and that they must have rowed to a wrong island; but when they looked better about them, they saw they were come to the old place.

Then they soon found out it must be he whom they had rowed out the day before who had brought the beggars on the island all this state and bravery; and as soon as they got back to the palace, they were not slow to tell how the man, whom they had rowed over the day before, had dressed out all the beggars so fine and grand that precious things fell from their clothes.

'And as for the porridge and cheese we took, they wouldn't even taste them, so proud have they got', they said.

One of them, too, had smelt out that the lad had a pair of scissors which he cut out the clothes with.

'When he only snips with those scissors up in the air he snips and cuts out nothing but silk and satin', said he.

So, when the Princess heard that, she had neither peace nor rest till she saw the lad and his scissors that cut out silk and satin from the air; such a pair was worth having, she thought, for with its help she would soon get all the finery she wished for. Well, she begged the king so long and hard, he was forced to send a messenger for the lad who owned the scissors; and when he came to the palace, the Princess asked him if it were true that he had such and such a pair of scissors, and if he would sell it to her. Yes, it was all true he had such a pair, said Boots, but sell it he wouldn't; and with that he took the scissors out of his pocket, and snipped and snipped with them in the air till strips of silk and satin flew all about him.

'Nay, but you must sell me these scissors', said the Princess. 'You may ask what you please for them, but have them I must.'

No! Such a pair of scissors he wouldn't sell at any price, for he could never get such a pair again; and while they stood and haggled for the scissors, the Princess had time to look better at Boots, and she too thought with the innkeepers' wives that she had never seen such a handsome fellow before. So she began to bargain for the scissors over again, and begged and prayed Boots to let her have them; he might ask many, many hundred dollars for them, 'twas all the same to her, so she got them.

'No! sell them I won't', said Boots; 'but all the same, if I can get leave to sleep one night on the floor of the Princess' bedroom, close by the door, I'll give her the scissors. I'll do her no harm, but if she's afraid, she may have two men to watch inside the room.'

Yes! the Princess was glad enough to give him leave, for she was ready to grant him anything if she only got the scissors. So Boots lay on the floor inside the Princess' bedroom that night, and two men stood watch there too; but the Princess didn't get much rest after all; for when she ought to have been asleep, she must open her eyes to look at Boots, and so it went on the whole night. If she shut her eyes for a minute, she peeped out at him again the next, such a handsome fellow he seemed to her to be.

Next morning Boots was rowed over to the Beggars' isle again; but when they came with the porridge scrapings and cheese parings from the palace, there was no one who would taste them that day either, and so those who brought the food were more astonished than ever. But one of those who brought the food contrived to smell out that the lad who had owned the scissors owned also a table-cloth, which he only needed to spread out, and it was covered with all the good things he could wish for. So when he got back to the palace, he wasn't long before he said:

'Such hot joints and such custards I never saw the like of in the king's palace.'

And when the Princess heard that, she told it to the king, and begged and prayed so long, that he was forced to send a messenger out to the island to fetch the lad who owned the table-cloth; and so Boots came back to the palace. The Princess must and would have the cloth of him, and offered him gold and green woods for it, but Boots wouldn't sell it at any price.

'But if I may have leave to lie on the bench by the Princess' bed- side to-night, she shall have the cloth; but if she's afraid, she is welcome to set four men to watch inside the room.'

Yes! the Princess agreed to this, so Boots lay down on the bench by the bed-side, and the four men watched; but if the Princess hadn't much sleep the night before, she had much less this, for she could scarce get a wink of sleep; there she lay wide awake looking at the lovely lad the whole night through, and after all, the night seemed too short.

Next morning Boots was rowed off again to the Beggars' island, though sorely against the Princess' will, so happy was she to be near him; but it was past praying for; to the island he must go, and there was an end of it. But when those who brought the food to the beggars came with the porridge scrapings and cheese parings, there wasn't one of them who would even look at what the king sent, and those who brought it didn't wonder either; though they all thought it strange that none of them were thirsty. But just then, one of the king's guard smelled out that the lad who had owned the scissors and the table-cloth had a tap besides, which, if one only turned it a little, gave out the rarest drink, both ale, and mead, and wine. So when he came back to the palace, he couldn't keep his mouth shut this time any more than before; he went about telling high and low about the tap, and how easy it was to draw all sorts of drink out of it.

'And as for that mead and ale, I've never tasted the like of them in the king's palace; honey and syrup are nothing to them for sweetness.'

So when the Princess heard that, she was all for getting the tap, and was nothing loath to strike a bargain with the owner either. So she went again to the king, and begged him to send a messenger to the Beggars' Isle after the lad who had owned the scissors and cloth, for now he had another thing worth having, she said; and when the king heard it was a tap, that was good to give the best ale and wine any one could drink, when one gave it a turn, he wasn't long in sending the messenger, I should think.

So when Boots came up to the palace, the Princess asked whether it were true he had a tap which could do such and such things? 'Yes! he had such a tap in his waistcoat pocket', said Boots; but when the Princess wished with all her might to buy it, Boots said, as he had said twice before, he wouldn't sell it, even if the Princess bade half the kingdom for it.

'But all the same', said Boots; 'if I may have leave to sleep on the Princess' bed to-night, outside the quilt, she shall have my tap. I'll not do her any harm; but, if she's afraid, she may set eight men to watch in her room.'

'Oh, no!' said the Princess, 'there was no need of that, she knew him now so well'; and so Boots lay outside the Princess' bed that night. But if she hadn't slept much the two nights before, she had less sleep that night; for she couldn't shut her eyes the livelong night, but lay and looked at Boots, who lay alongside her outside the quilt.

So, when she got up in the morning, and they were going to row Boots back to the island, she begged them to hold hard a little bit; and in she ran to the king, and begged him so prettily to let her have Boots for a husband, she was so fond of him, and, unless she had him, she did not care to live.

'Well, well!' said the king, 'you shall have him if you must; for he who has such things is just as rich as you are.'

So Boots got the Princess and half the kingdom--the other half he was to have when the king died; and so everything went smooth and well; but as for his brothers, who had always been so bad to him, he packed them off to the Beggars' island.

'There', said Boots, 'perhaps they may find out which is best off, the man who has his pockets full of money, or the man whom all women fall in love with.'

Nor, to tell you the truth, do I think it would help them much to wander about upon the Beggars' island pulling pieces of money out of their pockets; and so, if Boots hasn't taken them off the island, there they are still walking about to this very day, eating cheese- parings and the scrapings of the porridge-pots.

THE THREE BILLY-GOATS GRUFF

Once on a time there were three Billy-goats, who were to go up to the hill-side to make themselves fat, and the name of all three was 'Gruff'. On the way up was a bridge over a burn they had to cross; and under the bridge lived a great ugly Troll, with eyes as big as saucers, and a nose as long as a poker.

So first of all came the youngest billy-goat Gruff to cross the bridge.

'Trip, trap; trip, trap!' went the bridge.

'WHO'S THAT tripping over my bridge?' roared the Troll.

'Oh! it is only I, the tiniest billy-goat Gruff; and I'm going up to the hill-side to make myself fat', said the billy-goat, with such a small voice.

'Now, I'm coming to gobble you up', said the Troll.

'Oh, no! pray don't take me. I'm too little, that I am', said the billy-goat; 'wait a bit till the second billy-goat Gruff comes, he's much bigger.'

'Well! be off with you', said the Troll.

A little while after came the second billy-goat Gruff to cross the bridge.

'TRIP, TRAP! TRIP, TRAP! TRIP, TRAP!' went the bridge.

'WHO'S THAT tripping over my bridge?' roared the Troll.

'Oh! it's the second billy-goat Gruff, and I'm going up to the hill- side to make myself fat', said the billy-goat, who hadn't such a small voice.

'Now, I'm coming to gobble you up', said the Troll.

'Oh, no! don't take me, wait a little till the big billy-goat Gruff comes, he's much bigger.'

'Very well! be off with you', said the Troll.

But just then up came the big billy-goat Gruff.

'TRIP, TRAP! TRIP, TRAP! TRIP, TRAP!' went the bridge, for the billy- goat was so heavy that the bridge creaked and groaned under him.

'WHO'S THAT tramping over my bridge?' roared the Troll.

'IT'S I! THE BIG BILLY-GOAT GRUFF', said the billy-goat, who had an ugly hoarse voice of his own.

'Now, I'm coming to gobble you up', roared the Troll.

Well, come along! I've got two spears,   And I'll poke your eyeballs out at your ears;   I've got besides two curling-stones,   And I'll crush you to bits, body and bones.

That was what the big billy-goat said; and so he flew at the Troll and poked his eyes out with his horns, and crushed him to bits, body and bones, and tossed him out into the burn, and after that he went up to the hill-side. There the billy-goats got so fat they were scarce able to walk home again; and if the fat hasn't fallen off them, why they're still fat; and so:

Snip, snap, snout,   This tale's told out.

WELL DONE AND ILL PAID

Once on a time there was a man, who had to drive his sledge to the wood for fuel. So a Bear met him.

'Out with your horse', said the Bear, 'or I'll strike all your sheep dead by summer.'

'Oh! heaven help me then', said the man; 'there's not a stick of firewood in the house; you must let me drive home a load of fuel, else we shall be frozen to death. I'll bring the horse to you to- morrow morning.'

Yes! on those terms he might drive the wood home, that was a bargain; but Bruin said, 'if he didn't come back, he should lose all his sheep by summer'.

So the man got the wood on the sledge and rattled homewards, but he wasn't over pleased at the bargain you may fancy. So just then a Fox met him.

'Why, what's the matter?' said the Fox; 'why are you so down in the mouth?'

'Oh, if you want to know', said the man; 'I met a Bear up yonder in the wood, and I had to give my word to him to bring Dobbin back to- morrow, at this very hour; for if he didn't get him, he said he would tear all my sheep to death by sum- mer.'

'Stuff, nothing worse than that', said the Fox; 'if you'll give me your fattest wether, I'll soon set you free; see if I don't.'

Yes! the man gave his word, and swore he would keep it too.

'Well, when you come with Dobbin to-morrow for the bear', said the Fox, 'I'll make a clatter up in that heap of stones yonder, and so when the bear asks what that noise is, you must say 'tis Peter the Marksman, who is the best shot in the world; and after that you must help yourself.'

Next day off set the man, and when he met the Bear, something began to make a clatter up in the heap of stones.

'Hist! what's that?' said the Bear.

'Oh! that's Peter the Marksman, to be sure', said the than; 'he's the best shot in the world. I know him by his voice.'

'Have you seen any bears about here, Eric?' shouted out a voice in the wood.

'Say, no!' said the Bear.

'No, I haven't seen any', said Eric.

'What's that then, that stands alongside your sledge?' bawled out the voice in the wood.

'Say it's an old fir-stump', said the Bear.

'Oh, it's only an old fir-stump', said the man.

'Such fir-stumps we take in our country and roll them on our sledges', bawled out the voice; 'if you can't do it yourself, I'll come and help you.'

'Say you can help yourself, and roll me up on the sledge', said the Bear.

'No, thank ye, I can help myself well enough', said the man, and rolled the Bear on to the sledge.

'Such fir-stumps we always bind fast on our sledges in our part of the world', bawled out the voice; 'shall I come and help you?'

'Say you can help yourself, and bind me fast, do', said the Bear.

'No, thanks, I can help myself well enough', said the man, who set to binding Bruin fast with all the ropes he had, so that at last the bear couldn't stir a paw.

'Such fir-stumps we always drive our axes into, in our part of the world', bawled out the voice; 'for then we guide them better going down the steep pitches.'

'Pretend to drive your axe into me, do now', said the bear. Then the man took up his axe, and at one blow split the bear's skull, so that Bruin lay dead in a trice, and so the man and the Fox were great friends, and on the best terms. But when they came near the farm, the Fox said:

'I've no mind to go right home with you, for I can't say I like your tykes; so I'll just wait here, and you can bring the wether to me, but mind and pick out one nice and fat.'

Yes! the man would be sure to do that, and thanked the Fox much for his help. So when he had put up Dobbin, he went across to the sheep- stall.

'Whither away, now?' asked his old dame.

'Oh!' said the man, 'I'm only going to the sheep-stall to fetch a fat wether for that cunning Fox, who set our Dobbin free. I gave him my word I would.'

'Whither, indeed', said the old dame; 'never a one shall that thief of a Fox get. Haven't we got Dobbin safe, and the bear into the bargain; and as for the Fox, I'll be bound he's stolen more of our geese than the wether is worth; and even if he hasn't stolen them, he will. No, no; take a brace of your swiftest hounds in a sack, and slip them loose after him; and then, perhaps, we shall be rid of this robbing Reynard.'

Well, the man thought that good advice; so he took two fleet red hounds, put them into a sack, and set off with them.

'Have you brought the wether?' said the Fox.

'Yes, come and take it', said the man, as he untied the sack and let slip the hounds.

'HUF', said the Fox, and gave a great spring; 'true it is what the old saw says, "Well done is often ill paid"; and now, too, I see the truth of another saying, "The worst foes are those of one's own house."' That was what the Fox said as he ran off, and saw the red foxy hounds at his heels.

THE HUSBAND WHO WAS TO MIND THE HOUSE

Once on a time there was a man, so surly and cross, he never thought his wife did anything right in the house. So, one evening, in hay-making time, he came home, scolding and swearing, and showing his teeth and making a dust.

'Dear love, don't be so angry; there's a good man', said his goody; 'to-morrow let's change our work. I'll go out with the mowers and mow, and you shall mind the house at home.'

Yes! the husband thought that would do very well. He was quite willing, he said.

So, early next morning, his goody took a scythe over her neck, and went out into the hay-field with the mowers, and began to mow; but the man was to mind the house, and do the work at home.

First of all, he wanted to churn the butter; but when he had churned a while, he got thirsty, and went down to the cellar to tap a barrel of ale. So, just when he had knocked in the bung, and was putting the tap into the cask, he heard overhead the pig come into the kitchen. Then off he ran up the cellar steps, with the tap in his hand, as fast as he could, to look after the pig, lest it should upset the churn; but when he got up, and saw the pig had already knocked the churn over, and stood there, routing and grunting amongst the cream which was running all over the floor, he got so wild with rage that he quite forgot the ale-barrel, and ran at the pig as hard as he could. He caught it, too, just as it ran out of doors, and gave it such a kick, that piggy lay for dead on the spot.

Then all at once he remembered he had the tap in his hand; but when he got down to the cellar, every drop of ale had run out of the cask.

Then he went into the dairy and found enough cream left to fill the churn again, and so he began to churn, for butter they must have at dinner. When he had churned a bit, he remembered that their milking cow was still shut up in the byre, and hadn't had a bit to eat or a drop to drink all the morning, though the sun was high. Then all at once he thought 'twas too far to take her down to the meadow, so he'd just get her up on the house top-for the house, you must know, was thatched with sods, and a fine crop of grass was growing there. Now their house lay close up against a steep down, and he thought if he laid a plank across to the thatch at the back he'd easily get the cow up.

But still he couldn't leave the churn, for there was his little babe crawling about on the floor, and 'if I leave it', he thought, 'the child is safe to upset it'. So he took the churn on his back, and went out with it; but then he thought he'd better first water the cow before he turned her out on the thatch; so he took up a bucket to draw water out of the well; but, as he stooped down at the well's brink, all the cream ran out of the churn over his shoulders, and so down into the well.

Now it was near dinner-time, and he hadn't even got the butter yet; so he thought he'd best boil the porridge, and filled the pot with water, and hung it over the fire. When he had done that, he thought the cow might perhaps fall off the thatch and break her legs or her neck. So he got up on the house to tie her up. One end of the rope he made fast to the cow's neck and the other he slipped down the chimney and tied round his own thigh; and he had to make haste, for the water now began to boil in the pot, and he had still to grind the oatmeal.

So he began to grind away; but while he was hard at it, down fell the cow off the house-top after all, and as she fell, she dragged the man up the chimney by the rope. There he stuck fast; and as for the cow, she hung half-way down the wall, swinging between heaven and earth, for she could neither get down nor up.

And now the goody had waited seven lengths and seven breadths for her husband to come and call them home to dinner; but never a call they had. At last she thought she'd waited long enough, and went home. But when she got there and saw the cow hanging in such an ugly place, she ran up and cut the rope in two with her scythe. But as she did this, down came her husband out of the chimney; and so when his old dame came inside the kitchen, there she found him standing on his head in the porridge pot.

DAPPLEGRIM

Once on a time there was a rich couple who had twelve sons; but the youngest when he was grown up, said he wouldn't stay any longer at home, but be off into the world to try his luck. His father and mother said he did very well at home, and had better stay where he was. But no, he couldn't rest; away he must and would go. So at last they gave him leave. And when he had walked a good bit, he came to a king's palace, where he asked for a place, and got it.

Now the daughter of the king of that land had been carried off into the hill by a Troll, and the king had no other children; so he and all his land were in great grief and sorrow, and the king gave his word that any one who could set her free should have the Princess and half the kingdom. But there was no one who could do it, though many tried.

So when the lad had been there a year or so, he longed to go home again and see his father and mother, and back he went, but when he got home his father and mother were dead, and his brothers had shared all that the old people owned between them, and so there was nothing left for the lad.

'Shan't I have anything at all, then, out of father's and mother's goods?' said the lad.

'Who could tell you were still alive, when you went gadding and wandering about so long?' said his brothers. 'But all the same; there are twelve mares up on the hill which we haven't yet shared among us; if you choose to take them for your share, you're quite welcome.'

Yes! the lad was quite content; so he thanked his brothers, and went at once up on the hill, where the twelve mares were out at grass. And when he got up there and found them, each of them had a foal at her side, and one of them had besides, along with her, a big dapple-gray foal, which was so sleek that the sun shone from its coat.

'A fine fellow you are, my little foal', said the lad.

'Yes', said the foal; 'but if you'll only kill all the other foals, so that I may run and suck all the mares one year more, you'll see how big and sleek I'll be then.'

Yes! the lad was ready to do that; so he killed all those twelve foals, and went home again.

So when he came back the next year to look after his foal and mares, the foal was so fat and sleek, that the sun shone from its coat, and it had grown so big, the lad had hard work to mount it. As for the mares, they had each of them another foal.

'Well, it's quite plain I lost nothing by letting you suck all my twelve mares', said the lad to the yearling, 'but now you're big enough to come along with me.'

'No', said the colt, 'I must bide here a year longer; and now kill all the twelve foals, that I may suck all the mares this year too, and you'll see how big and sleek I'll be by summer.'

Yes! the lad did that; and next year when he went up on the hill to look after his colt and the mares, each mare had her foal, but the dapple colt was so tall the lad couldn't reach up to his crest when he wanted to feel how fat he was; and so sleek he was too, that his coat glistened in the sunshine.

'Big and beautiful you were last year, my colt', said the lad, 'but this year you're far grander. There's no such horse in the king's stable. But now you must come along with me.'

'No', said Dapple again, 'I must stay here one year more. Kill the twelve foals as before, that I may suck the mares the whole year, and then just come and look at me when the summer comes.'

Yes! the lad did that; he killed the foals, and went away home.

But when he went up next year to look after Dapple and the mares, he was quite astonished. So tall, and stout, and sturdy, he never thought a horse could be; for Dapple had to lie down on all fours before the lad could bestride him, and it was hard work to get up even then, although he lay flat; and his coat was so smooth and sleek, the sunbeams shone from it as from a looking-glass.

This time Dapple was willing enough to follow the lad, so he jumped up on his back, and when he came riding home to his brothers, they all clapped their hands and crossed themselves, for such a horse they had never heard of nor seen before.

'If you will only get me the best shoes you can for my horse, and the grandest saddle and bridle that are to be found', said the lad, 'you may have my twelve mares that graze up on the hill yonder, and their twelve foals into the bargain.' For you must know that this year too every mare had her foal.

Yes, his brothers were ready to do that, and so the lad got such strong shoes under his horse, that the stones flew high aloft as he rode away across the hills; and he had a golden saddle and a golden bridle, which gleamed and glistened a long way off.

'Now we're off to the king's palace', said Dapplegrim--that was his name; 'but mind you ask the king for a good stable and good fodder for me.'

Yes! the lad said he would mind; he'd be sure not to forget; and when he rode off from his brothers' house, you may be sure it wasn't long, with such a horse under him, before he got to the king's palace.

When he came there the king was standing on the steps, and stared and stared at the man who came riding along.

'Nay, nay!', said he, 'such a man and such a horse I never yet saw in all my life.'

But when the lad asked if he could get a place in the king's household, the king was so glad he was ready to jump and dance as he stood on the steps.

Well, they said, perhaps he might get a place there.

'Aye', said the lad, 'but I must have good stable-room for my horse, and fodder that one can trust.'

Yes! he should have meadow-hay and oats, as much as Dapple could cram, and all the other knights had to lead their horses out of the stable that Dapplegrim might stand alone, and have it all to himself.

But it wasn't long before all the others in the king's household began to be jealous of the lad, and there was no end to the bad things they would have done to him, if they had only dared. At last they thought of telling the king he had said he was man enough to set the king's daughter free--whom the Troll had long since carried away into the hill--if he only chose. The king called the lad before him, and said he had heard the lad said he was good to do so and so; so now he must go and do it. If he did it, he knew how the king had promised his daughter and half the kingdom, and that promise would be faithfully kept; if he didn't, he should be killed.

The lad kept on saying he never said any such thing; but it was no good--the king wouldn't even listen to him; and so the end of it was he was forced to say he'd go and try.

So he went into the stable, down in the mouth and heavy-hearted, and then Dapplegrim asked him at once why he was in such dumps.

Then the lad told him all, and how he couldn't tell which way to turn:

'For as for setting the Princess free, that's downright stuff.'

'Oh! but it might be done, perhaps', said Dapplegrim. 'I'll help you through; but you must first have me well shod. You must go and ask for ten pound of iron and twelve pound of steel for the shoes, and one smith to hammer and another to hold.'

Yes, the lad did that, and got for answer 'Yes!' He got both the iron and the steel, and the smiths, and so Dapplegrim was shod both strong and well, and off went the lad from the court-yard in a cloud of dust.

But when he came to the hill into which the Princess had been carried, the pinch was how to get up the steep wall of rock where the Troll's cave was, in which the Princess had been hid. For you must know the hill stood straight up and down right on end, as upright as a house-wall, and as smooth as a sheet of glass.

The first time the lad went at it he got a little way up; but then Dapple's fore-legs slipped, and down they went again, with a sound like thunder on the hill.

The second time he rode at it he got some way further up; but then one fore-leg slipped, and down they went with a crash like a landslip.

But the third time Dapple said:

'Now we must show our mettle'; and went at it again till the stones flew heaven-high about them, and so they got up.

Then the lad rode right into the cave at full speed, and caught up the Princess, and threw her over his saddle-bow and out and down again before the Troll had time even to get on his legs; and so the Princess was freed.

When the lad came back to the palace, the king was both happy and glad to get his daughter back; that you may well believe; but somehow or other, though I don't know how, the others about the court had so brought it about that the king was angry with the lad after all.

'Thanks you shall have for freeing my Princess', said he to the lad, when he brought the Princess into the hall, and made his bow.

'She ought to be mine as well as yours; for you're a word-fast man, I hope', said the lad.

'Aye, aye!' said the king, 'have her you shall, since I said it; but first of all, you must make the sun shine into my palace hall.'

Now, you must know there was a high steep ridge of rock close outside the windows, which threw such a shade over the hall that never a sunbeam shone into it.

'That wasn't in our bargain', answered the lad; 'but I see this is past praying against; I must e'en go and try my luck, for the Princess I must and will have.'

So down he went to Dapple, and told him what the king wanted, and Dapplegrim thought it might easily be done, but first of all he must be new shod; and for that ten pound of iron, and twelve pound of steel besides, were needed, and two smiths, one to hammer and the other to hold, and then they'd soon get the sun to shine into the palace hall.

So when the lad asked for all these things, he got them at once--the king couldn't say nay for very shame; and so Dapplegrim got new shoes, and such shoes! Then the lad jumped upon his back, and off they went again; and for every leap that Dapplegrim gave, down sank the ridge fifteen ells into the earth, and so they went on till there was nothing left of the ridge for the king to see.

When the lad got back to the king's palace, he asked the king if the Princess were not his now; for now no one could say that the sun didn't shine into the hall. But then the others set the king's back up again, and he answered the lad should have her of course, he had never thought of anything else; but first of all he must get as grand a horse for the bride to ride on to church as the bridegroom had himself.

The lad said the king hadn't spoken a word about this before, and that he thought he had now fairly earned the Princess; but the king held to his own; and more, if the lad couldn't do that he should lose his life; that was what the king said. So the lad went down to the stable in doleful dumps, as you may well fancy, and there he told Dapplegrim all about it; how the king had laid that task on him, to find the bride as good a horse as the bridegroom had himself, else he would lose his life.

'But that's not so easy', he said, 'for your match isn't to be found in the wide world.'

'Oh yes, I have a match', said Dapplegrim; 'but 'tisn't so easy to find him, for he abides in Hell. Still we'll try. And now you must go up to the king and ask for new shoes for me, ten pound of iron, and twelve pound of steel; and two smiths, one to hammer and one to hold; and mind you see that the points and ends of these shoes are sharp; and twelve sacks of rye, and twelve sacks of barley, and twelve slaughtered oxen, we must have with us; and mind, we must have the twelve ox-hides, with twelve hundred spikes driven into each; and, let me see, a big tar-barrel--that's all we want.'

So the lad went up to the king and asked for all that Dapplegrim had said, and the king again thought he couldn't say nay, for shame's sake, and so the lad got all he wanted.

Well, he jumped up on Dapplegrim's back, and rode away from the palace, and when he had ridden far far over hill and heath, Dapple asked:

'Do you hear anything?'

'Yes, I hear an awful hissing and rustling up in the air,' said the lad; 'I think I'm getting afraid.'

'That's all the wild birds that fly through the wood. They are sent to stop us; but just cut a hole in the corn-sacks, and then they'll have so much to do with the corn, they'll forget us quite.'

Yes! the lad did that; he cut holes in the corn-sacks, so that the rye and barley ran out on all sides. Then all the wild birds that were in the wood came flying round them so thick that the sunbeams grew dark; but as soon as they saw the corn, they couldn't keep to their purpose, but flew down and began to pick and scratch at the rye and barley, and after that they began to fight among themselves. As for Dapplegrim and the lad, they forgot all about them, and did them no harm.

So the lad rode on and on--far far over mountain and dale, over sand- hills and moor. Then Dapplegrim began to prick up his ears again, and at last he asked the lad if he heard anything?

'Yes! now I hear such an ugly roaring and howling in the wood all round, it makes me quite afraid.'

'Ah!' said Dapplegrim, 'that's all the wild beasts that range through the wood, and they're sent out to stop us. But just cast out the twelve carcasses of the oxen, that will give them enough to do, and so they'll forget us outright.'

Yes! the lad cast out the carcasses, and then all the wild beasts in the wood, both bears, and wolves, and lions--all fell beasts of all kinds--came after them. But when they saw the carcasses, they began to fight for them among themselves till blood flowed in streams; but Dapplegrim and the lad they quite forgot.

So the lad rode far away, and they changed the landscape many many times, for Dapplegrim didn't let the grass grow under him, as you may fancy. At last Dapple gave a great neigh.

'Do you hear anything?' he said.

'Yes, I hear something like a colt neighing loud, a long long way off', answered the lad.

'That's a full-grown colt then', said Dapplegrim, 'if we hear him neigh so loud such a long way off.'

After that they travelled a good bit, changing the landscape once or twice, maybe. Then Dapplegrim gave another neigh.

'Now listen, and tell me if you hear anything', he said.

'Yes, now I hear a neigh like a full-grown horse', answered the lad.

'Aye! aye!' said Dapplegrim, 'you'll hear him once again soon, and then you'll hear he's got a voice of his own.'

So they travelled on and on, and changed the landscape once or twice, perhaps, and then Dapplegrim neighed the third time; but before he could ask the lad if he heard anything, something gave such a neigh across the heathy hill-side, the lad thought hill and rock would surely be rent asunder.

'Now, he's here!' said Dapplegrim; 'make haste, now, and throw the ox hides, with the spikes in them, over me, and throw down the tar- barrel on the plain; then climb up into that great spruce-fir yonder. When it comes fire will flash out of both nostrils, and then the tar- barrel will catch fire. Now, mind what I say. If the flame rises, I win; if it falls, I lose; but if you see me winning take and cast the bridle--you must take it off me--over its head, and then it will be tame enough.'

So just as the lad had done throwing the ox hides, with the spikes, over Dapple-grim, and had cast down the tar-barrel on the plain, and had got well up into the spruce-fir, up galloped a horse, with fire flashing out of his nostrils, and the flame caught the tar-barrel at once. Then Dapplegrim and the strange horse began to fight till the stones flew heaven high. They fought and bit, and kicked, both with fore-feet and hind-feet, and sometimes the lad could see them, and sometimes he couldn't; but at last the flame began to rise; for wherever the strange horse kicked or bit, he met the spiked hides, and at last he had to yield. When the lad saw that, he wasn't long in getting down from the tree, and in throwing the bridle over its head, and then it was so tame you could hold it with a pack-thread.

And what do you think? that horse was dappled too, and so like Dapplegrim, you couldn't tell which was which. Then the lad bestrode the new Dapple he had broken, and rode home to the palace, and old Dapplegrim ran loose by his side. So when he got home, there stood the king out in the yard.

'Can you tell me now', said the lad, 'which is the horse I have caught and broken, and which is the one I had before. If you can't, I think your daughter is fairly mine.'

Then the king went and looked at both Dapples, high and low, before and behind, but there wasn't a hair on one which wasn't on the other as well. 'No', said the king, 'that I can't; and since you've got my daughter such a grand horse for her wedding, you shall have her with all my heart. But still, we'll have one trial more, just to see whether you're fated to have her. First, she shall hide herself twice, and then you shall hide yourself twice. If you can find out her hiding-place, and she can't find out yours, why then you're fated to have her, and so you shall have her.'

'That's not in the bargain either', said the lad; 'but we must just try, since it must be so'; and so the Princess went off to hide herself first.

So she turned herself into a duck, and lay swimming on a pond that was close to the palace. But the lad only ran down to the stable, and asked Dapplegrim what she had done with herself.

'Oh, you only need to take your gun', said Dapplegrim, 'and go down to the brink of the pond, and aim at the duck which lies swimming about there, and she'll soon show herself.'

So the lad snatched up his gun and ran off to the pond. 'I'll just take a pop at this duck', he said, and began to aim at it.

'Nay, nay, dear friend, don't shoot. It's I', said the Princess.

So he had found her once.

The second time the Princess turned herself into a loaf of bread, and laid herself on the table among four other loaves; and so like was she to the others, no one could say which was which.

But the lad went again down to the stable to Dapplegrim, and said how the Princess had hidden herself again, and he couldn't tell at all what had become of her.

'Oh, just take and sharpen a good bread-knife', said Dapplegrim,' and do as if you were going to cut in two the third loaf on the left hand of those four loaves which are lying on the dresser in the king's kitchen, and you'll find her soon enough.'

Yes! the was down in the kitchen in no time, and began to sharpen the biggest bread-knife he could lay hands on; then he caught hold of the third loaf on the left hand, and put the knife to it, as though he was going to cut it in two. I'll just have a slice off this loaf', he said,

Nay, dear friend', said the Princess, 'don't cut. It's I' So he had found her twice.

Then he was to go and hide; but he and Dapplegrim had settled it all so well beforehand, it wasn't easy to find him. First he turned himself into a tick, and hid himself in Dapplegrim's left nostril; and the Princess went about hunting him everywhere, high and low; at last she wanted to go into Dapplegrim's stall, but he began to bite and kick, so that she daren't go near him, and so she couldn't find the lad.

'Well', she said, 'since I can't find you, you must show where you are yourself'; and in a trice the lad stood there on the stable floor.

The second time Dapplegrim told him again what to do; and then he turned himself into a clod of earth, and stuck himself between Dapple's hoof and shoe on the near forefoot. So the Princess hunted up and down, out and in, everywhere; at last she came into the stable, and wanted to go into Dapplegrim's loose-box. This time he let her come up to him, and she pried high and low, but under his hoofs she couldn't come, for he stood firm as a rock on his feet, and so she couldn't find the lad.

'Well; you must just show yourself, for I'm sure I can't find you', said the Princess, and as she spoke the lad stood by her side on the stable floor.

'Now you are mine indeed', said the lad; 'for now you can see I'm fated to have you.' This he said both to the father and daughter.

'Yes; it is so fated', said the king; 'so it must be.' Then they got ready the wedding in right down earnest, and lost no time about it; and the lad got on Dapplegrim, and the Princess on Dapplegrim's match, and then you may fancy they were not long on their way to the church.

FARMER WEATHERSKY

O nce on a time there was a man and his wife, who had an only son, and his name was Jack. The old dame thought it high time for her son to go out into the world to learn a trade, and bade her husband be off with him.

'But all you do', she said, 'mind you bind him to some one who can teach him to be master above all masters'; and with that she put some food and a roll of tobacco into a bag, and packed them off.

Well! they went to many masters; but one and all said they could make the lad as good as themselves, but better they couldn't make him. So when the man came home again to his wife with that answer, she said:

'I don't care what you make of him; but this I say and stick to, you must bind him to some one where he can learn to be master above all masters'; and with that she packed up more food and another roll of tobacco, and father and son had to be off again.

Now when they had walked a while they got upon the ice, and there they met a man who came whisking along in a sledge, and drove a black horse.

'Whither away?' said the man.

'Well!' said the father, 'I'm going to bind my son to some one who is good to teach him a trade; but my old dame comes of such fine folk, she will have him taught to be master above all masters.'

'Well met then', said the driver; 'I'm just the man for your money, for I'm looking out for such an apprentice. Up with you behind!' he added to the lad, and whisk! off they went, both of them, and sledge and horse, right up into the air.

'Nay, nay!' cried the lad's father, 'you haven't told me your name, nor where you live.'

'Oh!' said the master, 'I'm at home alike north and south, and east and west, and my name's **Farmer Weathersky**. In a year and a day you may come here again, and then I'll tell you if I like him.' So away they went through the air, and were soon out of sight.

So when the man got home, his old dame asked what had become of her son.

'Well', said the man, 'Heaven knows, I'm sure I don't. They went up aloft'; and so he told her what had happened. But when the old dame heard that her husband couldn't tell at all when her son's apprenticeship would be out, nor whither he had gone, she packed him off again, and gave him another bag of food and another roll of tobacco.

So, when he had walked a bit, he came to a great wood, which stretched on and on all day as he walked through it. When it got dark he saw a great light, and he went towards it. After a long, long time he came to a little but under a rock, and outside stood an old hag drawing water out of a well with her nose, so long was it.

'Good evening, mother!' said the man.

'The same to you', said the old hag. 'It's hundreds of years since any one called me mother.'

'Can I have lodging here to-night?' asked the man.

'No! that you can't', said she.

But then the man pulled out his roll of tobacco, lighted his pipe, and gave the old dame a whiff, and a pinch of snuff. Then she was so happy she began to dance for joy, and the end was, she gave the man leave to stop the night.

So next morning he began to ask after Farmer Weathersky. 'No! she never heard tell of him, but she ruled over all the four-footed beasts; perhaps some of them might know him.' So she played them all home with a pipe she had, and asked them all, but there wasn't one of them who knew anything about Farmer Weathersky.

'Well!' said the old hag, 'there are three sisters of us; maybe one of the other two know where he lives. I'll lend you my horse and sledge, and then you'll be at her house by night; but it's at least three hundred miles off, the nearest way.'

Then the man started off, and at night reached the house, and when he came there, there stood another old hag before the door, drawing water out of the well with her nose.

'Good evening, mother!' said the man.

'The same to you', said she; 'it's hundreds of years since any one called me mother.'

'Can I lodge here to-night?' asked the man.

'No!' said the old hag.

But he took out his roll of tobacco, lighted his pipe, and gave the old dame a whiff, and a good pinch of snuff besides, on the back of her hand. Then she was so happy that she began to jump and dance for joy, and so the man got leave to stay the night. When that was over, he began to ask after Farmer Weathersky. 'No! she had never heard tell of him; but she ruled all the fish in the sea; perhaps some of them might know something about him.' So she played them all home with a pipe she had, and asked them, but there wasn't one of them who knew anything about Farmer Weathersky.

'Well, well!' said the old hag, 'there's one sister of us left; maybe she knows something about him. She lives six hundred miles off, but I'll lend you my horse and sledge, and then you'll get there by nightfall.'

Then the man started off, and reached the house by nightfall, and there he found another old hag who stood before the grate, and stirred the fire with her nose, so long and tough it was.

'Good evening, mother!' said the man.

'The same to you', said the old hag; 'it's hundreds of years since any one called me mother.'

'Can I lodge here to-night?' asked the man.

'No', said the old hag.

Then the man pulled out his roll of tobacco again, and lighted his pipe, and gave the old hag such a pinch of snuff it covered the whole back of her hand. Then she got so happy she began to dance for joy, and so the man got leave to stay. But when the night was over, he began to ask after Farmer Weathersky. She never heard tell of him she said; but she ruled over all the birds of the air, and so she played them all home with a pipe she had, and when she had mustered them all, the Eagle was missing. But a little while after he came flying home, and when she asked him, he said he had just come straight from Farmer Weathersky. Then the old hag said he must guide the man thither; but the eagle said he must have something to eat first, and besides he must rest till the next day; he was so tired with flying that long way, he could scarce rise from the earth.

So when he had eaten his fill and taken a good rest, the old hag pulled a feather out of the Eagle's tail, and put the man there in its stead; so the Eagle flew off with the man, and flew, and flew, but they didn't reach Farmer Weathersky's house before midnight.

So when they got there, the Eagle said

'There are heaps of dead bodies lying about outside but you mustn't mind them. Inside the house every man Jack of them are so sound asleep, 't will be hard work to wake them; but you must go straight to the table drawer, and take out of it three crumbs of bread, and when you hear some one snoring loud, pull three feathers out of his head; he won't wake for all that.'

So the man did as he was told, and after he had taken the crumbs of bread, he pulled out the first feather.

'OOF!' growled Farmer Weathersky, for it was he who snored.

So the man pulled out another feather.

'OOF!' he growled again.

But when he pulled out the third, Farmer Weathersky roared so, the man thought roof and wall would have flown asunder, but for all that the snorer slept on.

After that the Eagle told him what he was to do. He went to the yard, and there at the stable-door he stumbled against a big gray stone, and that he lifted up; underneath it lay three chips of wood, and those he picked up too; then he knocked at the stable-door, and it opened of itself. Then he threw down the three crumbs of bread, and a hare came and ate them up; that hare he caught and kept. After that the Eagle bade him pull three feathers out of his tail, and put the hare, the stone, the chips, and himself there instead, and then he would fly away home with them all.

So when the Eagle had flown a long way, he lighted on a rock to rest.

'Do you see anything?' it asked.

'Yes', said the man, 'I see a flock of crows coming flying after us.'

'We'd better be off again, then', said the Eagle, who flew away.

After a while it asked again:

'Do you see anything now?'

'Yes', said the man; 'now the crows are close behind us.'

'Drop now the three feathers you pulled out of his head, said the Eagle.

Well, the man dropped the feathers, and as soon as ever he dropped them they became a flock of ravens which drove the crows home again. Then the Eagle flew on far away with the man, and at last it lighted on another stone to rest.

'Do you see anything?' it said.

'I'm not sure', said the man; 'I fancy I see something coming far far away'.

'We'd better get on then', said the Eagle; and after a while it said again:

'Do you see anything?'

'Yes', said the man, 'now he's close at our heels.'

'Now, you must let fall the chips of wood which you took from under the gray stone at the stable door', said the Eagle.

Yes! the man let them fall, and they grew at once up into tall thick wood, so that Farmer Weathersky had to go back home to fetch an axe to hew his way through. While he did this, the Eagle flew ever so far, but when it got tired, it lighted on a fir to rest.

'Do you see anything?' it said.

'Well! I'm not sure', said the man; 'but I fancy I catch a glimpse of something far away.'

'We'd best be off then', said the Eagle; and off it flew as fast as it could. After a while it said:

'Do you see anything now?'

'Yes! now he's close behind us', said the man.

'Now, you must drop the big stone you lifted up at the stable door', said the Eagle.

The man did so, and as it fell it became a great high mountain, which Farmer Weathersky had to break his way through. When he had got half through the mountain, he tripped and broke one of his legs, and so he had to limp home again and patch it up.

But while he was doing this, the Eagle flew away to the man's house with him and the hare, and as soon as they got home, the man went into the churchyard and sprinkled Christian mould over the hare, and lo! it turned into 'Jack', his son.

Well, you may fancy the old dame was glad to get her son again, but still she wasn't easy in her mind about his trade, and she wouldn't rest till he gave her a proof that he was 'master above all masters'.

So when the fair came round, the lad changed himself into a bay horse, and told his father to lead him to the fair. 'Now, when any one comes', he said, 'to buy me, you may ask a hundred dollars for me; but mind you don't forget to take the headstall off me; if you do, Farmer Weathersky will keep me for ever, for he it is who will come to deal with you.'

So it turned out. Up came a horse-dealer, who had a great wish to deal for the horse, and he gave a hundred dollars down for him; but when the bargain was struck, and Jack's father had pocketed the money, the horse-dealer wanted to have the headstall. 'Nay, nay!' said the man, 'there's nothing about that in the bargain; and besides, you can't have the headstall, for I've other horses at home to bring to town to-morrow.'

So each went his way; but they hadn't gone far before Jack took his own shape and ran away, and when his father got home, there sat Jack in the ingle.

Next day he turned himself into a brown horse, and told his father to drive him to the fair.

'And when any one comes to buy me, you may ask two hundred dollars for me--he'll give that and treat you besides; but whatever you do, and however much you drink, don't forget to take the headstall off me, else you'll never set eyes on me again.'

So all happened as he had said; the man got two hundred dollars for the horse and a glass of drink besides, and when the buyer and seller parted, it was as much as he could do to remember to take off the headstall. But the buyer and the horse hadn't got far on the road before Jack took his own shape, and when the man got home, there sat Jack in the ingle.

The third day, it was the same story over again: the lad turned himself into a black horse, and told his father some one would come and bid three hundred dollars for him, and fill his skin with meat and drink besides; but however much he ate or drank, he was to mind and not forget to take the headstall off, else he'd have to stay with Farmer Weathersky all his life long.

'No, no; I'll not forget, never fear', said the man.

So when he came to the fair, he got three hundred dollars for the horse, and as it wasn't to be a dry bargain, Farmer Weathersky made him drink so much that he quite forgot to take the headstall off, and away went Farmer Weathersky with the horse. Now when he had gone a little way, Farmer Weathersky thought he would just stop and have another glass of brandy; so he put a barrel of red-hot nails under his horse's nose, and a sieve of oats under his tail, hung the halter, upon a hook, and went into the inn. So the horse stood there and stamped and pawed, and snorted and reared. Just then out came a lassie, who thought it a shame to treat a horse so.

'Oh, poor beastie', she said, 'what a cruel master you must have to treat you so', and as she said this she pulled the halter off the hook, so that the horse might turn round and taste the oats.

'I'M AFTER YOU', roared Farmer Weathersky, who came rushing out of the door.

But the horse had already shaken off the headstall, and jumped into a duck-pond, where he turned himself into a tiny fish. In went Farmer Weathersky after him, and turned himself into a great pike. Then Jack turned himself into a dove, and Farmer Weathersky made himself into a hawk, and chased and struck at the dove. But just then a Princess stood at the window of the palace and saw this struggle.

'Ah! poor dove', she cried, 'if you only knew what I know, you'd fly to me through this window.'

So the dove came flying in through the window, and turned itself into Jack again, who told his own tale.

'Turn yourself into a gold ring, and put yourself on my finger', said the Princess.

'Nay, nay!' said Jack, 'that'll never do, for then Farmer Weathersky will make the king sick, and then there'll be no one who can make him well again till Farmer Weathersky comes and cures him, and then, for his fee, he'll ask for that gold ring.'

'Then I'll say I had it from my mother, and can't part with it', said the Princess.

Well, Jack turned himself into a gold ring, and put himself on the Princess' finger, and so Farmer Weathersky couldn't get at him. But then followed what the lad had foretold; the king fell sick, and there wasn't a doctor in the kingdom who could cure him till Farmer Weathersky came, and he asked for the ring off the Princess' finger for his fee. So the king sent a messenger to the Princess for the ring; but the Princess said she wouldn't part with it, her mother had left it her. When the king heard that, he flew into a rage, and said he would have the ring, whoever left it to her.

'Well', said the Princess, 'it's no good being cross about it. I can't get it off, and if you must have the ring, you must take my finger too.'

'If you'll let me try, I'll soon get the ring off', said Farmer Weathersky.

'No, thanks, I'll try myself', said the Princess, and flew off to the grate and put ashes on her finger. Then the ring slipped off and was lost among the ashes. So Farmer Weathersky turned himself into a cock, who scratched and pecked after the ring in the grate, till he was up to the ears in ashes. But while he was doing this, Jack turned himself into a fox, and bit off the cock's head; and so if the Evil One was in Farmer Weathersky, it is all over with him now.

LORD PETER

Once on a time there was a poor couple, and they had nothing in the world but three sons. What the names the two elder had I can't say, but the youngest he was called Peter. So when their father and mother died, the sons were to share what was left, but there was nothing but a porridge-pot, a griddle, and a cat.

The eldest, who was to have first choice, he took the pot; 'for', said he, 'whenever I lend the pot to any one to boil porridge, I can always get leave to scrape it'.

The second took the griddle; 'for', said he, 'whenever I lend it to any one, I'll always get a morsel of dough to make a bannock.'

But the youngest, he had no choice left him; if he was to choose anything it must be the cat.

'Well!' said he, 'if I lend the cat to any one I shan't get much by that; for if pussy gets a drop of milk, she'll want it all herself. Still, I'd best take her along with me; I shouldn't like her to go about here and starve.'

So the brothers went out into the world to try their luck, and each took his own way; but when the youngest had gorse a while, the cat said:

'Now you shall have a good turn, because you wouldn't let me stay behind in the old cottage and starve. Now, I'm off to the wood to lay hold of a fine fat head of game, and then you must go up to the king's palace that you see yonder, and say you are come with a little present for the king; and when he asks who sends it, you must say, "Why, who should it be from but Lord Peter."'

Well! Peter hadn't waited long before back came the cat with a reindeer from the wood; she had jumped up on the reindeer's head, between his horns, and said, 'If you don't go straight to the king's palace I'll claw your eyes out.'

So the reindeer had to go whether he liked it or no.

And when Peter got to the palace he went into the kitchen with the deer, and said: 'Here I'm come with a little present for the king, if he won't despise it.'

Then the King went out into the kitchen, and when he saw the fine plump reindeer, he was very glad.

'But, my dear friend', he said, 'who in the world is it that sends me such a fine gift?'

'Oh!' said Peter, 'who should send it but Lord Peter.'

'Lord Peter! Lord Peter!' said the King. 'Pray tell me where he lives'; for he thought it a shame not to know so great a man. But that was just what the lad wouldn't tell him; he daren't do it, he said, because his master had forbidden him.

So the King gave him a good bit of money to drink his health, and bade him be sure and say all kind of pretty things, and many thanks for the present to his master when he got home.

Next day the Cat went again into the wood, and jumped up on a red deer's head, and sat between his horns, and forced him to go to the palace. Then Peter went again into the kitchen, and said he was come with a little present for the King, if he would be pleased to take it. And the King was still more glad to get the red deer than he had been to get the reindeer, and asked again who it was that sent so fine a present.

'Why, it's Lord Peter, of course', said the lad; but when the King wanted to know where Lord Peter lived, he got the same answer as the day before; and this day, too, he gave Peter a good lump of money to drink his health with.

The third day the Cat came with an elk. And so when Peter got into the palace kitchen, and said he had a little present for the King, if he'd be pleased to take it, the King came out at once into the kitchen; and when he saw the grand big elk, he was so glad he scarce knew which leg to stand on; and this day, too, he gave Peter many many more dollars--at least a hundred. He wished now, once for all, to know where this Lord Peter lived, and asked and asked about this thing and that, but the lad said he daren't say, for his master's sake, who had strictly forbidden him to tell.

'Well, then', said the King, 'beg Lord Peter to come and see me.'

Yes, the lad would take that message; but when Peter got out into the yard again, and met the Cat, he said,

'A pretty scrape you've got me into now, for here's the King, who wants me to come and see him, and you know I've nothing to go in but these rags I stand and walk in.'

'Oh, don't be afraid about that', said the Cat; 'in three days you shall have coach and horses, and fine clothes, so fine that the gold falls from them, and then you may go and see the king very well. But mind, whatever you see in the king's palace, you must say you have far finer and grander things of your own. Don't forget that.'

No, no, Peter would bear that in mind, never fear.

So when three days were over, the Cat came with a coach and horses, and clothes, and all that Peter wanted, and altogether it was as grand as anything you ever set eyes on; so off he set, and the Cat ran alongside the coach. The King met him well and graciously; but whatever the King offered him, and whatever he showed him, Peter said, 'twas all very well, but he had far finer and better things in his own house. The King seemed not quite to believe this, but Peter stuck to what he said, and at last the King got so angry, he couldn't bear it any longer.

'Now I'll go home with you', he said, 'and see if it be true what you've been telling me, that you have far finer and better things of your own. But if you've been telling a pack of lies, Heaven help you, that's all I say.'

'Now, you've got me into a fine scrape', said Peter to the Cat, 'for here's the King coming home with me; but my home, that's not so easy to find, I think.'

'Oh! never mind', said the Cat; 'only do you drive after me as I run before.'

So off they set; first Peter, who drove after his Cat, and then the King and all his court.

But when they had driven a good bit, they came to a great flock of fine sheep, that had wool so long it almost touched the ground.

'If you'll only say', said the Cat to the Shepherd, 'this flock of sheep belongs to Lord Peter, when the King asks you, I'll give you this silver spoon', which she had taken with her from the King's palace.

Yes! he was willing enough to do that. So when the king came up, he said to the lad who watched the sheep,

'Well, I never saw so large and fine a flock of sheep in my life! Whose is it? my little lad.'

'Why', said the lad, 'whose should it be but Lord Peter's.'

A little while after they came to a great, great herd of fine brindled kine, who were all so sleek the sun shone from them.

'If you'll only say', said the Cat to the neat-herd, 'this herd is Lord Peter's, when the King asks you, I'll give you this silver ladle'; and the ladle too she had taken from the King's palace.

'Yes! with all my heart', said the neat-herd.

So when the King came up, he was quite amazed at the fine fat herd, for such a herd he had never seen before, and so he asked the neat- herd who owned those brindled kine.

'Why! who should own them but Lord Peter', said the neat-herd.

So they went on a little further, and came to a great, great drove of horses, the finest you ever saw, six of each colour, bay, and black, and brown, and chesnut.

'If you'll only say this drove of horses is Lord Peter's when the King asks you', said the Cat, 'I'll give you this silver stoop'; and the stoop too she had taken from the palace.

Yes! the lad was willing enough; and so when the King came up, he was quite amazed at the grand drove of horses, for the matches of such horses he had never yet set eyes on, he said.

So he asked the lad who watched them, whose all these blacks, and bays, and browns, and chesnuts were?

'Whose should they be', said the lad, 'but Lord Peter's.'

So when they had gone a good bit farther, they came to a castle; first there was a gate of tin, and next there was a gate of silver, and next a gate of gold. The castle itself was of silver, and so dazzling white, that it quite hurt one's eyes to look at in the sunbeams which fell on it just as they reached it.

So they went into it, and the Cat told Peter to say this was his house. As for the castle inside, it was far finer than it looked outside, for everything was pure gold-- chairs, and tables, and benches, and all. And when the King had gone all over it, and seen everything high and low, he got quite shameful and downcast.

'Yes', he said at last; 'Lord Peter has everything far finer than I have, there's no gainsaying that', and so he wanted to be off home again.

But Peter begged him to stay to supper, and the King stayed, but he was sour, and surly the whole time.

So as they sat at supper, back came the Troll who owned the castle, and gave such a great knock at the door.

'WHO'S THIS EATING MY MEAT AND DRINKING MY MEAD LIKE SWINE IN HERE', roared out the Troll.

As soon as the Cat heard that, she ran down to the gate.

'Stop a bit', she said, 'and I'll tell you how the farmer sets to work to get in his winter rye.'

And so she told him such a long story about the winter rye.

'First of all, you see, he ploughs his field, and then he dungs it, and then he ploughs it again, and then he harrows it'; and so she went on till the sun rose.

'Oh, do look behind you, and there you'll see such a lovely lady', said the Cat to the Troll.

So the Troll turned round, and, of course, as soon as he saw the sun he burst.

'Now all this is yours', said the Cat to Lord Peter. 'Now, you must cut off my head; that's all I ask for what I have done for you.'

'Nay, nay', said Lord Peter, 'I'll never do any such thing, that's flat.'

'If you don't', said the Cat,' see if I don't claw your eyes out.'

Well! so Lord Peter had to do it, though it was sore against his will. He cut off the Cat's head, but there and then she became the loveliest Princess you ever set eyes on, and Lord Peter fell in love with her at once.

'Yes! all this greatness was mine first', said the Princess, 'but a Troll bewitched me to be a Cat in your father's and mother's cottage. Now you may do as you please, whether you take me as your queen or not, for you are now king over all this realm.'

Well, well; there was little doubt Lord Peter would be willing enough to have her as his queen, and so there was a wedding that lasted eight whole days, and a feast besides; and after it was over, I stayed no longer with Lord Peter and his lovely queen, and so I can't say anything more about them.

THE SEVEN FOALS

O nce on a time there was a poor couple who lived in a wretched hut, far far away in the wood. How they lived I can't tell, but I'm sure it was from hand to mouth, and hard work even then; but they had three sons, and the youngest of them was Boots, of course, for he did little else than lie there and poke about in the ashes.

So one day the eldest lad said he would go out to earn his bread, and he soon got leave, and wandered out into the world. There he walked and walked the whole day, and when evening drew in, he came to a king's palace, and there stood the King out on the steps, and asked whither he was bound.

'Oh, I'm going about, looking after a place', said the lad.

'Will you serve me?' asked the King, 'and watch my seven foals. If you can watch them one whole day, and tell me at night what they eat and what they drink, you shall have the Princess to wife, and half my kingdom; but if you can't, I'll cut three red stripes out of your back. Do you hear?'

Yes! that was an easy task, the lad thought; he'd do that fast enough, never fear.

So next morning, as soon as the first peep of dawn came, the king's coachman let out the seven foals. Away they went, and the lad after them. You may fancy how they tore over hill and dale, through bush and bog. When the lad had run so a long time, he began to get weary, and when he had held on a while longer, he had more than enough of his watching, and just there, he came to a cleft in a rock, where an old hag sat and spun with a distaff. As soon as she saw the lad who was running after the foals till the sweat ran down his brow, this old hag bawled out:

'Come hither, come hither, my pretty son, and let me comb your hair.'

Yes! the lad was willing enough; so he sat down in the cleft of the rock with the old hag, and laid his head on her lap, and she combed his hair all day whilst he lay there, and stretched his lazy bones.

So, when evening drew on, the lad wanted to go away. 'I may just as well toddle straight home now', said he, 'for it's no use my going back to the palace.'

'Stop a bit till it's dark', said the old hag, 'and then the king's foals will pass by here again, and then you can run home with them, and then no one will know that you have lain here all day long, instead of watching the foals.'

So, when they came, she gave the lad a flask of water and a clod of turf. Those he was to show to the King, and say that was what his seven foals ate and drank.

'Have you watched true and well the whole day, now?' asked the King, when the lad came before him in the evening.

'Yes, I should think so', said the lad.

'Then you can tell me what my seven foals eat and drink', said the King.

'Yes!' and so the lad pulled out the flask of water and the clod of turf, which the old hag had given him.

'Here you see their meat, and here you see their drink', said the lad.

But then the King saw plain enough how he had watched, and he got so wroth, he ordered his men to chase him away home on the spot; but first they were to cut three red stripes out of his back, and rub salt into them. So when the lad got home again, you may fancy what a temper he was in. He'd gone out once to get a place, he said, but he'd never do so again.

Next day the second sons aid he would go out into the world to try his luck. His father and mother said 'No', and bade him look at his brother's back; but the lad wouldn't give in; he held to his own, and at last he got leave to go, and set off. So when he had walked the whole day, he, too, came to the king's palace. There stood the King out on the steps, and asked whither he was bound? and when the lad said he was looking about for a place, the King said he might have a place there, and watch his seven foals. But the king laid down the same punishment, and the same reward, as he had settled for his brother. Well, the lad was willing enough; he took the place at once with the King, for he thought he'd soon watch the foals, and tell the King what they ate and drank. So, in the gray of the morning, the coachman let out the seven foals, and off they went again over hill and dale, and the lad after them. But the same thing happened to him as had befallen his brother. When he had run after the foals a long long time, till he was both warm and weary, he passed by the cleft in a rock, where an old hag sat and spun with a distaff, and she bawled out to the lad:

'Come hither, come hither, my pretty son, and let me comb your hair.'

That the lad thought a good offer, so he let the foals run on their way, and sat down in the cleft with the old hag. There he sat, and there he lay, taking his ease, and stretching his lazy bones the whole day.

When the foals came back at nightfall, he too got a flask of water and clod of turf from the old hag to show to the King. But when the King asked the lad:

'Can you tell me now, what my seven foals eat and drink?' and the lad pulled out the flask and the clod, and said:

'Here you see their meat, and here you see their drink.'

Then the King got wroth again, and ordered them to cut three red stripes out of the lad's back, and rub salt in, and chase him home that very minute. And so when the lad got home, he also told how he had fared, and said, he had gone out once to get a place, but he'd never do so any more.

The third day Boots wanted to set out; he had a great mind to try and watch the seven foals, he said. The others laughed at him, and made game of him, saying:

'When we fared so ill, you'll do it better--a fine joke; you look like it--you, who have never done anything but lie there and poke about in the ashes.'

'Yes!' said Boots, 'I don't see why I shouldn't go, for I've got it into my head, and can't get it out again.'

And so, in spite of all the jeers of the others and the prayers of the old people, there was no help for it, and Boots set out.

So after he had walked the whole day, he too came at dusk to the king's palace. There stood the King out on the steps, and asked whither he was bound.

'Oh', said Boots, 'I'm going about seeing if I can hear of a place.'

'Whence do you come then?' said the King, for he wanted to know a little more about them before he took any one into his service.

So Boots said whence he came, and how he was brother to those two who had watched the king's seven foals, and ended by asking if he might try to watch them next day.

'Oh, stuff!' said the King, for he got quite cross if he even thought of them; 'if you're brother to those two, you're not worth much, I'll be bound. I've had enough of such scamps.'

'Well', said Boots; but since I've come so far, I may just as well get leave to try, I too.'

'Oh, very well; with all my heart', said the King, 'if you **will** have your back flayed, you're quite welcome.'

'I'd much rather have the Princess', said Boots.

So next morning, at gray of dawn, the coachman let out the seven foals again, and away they went over hill and dale, through bush and bog, and Boots behind them. And so, when he too had run a long while, he came to the cleft in the rock, where the old hag sat, spinning at her distaff. So she bawled out to Boots:

'Come hither, come hither, my pretty son, and let me comb your hair.'

'Don't you wish you may catch me', said Boots. 'Don't you wish you may catch me', as he ran along, leaping and jumping, and holding on by one of the foal's tails. And when he had got well past the cleft in the rock, the youngest foal said:

'Jump up on my back, my lad, for we've a long way before us still.'

So Boots jumped up on his back.

So they went on, and on, a long, long way.

'Do you see anything now', said the Foal.

'No', said Boots.

So they went on a good bit farther.

'Do you see anything now?' asked the Foal.

'Oh no', said the lad.

So when they had gone a great, great way farther--I'm sure I can't tell how far--the Foal asked again:

'Do you see anything now?'

'Yes', said Boots; 'now I see something that looks white--just like a tall, big birch trunk.'

'Yes', said the Foal; 'we're going into that trunk.' So when they got to the trunk, the eldest foal took and pushed it on one side, and then they saw a door where it had stood, and inside the door was a little room, and in the room there was scarce anything but a little fireplace and one or two benches; but behind the door hung a great rusty sword and a little pitcher.

'Can you brandish the sword?' said the Foals; 'try.' So Boots tried, but he couldn't; then they made him take a pull at the pitcher; first once, then twice, and then thrice, and then he could wield it like anything.

'Yes', said the Foals, 'now you may take the sword with you, and with it you must cut off all our seven heads on your wedding-day, and then we'll be princes again as we were before. For we are brothers of that Princess whom you are to have when you can tell the King what we eat and drink; but an ugly Troll has thrown this shape over us. Now mind, when you have hewn off our heads, to take care to lay each head at the tail of the trunk which it belonged to before, and then the spell will have no more power over us.'

Yes! Boots promised all that, and then on they went. And when they had travelled a long long way, the Foal asked:

'Do you see anything?'

'No', said Boots.

So they travelled a good bit still.

'And now?' asked the Foal.

'No, I see nothing', said Boots.

So they travelled many many miles again, over hill and dale.

'Now then', said the Foal, 'do you see anything now?'

'Yes', said Boots, 'now I see something like a blue stripe, far far away.'

'Yes', said the Foal, 'that's a river we've got to cross.' Over the river was a long, grand bridge; and when they had got over to the other side, they travelled on a long, long way. At last the Foal asked again:

'If Boots didn't see anything?'

'Yes, this time he saw something that looked black far far away, just as though it were a church steeple.'

'Yes', said the Foal, 'that's where we're going to turn in.'

So when the foals got into the churchyard, they became men again, and looked like Princes, with such fine clothes that it glistened from them; and so they went into the church, and took the bread and wine from the priest who stood at the altar. And Boots he went in too; but when the priest had laid his hands on the Princes, and given them the blessing, they went out of the church again, and Boots went out too; but he took with him a flask of wine and a wafer. And soon as ever the seven Princes came out into the churchyard, they were turned into foals again, and so Boots got up on the back of the youngest, and so they all went back the same way that they had come; only they went much, much faster. First they crossed the bridge, next they passed the trunk, and then they passed the old hag, who sat at the cleft and span, and they went by her so fast, that Boots couldn't hear what the old hag screeched after him; but he heard so much as to know she was in an awful rage.

It was almost dark when they got back to the palace, and the King himself stood out on the steps and waited for them. 'Have you watched well and true the whole day?' said he to Boots.

'I've done my best', answered Boots.

'Then you can tell me what my seven foals eat and drink', said the King.

Then Boots pulled out the flask of wine and the wafer, and showed them to the King.

'Here you see their meat, and here you see their drink', said he.

'Yes', said the King, 'you have watched true and well, and you shall have the Princess and half the kingdom.'

So they made ready the wedding-feast, and the King said it should be such a grand one, it should be the talk far and near.

But when they sat down to the bridal feast, the bridegroom got up and went down to the stable, for he said he had forgotten something, and must go to fetch it. And when he got down there, he did as the Foals had said, and hewed their heads off, all seven, the eldest first, and the others after him; and at the same time he took care to lay each head at the tail of the foal to which it belonged; and as he did this, lo! they all became Princes again.

So when he went into the bridal hall with the seven princes, the King was so glad he both kissed Boots and patted him on the back, and his bride was still more glad of him than she had been before.

'Half the kingdom you have got already', said the King, 'and the other half you shall have after my death; for my sons can easily get themselves lands and wealth, now they are princes again.'

And so, like enough, there was mirth and fun at that wedding. I was there too; but there was no one to care for poor me; and so I got nothing but a bit of bread and butter, and I laid it down on the stove, and the bread was burnt and the butter ran, and so I didn't get even the smallest crumb. Wasn't that a great shame?

THE WIDOW'S SON

Once on a time there was a poor, poor widow, who had an only son. She dragged on with the boy till he had been confirmed, and then she said she couldn't feed him any longer, he must just go out and earn his own bread. So the lad wandered out into the world, and when he had walked a day or so, a strange man met him.

'Whither away?' asked the man.

'Oh, I'm going out into the world to try and get a place', said the lad.

'Will you come and serve me?' said the man.

'Oh yes; just as soon you as any one else', said the lad.

'Well, you'll have a good place with me', said the man; 'for you'll only have to keep me company, and do nothing at all else beside.'

So the lad stopped with him, and lived on the fat of the land, both in meat and drink, and had little or nothing to do; but he never saw a living soul in that man's house.

So one day the man said:

'Now, I'm going off for eight days, and that time you'll have to spend here all alone; but you must not go into any one of these four rooms here. If you do, I'll take your life when I come back.'

'No', said the lad, he'd be sure not to do that. But when the man had been gone three or four days, the lad couldn't bear it any longer, but went into the first room, and when he got inside he looked round, but he saw nothing but a shelf over the door where a bramble-bush rod lay.

Well, indeed! thought the lad; a pretty thing to forbid my seeing this.

So when the eight days were out, the man came home, and the first thing he said was:

'You haven't been into any of these rooms, of course.'

'No, no; that I haven't', said the lad.

'I'll soon see that', said the man, and went at once into the room where the lad had been.

'Nay, but you have been in here', said he; 'and now you shall lose your life.'

Then the lad begged and prayed so hard that he got off with his life, but the man gave him a good thrashing. And when it was over, they were as good friends as ever.

Some time after the man set off again, and said he should be away fourteen days; but before he went he forbade the lad to go into any of the rooms he had not been in before; as for that he had been in, he might go into that, and welcome. Well, it was the same story aver again, except that the lad stood out eight days before he went in. In this room, too, he saw nothing but a shelf over the door, and a big stone, and a pitcher of water on it. Well, after all, there's not much to be afraid of my seeing here, thought the lad.

But when the man came back, he asked if he had been into any of the rooms. No, the lad hadn't done anything of the kind.

'Well, well; I'll soon see that,' said the man; and when he saw that the lad had been in them after all, he said, 'Ah! now I'll spare you no longer; now you must lose your life.'

But the lad begged and prayed for himself again, and so this time too he got off with stripes; though he got as many as his skin could carry. But when he got sound and well again, he led just as easy a life as ever, and he and the man were just as good friends.

So a while after the man was to take another journey, and now he said he should be away three weeks, and he forbade the lad anew to go into the third room, for if he went in there he might just make up his mind at once to lose his life. Then after fourteen days the lad couldn't bear it, but crept into the room, but he saw nothing at all in there but a trap door on the floor; and when he lifted it up and looked down, there stood a great copper cauldron which bubbled and boiled away down there; but he saw no fire under it.

'Well, I should just like to know if it's hot,' thought the lad, and stuck his finger down into the broth, and when he pulled it out again, lo! it was gilded all over. So the lad scraped and scrubbed it, but the gilding wouldn't go off, so he bound a piece of rag round it; and when the man came back, and asked what was the matter with his finger, the lad said he'd given it such a bad cut. But the man tore off the rag, and then he soon saw what was the matter with the finger. First he wanted to kill the lad outright, but when he wept, and begged, he only gave him such a thrashing that he had to keep his bed three days. After that the man took down a pot from the wall, and rubbed him over with some stuff out of it, and so the lad was sound and fresh as ever.

So after a while the man started off again, and this time he was to be away a month. But before he went, he said to the lad, if he went into the fourth room he might give up all hope of saving his life.

Well, the lad stood out for two or three weeks, but then he couldn't holdout any longer; he must and would go into that room, and so in he stole. There stood a great black horse tied up in a stall by himself, with a manger of red-hot coals at his head, and a truss of hay at his tail. Then the lad thought this all wrong, so he changed them about, and put the hay at his head. Then said the Horse:

'Since you are so good at heart as to let me have some food, I'll set you free, that I will. For if the Troll comes back and finds you here, he'll kill you outright. But now you must go up to the room which lies just over this, and take a coat of mail out of those that hang there; and mind, whatever you do, don't take any of the bright ones, but the most rusty of all you see, that's the one to take; and sword and saddle you must choose for yourself just in the same way.'

So the lad did all that; but it was a heavy load for him to carry them all down at once.

When he came back, the Horse told him to pull off his clothes and get into the cauldron which stood and boiled in the other room, and bathe himself there. 'If I do', thought the lad, 'I shall look an awful fright'; but for all that, he did as he was told. So when he had taken his bath, he became so handsome and sleek, and as red and white as milk and blood, and much stronger than he had been before.

'Do you feel any change?' asked the Horse.

'Yes', said the lad.

'Try to lift me, then', said the Horse.

Oh yes! he could do that, and as for the sword, he brandished it like a feather.

'Now saddle me', said the Horse, 'and put on the coat of mail, and then take the bramble-bush rod, and the stone, and the pitcher of water, and the pot of ointment, and then we'll be off as fast as we can.'

So when the lad had got on the horse, off they went at such a rate, he couldn't at all tell how they went. But when he had ridden awhile, the Horse said,

'I think I hear a noise; look round! can you see anything?'

'Yes; there are ever so many coming after us, at least a score', said the lad.

'Aye, aye, that's the Troll coming', said the Horse; 'now he's after us with his pack.'

So they rode on a while, until those who followed were close behind them.

'Now throw your bramble-bush rod behind you, over your shoulder', said the Horse; 'but mind you throw it a good way off my back.'

So the lad did that, and all at once a close, thick bramble-wood grew up behind them. So the lad rode on a long, long time, while the Troll and his crew had to go home to fetch something to hew their way through the wood. But at last, the Horse said again.

'Look behind you! can you see anything now?'

'Yes, ever so many', said the lad, 'as many as would fill a large church.'

'Aye, aye, that's the Troll and his crew', said the Horse; 'now he's got more to back him; but now throw down the stone, and mind you throw it far behind me.'

And as soon as the lad did what the Horse said, up rose a great black hill of rock behind him. So the Troll had to be off home to fetch something to mine his way through the rock; and while the Troll did that, the lad rode a good bit further on. But still the Horse begged him to look behind him, and then he saw a troop like a whole army behind him, and they glistened in the sunbeams.

'Aye, aye', said the Horse, 'that's the Troll, and now he's got his whole band with him, so throw the pitcher of water behind you, but mind you don't spill any of it upon me.'

So the lad did that; but in spite of all the pains he took, he still spilt one drop on the horse's flank. So it became a great deep lake; and because of that one drop, the horse found himself far out in it, but still he swam safe to land. But when the Trolls came to the lake, they lay down to drink it dry; and so they swilled and swilled till they burst.

'Now we're rid of them', said the Horse.

So when they had gone a long, long while, they came to a green patch in a wood.

'Now, strip off all your arms', said the Horse, 'and only put on your ragged clothes, and take the saddle off me, and let me loose, and hang all my clothing and your arms up inside that great hollow lime- tree yonder. Then make yourself a wig of fir-moss, and go up to the king's palace, which lies close here, and ask for a place. Whenever you need me, only come here and shake the bridle, and I'll come to you.'

Yes! the lad did all his Horse told him, and as soon as ever he put on the wig of moss he became so ugly, and pale, and miserable to look at, no one would have known him again. Then he went up to the king's palace and begged first for leave to be in the kitchen, and bring in wood and water for the cook, but then the kitchen-maid asked him:

'Why do you wear that ugly wig? Off with it. I won't have such a fright in here.'

'No, I can't do that', said the lad; 'for I'm not quite right in my head.'

'Do you think then I'll have you in here about the food', cried the cook. 'Away with you to the coachman; you're best fit to go and clean the stable.'

But when the coachman begged him to take his wig off, he got the same answer, and he wouldn't have him either. 'You'd best go down to the gardener', said he; 'you're best fit to go about and dig in the garden.'

So he got leave to be with the gardener, but none of the other servants would sleep with him, and so he had to sleep by himself under the steps of the summer-house. It stood upon beams, and had a high staircase. Under that he got some turf for his bed, and there he lay as well as he could.

So, when he had been some time at the palace, it happened one morning, just as the sun rose, that the lad had taken off his wig, and stood and washed himself, and then he was so handsome, it was a joy to look at him.

So the Princess saw from her window the lovely gardener's boy, and thought she had never seen any one so handsome. Then she asked the gardener why he lay out there under the steps.

'Oh', said the gardener, 'none of his fellow-servants will sleep with him; that's why.'

'Let him come up to-night, and lie at the door inside my bedroom, and then they'll not refuse to sleep with him any more', said the Princess.

So the gardener told that to the lad.

'Do you think I'll do any such thing?' said the lad. 'Why they'd say next there was something between me and the Princess.'

'Yes', said the gardener, 'you've good reason to fear any such thing, you who are so handsome.'

'Well, well', said the lad, 'since it's her will, I suppose I must go.'

So, when he was to go up the steps in the evening, he tramped and stamped so on the way, that they had to beg him to tread softly lest the King should come to know it. So he came into the Princess' bedroom, lay down, and began to snore at once. Then the Princess said to her maid:

'Go gently, and just pull his wig off'; and she went up to him.

But just as she was going to whisk it off, he caught hold of it with both hands, and said she should never have it. After that he lay down again, and began to snore. Then the Princess gave her maid a wink, and this time she whisked off the wig; and there lay the lad so lovely, and white and red, just as the Princess had seen him in the morning sun.

After that the lad slept every night in the Princess' bedroom.

But it wasn't long before the King came to hear how the gardener's lad slept every night in the Princess' bedroom; and he got so wroth he almost took the lad's life. He didn't do that, however, but threw him into the prison tower; and as for his daughter, he shut her up in her own room, whence she never got leave to stir day or night. All that she begged, and all that she prayed, for the lad and herself, was no good. The King was only more wroth than ever.

Some time after came a war and uproar in the land, and the king had to take up arms against another king who wished to take the kingdom from him. So when the lad heard that, he begged the gaoler to go to the king and ask for a coat of mail and a sword, and for leave to go to the war. All the rest laughed when the gaoler told his errand, and begged the king to let him have an old worn-out suit, that they might have the fun of seeing such a wretch in battle. So he got that, and an old broken-down hack besides, which went upon three legs and dragged the fourth after it.

Then they went out to meet the foe; but they hadn't got far from the palace before the lad got stuck fast in a bog with his hack. There he sat and dug his spurs in, and cried, 'Gee up, gee up!' to his hack. And all the rest had their fun out of this, and laughed, and made game of the lad as they rode past him. But they were scarcely gone, before he ran to the lime-tree, threw on his coat of mail, and shook the bridle, and there came the horse in a trice, and said 'Do now your best, and I'll do mine.'

But when the lad came up the battle had begun, and the king was in a sad pinch; but no sooner had the lad rushed into the thick of it than the foe was beaten back, and put to flight. The king and his men wondered and wondered who it could be who had come to help them, but none of them got so near him as to be able to talk to him, and as soon as the fight was over he was gone. When they went back, there sat the lad still in the bog, and dug his spurs into his three-legged hack, and they all laughed again.

'No! only just look', they said; 'there the fool sits still.'

The next day when they went out to battle, they saw the lad sitting there still, so they laughed again, and made game of him; but as soon as ever they had ridden by, the lad ran again to the lime-tree, and all happened as on the first day. Every one wondered what strange champion it could be that had helped them, but no one got so near him as to say a word to him; and no one guessed it could be the lad; that's easy to understand.

So when they went home at night, and saw the lad still sitting there on his hack, they burst out laughing at him again, and one of them shot an arrow at him and hit him in the leg. So he began to shriek and to bewail; 'twas enough to break one's heart; and so the king threw his pocket-handkerchief to him to bind his wound.

When they went out to battle the third day, the lad still sat there.

'Gee up! gee up!' he said to his hack.

'Nay, nay', said the king's men; 'if he won't stick there till he's starved to death.'

And then they rode on, and laughed at him till they were fit to fall from their horses. When they were gone, he ran again to the lime, and came up to the battle just in the very nick of time. This day he slew the enemy's king, and then the war was over at once.

When the battle was over, the king caught sight of his handkerchief, which the strange warrior had bound round his leg, and so it wasn't hard to find him out. So they took him with great joy between them to the palace, and the Princess, who saw him from her window, got so glad, no one can believe it.

'Here comes my own true love', she said.

Then he took the pot of ointment and rubbed himself on the leg, and after that he rubbed all the wounded, and so they all got well again in a moment.

So he got the Princess to wife; but when he went down into the stable where his horse was on the day the wedding was to be, there it stood so dull and heavy, and hung its ears down, and wouldn't eat its corn. So when the young king--for he was now a king, and had got half the kingdom--spoke to him, and asked what ailed him, the Horse said:

'Now I have helped you on, and now I won't live any longer. So just take the sword, and cut my head off.'

'No, I'll do nothing of the kind', said the young king; 'but you shall have all you want, and rest all your life.'

'Well', said the Horse, 'If you don't do as I tell you, see if I don't take your life somehow.'

So the king had to do what he asked; but when he swung the sword and was to cut his head off, he was so sorry he turned away his face, for he would not see the stroke fall. But as soon as ever he had cut off the head, there stood the loveliest Prince on the spot where the horse had stood.

'Why, where in all the world did you come from?' asked the king.

'It was I who was a horse', said the Prince; 'for I was king of that land whose king you slew yesterday. He it was who threw this Troll's shape over me, and sold me to the Troll. But now he is slain I get my own again, and you and I will be neighbour kings, but war we will never make on one another.'

And they didn't either; for they were friends as long as they lived, and each paid the other very many visits.

BUSHY BRIDE

Once on a time there was a widower, who had a son and a daughter by his first marriage. Both were good children, and loved each other dearly. Some time after the man married a widow, who had a daughter by her first husband, and she was both ugly and bad, like her mother. So from the day the new wife came into the house there was no peace for her stepchildren in any corner; and at last the lad thought he'd best go out into the world, and try to earn his own bread. And when he had wandered a while he came to a king's palace, and got a place under the coachman, and quick and willing he was, and the horses he looked after were so sleek and clean that their coats shone again.

But the sister who stayed at home was treated worse than badly; both her stepmother and stepsister were always at her, and wherever she went, and whatever she did, they scolded and snarled so, the poor lassie hadn't an hour's peace. All the hard work she was forced to do, and early and late she got nothing but bad words, and little food besides.

So one day they had sent her to the burn to fetch water: and what do you think? up popped an ugly, ugly head out of the pool, and said:

'Wash me, you lassie.'

'Yes, with all my heart I'll wash you', said the lassie. So she began to wash and scrub the ugly head; but truth to say, she thought it nasty work.

Well, as soon as she had done washing it, up popped another head out of the pool, and this was uglier still.

'Brush me, you lassie', said the head.

'Yes, with all my heart I'll brush you.'

And with that she took in hand the matted locks, and you may fancy she hadn't very pleasant work with them. But when she had got over that, if a third head didn't pop up out of the pool, and this was far more ugly and loathsome than both the others put together.

'Kiss me, you lassie!'

'Yes, I'll kiss you', said the lassie, and she did it too, though she thought it the worst work she had ever had to do in her life.

Then the heads began to chatter together, and each asked what they should do for the lassie who was so kind and gentle.

'That she be the prettiest lassie in the world, and as fair as the bright day', said the first head.

'That gold shall drop from her hair, every time she brushes it', said the second head.

'That gold shall fall from her mouth every time she speaks', said the third head.

So when the lassie came home looking so lovely, and beaming as the bright day itself, her stepmother and her stepsister got more and more cross, and they got worse still when she began to talk, and they saw how golden guineas fell from her mouth. As for the stepmother, she got so mad with rage, she chased the lassie into the pigsty. That was the right place for all her gold stuff, but as for coming into the house, she wouldn't hear of it.

Well, it wasn't long before the stepmother wished her own daughter to go to the burn to fetch water. So when she came to the water's edge with her buckets, up popped the first head.

'Wash me, you lassie', it said.

'The Deil wash you', said the stepdaughter.

So the second head popped up.

'Brush me, you lassie', it said.

'The Deil brush you', said the stepdaughter.

So down it went to the bottom, and the third head popped up.

'Kiss me, you lassie', said the head.

'The Deil kiss you, you pig's-snout', said the girl.

Then the heads chattered together again, and asked what they should do to the girl who was so spiteful and cross-grained; and they all agreed she should have a nose four ells long, and a snout three ells long, and a pine bush right in the midst of her forehead, and every time she spoke, ashes were to fall out of her mouth.

So when she got home with her buckets, she bawled out to her mother:

'Open the door.'

'Open it yourself, my darling child', said the mother.

'I can't reach it because of my nose', said the daughter.

So, when the mother came out and saw her, you may fancy what a way she was in, and how she screamed and groaned; but, for all that, there were the nose and the snout and the pine bush, and they got no smaller for all her grief.

Now the brother, who had got the place in the King's stable, had taken a little sketch of his sister, which he carried away with him, and every morning and every evening he knelt down before the picture and prayed to Our Lord for his sister, whom he loved so dearly. The other grooms had heard him praying, so they peeped through the key-hole of his room, and there they saw him on his knees before the picture. So they went about saying how the lad every morning and every evening knelt down and prayed to an idol which he had, and at last they went to the king himself and begged him only to peep through the key-hole, and then His Majesty would see the lad, and what things he did. At first the King wouldn't believe it, but at last they talked him over, and he crept on tiptoe to the door and peeped in. Yes, there was the lad on his knees before the picture, which hung on the wall, praying with clasped hands.

'Open the door!' called out the King; but the lad didn't hear him.

So the King called out in a louder voice, but the lad was so deep in his prayers he couldn't hear him this time either. 'OPEN THE DOOR, I SAY!' roared out the King; 'It's I, the King, who want to come in.'

Well, up jumped the lad and ran to the door, and unlocked it, but in his hurry he forgot to hide the picture. But when the King came in and saw the picture, he stood there as if he were fettered, and couldn't stir from the spot, so lovely he thought the picture.

'So lovely a woman there isn't in all the wide world', said the King.

But the lad told him she was his sister whom he had drawn, and if she wasn't prettier than that, at least she wasn't uglier.

'Well, if she's so lovely', said the King, 'I'll have her for my queen'; and then he ordered the lad to set off home that minute, and not be long on the road either. So the lad promised to make as much haste as he could, and started off from the King's palace.

When the brother came home to fetch his sister, the step-mother and stepsister said they must go too. So they all set out, and the good lassie had a casket in which she kept her gold, and a little dog, whose name was 'Little Flo'; those two things were all her mother left her. And when they had gone a while, they came to a lake which they had to cross; so the brother sat down at the helm, and the stepmother and the two girls sat in the bow foreward, and so they sailed a long, long way.

At last they caught sight of land.

'There', said the brother, 'where you see the white strand yonder, there's where we're to land'; and as he said this he pointed across the water.

'What is it my brother says?' asked the good lassie.

'He says you must throw your casket overboard', said the stepmother.

'Well, when my brother says it, I must do it', said the lassie, and overboard went the casket.

When they had sailed a bit farther, the brother pointed again across the lake.

'There you see the castle we're going to.'

'What is it my brother says?' asked the lassie.

'He says now you must throw your little dog overboard', said the stepmother.

Then the lassie wept and was sore grieved, for Little Flo was the dearest thing she had in the world, but at last she threw him overboard.

'When my brother says it, I must do it, but heaven knows how it hurts me to throw you over, Little Flo', she said.

So they sailed on a good bit still.

'There you see the King coming down to meet us', said the brother, and pointed towards the strand.

'What is it my brother says', asked the lassie.

'Now he says you must make haste and throw yourself overboard', said the stepmother.

Well, the lassie wept and moaned; but when her brother told her to do that, she thought she ought to do it, and so she leapt down into the lake.

But when they came to the palace, and the King saw the loathly bride, with a nose four ells long, and a snout three ells long, and a pine- bush in the midst of her forehead, he was quite scared out of his wits; but the wedding was all ready, both in brewing and baking, and there sat all the wedding guests, waiting for the bride; and so the King couldn't help himself, but was forced to take her for better for worse. But angry he was, that any one can forgive him, and so he had the brother thrown into a pit full of snakes.

Well, the first Thursday evening after the wedding, about midnight, in came a lovely lady into the palace-kitchen, and begged the kitchen-maid, who slept there, so prettily, to lend her a brush. That she got, and then she brushed her hair, and as she brushed, down dropped gold, A little dog was at her heel, and to him she said:

'Run out, Little Flo, and see if it will soon be day.'

This she said three times, and the third time she sent the dog it was just about the time the dawn begins to peep. Then she had to go, but as she went she sung:

Out on you, ugly Bushy Bride,
Lying so warm by the King's left side;
While I on sand and gravel sleep,
And over my brother adders creep,
And all without a tear.

'Now I come twice more, and then never again.'

So next morning the kitchen-maid told what she had seen and heard, and the King said he'd watch himself next Thursday night in the kitchen, and see if it were true, and as soon as it got dark, out he went into the kitchen to the kitchen-maid. But all he could do, and however much he rubbed his eyes and tried to keep himself awake, it was no good; for the Bushy Bride chaunted and sang till his eyes closed, and so when the lovely lady came, there he slept and snored. This time, too, as before, she borrowed a brush, and brushed her hair till the gold dropped, and sent her dog out three times, and as soon as it was gray dawn, away she went singing the same words, and adding:

'Now I come once more, and then never again.'

The third Thursday evening the King said he would watch again; and he set two men to hold him, one under each arm, who were to shake and jog him every time he wanted to fall asleep; and two men he set to watch his Bushy Bride. But when the night wore on, the Bushy Bride began to chaunt and sing, so that his eyes began to wink, and his head hung down on his shoulders. Then in came the lovely lady, and got the brush and brushed her hair, till the gold dropped from it; after that she sent Little Flo out again to see if it would soon be day, and this she did three times. The third time it began, to get gray in the east; then she sang,

> Out on you, ugly Bushy Bride,
> Lying so warm by the King's left side;
> While I on sand and gravel sleep,
> And over my brother adders creep,
> And all without a tear.

'Now I come back never more', she said, and went towards the door. But the two men who held the King under the arms, clenched his hands together, and put a knife into his grasp; and so, somehow or other, they got him to cut her in her little finger, and drew blood. Then the true bride was freed, and the King woke up, and she told him now the whole story, and how her stepmother and sister had deceived her. So the King sent at once and took her brother out of the pit of snakes, and the adders hadn't done him the least harm, but the stepmother and her daughter were thrown into it in his stead.

And now no one can tell how glad the King was to be rid of that ugly Bushy Bride, and to get a Queen who was as lovely and bright as the day itself. So the true wedding was held, and every one talked of it over seven kingdoms; and then the King and Queen drove to church in their coach, and Little Flo went inside with them too, and when the blessing was given they drove back again, and after that I saw nothing more of them.

BOOTS AND HIS BROTHERS

Once on a time there was a man who had three sons, Peter, Paul, and John. John was Boots, of course, because he was the youngest. I can't say the man had anything more than these three sons, for he hadn't one penny to rub against another; and so he told his sons over and over again they must go out into the world and try to earn their bread, for there at home there was nothing to be looked for but starving to death.

Now, a bit off the man's cottage was the king's palace, and you must know, just against the king's windows a great oak had sprung up, which was so stout and big that it took away all the light from the king's palace. The King had said he would give many, many dollars to the man who could fell the oak, but no one was man enough for that, for as soon as ever one chip of the oak's trunk flew off, two grew in its stead. A well, too, the King had dug, which was to hold water for the whole year; for all his neighbours had wells, but he hadn't any, and that he thought a shame. So the King said he would give any one who could dig him such a well as would hold water for a whole year round, both money and goods; but no one could do it, for the King's palace lay high, high up on a hill, and they hadn't dug a few inches before they came upon the living rock.

But as the King had set his heart on having these two things done, he had it given out far and wide, in all the churches of his kingdom, that he who could fell the big oak in the king's court-yard, and get him a well that would hold water the whole year round, should have the Princess and half the kingdom. Well! you may easily know there was many a man who came to try his luck; but for all their hacking and hewing, and all their digging and delving, it was no good. The oak got bigger and stouter at every stroke, and the rock didn't get softer either. So one day those three brothers thought they'd set off and try too, and their father hadn't a word against it; for even if they didn't get the Princess and half the kingdom, it might happen they might get a place somewhere with a good master; and that was all he wanted. So when the brothers said they thought of going to the palace, their father said 'yes' at once. So Peter, Paul, and Jack went off from their home.

Well! they hadn't gone far before they came to a fir wood, and up along one side of it rose a steep hill-side, and as they went, they heard something hewing and hacking away up on-the hill among the trees.

'I wonder now what it is that is hewing away up yonder?' said Jack.

'You're always so clever with your wonderings', said Peter and Paul both at once. 'What wonder is it, pray, that a woodcutter should stand and hack up on a hill-side?'

'Still, I'd like to see what it is, after all', said Jack; and up he went.

'Oh, if you're such a child, 'twill do you good to go and take a lesson', bawled out his brothers after him.

But Jack didn't care for what they said; he climbed the steep hill- side towards where the noise came, and when he reached the place, what do you think he saw? why, an axe that stood there hacking and hewing, all of itself, at the trunk of a fir.

'Good day!' said Jack. 'So you stand here all alone and hew, do you?'

'Yes; here I've stood and hewed and hacked a long long time, waiting for you', said the Axe.

'Well, here I am at last', said Jack, as he took the axe, pulled it off its haft, and stuffed both head and haft into his wallet.

So when he got down again to his brothers, they began to jeer and laugh at him.

'And now, what funny thing was it you saw up yonder on the hill- side?' they said.

'Oh, it was only an axe we heard', said Jack.

So when they had gone a bit farther, they came under a steep spur of rock, and up there they heard something digging and shovelling.

'I wonder now,' said Jack, 'what it is digging and shovelling up yonder at the top of the rock.'

'Ah, you're always so clever with your wonderings', said Peter and Paul again, 'as if you'd never heard a woodpecker hacking and pecking at a hollow tree.'

'Well, well', said Jack, 'I think it would be a piece of fun just to see what it really is.'

And so off he set to climb the rock, while the others laughed and made game of him. But he didn't care a bit for that; up he clomb, and when he got near the top, what do you think he saw? Why, a spade that stood there digging and delving.

'Good day!' said Jack. 'So you stand here all alone, and dig and delve!'

'Yes, that's what I do', said the Spade, 'and that's what I've done this many a long day, waiting for you.'

'Well, here I am', said Jack again, as he took the spade and knocked it off its handle, and put it into his wallet, and then down again to his brothers.

'Well, what was it, so rare and strange', said Peter and Paul, 'that you saw up there at the top of the rock?'

'Oh,', said Jack, 'nothing more than a spade; that was what we heard.'

So they went on again a good bit, till they came to a brook. They were thirsty, all three, after their long walk, and so they lay down beside the brook to have a drink.

'I wonder now', said Jack, 'where all this water comes from.'

'I wonder if you're right in your head', said Peter and Paul, in one breath. 'If you're not mad already, you'll go mad very soon, with your wonderings. Where the brook comes from, indeed! Have you never heard how water rises from a spring in the earth?'

'Yes! but still I've a great fancy to see where this brook comes from', said Jack.

So up alongside the brook he went, in spite of all that his brothers bawled after him. Nothing could stop him. On he went. So, as he went up and up, the brook got smaller and smaller, and at last, a little way farther on, what do you think he saw? Why, a great walnut, and out of that the water trickled.

'Good-day!' said Jack again. 'So you lie here, and trickle and run down all alone?'

'Yes, I do,' said the Walnut; 'and here have I trickled and run this many a long day, waiting for you.'

'Well, here I am', said Jack, as he took up a lump of moss and plugged up the hole, that the water mightn't run out. Then he put the walnut into his wallet, and ran down to his brothers.

'Well now', said Peter and Paul, 'have you found out where the water comes from? A rare sight it must have been!'

'Oh, after all, it was only a hole it ran out of', said Jack; and so the others laughed and made game of him again, but Jack didn't mind that a bit.

'After all, I had the fun of seeing it', said he. So when they had gone a bit farther, they came to the king's palace; but as every one in the kingdom had heard how they might win the Princess and half the realm, if they could only fell the big oak and dig the king's well, so many had come to try their luck that the oak was now twice as stout and big as it had been at first, for two chips grew for every one they hewed out with their axes, as I daresay you all bear in mind. So the King had now laid it down as a punishment, that if any one tried and couldn't fell the oak, he should be put on a barren island, and both his ears were to be clipped off. But the two brothers didn't let themselves be scared by that; they were quite sure they could fell the oak, and Peter, as he was eldest, was to try his hand first; but it went with him as with all the rest who had hewn at the oak; for every chip he cut out, two grew in its place. So the king's men seized him, and clipped off both his ears, and put him out on the island.

Now Paul, he was to try his luck, but he fared just the same; when he had hewn two or three strokes, they began to see the oak grow, and so the king's men seized him too, and clipped his ears, and put him out on the island; and his ears they clipped closer, because they said he ought to have taken a lesson from his brother.

So now Jack was to try.

'If you *will* look like a marked sheep, we're quite ready to clip your ears at once, and then you'll save yourself some bother', said the King; for he was angry with him for his brothers' sake.

'Well, I'd like just to try first', said Jack, and so he got leave. Then he took his axe out of his wallet and fitted it to its haft.

'Hew away!' said he to his axe; and away it hewed, making the chips fly again, so that it wasn't long before down came the oak.

When that was done, Jack pulled out his spade, and fitted it to its handle.

'Dig away!' said he to the spade; and so the spade began to dig and delve till the earth and rock flew out in splinters, and so he had the well soon dug out, you may think.

And when he had got it as big and deep as he chose, Jack took out his walnut and laid it in one corner of the well, and pulled the plug of moss out.

'Trickle and run', said Jack; and so the nut trickled and ran, till the water gushed out of the hole in a stream, and in a short time the well was brimfull.

Then Jack had felled the oak which shaded the king's palace, and dug a well in the palace-yard, and so he got the Princess and half the kingdom, as the King had said; but it was lucky for Peter and Paul that they had lost their ears, else they had heard each hour and day, how every one said, 'Well, after all, Jack wasn't so much out of his mind when he took to wondering.'

BIG PETER AND LITTLE PETER

Once on a time there were two brothers, both named Peter, and so the elder was called Big Peter, and the younger Little Peter. When his father was dead, Big Peter took him a wife with lots of money, but Little Peter was at home with his mother, and lived on her means till he grew up. So when he was of age he came into his heritage, and then Big Peter said he mustn't stay any longer in the old house, and eat up his mother's substance; 'twere better he should go out into the world and do something for himself.

Yes; Little Peter thought that no bad plan; so he bought himself a fine horse and a load of butter and cheese, and set off to the town; and with the money he got for his goods he bought brandy, and wine, and beer, and as soon as ever he got home again it was one round of holiday-keeping and merry-making; he treated all his old friends and neighbours, and they treated him again; and so he lived in fun and frolic so long as his money lasted. But when his last shilling was spent, and Little Peter hadn't a penny in his purse, he went back home again to his old mother, and brought nothing with him but a calf. When the spring came he turned out the calf and let it graze on Big Peter's meadow. Then Big Peter got cross and killed the calf at one blow; but Little Peter, he flayed the calf, and hung the skin up in the bathroom till it was thoroughly dry; then he rolled it up, stuffed it into a sack, and went about the country trying to sell it; but wherever he came, they only laughed at him, and said they had no need of smoked calfskin. So when he had walked on a long way, he came to a farm, and there he turned in and asked for a night's lodging.

'Nay, nay', said the Goody, 'I can't give you lodging, for my husband is up at the shieling on the hill, and I'm alone in the house. You must just try to get shelter at our next neighbour's; but still if they won't take you in, you may come back, for you must have a house over your head, come what may.'

So as little Peter passed by the parlour window, he saw that there was a priest in there, with whom the Goody was making merry, and she was serving him up ale and brandy, and a great bowl of custard. But just as the priest had sat down to eat and drink, back came the husband, and as soon as ever the Goody heard him in the passage, she was not slow; she took the bowl of custard, and put it under the kitchen grate, and the ale and brandy into the cellar, and as for the priest, she locked him up in a great chest which stood there. All this Little Peter stood outside and saw, and as soon as the husband was well inside Little Peter went up to the door and asked if he might have a night's lodging.

'Yes, to be sure', said the man, 'we'll take you in'; and so he begged Little Peter to sit down at the table and eat. Yes, Little Peter sat down, and took his calfskin with him, and laid it down at his feet.

So, when they had sat a while, Little Peter began to mutter to his skin:

'What are you saying now? can't you hold your tongue', said Little Peter.

'Who is it you're talking with?' asked the man.

'Oh!' answered Little Peter, 'it's only a spae-maiden whom I've got in my calf-skin.'

'And pray what does she spae?' asked the man again.

'Why, she says that no one can say there isn't a bowl of custard standing under the grate', said Little Peter.

'She may spae as much as she pleases', answered the man, 'but we haven't had custards in this house for a year and a day.'

But Peter begged him only to look, and he did so; and he found the custard-bowl. So they began to make merry with it, but just as they sat and took their ease, Peter muttered something again to the calfskin.

'Hush!' he said, 'can't you hold your jaw?'

'And pray what does the spae-maiden say now?' asked the man.

'Oh! she says no one can say there isn't brandy and ale standing just under the trap-door which goes down into the cellar', answered Peter.

'Well! if she never spaed wrong in her life, she spaes wrong now', said the man. 'Brandy and ale! why, I can't call to mind the day when we had such things in the house!'

'Just look', said Peter; and the man did so, and there, sure enough, he found the drink, and you may fancy how merry and jolly he was.

'What did you give for that spae-maiden?' said the man, 'for I must have her, whatever you ask for her.'

'She was left me by my father', said Peter, 'and so she didn't cost me much. To tell you the truth, I've no great mind to part with her, but, all the same, you may have her, if you'll let me have, instead of her, that old chest that stands in the parlour yonder.'

'The chest's locked and the key lost', screamed the old dame.

'Then I'll take it without the key, that I will', said Peter. And so he and the man soon struck the bargain. Peter got a rope instead of the key, and the man helped him to get the chest up on his back, and then off he stumped with it. So when he had walked a bit he came on to a bridge, and under the bridge ran a river in such a headlong stream; it leapt, and foamed, and made such a roar, that the bridge shook again.

'Ah!' said Peter, 'that brandy-that brandy! Now I can feel I've had a drop too much. What's the good of my dragging this chest about? If I hadn't been drunk and mad, I shouldn't have gone and swopped away my spae-maiden for it. But now this chest shall go out into the river this very minute.'

And with that he began to untie the rope.

'Au! Au! do for God's sake set me free. The priest's life is at stake; he it is whom you have got in the chest', screamed out some one inside.

'This must be the Deil himself', said Peter, 'who wants to make me believe he has turned priest; but whether he makes himself priest or clerk, out he goes into the river.' 'Oh no! oh no! 'roared out the priest. 'The parish priest is at stake. He was on a visit to the Goody for her soul's health, but her husband is rough and wild, and so she had to hide me in the chest. Here I have a gold watch and a silver watch in my fob; you shall have them both, and eight hundred dollars beside, if you will only let me out.'

'Nay, nay', said Peter; 'is it really your reverence after all'; and with that he took up a stone, and knocked the lid of the chest to pieces. Then the priest got out, and off he set home to his parsonage both fast and light, for he no longer had his watches and money to weigh him down.

As for Little Peter, he went home again, and said to Big Peter, 'There was a good sale to-day for calfskins at the market.'

'Why, what did you get for your tattered one, now?' asked Big Peter.

'Quite as much as it was worth. I got eight hundred dollars for it, but bigger and stouter calves-skins fetched twice as much', said Little Peter, and showed his dollars.

''Twas well you told me this', answered Big Peter, who went and slaughtered all his kine and calves, and set off on the road to town with their skins and hides. So when he got to the market, and the tanners asked what he wanted for his hides, Big Peter said he must have eight hundred dollars for the small ones, and so on, more and more for the big ones. But all the folk only laughed and made game of him, and said he oughtn't to come there; he'd better turn into the madhouse for a better bargain, and so he soon found out how things had gone, and that Little Peter had played him a trick. But when he got home again, he was not very soft-spoken, and he swore and cursed; so help him, if he wouldn't strike Little Peter dead that very night. All this Little Peter stood and listened to; and so, when he had gone to bed with his mother, and the night had worn on a little, he begged her to change sides with him, for he was well-nigh frozen, he said, and might be 'twas warmer next the wall. Yes, she did that, and in a little while came Big Peter with an axe in his hand, and crept up to the bedside, and at one blow chopped off his mother's head.

Next morning, in went Little Peter into Big Peter's sitting-room.

'Heaven better and help you', he said; 'you who have chopped our mother's head off. The Sheriff will not be over-pleased to hear that you pay mother's dower in this way.'

Then Big Peter got so afraid, he begged Little Peter, for God's sake, to say nothing about what he knew. If he would only do that, he should have eight hundred dollars.

Well, Little Peter swept up the money; set his mother's head on her body again; put her on a hand-sledge, and so drew her to market. There he set her up with an apple-basket on each arm, and an apple in each hand. By and by came a skipper walking along; he thought she was an apple-woman, and asked if she had apples to sell, and how many he might have for a penny. But the old woman made no answer. So the skipper asked again. No! she hadn't a word to say for herself.

'How many may I have for a penny', he bawled the third time, but the old dame sat bolt upright, as though she neither saw him, nor heard what he said. Then the skipper flew into such a rage that he gave her one under the ear, and so away rolled her head across the market- place. At that moment, up came Little Peter with a bound; he fell a- weeping and bewailing, and threatened to make the skipper smart for it, for having dealt his old mother her death blow.

'Dear friend, only hold your tongue about what you know', said the skipper, 'and you shall have eight hundred dollars.'

And so they made it up.

When Little Peter got home again, he said to Big Peter:

'Old women fetch a fine price at market to-day. I got eight hundred dollars for mother; just look', and so he showed him the money.

''Twas well I came to know this', said Big Peter.

Now, you must know he had an old stepmother, so he took and killed her out of hand, and strode off to sell her. But when they heard how he went about trying to sell dead bodies, the neighbours were all for handing him over to the Sheriff, and it was as much as he could do to get out of the scrape.

When Big Peter got home again, he was so wroth and mad against Little Peter, he threatened to strike him dead there and then; he needn't hope for mercy, die he must.

'Well! well!' said Little Peter, 'that's the way we must all trudge, and betwixt to-day and to-morrow, there's only a night to come. But if I must set off now, I've only one thing to ask; stuff me into that sack that hangs yonder, and take and toss me into the river.'

Well! Big Peter had nothing to say against that, he stuffed him into the sack and set off. But he hadn't gone far on his way, before it came into his mind that he had forgotten something which he must go back to fetch; meanwhile, he set the sack down by the road side. Just then came a man driving a fine fat flock of sheep.

To Kingdom-come, to Paradise.
To Kingdom-come, to Paradise.

roared out Little Peter, who lay inside the sack, and that he kept bawling and bellowing out.

'Mayn't I get leave to go with you', asked the man who drove the sheep.

'Of course you may', said Little Peter. 'If you'll only untie the sack, and creep into it in my stead, you'll soon get there. As for me, I don't mind biding here till next time, that I don't. But you must keep on calling out the words I bawled out, else you'll not go to the right place.'

Then the man untied the sack, and got into it in Little Peter's place: Peter tied the sack up again and the man began to bawl out:

To Kingdom-come, to Paradise.
To Kingdom-come, to Paradise.

and to that text he stuck.

When Peter had got him well into the sack, he wasn't slow; off he went with the flock of sheep, and soon put a good bit of the road behind him. Meantime, back came Big Peter, took the sack on his shoulders, and bore it across the country to the river, and all the while he went, the drover sat inside bawling out:

To Kingdom-come, to Paradise.
To Kingdom-come, to Paradise.

'Aye, aye', said Big Peter; 'try now to find the way for yourself'; and with that, he tossed him out into the stream.

So when Big Peter had done that, and was going back home, whom should he overtake but his brother, who went along driving the flock of sheep before him. Big Peter could scarce believe his eyes, and asked how Little Peter had got out of the river, and whence the fine flock of sheep came.

'Ah!' said Little Peter, 'that just was a good brotherly turn you did me, when you threw me into the river. I sank right down to the bottom like a stone, and there I just did see flocks of sheep; you'd scarce believe now, that they go about down there by thousands, one flock bigger than the other. And just look here! here are fleeces for you!'

'Well', said Big Peter, 'I'm very glad you told me.'

So off he ran home to his old dame; made her come with him to the river; crept into a sack, and bade her make haste to tie it up, and toss him over the bridge.

'I'm going after a flock of sheep', he said, 'but if I stay too long, and you think I can't get along with the flock by myself, just jump over and help me; do you hear?'

'Well, don't stay too long', said his wife, 'for my heart is set on seeing those sheep.'

There she stood and waited a while, but then she thought, perhaps her husband couldn't keep the flock well together, and so down she jumped after him.

And so Little Peter was rid of them all, and the farm and fields came to him as heir, and horses and cattle too; and, besides, he had money in his pocket to buy milch kine to tether in his byre.

TATTERHOOD

Once on a time there was a king and a queen who had no children, and that gave the queen much grief; she scarce had one happy hour. She was always bewailing and bemoaning herself, and saying how dull and lonesome it was in the palace.

'If we had children there'd be life enough', she said.

Wherever she went in all her realm she found God's blessing in children, even in the vilest hut; and wherever she came she heard the Goodies scolding the bairns, and saying how they had done that and that wrong. All this the queen heard, and thought it would be so nice to do as other women did. At last the king and queen took into their palace a stranger lassie to rear up, that they might have her always with them, to love her if she did well, and scold her if she did wrong, like their own child.

So one day the little lassie whom they had taken as their own, ran down into the palace yard, and was playing with a gold apple. Just then an old beggar wife came by, who had a little girl with her, and it wasn't long before the little lassie and the beggar's bairn were great friends, and began to play together, and to toss the gold apple about between them. When the Queen saw this, as she sat at a window in the palace, she tapped on the pane for her foster-daughter to come up. She went at once, but the beggar-girl went up too; and as they went into the Queen's bower, each held the other by the hand. Then the Queen began to scold the little lady, and to say:

'You ought to be above running about and playing with a tattered beggar's brat.'

And so she wanted to drive the lassie downstairs.

'If the Queen only knew my mother's power, she'd not drive me out', said the little lassie; and when the Queen asked what she meant more plainly, she told her how her mother could get her children if she chose. The Queen wouldn't believe it, but the lassie held her own, and said every word of it was true, and bade the Queen only to try and make her mother do it. So the Queen sent the lassie down to fetch up her mother.

'Do you know what your daughter says?' asked the Queen of the old woman, as soon as ever she came into the room.

No; the beggar wife knew nothing about it.

'Well, she says you can get me children if you will', answered the Queen.

'Queens shouldn't listen to beggar lassies' silly stories', said the old wife, and strode out of the room.

Then the Queen got angry, and wanted again to drive out the little lassie; but she declared it was true every word that she had said.

'Let the Queen only give my mother a drop to drink,' said the lassie; 'when she gets merry she'll soon find out a way to help you.'

The Queen was ready to try this; so the beggar wife was fetched up again once more, and treated both with wine and mead as much as she chose; and so it was not long before her tongue began to wag. Then the Queen came out again with the same question she had asked before.

'One way to help you perhaps I know', said the beggar wife. 'Your Majesty must make them bring in two pails of water some evening before you go to bed. In each of them you must wash yourself, and afterwards throw away the water under the bed. When you look under the bed next morning, two flowers will have sprung up, one fair and one ugly. The fair one you must eat, the ugly one you must let stand; but mind you don't forget the last.'

That was what the beggar wife said.

Yes; the Queen did what the beggar wife advised her to do; she had the water brought up in two pails, washed herself in them, and emptied them under the bed; and lo! when she looked under the bed next morning, there stood two flowers; one was ugly and foul, and had black leaves; but the other was so bright, and fair, and lovely, she had never seen its like; so she ate it up at once. But the pretty flower tasted so sweet, that she couldn't help herself. She ate the other up too, for, she thought, 'it can't hurt or help one much either way, I'll be bound'.

Well, sure enough, after a while the Queen was brought to bed. First of all, she had a girl who had a wooden spoon in her hand, and rode upon a goat; loathly and ugly she was, and the very moment she came into the world, she bawled out 'Mamma'.

'If I'm your mamma', said the Queen, 'God give me grace to mend my ways.'

'Oh, don't be sorry', said the girl, who rode on the goat, 'for one will soon come after me who is better looking.'

So, after a while, the Queen had another girl, who was so fair and sweet, no one had ever set eyes on such a lovely child, and with her you may fancy the Queen was very well pleased. The elder twin they called 'Tatterhood', because she was always so ugly and ragged, and because she had a hood which hung about her ears in tatters. The Queen could scarce bear to look at her, and the nurses tried to shut her up in a room by herself, but it was all no good; where the younger twin was, there she must also be, and no one could ever keep them apart.

Well, one Christmas eve, when they were half grown up, there rose such a frightful noise and clatter in the gallery outside the Queen's bower. So Tatterhood asked what it was that dashed and crashed so out in the passage.

'Oh!' said the Queen, 'it isn't worth asking about.'

But Tatterhood wouldn't give over till she found out all about it and so the Queen told her it was a pack of Trolls and witches who had come there to keep Christmas. So Tatterhood said she'd just go out and drive them away; and in spite of all they could say, and however much they begged and prayed her to let the Trolls alone, she must and would go out to drive the witches off; but she begged the Queen to mind and keep all the doors close shut, so that not one of them came so much as the least bit ajar. Having said this, off she went with her wooden spoon, and began to hunt and sweep away the hags; and all this while there was such a pother out in the gallery, the like of it was never heard. The whole Palace creaked and groaned as if every joint and beam were going to be torn out of its place. Now, how it was, I'm sure I can't tell; but somehow or other one door did get the least bit ajar, then her twin sister just peeped out to see how things were going with Tatterhood, and put her head a tiny bit through the opening. But, POP! up came an old witch, and whipped off her head, and stuck a calf's head on her shoulders instead; and so the Princess ran back into the room on all-fours, and began to 'moo' like a calf. When

Tatterhood came back and saw her sister, she scolded them all round, and was very angry because they hadn't kept better watch, and asked them what they thought of their heedlessness now, when her sister was turned into a calf.

'But still I'll see if I can't set her free', she said.

Then she asked the King for a ship in full trim, and well fitted with stores; but captain and sailors she wouldn't have. No; she would sail away with her sister all alone; and as there was no holding her back, at last they let her have her own way.

Then Tatterhood sailed off, and steered her ship right under the land where the witches dwelt, and when she came to the landing-place, she told her sister to stay quite still on board the ship; but she herself rode on her goat up to the witches' castle. When she got there, one of the windows in the gallery was open, and there she saw her sister's head hung up on the window frame; so she leapt her goat through the window into the gallery, snapped up the head, and set off with it. After her came the witches to try to get the head again, and they flocked about her as thick as a swarm of bees or a nest of ants; but the goat snorted, and puffed, and butted with his horns, and Tatterhood beat and banged them about with her wooden spoon; and so the pack of witches had to give it up. So Tatterhood got back to her ship, took the calf's head off her sister, and put her own on again, and then she became a girl as she had been before. After that she sailed a long, long way, to a strange king's realm.

Now the king of that land was a widower, and had an only son. So when he saw the strange sail, he sent messengers down to the strand to find out whence it came, and who owned it; but when the king's men came down there, they saw never a living soul on board but Tatterhood, and there she was, riding round and round the deck on her goat at full speed, till her elf locks streamed again in the wind. The folk from the palace were all amazed at this sight, and asked, were there not more on board? Yes, there were; she had a sister with her, said Tatterhood. Her, too, they wanted to see, but Tatterhood said 'No':

'No one shall see her, unless the king comes himself', she said; and so she began to gallop about on her goat till the deck thundered again.

So when the servants got back to the palace, and told what they had seen and heard down at the ship, the king was for setting out at once, that he might see the lassie that rode on the goat. When he got down, Tatterhood led out her sister, and she was so fair and gentle, the king fell over head and ears in love with her as he stood. He brought them both back with him to the Palace, and wanted to have the sister for his queen; but Tatterhood said 'No'; the king couldn't have her in any way, unless the king's son chose to have Tatterhood. That you may fancy the prince was very loath to do, such an ugly hussy as Tatterhood was; but at last the king and all the others in the palace talked him over, and he yielded, giving his word to take her for his queen; but it went sore against the grain, and he was a doleful man.

Now they set about the wedding, both with brewing and baking; and when all was ready, they were to go to church; but the prince thought it the weariest churching he had ever had in all his life. First, the king drove off with his bride, and she was so lovely and so grand, all the people stopped to look after her all along the road, and they stared at her till she was out of sight. After them came the prince on horseback by the side of Tatterhood, who trotted along on her goat with her wooden spoon in her fist, and to look at him, it was more like going to a burial than a wedding, and that his own; so sorrowful he seemed, and with never a word to say.

'Why don't you talk?' asked Tatterhood, when they had ridden a bit.

'Why, what should I talk about?' answered the prince.

'Well, you might at least ask me why I ride upon this ugly goat', said Tatterhood.

'Why do you ride on that ugly goat?' asked the prince.

'Is it an ugly goat? why, it's the grandest horse bride ever rode on', answered Tatterhood; and in a trice the goat became a horse, and that the finest the prince had ever set eyes on.

Then they rode on again a bit, but the prince was just as woeful as before, and couldn't get a word out. So Tatterhood asked him again why he didn't talk, and when the Prince answered he didn't know what to talk about, she said:

'You can at least ask me why I ride with this ugly spoon in my fist.'

'Why do you ride with that ugly spoon? 'asked the prince.

'Is it an ugly spoon? why, it's the loveliest silver wand bride ever bore', said Tatterhood; and in a trice it became a silver wand, so dazzling bright, the sunbeams glistened from it.

So they rode on another bit, but the Prince was just as sorrowful, and said never a word. In a little while, Tatterhood asked him again why he didn't talk, and bade him ask why she wore that ugly grey hood on her head.

'Why do you wear that ugly grey hood on your head?' asked the Prince.

'Is it an ugly hood? why, it's the brightest golden crown bride ever wore', answered Tatterhood, and it became a crown on the spot.

Now, they rode on a long while again, and the Prince was so woeful, that he sat without sound or speech just as before. So his bride asked him again why he didn't talk, and bade him ask now, why her face was so ugly and ashen-grey?

'Ah!' asked the Prince, 'why is your face so ugly and ashen-grey?'

'I ugly', said the bride; 'you think my sister pretty, but I am ten times prettier'; and lo! when the Prince looked at her, she was so lovely, he thought there never was so lovely a woman in all the world. After that, I shouldn't wonder if the Prince found his tongue, and no longer rode along hanging down his head.

So they drank the bridal cup both deep and long, and, after that, both Prince and King set out with their brides to the Princess's father's palace, and there they had another bridal feast, and drank anew, both deep and long. There was no end to the fun; and, if you make haste and run to the King's palace, I dare say you'll find there's still a drop of the bridal ale left for you.

THE COCK AND HEN THAT WENT TO THE DOVREFELL

Once on a time there was a Hen that had flown up, and perched on an oak-tree for the night. When the night came, she dreamed that unless she got to the Dovrefell, the world would come to an end. So that very minute she jumped down, and set out on her way. When she had walked a bit she met a Cock.

'Good day, Cocky-Locky', said the Hen.

'Good day, Henny-Penny', said the Cock, 'whither away so early.'

'Oh, I'm going to the Dovrefell, that the world mayn't come to an end', said the Hen.

'Who told you that, Henny-Penny', said the Cock.

'I sat in the oak and dreamt it last night', said the Hen.

'I'll go with you', said the Cock.

Well! they walked on a good bit, and then they met a Duck.

'Good day, Ducky-Lucky', said the Cock.

'Good day, Cocky-Locky', said the Duck, 'whither away so early?'

'Oh, I'm going to the Dovrefell, that the world mayn't come to an end', said the Cock.

'Who told you that, Cocky-Locky?'

'Henny-Penny', said the Cock.

'Who told you that, Henny-Penny?' said the Duck.

'I sat in the oak and dreamt it last night', said the Hen.

'I'll go with you', said the Duck.

So they went off together, and after a bit they met a Goose.

'Good day, Goosey-Poosey', said the Duck.

'Good day, Ducky-Lucky', said the Goose, 'whither away so early?'

'I'm going to the Dovrefell, that the world mayn't come to an end', said the Duck.

'Who told you that, Ducky-Lucky?' asked the Goose.

'Cocky-Locky.'

'Who told you that, Cocky-Locky?'

'Henny-Penny.'

'How you do know that, Henny-Penny?' said the Goose.

'I sat in the oak and dreamt it last night, Goosey-Poosey', said the Hen.

'I'll go with you', said the Goose.

Now when they had all walked along for a bit, a Fox met them.

'Good day, Foxsy-Cocksy', said the Goose.

'Good day, Goosey-Poosey.'

'Whither away, Foxy-Cocksy?'

'Whither away yourself, Goosey-Poosey?'

'I'm going to the Dovrefell that the world mayn't come to an end', said the Goose.

'Who told you that, Goosey-Poosey?' asked the Fox.

'Ducky-Lucky.'

'Who told you that, Ducky-Lucky?'

'Cocky-Locky.'

'Who told you that, Cocky-Locky?'

'Henny-Penny.'

'How do you know that, Henny-Penny?'

'I sat in the oak and dreamt last night, that if we don't get to the Dovrefell, the world will come to an end', said the Hen.

'Stuff and nonsense', said the Fox; 'the world won't come to an end if you don't get thither. No! come home with me to my earth. That's far better, for it's warm and jolly there.'

Well, they went home with the Fox to his earth, and when they got in, the Fox laid on lots of fuel, so that they all got very sleepy.

The Duck and the Goose, they settled themselves down in a corner, but the Cock and Hen flew up on a post. So when the Goose and Duck were well asleep, the

Fox, took the Goose and laid him on the embers, and roasted him. The Hen smelt the strong roast meat, and sprang up to a higher peg, and said, half asleep:

Faugh, what a nasty smell!
What a nasty smell!

'Oh, stuff', said the Fox; 'it's only the smoke driven down the chimney; go to sleep again, and hold your tongue.' So the Hen went off to sleep again.

Now the Fox had hardly got the Goose well down his throat, before he did the very same with the Duck. He took and laid him on the embers, and roasted him for a dainty bit. Then the hen woke up again, and sprung up to a higher peg still.

Faugh, what a nasty smell!
What a nasty smell!

She said again, and then she got her eyes open, and came to see how the Fox had eaten both the twain, goose and duck; so she flew up to the highest peg of all, and perched there, and peeped up through the chimney.

'Nay, nay; just see what a lovely lot of geese flying yonder', she said to the Fox.

Out ran Reynard to fetch a fat roast. But while he was gone, the Hen woke up the Cock, and told him how it had gone with Goosey-Poosey and Ducky-Lucky; and so Cocky-Lucky and Henny-Penny flew out through the chimney, and if they hadn't got to the Dovrefell, it surely would have been all over with the world.

KATIE WOODENCLOAK

Once on a time there was a King who had become a widower. By his Queen he had one daughter, who was so clever and lovely, there wasn't a cleverer or lovelier Princess in all the world. So the King went on a long time sorrowing for the Queen, whom he had loved so much, but at last he got weary of living alone, and married another Queen, who was a widow, and had, too, an only daughter; but this daughter was just as bad and ugly as the other was kind, and clever, and lovely, The stepmother and her daughter were jealous of the Princess, because she was so lovely; but so long as the King was at home, they daredn't do her any harm, he was so fond of her.

Well, after a time, he fell into war with another King, and went out to battle with his host, and then the stepmother thought she might do as she pleased; and so she both starved and beat the Princess, and was after her in every hole and corner of the house. At last she thought everything too good for her, and turned her out to herd cattle. So there she went about with the cattle, and herded them in the woods and on the fells. As for food, she got little or none, and she grew thin and wan, and was always sobbing and sorrowful. Now in the herd there was a great dun bull, which always kept himself so neat and sleek, and often and often he came up to the Princess, and let her pat him. So one day when she sat there, sad, and sobbing, and sorrowful, he came up to her and asked her outright why she was always in such grief. She answered nothing, but went on weeping.

'Ah!' said the Bull, 'I know all about it quite well, though you won't tell me; you weep because the Queen is bad to you, and because she is ready to starve you to death. But food you've no need to fret about, for in my left ear lies a cloth, and when you take and spread it out, you may have as many dishes as you please.'

So she did that, took the cloth and spread it out on the grass, and lo! it served up the nicest dishes one could wish to have; there was wine too, and mead, and sweet cake. Well, she soon got up her flesh again, and grew so plump, and rosy, and white, that the Queen and her scrawny chip of a daughter turned blue and yellow for spite. The Queen couldn't at all make out how her stepdaughter got to look so well on such bad fare, so she told one of her maids to go after her in the wood, and watch and see how it all was, for she thought some of the servants in the house must give her food. So the maid went after her, and watched in the wood, and then she saw how the stepdaughter took the cloth out of the Bull's ear, and spread it out, and how it served up the nicest dishes, which the stepdaughter ate and made good cheer over. All this the maid told the Queen when she went home.

And now the King came home from war, and had won the fight against the other king with whom he went out to battle. So there was great joy throughout the palace, and no one was gladder than the King's daughter. But the Queen shammed sick, and took to her bed, and paid the doctor a great fee to get him to say she could never be well again unless she had some of the Dun Bull's flesh to eat. Both the king's daughter and the folk in the palace asked the doctor if nothing else would help her, and prayed hard for the Bull, for every one was fond of him, and they all said there wasn't that Bull's match in all the land. But, no; he must and should be slaughtered, nothing else would do. When the king's daughter heard that, she got very sorrowful, and went down into the byre to the Bull. There, too, he stood and hung down his head, and looked so downcast that she began to weep over him.

'What are you weeping for?' asked the Bull.

So she told him how the King had come home again, and how the Queen had shammed sick and got the doctor to say she could never be well and sound again unless she got some of the Dun Bull's flesh to eat, and so now he was to be slaughtered.

'If they get me killed first', said the Bull, 'they'll soon take your life too. Now, if you're of my mind, we'll just start off, and go away to-night.'

Well, the Princess thought it bad, you may be sure, to go and leave her father, but she thought it still worse to be in the house with the Queen; and so she gave her word to the Bull to come to him.

At night, when all had gone to bed, the Princess stole down to the byre to the Bull, and so he took her on his back, and set off from the homestead as fast as ever he could. And when the folk got up at cockcrow next morning to slaughter the Bull, why, he was gone; and when the King got up and asked for his daughter, she was gone too. He sent out messengers on all sides to hunt for them, and gave them out in all the parish churches; but there was no one who had caught a glimpse of them. Meanwhile, the Bull went through many lands with the King's daughter on his back, and so one day they came to a great copper-wood, where both the trees, and branches, and leaves, and flowers, and everything, were nothing but copper.

But before they went into the wood, the Bull said to the King's daughter:

'Now, when we get into this wood, mind you take care not to touch even a leaf of it, else it's all over both with me and you, for here dwells a Troll with three heads who owns this wood.'

No, bless her, she'd be sure to take care not to touch anything. Well, she was very careful, and leant this way and that to miss the boughs, and put them gently aside with her hands; but it was such a thick wood, 'twas scarce possible to get through; and so, with all her pains, somehow or other she tore off a leaf, which she held in her hand.

'AU! AU! what have you done now?' said the Bull; 'there's nothing for it now but to fight for life or death; but mind you keep the leaf safe.'

Soon after they got to the end of the wood, and a Troll with three heads came running up:

'Who is this that touches my wood?' said the Troll.

'It's just as much mine as yours', said the Bull.

'Ah!' roared the Troll, 'we'll try a fall about that.'

'As you choose', said the Bull.

So they rushed at one another, and fought; and the Bull he butted, and gored, and kicked with all his might and main; but the Troll gave him as good as he brought, and it lasted the whole day before the Bull got the mastery; and then he was so full of wounds, and so worn out, he could scarce lift a leg. Then they were forced to stay there a day to rest, and then the Bull bade the King's daughter to take the horn of ointment which hung at the Troll's belt, and rub him with it. Then he came to himself again, and the day after they trudged on again. So they travelled many, many days, until, after a long long time, they came to a silver wood, where both the trees, and branches, and leaves, and flowers, and everything, were silvern.

Before the Bull went into the wood, he said to the King's daughter:

'Now, when we get into this wood, for heaven's sake mind you take good care; you mustn't touch anything, and not pluck off so much as one leaf, else it is all over both with me and you; for here is a Troll with six heads who owns it, and him I don't think I should be able to master.'

'No', said the King's daughter; 'I'll take good care and not touch anything you don't wish me to touch.'

But when they got into the wood, it was so close and thick, they could scarce get along. She was as careful as careful could be, and leant to this side and that to miss the boughs, and put them on one side with her hands, but every minute the branches struck her across the eyes, and in spite of all her pains, it so happened she tore off a leaf.

'AU! AU! what have you done now?' said the Bull. 'There's nothing for it now but to fight for life and death, for this Troll has six heads, and is twice as strong as the other, but mind you keep the leaf safe, and don't lose it.'

Just as he said that, up came the Troll:

'Who is this', he said, 'that touches my wood?'

'It's as much mine as yours', said the Bull.

'That we'll try a fall about', roared the Troll.

'As you choose', said the Bull, and rushed at the Troll, and gored out his eyes, and drove his horns right through his body, so that the entrails gushed out; but the Troll was almost a match for him, and it lasted three whole days before the Bull got the life gored out of him. But then he, too, was so weak and wretched, it was as much as he could do to stir a limb, and so full of wounds, that the blood streamed from him. So he said to the King's daughter she must take the horn of ointment that hung at the Troll's belt, and rub him with it. Then she did that, and he came to himself; but they were forced to stay there a week to rest before the Bull had strength enough to go on.

At last they set off again, but the Bull was still poorly, and they went rather slowly at first. So, to spare time, the King's daughter said, as she was young and light of foot, she could very well walk, but she couldn't get leave to do that. No; she must seat herself up on his back again. So on they travelled through many lands a long time, and the King's daughter did not know in the least whither they went; but after a long, long time they came to a gold wood. It was so grand, the gold dropped from every twig, and all the trees, and boughs, and flowers, and leaves, were of pure gold. Here, too, the same thing happened as had happened in the silver wood and copper wood. The Bull told the King's daughter she mustn't touch it for anything, for there was a Troll with nine heads who owned it, and he was much bigger and stouter than both the others put together; and he didn't think he could get the better of him. No; she'd be sure to take heed not to touch it; that he might know very well. But when they got into the wood, it was far thicker and closer than the silver wood, and the deeper they went into it, the worse it got. The wood went on, getting thicker and thicker, and closer and closer; and at last she thought there was no way at all to get through it. She was in such an awful fright of plucking off anything, that she sat, and twisted, and turned herself this way and that, and hither and thither, to keep clear of the boughs, and she put them on one side with her hands; but every moment the branches struck her across the eyes, so that she couldn't see what she was clutching at; and lo! before she knew how it came about, she had a gold apple in her hand. Then she was so bitterly sorry, she burst into tears, and wanted to throw it away; but the Bull said, she must keep it safe and watch it well, and comforted her as well as he could; but he thought it would be a hard tussle, and he doubted how it would go.

Just then up came the Troll with the nine heads, and he was so ugly, the King's daughter scarcely dared to look at him.

'WHO IS THIS THAT TOUCHES MY WOOD?' he roared.

'It's just as much mine as yours', said the Bull.

'That we'll try a fall about', roared the Troll again.

'Just as you choose', said the Bull; and so they rushed at one another, and fought, and it was such a dreadful sight, the King's daughter was ready to swoon away. The Bull gored out the Troll's eyes, and drove his horns through and through his body, till the entrails came tumbling out; but the Troll fought bravely; and when the Bull got one head gored to death, the rest breathed life into it again, and so it lasted a whole week before the Bull was able to get the life out of them all. But then he was utterly worn out and wretched. He couldn't stir a foot, and his body was all one wound. He couldn't so much as ask the King's daughter to take the horn of ointment which hung at the Troll's belt, and rub it over him. But she did it all the same, and then he came to himself by little and little; but they had to lie there and rest three weeks before he was fit to go on again.

Then they set off at a snail's pace, for the Bull said they had still a little further to go, and so they crossed over many high hills and thick woods. So after awhile they got upon the fells.

'Do you see anything?' asked the Bull.

'No, I see nothing but the sky, and the wild fell', said the King's daughter.

So when they clomb higher up, the fell got smoother, and they could see further off.

'Do you see anything now?' asked the Bull.

'Yes, I see a little castle far, far away', said the Princess.

'That's not so little though', said the Bull.

After a long, long time, they came to a great cairn, where there was a spur of the fell that stood sheer across the way.

'Do you see anything now?' asked the Bull.

'Yes, now I see the castle close by', said the King's daughter, 'and now it is much, much bigger.'

'Thither you're to go', said the Bull. 'Right underneath the castle is a pig-sty, where you are to dwell. When you come thither you'll find a wooden cloak, all made of strips of lath; that you must put on, and go up to the castle and say your name is "Katie Woodencloak", and ask for a place. But before you go, you must take your penknife and cut my head off, and then you must flay me, and roll up the hide, and lay it under the wall of rock yonder, and under the hide you must lay the copper leaf, and the silver leaf, and the golden apple. Yonder, up against the rock, stands a stick; and when you want anything, you've only got to knock on the wall of rock with that stick.'

At first she wouldn't do anything of the kind; but when the Bull said it was the only thanks he would have for what he had done for her, she couldn't help herself. So, however much it grieved her heart, she hacked and cut away with her knife at the big beast till she got both his head and his hide off, and then she laid the hide up under the wall of rock, and put the copper leaf, and the silvern leaf, and the golden apple inside it.

So when she had done that, she went over to the pig-sty, but all the while she went she sobbed and wept. There she put on the wooden cloak, and so went up to the palace. When she came into the kitchen she begged for a place, and told them her name was Katie Woodencloak. Yes, the cook said she might have a place--she might have leave to be there in the scullery, and wash up, for the lassie who did that work before had just gone away.

'But as soon as you get weary of being here, you'll go your way too, I'll be bound.'

No; she was sure she wouldn't do that.

So there she was, behaving so well, and washing up so handily. The Sunday after there were to be strange guests at the palace, so Katie asked if she might have leave to carry up water for the Prince's bath; but all the rest laughed at her, and said:

'What should you do there? Do you think the Prince will care to look at you, you who are such a fright!'

But she wouldn't give it up, and kept on begging and praying; and at last she got leave. So when she went up the stairs, her wooden cloak made such a clatter, the Prince came out and asked:

'Pray who are you?'

'Oh! I was just going to bring up water for your Royal Highness's bath', said Katie.

'Do you think now', said the Prince, 'I'd have anything to do with the water you bring?' and with that he threw the water over her.

So she had to put up with that, but then she asked leave to go to church; well, she got that leave too, for the church lay close by. But, first of all, she went to the rock, and knocked on its face with the stick which stood there, just as the Bull had said. And straightway out came a man, who said:

'What's your will?'

So the Princess said she had got leave to go to church and hear the priest preach, but she had no clothes to go in. So he brought out a kirtle, which was as bright as the copper wood, and she got a horse and saddle beside. Now, when she got to the church she was so lovely and grand, all wondered who she could be, and scarce one of them listened to what the priest said, for they looked too much at her. As for the Prince, he fell so deep in love with her, he didn't take his eyes off her for a single moment.

So, as she went out of church, the Prince ran after her, and held the church door open for her; and so he got hold of one of her gloves, which was caught in the door. When she went away and mounted her horse, the Prince went up to her again, and asked whence she came.

'Oh! I'm from Bath', said Katie; and while the Prince took out the glove to give it to her, she said:

Bright before and dark behind,   Clouds come rolling on the wind;   That this Prince may never see   Where my good steed goes with me.

The Prince had never seen the like of that glove, and went about far and wide asking after the land whence the proud lady, who rode off without her glove, said she came; but there was no one who could tell where 'Bath' lay.

Next Sunday some one had to go up to the Prince with a towel.

'Oh! may I have leave to go up with it?' said Katie.

'What's the good of your going?' said the others; 'you saw how it fared with you last time.'

But Katie wouldn't give in; she kept on begging and praying, till she got leave; and then she ran up the stairs, so that her wooden cloak made a great clatter. Out came the Prince, and when he saw it was Katie, he tore the towel out of her hand, and threw it into her face.

'Pack yourself off, you ugly Troll', he cried; 'do you think I'd have a towel which you have touched with your smutty fingers?'

After that the Prince set off to church, and Katie begged for leave to go too. They all asked what business she had at church--she who had nothing to put on but that wooden cloak, which was so black and ugly. But Katie said the priest was such a brave man to preach, what he said did her so much good; and so she at last got leave. Now she went again to the rock and knocked, and so out came the man, and gave her a kirtle far finer than the first one; it was all covered with silver, and it shone like the silver wood; and she got besides a noble steed, with a saddle-cloth broidered with silver, and a silver bit.

So when the King's daughter got to the church, the folk were still standing about in the churchyard. And all wondered and wondered who she could be, and the Prince was soon on the spot, and came and wished to hold her horse for her while she got off. But she jumped down, and said there was no need, for her horse was so well broke, it stood still when she bid it, and came when she called it. So they all went into church; but there was scarce a soul that listened to what the priest said, for they looked at her a deal too much; and the Prince fell still deeper in love than the first time.

When the sermon was over, and she went out of church and was going to mount her horse, up came the Prince again, and asked her whence she came.

'Oh! I'm from Towelland', said the King's daughter; and as she said that, she dropped her riding-whip, and when the Prince stooped to pick it up, she said:

Bright before and dark behind,   Clouds come rolling on the wind;   That this Prince may never see   Where my good steed goes with me.

So away she was again; and the Prince couldn't tell what had become of her. He went about far and wide asking after the land whence she said she came, but there was no one who could tell him where it lay; and so the Prince had to make the best he could of it.

Next Sunday some one had to go up to the Prince with a comb. Katie begged for leave to go up with it, but the others put her in mind how she had fared the last time, and scolded her for wishing to go before the Prince--such a black and ugly fright as she was in her wooden cloak. But she wouldn't leave off asking till they let her go up to the Prince with his comb. So, when she came clattering up the stairs again, out came the Prince, and took the comb, and threw it at her, and bade her be off as fast as she could. After that the Prince went to church, and Katie begged for leave to go too. They asked again what business she had there, she who was so foul and black, and who had no clothes to show herself in. Might be the Prince or some one else would see her, and then both she and all the others would smart for it; but Katie said they had something else to do than to look at her; and she wouldn't leave off begging and praying till they gave her leave to go.

So the same thing happened now as had happened twice before. She went to the rock and knocked with the stick, and then the man came out and gave her a kirtle which was far grander than either of the others. It was almost all pure gold, and studded with diamonds; and she got besides a noble steed, with a gold broidered saddle-cloth and a golden bit.

Now when the King's daughter got to the church, there stood the priest and all the people in the churchyard waiting for her. Up came the Prince running, and wanted to hold her horse, but she jumped off, and said:

'No; thanks--there's no need, for my horse is so well broke, it stands still when I bid him.'

So they all hastened into church, and the priest got into the pulpit, but no one listened to a word he said; for they all looked too much at her, and wondered whence she came; and the Prince, he was far deeper in love than either of the former times. He had no eyes, or ears, or sense for anything, but just to sit and stare at her.

So when the sermon was over, and the King's daughter was to go out of the church, the Prince had got a firkin of pitch poured out in the porch, that he might come and help her over it; but she didn't care a bit--she just put her foot right down into the midst of the pitch, and jumped across it; but then one of her golden shoes stuck fast in it, and as she got on her horse, up came the Prince running out of the church, and asked whence she came.

'I'm from Combland', said Katie. But when the Prince wanted to reach her the gold shoe, she said,

Bright before and dark behind,   Clouds come rolling on the wind;   That this Prince may never see   Where my good steed goes with me.

So the Prince couldn't tell still what had become of her, and he went about a weary time all over the world asking for 'Combland'; but when no one could tell him where it lay, he ordered it to be given out everywhere that he would wed the woman whose foot could fit the gold shoe.

So many came of all sorts from all sides, fair and ugly alike; but there was no one who had so small a foot as to be able to get on the gold shoe. And after a long, long time, who should come but Katie's wicked stepmother, and her daughter, too, and her the gold shoe fitted; but ugly she was, and so loathly she looked, the Prince only kept his word sore against his will. Still they got ready the wedding-feast, and she was dressed up and decked out as a bride; but as they rode to church, a little bird sat upon a tree and sang:

A bit off her heel,   And a bit off her toe;   Katie Woodencloak's tiny shoe   Is full of blood--that's all I know.

And, sure enough, when they looked to it the bird told the truth, for blood gushed out of the shoe.

Then all the maids and women who were about the palace had to go up to try on the shoe, but there was none of them whom it would fit at all.

'But where's Katie Woodencloak?' asked the Prince, when all the rest had tried the shoe, for he understood the song of birds very well, and bore in mind what the little bird had said.

'Oh! she think of that!' said the rest; 'it's no good her coming forward. Why, she's legs like a horse.'

'Very true, I daresay', said the Prince; 'but since all the others have tried, Katie may as well try too.'

'Katie', he bawled out through the door; and Katie came trampling upstairs, and her wooden cloak clattered as if a whole regiment of dragoons were charging up.

'Now, you must try the shoe on, and be a Princess, you too,' said the other maids, and laughed and made game of her.

So Katie took up the shoe, and put her foot into it like nothing, and threw off her wooden cloak; and so there she stood in her gold kirtle, and it shone so that the sunbeams glistened from her; and, lo! on her other foot she had the fellow to the gold shoe.

So when the Prince knew her again, he grew so glad, he ran up to her and threw his arms round her, and gave her a kiss; and when he heard she was a King's daughter, he got gladder still, and then came the wedding feast; and so,

Snip, snip, snover, This story's over.

THUMBIKIN

Once on a time there was a woman who had an only son, and he was no taller than your thumb; and so they called him Thumbikin.

Now, when he had come to be old enough to know right and wrong, his mother told him to go out and woo him a bride, for now she said it was high time he thought about getting a wife. When Thumbikin heard that, he was very glad; so they got their driving gear in order and set off, and his mother put him into her bosom. Now they were going to a palace where there was an awfully big Princess, but when they had gone a bit of the way, Thumbikin was lost and gone. His mother hunted for him everywhere, and bawled to him, and wept because he was lost, and she couldn't find him again.

'*Pip, Pip*', said Thumbikin, 'here I am'; and he had hidden himself in the horse's mane.

So he came out, and had to give his word to his mother that he wouldn't do so any more. But when they had driven a bit further on, Thumbikin was lost again. His mother hunted for him, and called him, and wept; but gone he was, and gone he stayed.

'*Pip, Pip*', said Thumbikin at last; and then she heard how he laughed and tittered, but she couldn't find him at all for the life of her.

'*Pip, Pip*, why, here I am now!' said Thumbikin, and came out of the horse's ear.

So he had to give his word that he wouldn't hide himself again; but they had scarce driven a bit further before he was gone again. He couldn't help it. As for his mother, she hunted, and wept, and called him by name; but gone he was, and gone he stayed; and the more she hunted, the less she could find him in any way.

'*Pip, Pip*, here I am then', said Thumbikin.

But she couldn't make out at all where he was, his voice sounded so dull, and muffled.

So she hunted, and he kept on saying, 'Pip, here I am', and laughed and chuckled, but she couldn't find him; but all at once the horse snorted, and it snorted Thumbikin out, for he had crept up one of his nostrils.

Then his mother took him and put him into a bag; she knew no other way, for she saw well enough he couldn't help hiding himself.

So, when they came to the palace, the match was soon made, for the Princess thought him a pretty little chap, and it wasn't long before the wedding came on too.

Now, when they were going to sit down to the wedding-feast, Thumbikin sat at the table by the Princess's side; but he had worse than no seat, for when he was to eat he couldn't reach up to the table; and so if the Princess hadn't helped him up on to it, he wouldn't have got a bit to eat.

Now it went good and well so long as he had to eat off a plate, but then there came a great bowl of porridge--that he couldn't reach up to; but Thumbikin soon found out a way to help himself; he climbed up and sat on the lip of the bowl. But then there was a pat of melting butter right in the middle of the bowl, and that he couldn't reach to dip his porridge into it, and so he went on and took his seat at the edge of the melting butter; but just then who should come but the Princess, with a great spoonful of porridge to dip it into the butter; and, alas! she went too near to Thumbikin, and tipped him over; and so he fell over head and ears, and was drowned in the melted butter.

DOLL I' THE GRASS

Once on a time there was a King who had twelve sons. When they were grown big he told them they must go out into the world and win themselves wives, but these wives must each be able to spin, and weave, and sew a shirt in one day, else he wouldn't have them for daughters-in-law.

To each he gave a horse and a new suit of mail, and they went out into the world to look after their brides; but when they had gone a bit of the way, they said they wouldn't have Boots, their youngest brother, with them--he wasn't fit for anything.

Well, Boots had to stay behind, and he didn't know what to do or whither to turn; and so he grew so downcast, he got off his horse, and sat down in the tall grass to weep. But when he had sat a little while, one of the tufts in the grass began to stir and move, and out of it came a little white thing, and when it came nearer, Boots saw it was a charming little lassie, only such a tiny bit of a thing. So the lassie went up to him, and asked if he would come down below and see 'Doll i' the Grass'.

Yes, he'd be very happy, and so he went.

Now, when he got down; there sat Doll i' the Grass on a chair; she was so lovely and so smart, and she asked Boots whither he was going, and what was his business.

So he told her how there were twelve brothers of them, and how the King had given them horses and mail, and said they must each go out into the world and find them a wife who could spin, and weave, and sew a shirt in a day.

'But if you'll only say at once you'll be my wife, I'll not go a step further', said Boots to Doll i' the Grass.

Well, she was willing enough, and so she made haste and span, and wove, and sewed the shirt, but it was so tiny, tiny little. It wasn't longer than so--------long.

So Boots set off home with it, but when he brought it out he was almost ashamed, it was so small. Still the King said he should have her, and so Boots set off, glad and happy to fetch his little sweetheart. So when he got to Doll i' the Grass, he wished to take her up before him on his horse; but she wouldn't have that, for she said she would sit and drive along in a silver spoon, and that she had two small white horses to draw her. So off they set, he on his horse and she on her silver spoon, and the two horses that drew her were two tiny white mice; but Boots always kept the other side of the road, he was so afraid lest he should ride over her, she was so little. So, when they had gone a bit of the way, they came to a great piece of water. Here Boots' horse got frightened, and shied across the road and upset the spoon, and Doll i' the Grass tumbled into the water. Then Boots got so sorrowful because he didn't know how to get her out again; but in a little while up came a merman with her, and now she was as well and full grown as other men and women, and far lovelier than she had been before. So he took her up before him on his horse, and rode home.

When Boots got home all his brothers had come back each with his sweetheart, but these were all so ugly, and foul, and wicked, that they had done nothing but fight with one another on the way home, and on their heads they had a kind of hat that was daubed over with tar and soot, and so the rain had run down off the hats on to their faces, till they got far uglier and nastier than they had been before. When his brothers saw Boots and his sweetheart, they were all as jealous as jealous could be of her; but the King was so overjoyed with them both, that he drove all the others away, and so Boots held his wedding-feast with Doll i' the Grass, and after that they lived well and happily together a long long time, and if they're not dead, why they're alive still.

THE LAD AND THE DEIL

Once on a time there was a lad who was walking along a road cracking nuts, so he found one that was worm-eaten, and just at that very moment he met the Deil.

'Is it true, now', said the lad, 'what they say, that the Deil can make himself as small as he chooses, and thrust himself in through a pinhole?'

'Yes it is', said the Deil.

'Oh! it is, is it? then let me see you do it, and just creep into this nut', said the lad.

So the Deil did it.

Now, when he had crept well in through the worm's hole, the lad stopped it up with a pin.

'Now, I've got you safe', he said, and put the nut into his pocket.

So when he had walked on a bit, he came to a smithy, and he turned in and asked the smith if he'd be good enough to crack that nut for him.

'Aye, that'll be an easy job', said the smith, and took his smallest hammer, laid the nut on the anvil, and gave it a blow, but it wouldn't break.

So he took another hammer a little bigger, but that wasn't heavy enough either.

Then he took one bigger still, but it was still the same story; and so the smith got wroth, and grasped his great sledge-hammer.

'Now, I'll crack you to bits', he said, and let drive at the nut with all his might and main. And so the nut flew to pieces with a bang that blew off half the roof of the smithy, and the whole house creaked and groaned as though it were ready to fall.

'Why! if I don't think the Deil must have been in that nut', said the smith.

'So he was; you're quite right', said the lad, as he went away laughing.

THE COCK AND HEN A-NUTTING

Once on a time the cock and the hen went out into the hazel-wood to pick nuts; and so the hen got a nutshell in her throat, and lay on her back, flapping her wings.

Off went the cock to fetch water for her; so he came to the Spring and said:

'Dear good friend Spring give me a drop of water, that I may give it to Dame Partlet, my mate, who lies at death's door in the hazel- wood.'

But the Spring answered:

'You'll get no water from me until I get leaves from you.'

So the Cock ran to the Linden, and said:

'Dear good friend Linden, give me some of your leaves, the leaves I'll give to the Spring, and the Spring'll give me water to give to Dame Partlet my mate, who lies at death's door in the hazel-wood.'

'You'll get no leaves from me', said the Linden, 'until I get a red ribbon with a golden edge from you.'

So the Cock ran to the Virgin Mary.

'Dear good Virgin Mary, give me a red ribbon with a golden edge, and I'll give the red ribbon to the Linden, the Linden'll give me leaves, the leaves I'll give to the Spring, the Spring'll give me water, and the water I'll give to Dame Partlet my mate, who lies at death's door, in the hazel-wood.'

'You'll get no red ribbon from me', answered the Virgin Mary, 'until I get shoes from you.'

So the Cock ran to the Shoemaker and said

'Dear good friend Shoemaker, give me shoes, and I'll give the shoes to the Virgin Mary, the Virgin Mary'll give me a red ribbon, the red ribbon I'll give to the

Linden, the Linden'll give me leaves, the leaves I'll give to the Spring, the Spring'll give me water, the water I'll give to Dame Partlet my mate, who lies at death's door in the hazel-wood.'

'You'll get no shoes from me', said the Shoemaker, 'until I get bristles from you.'

So the Cock ran to the Sow and said:

'Dear good friend Sow, give me bristles, the bristles I'll give to the Shoemaker, the Shoemaker'll give me shoes, the shoes I'll give to the Virgin Mary, the Virgin Mary'll give me a red ribbon, the red ribbon I'll give to the Linden, the Linden'll give me leaves, the leaves I'll give to the Spring, the Spring'll give me water, the water I'll give to Dame Partlet my mate, who lies at death's door in the hazel-wood.'

'You'll get no bristles from me', said the Sow, 'until I get corn from you.'

So the Cock ran to the Thresher and said:

'Dear good friend Thresher, give me corn, the corn I'll give to the Sow, the Sow'll give me bristles, the bristles I'll give to the Shoemaker, the Shoemaker'll give me shoes, the shoes I'll give to the Virgin Mary, the Virgin Mary'll give me a red ribbon, the red ribbon I'll give to the Linden, the Linden'll give me leaves, the leaves I'll give to the Spring, the Spring'll give me water, the water I'll give to Dame Partlet my mate, who lies at death's door in the hazel- wood.'

'You'll get no corn from me', said the Thresher, 'until I get a bannock from you.'

So the Cock ran to the Baker's wife and said:

'Dear good friend Mrs. Baker, give me a bannock, the bannock I'll give to the Thresher, the Thresher'll give me corn, the corn I'll give to the Sow, the Sow'll give me bristles, the bristles I'll give to the Shoemaker, the Shoemaker'll give me shoes, the shoes I'll give to the Virgin Mary, the Virgin Mary'll give me a red ribbon, the red ribbon I'll give to the Linden, the Linden'll give me leaves, the leaves I'll give to the Spring, the Spring'll give me water, the water I'll give to Dame Partlet my mate, who lies at death's door in the hazel-wood.'

'You'll get no bannock from me', said the Baker's wife, until I get wood from you.'

So the Cock ran to the Woodcutter and said:

'Dear good friend Woodcutter, give me wood, the wood I'll give to the Baker's wife, the Baker's wife'll give me a bannock, the bannock I'll give to the Thresher, the Thresher'll give me corn, the corn I'll give to the Sow, the Sow'll give me bristles, the bristles I'll give to the Shoemaker, the Shoemaker'll give me shoes, the shoes I'll give to the Virgin Mary, the Virgin Mary'll give me a red ribbon, the red ribbon I'll give to the Linden, the Linden'll give me leaves, the leaves I'll give to the Spring, the Spring'll give me water, the water I'll give to Dame Partlet my mate, who lies at death's door in the hazel-wood.'

'You'll get no wood from me', answered the Woodcutter, 'until I get an axe from you.'

So the Cock ran to the Smith and said:

'Dear good friend Smith, give me an axe, the axe I'll give to the Woodcutter, the Woodcutter'll give me wood, the wood I'll give to the Baker's wife, the Baker's wife'll give me a bannock, the bannock I'll give to the Thresher, the Thresher'll give me corn, the corn I'll give to the Sow, the Sow'll give me bristles, the bristles I'll give to the Shoemaker, the Shoemaker'll give me shoes, the shoes I'll give to the Virgin Mary, the Virgin Mary'll give me a red ribbon, the red ribbon I'll give to the Linden, the Linden'll give me leaves, the leaves I'll give to the Spring, the Spring'll give me water, the water I'll give to Dame Partlet my mate, who lies at death's door in the hazel-wood.'

'You'll get no axe from me', answered the Smith, 'until I get charcoal of you.'

So the Cock ran to the Charcoal-burner and said

'Dear good friend Charcoal-burner, give me charcoal, the charcoal I'll give to the Smith, the Smith'll give me an axe, the axe I'll give to the Woodcutter, the Woodcutter'll give me wood, the wood I'll give to the Baker's wife, the Baker's wife'll give me a bannock, the bannock I'll give to the Thresher, the Thresher'll give me corn, the corn I'll give to the Sow, the Sow'll give me bristles, the bristles I'll give to the Shoemaker, the Shoemaker'll give me shoes, the shoes I'll give to the Virgin Mary, the Virgin Mary'll give me a red ribbon, the red ribbon I'll give to the Linden, the Linden'll give me leaves, the leaves I'll give to the Spring, the Spring'll give me water, the water I'll give to Dame Partlet my mate, who lies at death's door in the hazel-wood.

So the Charcoal-burner took pity on the Cock, and gave him a bit of charcoal, and then the Smith got his coal, and the Woodcutter his axe, and the Baker's wife her wood, and the Thresher his bannock, and the Sow her corn, and the Shoemaker his bristles, and the Virgin Mary her shoes, and the Linden its red ribbon with a golden edge, and the Spring its leaves, and the Cock his drop of water, and he gave it to Dame Partlet, his mate, who lay there at death's door in the hazel- wood, and so she got all right again.

THE BIG BIRD DAN

Once on a time there was a king who had twelve daughters, and he was so fond of them they must always be at his side; but every day at noon, while the king slept, the Princesses went out to take a walk. So once, while the king was taking his noontide nap, and the Princesses had gone to take their walk, all at once they were missing, and worse, they never came home again. Then there was great grief and sorrow all over the land, but the most sorry of all was the king. He sent messengers out throughout his own and other realms, and gave out their names in all the churches, and had the bells tolled for them in all the steeples; but gone the Princesses were, and gone they stayed, and none could tell what was become of them. So it was as clear as day that they must have been carried off by some witchcraft.

Well, it wasn't long before these tidings spread far and wide, over land and town, aye, over many lands; and so the news came to a king ever so many lands off, who had twelve sons. So when these Princes heard of the twelve king's daughters, they asked leave of their father to go out and seek them. They had hard work to get his leave, for he was afraid lest he should never see them again, but they all fell down on their knees before the king, and begged so long, at last he was forced to let them go after all.

He fitted out a ship for them, and gave them Ritter Red, who was quite at home at sea, for a captain. So they sailed about a long, long time, landed on every shore they came to, and hunted and asked after the Princesses, but they could neither hear nor see anything of them. And now, a few days only were wanting to make up seven years since they set sail, when one day a strong storm rose, and such foul weather, they thought they should never come to land again, and all had to work so hard, they couldn't get a wink of sleep so long as the storm lasted. But when the third day was nearly over, the wind fell, and all at once it got as still as still could be. Now, they were all so weary with work and the rough weather, they fell fast asleep in the twinkling of an eye; all but the youngest Prince, he could get no rest, and couldn't go off to sleep at all.

So as he was pacing up and down the deck, the ship came to a little island, and on the island ran a little dog, and bayed and barked at the ship as if it wanted to come on board. So the Prince went to that side of the deck, and tried to coax the dog, and whistled and whistled to him, but the more he whistled and coaxed, the more the dog barked and snarled. Well, he thought it a shame the dog should run about there and starve, for he made up his mind that it must have come thither from a ship that had been cast away in the storm; but still he thought he should never be able to help it after all, for he couldn't put out the boat by himself, and as for the others, they all slept so sound, he wouldn't wake them for the sake of a dog. But then the weather was so calm and still; and at last he said to himself: 'Come what may, you must go on shore and save that dog', and so he began to try to launch the boat, and he found it far easier work than he thought. So he rowed ashore, and went up to the dog; but every time he tried to catch it, it jumped on one side, and so it went on till he found himself inside a great grand castle, before he knew where he was. Then the dog, all at once, was changed into a lovely Princess; and there, on the bench, sat a man so big and ugly, the Prince almost lost his wits for fear.

'YOU'VE NO NEED TO BE AFRAID', said the man--but the Prince, to tell you the truth, got far more afraid when he heard his gruff voice-- 'for I know well enough what you want. There are twelve Princes of you, and you are looking for the twelve Princesses that are lost. I know, too, very well whereabouts they are; they're with my lord and master, and there they sit, each of them on her chair, and comb his hair; for he has twelve heads. And now you have sailed seven years, but you'll have to sail seven years more before you find them. As for you, you might stay here and welcome, and have my daughter; but you must first slay him, for he's a hard master to all of us, and we're all weary of him, and when he's dead I shall be King in his stead; but first try if you can brandish this sword'.

Then the King's son took hold of a rusty old sword which hung on the wall, but he could scarce stir it.

'Now you must take a pull at this flask', said the Troll; and when he had done that he could stir it, and when he had taken another he could lift it, and when he had taken a third he could brandish the sword as easily as if it had been his own.

'Now, when you get on board', said the Troll Prince, 'you must hide the sword well in your berth, that Ritter Red mayn't set eyes on it; he's not man enough to wield it, but he'll get spiteful against you, and try to take your life. And when seven years are almost out all but three days', he went on to say, 'everything will happen just as now; foul weather will come on you, with a great storm, and when it is over you'll all be sleepy. Then you must take the sword and row ashore, and so you'll come to a castle where all sorts of guards will stand--wolves, and bears, and lions; but you needn't be afraid of them, for they'll all come and crouch at your feet. But when you come inside the castle, you'll soon see the Troll; he sits in a splendid chamber in grand attire and array; twelve heads he has of his own, and the Princesses sit round them, each on her chair, and comb his heads, and that's a work you may guess they don't much like. Then you must make haste, and hew off one head after the other as quick as you can; for if he wakes and sets his eyes on you, he'll swallow you alive'.

So the King's son went on board with the sword, and he bore in mind what he had come to know. The others still lay fast asleep and snored, and he hid the sword in his berth, so that neither Ritter Red nor any of the rest got sight of it. And now it began to blow again, so he woke up the others and said he thought they oughtn't to sleep any longer now when there was such a good wind. And there was none of them that marked he had been away. Well, after the seven years were all gone but three days, all happened as the Troll had said. A great storm and foul weather came on that lasted three days, and when it had blown itself out, all the rest grew sleepy and went to rest; but the youngest King's son rowed ashore, and the guards fell at his feet, and so he came to the castle. So when he got inside the chamber, there sat the King fast asleep as the Troll Prince had said, and the twelve Princesses sat each on her chair and combed one of his heads. The king's son beckoned to the Princesses to get out of the way; they pointed to the Troll, and beckoned to him again to go his way as quick as ever he could, but he kept on making signs to them to get out of the way, and then they understood that he wanted to set them free, and stole away softly one after the other, and as fast as they went, he hewed off the Troll King's heads, till at last the blood gushed out like a great brook. When the

Troll was slain he rowed on board and hid his sword. He thought now he had done enough, and as he couldn't get rid of the body by himself, he thought it only fair they should help him a little. So he woke them all up, and said it was a shame they should be snoring there, when he had found the Princesses, and set them free from the Troll. The others only laughed at him, and said he had been just as sound asleep as they, and only dreamt that he was man enough to do what he said; for if any one was to set the Princesses free, it was far more likely it would be one of them. But the youngest King's son told them all about it, and when they followed him to the land and saw first of all the brook of blood, and then the castle, and the Troll, and the twelve heads, and the Princesses, they saw plain enough that he had spoken the truth, and now the whole helped him to throw the body and the heads into the sea. So all were glad and happy, but none more so than the Princesses, who got rid of having to sit there and comb the Troll's hair all day. Of all the silver and gold and precious things that were there, they took as much as the ship could hold, and so they went on board altogether Princes and Princesses alike.

But when they had gone a bit out on the sea, the Princesses said they had forgotten in their joy their gold crowns; they lay behind in a press, and they would be so glad to have them. So when none of the others was willing to fetch them, the youngest King's son said:

'I have already dared so much, I can very well go back for the gold crowns too, if you will only strike sail and wait till I come again.'

Yes, that they would do. But when he had gone back so far that they couldn't see him any longer, Ritter Red, who would have been glad enough to have been their chief, and to have the youngest Princess, said, 'it was no use their lying there still waiting for him, for they might know very well he would never come back; they all knew, too, how the king had given him all power and authority to sail or not as he chose; and now they must all say 'twas he that had saved the Princesses, and if any one said anything else, he should lose his life'.

The Princes didn't dare to do anything else than what Ritter Red willed, and so they sailed away.

Meanwhile the youngest King's son rowed to land, went up to the castle, found the press with gold crowns in it, and at last lugged it down to the boat, and shoved off; but when he came where he ought to have seen the ship, lo! it was gone. Well, as he couldn't catch a glimpse of it anywhere, he could very soon tell how matters stood. To row after them was no good, and so he was forced to turn about and row back to land. He was rather afraid to stay alone in the castle all night, but there was no other house to be got, so he plucked up a heart, locked up all the doors and gates fast, and lay down in a room where there was a bed ready made. But fearful and woeful he was, and still more afraid he got when he had lain a while and something began to creak and groan and quake in wall and roof, as if the whole castle were being torn asunder. Then all at once down something plunged close by the side of his bed, as if it were a whole cartload of hay. Then all was still again; but after a while he heard a voice, which bade him not to be afraid, and said:

   Here am I the Big Bird Dan   Come to help you all I can.

'But the first thing you must do when you wake in the morning, will be to go to the barn and fetch four barrels of rye for me. I must fill my crop with them for breakfast, else I can't do anything'.

When he woke up, sure enough there he saw an awfully big bird, which had a feather at the nape of his neck, as thick and long as a half- grown spruce fir. So the King's son went down to the barn to fetch four barrels of rye for the Big Bird Dan, and when he had crammed them into his crop he told the King's son to hang the press with the gold crowns on one side of his neck, and as much gold and silver as would weigh it down on the other side, and after that to get on his back and hold fast by the feather in the nape of his neck. So away they went till the wind whistled after them, and so it wasn't long before they outstripped the ship. The King's son wanted to go on board for his sword, for he was afraid lest any one should get sight of it, for the Troll had told him that mustn't be; but Bird Dan said that mustn't be either.

'Ritter Red will never see it, never fear; but if you go on board, he'll try to take your life, for he has set his heart on having the youngest Princess; but make your mind quite easy about her, for she lays a naked sword by her side in bed every night.'

So after a long, long time, they came to the island where the Troll Prince was; and there the King's son was welcomed so heartily there was no end to it. The Troll Prince didn't know how to be good enough to him for having slain his Lord and Master, and so made him King of the Trolls, and if the King's son had been willing he might easily have got the Troll King's daughter, and half the kingdom. But he had so set his heart on the youngest of the twelve Princesses, he could take no rest, but was all for going after their ship time after time. So the Troll King begged him to be quiet a little longer, and said they had still nearly seven years to sail before they got home. As for the Princess the Troll said the same thing as the Big Bird Dan.

'You needn't fret yourself about her, for she lays a naked sword by her side every night in bed. And now if you don't believe what I say', said the Troll, 'you can go on board when they sail by here, and see for yourself, and fetch the sword too, for I may just as well have it again.'

So when they sailed by another great storm arose, and when the king's son went on board they all slept, and each Princess lay beside her Prince; but the youngest lay alone with a naked sword beside her in the bed, and on the floor by the bedside lay Ritter Red. Then the king's son took the sword and rowed ashore again, and none of them had seen that he had been on board. But still the King's son couldn't rest, and he often and often wanted to be off, and so at last when it got near the end of the seven years, and only three weeks were left, the Troll King said:

'Now you may get ready to go since you won't stay with us; and you shall have the loan of my iron boat, which sails of itself, if you only say:

Boat, boat, go on!

'In that boat there is an iron club, and that club you must lift a little when you see the ship straight a-head of you, and then they'll get such a rattling fair breeze, they'll forget to look at you; but when you get alongside them, you must lift the club a little again, and then they'll get such a foul wind and storm, they'll have something else to do than to stare at you; and when you have run past them, you must lift the club a third time, but you must always be sure and lay it down carefully again, else there'll be such a storm both you and they will be wrecked and lost. Now, when you have got to land, you've no need to bother yourself at all about the boat; just turn it about, and shove it off, and say:

Boat, boat, go back home!

When he set out they gave him so much gold and silver, and so many other costly things, and clothes and linen which the Troll Princess had sewn and woven for him all that long time, that he was far richer than any of his brothers.

Well, he had no sooner seated himself in the boat, and said,

Boat, boat, go on!

than away went the boat, and when he saw the ship right ahead he lifted up the club, and then they got such a fair breeze, they forgot to look at him. When he was alongside the ship, he lifted the club again, and then such a storm arose and such foul weather, that the white foam flew about the ship, and the billows rolled over the deck, and they had something else to do than to stare at him; and when he had run past them he lifted the club the third time, and then the storm and the wind rose so, they had still less time to look after him, and to make him out. So he came to land long, long before the ship; and when he had got all his goods out of the boat, he shoved it off again, and turned it about and said:

Boat, boat, go back home!

And off went the boat.

Then he dressed himself up as a sailor--whether the Troll king had told him that, or it was his own device, I'm sure I can't say--and went up to a wretched hut where an old wife lived, whom he got to believe that he was a poor sailor who had been on board a great ship that was wrecked, and that he was the only soul that had got ashore. After that he begged for house-room for himself and the goods he had saved.

'Heaven mend me!' said the old wife, 'how can I lend any one house- room? look at me and mine, why, I've no bed to sleep on myself, still less one for any one else to lie on.'

Well, well, it was all the same, said the sailor; if he only got a roof over his head, it didn't matter where he lay. So she couldn't turn him out of the house, when he was so thankful for what there was. That afternoon he fetched up his things, and the old wife, who was very eager to hear a bit of news to run about and tell, began at once to ask who he was, whence he came, whither he was bound, what it was he had with him, what his business was, and if he hadn't heard anything of the twelve Princesses who had been away the Lord knew how many years. All this she asked and much more, which it would be waste of time to tell. But he said he was so poorly and had such a bad headache after the awful weather he had been out in, that he couldn't answer any of her questions; she must just leave him alone and let him rest a few days till he came to himself after the hard work he'd had in the gale, and then she'd know all she wanted.

The very next day the old wife began to stir him up and ask again, but the sailor's head was still so bad he hadn't got his wits together, but somehow he let drop a word or two to show that he did know something about the Princesses. Off ran the old wife with what she had heard to all the gossips and chatterboxes round about, and soon the one came running after the other to ask about the Princesses, 'if he had seen them', 'if they would soon be there', 'if they were on the way', and much more of the same sort. He still went on groaning over his headache after the storm, so that he couldn't tell them all about it, but so much he told them, unless they had been lost in the great storm they'd make the land in about a fortnight or before perhaps; but he couldn't say for sure whether they were alive or no, for though he had seen them, it might very well be that they had been cast away in the storm since. So what did one of these old gossips do but run up to the Palace with this story, and say that there was a sailor down in such and such an old wife's hut, who had seen the Princesses, and that they were coming home in a fortnight or in a week's time. When the King heard that he sent a messenger down to the sailor to come up to him and tell the news himself.

'I don't see how it's to be', said the sailor, 'for I haven't any clothes fit to stand in before the King.'

But the King said he must come; for the King must and would talk with him, whether he were richly or poorly clad, for there was no one else who could bring him any tidings of the Princesses. So he went up at last to the Palace and went in before the King, who asked him if it were true that he had seen anything of the Princesses.

'Aye, aye', said the sailor, 'I've seen them sure enough, but I don't know whether they're still alive, for when I last caught sight of them, the weather was so foul we in our ship were cast away; but if they're still alive they'll come safe home in a fortnight or perhaps before.'

When the King heard that he was almost beside himself for joy; and when the time came that the sailor had said they would come, the King drove down to the strand to meet them in a great state; and there was joy and gladness over the whole land, when the ship came sailing in with the Princes and Princesses and Ritter Red. But no one was gladder than the old King, who had got his daughters back again. The eleven eldest Princesses too, were glad and merry, but the youngest who was to have Ritter Red, who said that he had set them all free and slain the Troll, she wept and was always sorrowful. The King took this ill, and asked why she wasn't cheerful and merry like the others; she hadn't anything to be sorry for now when she had got out of the Troll's clutches, and was to have such a husband as Ritter Red. But she daredn't say anything, for Ritter Red had said he would take the life of any one who told the truth how things had gone.

But now one day, when they were hard at work sewing and stitching the bridal array, in came a man in a great sailor's cloak with a pedlar's pack on his back, and asked if the Princesses wouldn't buy something fine of him for the wedding; he had so many wares and costly things, both gold and silver. Yes, they might do so perhaps, so they looked at his wares and they looked at him, for they thought they had seen both him and many of his costly things before.

'He who has so many fine things', said the youngest Princess, 'must surely have something still more precious, and which suits us better even than these.'

'Maybe I have', said the Pedlar.

But now all the others cried 'Hush', and bade her bear in mind what Ritter Red had said he would do.

Well, some time after the Princesses sat and looked out of the window, and then the King's son came again with the great sea-cloak thrown about him, and the press with the gold crowns at his back; and when he got into the palace hall he unlocked the press before the Princesses, and when each of them knew her own gold crown again, the youngest said:

'I think it only right that he who set us free should get the meed that is his due; and he is not Ritter Red, but this man who has brought us our gold crowns. He it is that set us free.'

Then the King's son cast off the sailor's cloak, and stood there far finer and grander than all the rest; and so the old King made them put Ritter Red to death. And now there was real right down joy in the palace; each took his own bride, and there just was a wedding! Why, it was heard of and talked about over twelve kings' realms.

SORIA MORIA CASTLE

Once on a time there was a poor couple who had a son whose name was Halvor. Ever since he was a little boy he would turn his hand to nothing, but just sat there and groped about in the ashes. His father and mother often put him out to learn this trade or that, but Halvor could stay nowhere; for, when he had been there a day or two, he ran away from his master, and never stopped till he was sitting again in the ingle, poking about in the cinders.

Well, one day a skipper came, and asked Halvor if he hadn't a mind to be with him, and go to sea, and see strange lands. Yes, Halvor would like that very much; so he wasn't long in getting himself ready.

How long they sailed I'm sure I can't tell; but the end of it was, they fell into a great storm, and when it was blown over, and it got still again, they couldn't tell where they were; for they had been driven away to a strange coast, which none of them knew anything about.

Well, as there was just no wind at all, they stayed lying wind-bound there, and Halvor asked the skipper's leave to go on shore and look about him; he would sooner go, he said, than lie there and sleep.

'Do you think now you're fit to show yourself before folk', said the skipper, 'why, you've no clothes but those rags you stand in?'

But Halvor stuck to his own, and so at last he got leave, but he was to be sure and come back as soon as ever it began to blow. So off he went and found a lovely land; wherever he came there were fine large flat corn-fields and rich meads, but he couldn't catch a glimpse of a living soul. Well, it began to blow, but Halvor thought he hadn't seen enough yet, and he wanted to walk a little farther just to see if he couldn't meet any folk. So after a while he came to a broad high road, so smooth and even, you might easily roll an egg along it. Halvor followed this, and when evening drew on he saw a great castle ever so far off, from which the sunbeams shone. So as he had now walked the whole day and hadn't taken a bit to eat with him, he was as hungry as a hunter, but still the nearer he came to the castle, the more afraid he got. In the castle kitchen a great fire was blazing, and Halvor went into it, but such a kitchen he had never seen in all his born days. It was so grand and fine; there were vessels of silver and vessels of gold, but still never a living soul. So when Halvor had stood there a while and no one came out, he went and opened a door, and there inside sat a Princess who span upon a spinning-wheel.

'Nay, nay, now!' she called out, 'dare Christian folk come hither? But now you'd best be off about your business, if you don't want the Troll to gobble you up; for here lives a Troll with three heads.'

'All one to me', said the lad, 'I'd be just as glad to hear he had four heads beside; I'd like to see what kind of fellow he is. As for going, I won't go at all. I've done no harm; but meat you must get me, for I'm almost starved to death.'

When Halvor had eaten his fill, the Princess told him to try if he could brandish the sword that hung against the wall; no, he couldn't brandish it, he couldn't even lift it up.

'Oh!' said the Princess, 'now you must go and take a pull of that flask that hangs by its side; that's what the Troll does every time he goes out to use the sword.'

So Halvor took a pull, and in the twinkling of an eye he could brandish the sword like nothing; and now he thought it high time the Troll came; and lo! just then up came the Troll puffing and blowing. Halvor jumped behind the door.

'HUTETU', said the Troll, as he put his head in at the door, 'what a smell of Christian man's blood!'

'Aye', said Halvor, 'you'll soon know that to your cost', and with that he hewed off all his heads.

Now the Princess was so glad that she was free, she both danced and sang, but then all at once she called her sisters to mind, and so she said:

'Would my sisters were free too'

'Where are they?' asked Halvor.

Well, she told him all about it; one was taken away by a Troll to his Castle which lay fifty miles off, and the other by another Troll to his Castle which was fifty miles further still.

'But now', she said, 'you must first help me to get this ugly carcass out of the house.'

Yes, Halvor was so strong he swept everything away, and made it all clean and tidy in no time. So they had a good and happy time of it, and next morning he set off at peep of grey dawn; he could take no rest by the way, but ran and walked the whole day. When he first saw the Castle he got a little afraid; it was far grander than the first, but here too there wasn't a living soul to be seen. So Halvor went into the kitchen, and didn't stop there either, but went strait further on into the house.

'Nay, nay', called out the Princess, 'dare Christian folk come hither? I don't know I'm sure how long it is since I came here, but in all that time I haven't seen a Christian man. 'Twere best you saw how to get away as fast as you came; for here lives a Troll, who has six heads.'

'I shan't go', said Halvor, 'if he has six heads besides.'

'He'll take you up and swallow you down alive', said the Princess.

But it was no good, Halvor wouldn't go; he wasn't at all afraid of the Troll, but meat and drink he must have, for he was half starved after his long journey. Well, he got as much of that as he wished, but then the Princess wanted him to be off again.

'No', said Halvor, 'I won't go, I've done no harm, and I've nothing to be afraid about.'

'He won't stay to ask that', said the Princess, 'for he'll take you without law or leave; but as you won't go, just try if you can brandish that sword yonder, which the Troll wields in war.'

He couldn't brandish it, and then the Princess said he must take a pull at the flask which hung by its side, and when he had done that he could brandish it.

Just then back came the Troll, and he was both stout and big, so that he had to go sideways to get through the door. When the Troll got his first head in he called out 'HUTETU, what a smell of Christian man's blood!'

But that very moment Halvor hewed off his first head, and so on, all the rest as they popped in. The Princess was overjoyed, but just then she came to think of her sisters, and wished out loud they were free. Halvor thought that might easily be done, and wanted to be off at once; but first he had to help the Princess to get the Troll's carcass out of the way, and so he could only set out next morning.

It was a long way to the Castle, and he had to walk fast and run hard to reach it in time; but about night-fall he saw the Castle, which was far finer and grander than either of the others. This time he wasn't the least afraid, but walked straight through the kitchen, and into the Castle. There sat a Princess who was so pretty, there was no end to her loveliness. She too like the others told him there hadn't been Christian folk there ever since she came thither, and bade him go away again, else the Troll would swallow him alive, and do you know, she said, he has nine heads.

'Aye, aye', said Halvor, 'if he had nine other heads, and nine other heads still, I won't go away', and so he stood fast before the stove. The Princess kept on begging him so prettily to go away, lest the Troll should gobble him up, but Halvor said:

'Let him come as soon as he likes.'

So she gave him the Troll's sword, and bade him take a pull at the flask, that he might be able to brandish and wield it.

Just then back came the Troll puffing and blowing and tearing along. He was far stouter and bigger than the other two, and he too had to go on one side to get through the door. So when he got his first head in, he said as the others had said:

'HUTETU what a smell of Christian man's blood!

That very moment Halvor hewed off the first head and then all the rest; but the last was the toughest of them all, and it was the hardest bit of work Halvor had to do, to get it hewn off, although he knew very well he had strength enough to do it.

So all the Princesses came together to that Castle, which was called ***Soria Moria Castle***, and they were glad and happy as they had never been in all their lives before, and they all were fond of Halvor and Halvor of them, and he might choose the one he liked best for his bride; but the youngest was fondest of him of all the three.

But there after a while, Halvor went about, and was so strange and dull and silent. Then the Princesses asked him what he lacked, and if he didn't like to live with them any longer? Yes, he did, for they had enough and to spare, and he was well off in every way, but still somehow or other he did so long to go home, for his father and mother were alive, and them he had such a great wish to see.

Well, they thought that might be done easily enough.

'You shall go thither and come back hither, safe and unscathed, if you will only follow our advice', said the Princesses.

Yes, he'd be sure to mind all they said. So they dressed him up till he was as grand as a king's son, and then they set a ring on his finger, and that was such a ring, he could wish himself thither and hither with it; but they told him to be sure not to take it off, and not to name their names, for there would be an end of all his bravery, and then he'd never see them more.

'If I only stood at home I'd be glad', said Halvor; and it was done as he had wished. Then stood Halvor at his father's cottage door before he knew a word about it. Now it was about dusk at even, and so, when they saw such a grand stately lord walk in, the old couple got so afraid they began to bow and scrape. Then Halvor asked if he couldn't stay there, and have a lodging there that night. No; that he couldn't.

'We can't do it at all', they said, 'for we haven't this thing or that thing which such a lord is used to have; 'twere best your lordship went up to the farm, no long way off, for you can see the chimneys, and there they have lots of everything.'

Halvor wouldn't hear of it--he wanted to stop; but the old couple stuck to their own, that he had better go to the farmer's; there he would get both meat and drink; as for them, they hadn't even a chair to offer him to sit down on.

'No', said Halvor, 'I won't go up there till to-morrow early, but let the just stay here to-night; worst come to the worst, I can sit in the chimney-corner.'

Well, they couldn't say anything against that; so Halvor sat down by the ingle, and began to poke about in the ashes, just as he used to do when he lay at home in old days, and stretched his lazy bones.

Well, they chattered and talked about many things; and they told Halvor about this thing and that; and so he asked them if they had never had any children.

'Yes, yes, they had once a lad whose name was Halvor, but they didn't know whither he had wandered; they couldn't even tell whether he were dead or alive.'

'Couldn't it be me, now?' said Halvor.

'Let me see; I could tell him well enough', said the old wife, and rose up. 'Our Halvor was so lazy and dull, he never did a thing; and besides, he was so ragged, that one tatter took hold of the next tatter on him. No; there never was the making of such a fine fellow in him as you are, master.'

A little while after the old wife went to the hearth to poke up the fire, and when the blaze fell on Halvor's face, just as when he was at home of old poking about in the ashes, she knew him at once.

'Ah! but is it you after all, Halvor?' she cried; and then there was such joy for the old couple, there was no end to it; and he was forced to tell how he had fared, and the old dame was so fond and proud of him, nothing would do but he must go up at once to the farmer's, and show himself to the lassies, who had always looked down on him. And off she went first, and Halvor followed after. So, when she got up there, she told them all how her Halvor had come home again, and now they should only just see how grand he was, for, said she, 'he looks like nothing but a king's son'.

'All very fine', said the lassies, and tossed up their heads. 'We'll be bound he's just the same beggarly ragged boy he always was.'

Just then in walked Halvor, and then the lassies were all so taken aback, they forgot their sarks in the ingle, where they were sitting darning their clothes, and ran out in their smocks. Well, when they were got back again, they were so shame-faced they scarce dared look at Halvor, towards whom they had always been proud and haughty.

'Aye, aye', said Halvor, 'you always thought yourselves so pretty and neat, no one could come near you; but now you should just see the eldest Princess I have set free; against her you look just like milkmaids, and the midmost is prettier still; but the youngest, who is my sweetheart, she's fairer than both sun and moon. Would to Heaven she were only here', said Halvor, 'then you'd see what you would see.'

He had scarce uttered these words before there they stood, but then he felt so sorry, for now what they had said came into his mind. Up at the farm there was a great feast got ready for the Princesses, and much was made of them, but they wouldn't stop there.

'No; we want to go down to your father and mother', they said to Halvor; 'and so we'll go out now and look about us.'

So he went down with them, and they came to a great lake just outside the farm. Close by the water was such a lovely green bank; here the Princesses said they would sit and rest a while; they thought it so sweet to sit down and look over the water.

So they sat down there, and when they had sat a while, the youngest Princess said:

'I may as well comb your hair a little, Halvor.'

Yes, Halvor laid his head on her lap, and so she combed his bonny locks, and it wasn't long before Halvor fell fast asleep. Then she took the ring from his finger, and put another in its stead; and so she said:

'Now hold me all together! and now would we were all in SORIA MORIA CASTLE.'

So when Halvor woke up, he could very well tell that he had lost the Princesses, and began to weep and wail; and he was so downcast, they couldn't comfort him at all. In spite of all his father and mother said, he wouldn't stop there, but took farewell of them, and said he was safe not to see them again; for if he couldn't find the Princesses again, he thought it not worth while to live.

Well, he had still three hundred dollars left, so he put them into his pocket, and set out on his way. So, when he had walked a while, he met a man with a tidy horse, and he wanted to buy it, and began to chaffer with the man.

'Aye', said the man, 'to tell the truth, I never thought of selling him; but if we could strike a bargain, perhaps----'

'What do you want for him', asked Halvor.

'I didn't give much for him, nor is he worth much; he's a brave horse to ride, but he can't draw at all; still he's strong enough to carry your knapsack and you too, turn and turn about', said the man.

At last they agreed on the price, and Halvor laid the knapsack on him, and so he walked a bit, and rode a bit, turn and turn about. At night he came to a green plain where stood a great tree, at the roots of which he sat down. There he let the horse loose, but he didn't lie down to sleep, but opened his knapsack and took a meal. At peep of day off he set again, for he could take no rest. So he rode and walked and walked and rode the whole day through the wide wood, where there were so many green spots and glades that shone so bright and lovely between the trees. He didn't know at all where he was or whither he was going, but he gave himself no more time to rest than when his horse cropped a bit of grass, and he took a snack out of his knapsack when they came to one of those green glades. So he went on walking and riding by turns, and as for the wood there seemed to be no end to it.

But at dusk the next day he saw a light gleaming away through the trees.

'Would there were folk hereaway', thought Halvor, 'that I might warm myself a bit and get a morsel to keep body and soul together.'

When he got up to it, he saw the light came from a wretched little hut, and through the window he saw an old old couple inside. They were as grey-headed as a pair of doves, and the old wife had such a nose! why, it was so long she used it for a poker to stir the fire as she sat in the ingle.

'Good evening', said Halvor.

'Good evening', said the old wife.

'But what errand can you have in coming hither?' she went on, 'for no Christian folk have been here these hundred years and more.'

Well, Halvor told her all about himself, and how he wanted to get to SORIA MORIA CASTLE, and asked if she knew the way thither.

'No', said the old wife, 'that I don't, but see now, here comes the Moon, I'll ask her, she'll know all about it, for doesn't she shine on everything?'

So when the Moon stood clear and bright over the tree-tops, the old wife went out.

'THOU MOON, THOU MOON', she screamed, 'canst thou tell me the way to SORIA MORIA CASTLE?'

'No', said the Moon, 'that I can't, for the last time I shone there a cloud stood before me.'

'Wait a bit still', said the old wife to Halvor, 'by and bye comes the West Wind; he's sure to know it, for he puffs and blows round every corner.'

'Nay, nay', said the old wife when she went out again, 'you don't mean to say you've got a horse too; just turn the poor beastie loose in our "toun", and don't let him stand there and starve to death at the door.'

Then she ran on:

'But won't you swop him away to me?--we've got an old pair of boots here, with which you can take twenty miles at each stride; those you shall have for your horse, and so you'll get all the sooner to SORIA MORIA CASTLE.'

That Halvor was willing to do at once; and the old wife was so glad at having the horse, she was ready to dance and skip for joy.

'For now', she said, 'I shall be able to ride to church. I too, think of that.'

As for Halvor, he had no rest, and wanted to be off at once, but the old wife said there was no hurry.

'Lie down on the bench with you and sleep a bit, for we've no bed to offer you, and I'll watch and wake you when the West Wind comes.'

So after a while up came the West Wind, roaring and howling along till the walls creaked and groaned again.

Out ran the old wife.

'THOU WEST WIND, THOU WEST WIND! Canst thou tell me the way to SORIA MORIA CASTLE? Here's one who wants to get thither.'

'Yes, I know it very well', said the West Wind, and now I'm just off thither to dry clothes for the wedding that's to be; if he's swift of foot he can go along with me.'

Out ran Halvor.

'You'll have to stretch your legs if you mean to keep up', said the West Wind.

So off he set over field and hedge, and hill and fell, and Halvor had hard work to keep up.

'Well', said the West Wind, 'now I've no time to stay with you any longer, for I've got to go away yonder and tear down a strip of spruce wood first before I go to the bleaching-ground to dry the clothes; but if you go alongside the hill you'll come to a lot of lassies standing washing clothes, and then you've not far to go to SORIA MORIA CASTLE.'

In a little while Halvor came upon the lassies who stood washing, and they asked if he had seen anything of the West Wind who was to come and dry the clothes for the wedding. 'Aye, aye, that I have', said Halvor, 'he's only gone to tear down a strip of spruce wood. It'll not be long before he's here', and then he asked them the way to SORIA MORIA CASTLE.

So they put him into the right way, and when he got to the Castle it was full of folk and horses; so full it made one giddy to look at them. But Halvor was so ragged and torn from having followed the West Wind through bush and brier and bog, that he kept on one side, and wouldn't show himself till the last day when the bridal feast was to be.

So when all, as was then right and fitting, were to drink the bride and bridegroom's health and wish them luck, and when the cupbearer was to drink to them all again, both knights and squires, last of all he came in turn to Halvor. He drank their health, but let the ring which the Princess had put upon his finger as he lay by the lake fall into the glass, and bade the cupbearer go and greet the bride and hand her the glass.

Then up rose the Princess from the board at once.

'Who is most worthy to have one of us', she said, 'he that has set us free, or he that here sits by me as bridegroom?'

Well they all said there could be but one voice and will as to that, and when Halvor heard that he wasn't long in throwing off his beggar's rags, and arraying himself as bridegroom.

'Aye, aye, here is the right one after all', said the youngest Princess as soon as she saw him, and so she tossed the other one out of the window, and held her wedding with Halvor.

BRUIN AND REYNARD

The Bear and the Fox had once bought a firkin of butter together; they were to have it at Yule and hid it till then under a thick spruce bush.

After that they went a little way off and lay down on a sunny bank to sleep. So when they had lain a while the Fox got up, shook himself, and bawled out 'yes'.

Then he ran off straight to the firkin and ate a good third part of it. But when he came back, and the Bear asked him where he had been, since he was so fat about the paunch, he said:

'Don't you believe then that I was bidden to barsel, to a christening feast.'

'So, so', said the Bear, 'and pray what was the bairn's name.'

'Just-begun', said the Fox.

So they lay down to sleep again. In a little while up jumped the Fox again, bawled out 'yes', and ran off to the firkin.

This time too he ate a good lump. When he came back, and the Bear asked him again where he had been, he said:

'Oh, wasn't I bidden to barsel again, don't you think.'

'And pray what was the bairn's name this time', asked the Bear.

'Half-eaten', said the Fox.

The Bear thought that a very queer name, but he hadn't wondered long over it before he began to yawn and gape and fell asleep. Well, he hadn't lain long before the Fox jumped up as he had done twice before, bawled out 'yes' and ran off to the firkin, which this time he cleared right out. When he got back he had been bidden to barsel again, and when the Bear wanted to know the bairn's name, he answered:

'Licked-to-the-bottom.'

After that they lay down again, and slept a long time; but then they were to go to the firkin to look at the butter, and when they found it eaten up, the Bear threw the blame on the Fox, and the Fox on the Bear; and each said the one had been at the firkin while the other slept.

'Well, well', said Reynard, 'we'll soon find this out, which of us has eaten the butter. We'll just lay down in the sunshine, and he whose cheeks and chaps are greasiest when we wake, he is the thief.'

Yes, that trial Bruin was ready to stand; and as he knew in his heart he had never so much as tasted the butter, he lay down without a care to sleep in the sun.

Then Reynard stole off to the firkin for a morsel of butter, which stuck there in a crack, and then he crept back to the Bear, and greased his chaps and cheeks with it; and then he, too, lay down to sleep as if nothing had happened.

So when they both woke, the sun had melted the butter, and the Bear's whiskers were all greasy; and so it was Bruin after all, and no one else, who had eaten the butter.

TOM TOTHERHOUSE

Once on a time there was a Goody who had a deaf husband. A good, easy man he was, but that was just why she thought more of the lad next door, whom they called 'Tom Totherhouse'. Now the lad that served the deaf man saw very well that the two had something between them, and one day he said to the Goody:

'Dare you wager ten dollars, mother, that I don't make you lay bare your own shame?'

'Yes I dare', said she; and so they wagered ten dollars. So one day, while the lad and the deaf man stood thrashing in the barn, the lad saw that Tom Totherhouse came to see the Goody. He said nothing, but a good while before dinnertime he turned toward the barn-door, and bawled out 'Halloa!'

'What! are we to go home already?' said the man, who hadn't given any heed to what the lad did.

'Yes, we must, since mother calls', said the lad.

So when they got into the passage, the lad began to hem and cough, that the Goody might get Tom Totherhouse out of the way. But when they came into the room, there stood a whole bowl of custards on the table.

'Nay, nay, mother', cried out the man; 'shall we have custards to- day?'

'Yes, that you shall, dear', said the Goody; but she was as sour as verjuice, and as cross as two sticks.

So when they had eaten and drank all the good cheer up, off they went again to their work, and the Goody said to Tom:

'Deil take that lad's sharp nose, this was all his fault; but now you must be off as fast as you can, and I'll come down to you in the mead with a snack between meals.'

This the lad stood outside in the passage and listened to.

'Do you know, father', he said, 'I think we'd best go down into the hollow and put our fence to rights, which is blown down, before the neighbours' swine get in and root up our meadow.'

'Aye, aye, let's go and do it', said the man; for he did all he was told, good, easy man.

So when the afternoon was half spent, down came the Goody sneaking along into the mead, with something under her apron.

'Nay, nay, mother', said the man, 'it can't be you any longer; are we to have a snack between meals too?'

'Yes, yes, that you shall', she said; but she was sourer and wilder than ever.

So they made merry, and crammed themselves with bannocks and butter, and had a drop of brandy into the bargain.

'I'll go off to Tom Totherhouse with a snack--shan't I, mother?' said the lad. 'He's had nothing between meals, I'll be bound.'

'Ah! do; there's a good fellow', said the Goody, who all at once got as mild as milk.

As he went along the lad broke a bannock to bits, and dropped the crumbs here and there as he walked. But when he got to Tom Totherhouse he said:

'Now, just you take care, for our old cock has found out that you come too often to see our Goody. He won't stand it any longer, and has sworn to drive his axe into you as soon as ever he can set eyes on you.'

As for Tom, he was so frightened he scarce knew which way to turn, and the lad went back again to his master.

'There's something wrong', he said, 'with Tom's plough, and he begs you to be so good as to take your axe, and go and see if you can't set it right.'

Yes, the man set off with his axe, but Tom Totherhouse had scarce caught sight of him before he took to his heels as fast as he could. The man turned and twisted the plough round and round, and looked at it on every side, and when he couldn't see anything wrong with it he went off home again; but on the way he picked up the bits of broken bannock which the lad had let fall. His old dame stood in the meadow and looked at him as he did this for a while, and wondered and wondered what it could be her husband was gathering up.

'Oh, I know', said the lad, 'master's picking up stones, I'll be bound; for he has marked how often this Tom Totherhouse runs over here; and the old fellow won't stand it any longer; and now he has sworn to stone mother to death.'

Off went the Goody as fast as her legs could carry her.

'What in the world is it that mother is running after now?' asked the man, when he reached the spot where she had stood.

'Oh', said the lad, 'maybe the house at home is on fire!'

So there ran the husband behind and the Goody before; and as she ran she screeched out:

'Ah! ah! don't stone me to death; don't stone me to death! and I'll give you my word never to let Tom Totherhouse come near me again.'

'Now the ten dollars are mine', bawled out the lad; and so they were.

LITTLE ANNIE THE GOOSE-GIRL

Once on a time there was a King who had so many geese he was forced to have a lassie to tend them and watch them; her name was Annie, and so they called her 'Annie the Goose-girl'. Now you must know there was a King's son from England who went out to woo; and as he came along Ann sat herself down in his way.

'Sitting all alone there, you little Annie?' said the King's son.

'Yes', said little Annie, 'here I sit and put stitch to stitch and patch on patch. I'm waiting to-day for the King's son from England.'

'Him you mustn't look to have', said the Prince.

'Nay, but if I'm to have him', said little Annie, 'have him I shall, after all.'

And now limners were sent out into all lands and realms to take the likenesses of the fairest Princesses, and the Prince was to chose between them. So he thought so much of one of them, that he set out to seek her, and wanted to wed her, and he was glad and happy when he got her for his sweetheart.

But now I must tell you this Prince had a stone with him which he laid by his bedside, and that stone knew everything, and when the Princess came little Annie told her, if so be she'd had a sweetheart before, or didn't feel herself quite free from anything which she didn't wish the Prince to know, she'd better not step on that stone which lay by the bedside.

'If you do, it will tell him all about you', said little Annie.

So when the Princess heard that she was dreadfully downcast, and she fell upon the thought to ask Annie if she would get into bed that night in her stead and lie down by the Prince's side; and then when he was sound asleep, Annie should get out and the Princess should get in, and so when he woke up in the morning he would find the right bride by his side.

So they did that, and when Annie the goose-girl came and stepped upon the stone the Prince asked:

'Who is this that steps into my bed?'

'A maid pure and bright', said the stone, and so they lay down to sleep; but when the night wore on the Princess came and lay down in Annie's stead.

But next morning, when they were to get up, the Prince asked the stone again:

'Who is this that steps out of my bed?'

'One that has had three bairns', said the stone. When the Prince heard that he wouldn't have her, you may know very well; and so he packed her off home again, and took another sweetheart.

But as he went to see her, little Annie went and sat down in his way again.

'Sitting all alone there, little Annie, the goose-girl', said the Prince.

'Yes, here I sit, and put stitch to stitch, and patch on patch; for I'm waiting to-day for the king's son from England', said Annie.

'Oh! you mustn't look to have him', said the king's son.

'Nay, but if I'm to have him, have him I shall, after all'; that was what Annie thought.

Well, it was the same story over again with the Prince; only this time, when his bride got up in the morning, the stone said she'd had six bairns.

So the Prince wouldn't have her either, but sent her about her business; but still he thought he'd try once more if he couldn't find one who was pure and spotless; and he sought far and wide in many lands, till at last he found one he thought he might trust. But when he went to see her, little Annie the goose-girl had put herself in his way again.

'Sitting all alone there, you little Annie, the goose-girl', said the Prince.

'Yes, here I sit, and put stitch to stitch, and patch on patch; for I'm waiting to-day for the king's son from England', said Annie.

'Him you mustn't look to have', said the Prince.

'Nay, but if I'm to have him, have him I shall, after all', said little Annie.

So when the Princess came, little Annie the goose-girl told her the same as she had told the other two, if she'd had any sweetheart before, or if there was anything else she didn't wish the Prince to know, she mustn't tread on the stone that the

Prince had put at his bedside; for, said she:

'It tells him everything.'

The Princess got very red and downcast when she heard that, for she was just as naughty as the others, and asked Annie if she would go in her stead and lie down with the Prince that night; and when he was sound asleep, she would come and take her place, and then he would have the right bride by his side when it was light next morning.

Yes! they did that. And when little Annie the goose-girl came and stepped upon the stone, the Prince asked:

'Who is this that steps into my bed.'

'A maid pure and bright', said the stone; and so they lay down to rest.

Farther on in the night the Prince put a ring on Annie's finger, and it fitted so tight she couldn't get it off again; for the Prince saw well enough there was something wrong, and so he wished to have a mark by which he might know the right woman again.

Well, when the Prince had gone off to sleep, the Princess came and drove Annie away to the pigsty, and lay down in her place. Next morning, when they were to get up, the Prince asked:

'Who is this that steps out of my bed?'

'One that's had nine bairns', said the stone.

When the Prince heard that he drove her away at once, for he was in an awful rage; and then he asked the stone how it all was with these Princesses who had stepped on it, for he couldn't understand it at all, he said.

So the stone told him how they had cheated him, and sent little Annie the goose-girl to him in their stead.

But as the Prince wished to have no mistake about it, he went down to her where she sat tending her geese, for he wanted to see if she had the ring too, and he thought, 'if she has it, 'twere best to take her at once for my queen'.

So when he got down he saw in a moment that she had tied a bit of rag round one of her fingers, and so he asked her why it was tied up.

'Oh! I've cut myself so badly', said little Annie the goose-girl.

So he must and would see the finger, but Annie wouldn't take the rag off. Then he caught hold of the finger; but Annie, she tried to pull it from him, and so between them the rag came off, and then he knew his ring.

So he took her up to the palace, and gave her much fine clothes and attire, and after that they held their wedding feast; and so little Annie the goose-girl came to have the king of England's son for her husband after all, just because it was written that she should have him.

INTRODUCTION TO APPENDIX

ANANZI STORIES

The Negroes in the West Indies still retain the tales and traditions which their fathers and grandfathers brought with them from Africa. Some thirty years back these 'Ananzi Stories', as they are called, were invariably told at the Negro wakes, which lasted for nine successive nights. The reciters were always men. In those days when the slaves were still half heathen, and when the awful **Obeah** was universally believed in, such of the Negroes as attended church or chapel kept their children away from these funeral gatherings. The wakes are now, it is believed, almost entirely discontinued, and with them have gone the stories. The Negroes are very shy of telling them, and both the clergyman of the Church of England, and the Dissenting Minister set their faces against them, and call them foolishness. The translator, whose early childhood was passed in those islands, remembers to have heard such stories from his nurse, who was an African born; but beyond a stray fragment here and there, the rich store which she possessed has altogether escaped his memory. The following stories have been taken down from the mouth of a West Indian nurse in his sister's house, who, born and bred in it, is rather regarded as a member of the family than as a servant. They are printed just as she told them, and both their genuineness and their affinity with the stories of other races will be self-evident. Thus we have the 'Wishing Tree' of the Hindoos, the **Kalpa Vriksha** of Somadeva, and of the German Fairy Tales in the 'Pumpkin Tree', which throws down as many pumpkins as the poor widow wishes. In one story we have 'Boots' to the life, while the man whom he outwits is own brother to the Norse Trolls. In another we find a 'speaking beast', which reminds us at once of the Egyptian story of Anessou and Satou, as well as of the 'Machandel-boom', and 'the Milk-white Doo'. We find here the woman who washes the dirty head rewarded, and the man who refuses to wash it punished, in the very words used in 'The Bushy Bride'. We find, too, in 'Nancy Fairy', the same story, both in groundwork and incident, as we have in 'the Lassie and her Godmother'; and most surprising of all, in the story of 'Ananzi and Quanqua', we find the very trait about a trick played with the tail of an ox, which is met with in a variation to 'Boots who ate a match with the Troll'. Here is the variation: 'Whilst he was with the Troll, the lad was to go out to watch the swine, so he drove them home to his father's house, but first he cut their tails off, and stuck them into the ground. Then he went home to the Troll, and begged him to come and see how his swine were going down to Hell. But when the Troll saw the swine's tails sticking out of the ground he wanted to pull them back again, so he caught hold of them and gave a great tug, and then down he fell with his heels up in the air, and the tails in his fist.'

They are called 'Ananzi Stories', because so many of them turn on the feats of Ananzi, whose character is a mixture of 'the Master-thief', and of 'Boots'; but the most curious thing about him, is that he illustrates the Beast Epic in a remarkable way. In all the West Indian Islands, 'Ananzi' is the name of spiders in general, and of a very beautiful spider with yellow stripes in particular.[1] The Negroes think that this spider is the 'Ananzi' of their stories, but that his superior cunning enables him to take any shape he pleases. In fact, he is the example which the African tribes from which these stories came, have chosen to take as pointing out the superior-ity of wit over brute strength. In this way they have matched the cleverness and dexterity of the Spider, against the bone and muscle of the Lion, invariably to the disadvantage of the latter.

After this introduction, we let the Tales speak for themselves, only premising that the 'Jack-Spaniard' in the first story is a very pretty fly of the wasp kind, and, like his European brother, very small in the waist; that the 'Cush-cush', is a little red yam which imparts a strong red dye to everything with which it is boiled; and that the 'Doukana' is a forest tree which bears a fruit, though of what kind it is hard to say.

---

1   Compare Crowther's **Yoruba Glossary**, where **Alansasa** is given as the Yoruban for **spider**. The change of **n** into **l** is not uncommon, even supposing the West Indian word to be uncorrupt.

APPENDIX

WHY THE JACK-SPANIARD'S WAIST IS SMALL

Ananzi and Mosquito were talking together one day, and boasting of their fathers' crops. Ananzi said his father had never had such a crop in his life before; and Mosquito said, he was sure his father's was bigger, for one yam they dug was as big as his leg. This tickled Jack-Spaniard so much, that he laughed till he broke his waist in two. That's why the Jack-Spaniard's waist is so small.

ANANZI AND THE LION

Once on a time Ananzi planned a scheme. He went to town and bought ever so many firkins of fat, and ever so many sacks, and ever so many balls of string, and a very big frying pan, then he went to the bay and blew a shell, and called the Head-fish in the sea, 'Green Eel', to him. Then he said to the fish, 'The King sends me to tell you that you must bring all the fish on shore, for he wants to give them new life.'

So 'Green Eel' said he would, and went to call them. Meanwhile Ananzi lighted a fire, and took out some of the fat, and got his frying pan ready, and as fast as the fish came out of the water he caught them and put them into the frying pan, and so he did with all of them until he got to the Head-fish, who was so slippery that he couldn't hold him, and he got back again into the water.

When Ananzi had fried all, the fish, he put them into the sacks, and took the sacks on his back and set off to the mountains. He had not gone very far when he met Lion, and Lion said to him':

'Well, brother Ananzi, where have you been? I have not seen you a long time.'

Ananzi said, 'I have been travelling about.'

'But what have you got there?' said the Lion.

'Oh! I have got my mother's bones--she has been dead these forty- eleven years, and they say I must not keep her here, so I am taking her up into the middle of the mountains to bury her.'

Then they parted. After he had gone a little way, the Lion said, 'I know that Ananzi is a great rogue; I daresay he has got something there that he doesn't want me to see, and I will just follow him'; but he took care not to let Ananzi see him.

Now, when Ananzi got into the wood he set his sacks down, and took one fish out and began to eat; then a fly came, and Ananzi said, 'I cannot eat any more, for there is some one near'; so he tied the sack up, and went on further into the mountains, where he set his sacks down, and took out two fish, which he ate; and no fly came, he said, 'There's no one near'; so he took out more fish. But when he had eaten about half-a-dozen, the Lion came up, and said:

'Well, brother Ananzi, a pretty tale you have told me.'

'Oh! brother Lion, I am so glad you have come; never mind what tale I have told you, but come and sit down--it was only my fun.'

So Lion sat down and began to eat; but before Ananzi had eaten two fish, Lion had emptied one of the sacks. Then said Ananzi to himself:

'Greedy fellow, eating up all my fish.'

'What do you say, sir?'

'I only said you do not eat half fast enough', for he was afraid the Lion would eat him up.

Then they went on eating, but Ananzi wanted to revenge himself, and he said to the Lion, 'Which of us do you think is the strongest?'

The Lion said, 'Why, I am, of course.'

Then Ananzi said, 'We will tie one another to the tree and we shall see which is the stronger.'

Now they agreed that the Lion should tie Ananzi first, and he tied him with some very fine string, and did not tie him tight. Ananzi twisted himself about two or three times, and the string broke.

Then it was Ananzi's turn to tie the Lion, and he took some very strong cord.

The Lion said, 'You must not tie me tight, for I did not tie you tight.' And Ananzi said, 'Oh! no, to be sure I will not.' But he tied him as tight as ever he could, and then told him to try and get loose.

The Lion tried and tried in vain--he could not get loose. Then Ananzi thought, now is my chance; so he got a big stick and beat him, and then went away and left him, for he was afraid to loose him lest he should kill him.

Now there was a woman called Miss Nancy, who was going out one morning to get some 'callalou' (spinach) in the wood, and as she was going, she heard some one say, 'Good morning, Miss Nancy!' She could not tell who spoke to her, but she looked where the voice came from, and saw the Lion tied to the tree.

'Good morning, Mr Lion, what are you doing there?'

He said, 'It is all that fellow Ananzi who has tied me to the tree, but will you loose me?'

But she said, 'No, for I am afraid, if I do, you will kill me.' But he gave, her his word he would not; still she could not trust him; but he begged her again and again, and said:

'Well, if I do try to eat you, I hope all the trees will cry out shame upon me.'

So at last she consented; but she had no sooner loosed him, than he came up to her to eat her, for he had been so many days without food that he was quite ravenous, but the trees immediately cried out 'shame', and so he could not eat her. Then she went away as fast as she could, and the Lion found his way home.

When Lion got home he told his wife and children all that happened to him, and how Miss Nancy had saved his life, so they said they would have a great dinner, and ask Miss Nancy. Now when Ananzi heard of it, he wanted to go to the dinner, so he went to Miss Nancy, and said she must take him with her as her child, but she said 'No'. Then he said, I can turn myself into quite a little child, and then you can take me, and at last she said 'Yes'; and he told her, when she was asked what pap her baby ate, she must be sure to tell them it did not eat pap, but the same food as every one else; and so they went, and had a very good dinner, and set off home again--but somehow one of the lion's sons fancied that all was not right, and he told his father he was sure it was Ananzi, and the Lion set out after him.

Now as they were going along, before the Lion got up to them, Ananzi begged Miss Nancy to put him down, that he might run, which she did, and he got away and ran along the wood, and the Lion ran after him. When he found the Lion was overtaking him, he turned himself into an old man with a bundle of wood on his head--and when the Lion got up to him, he said, 'Good-morning, Mr Lion', and the Lion said 'Good- morning, old gentleman.'

Then the old man said, 'What are you after now? 'and the Lion asked if he had seen Ananzi pass that way, but the old man said 'No, that fellow Ananzi is always meddling with some one; what mischief has he been up to now?'

Then the Lion told him, but the old man said it was no use to follow him any more, for he would never catch him, and so the Lion wished him good day, and turned and went home again.

ANANZI AND QUANQUA

Quanqua was a very clever fellow, and he had a large house full of all sorts of meat. But you must know he had a way of saying *Quan? qua?* (how? what?) when any one asked him anything and so they called him 'Quanqua'. One day when he was out, he met Atoukama, Ananzi's wife, who was going along driving an ox, but the ox would not walk, so Atoukama asked Quanqua to help her; and they got on pretty well, till they came to a river, when the ox would not cross through the water. Then Atoukama called to Quanqua to drive the ox across, but all she could get out of him was, 'QUAN? QUA? *Quan? qua?*' At last she said, 'Oh! you stupid fellow, you're no good; stop here and mind the ox while I go and get help to drive him across.' So off she went to fetch Ananzi. As soon as Atoukama was gone away, Quanqua killed the ox, and hid it all away, where Ananzi should not see it; but first he cut off the tail, then he dug a hole near the river side and stuck the tail partly in, leaving out the tip. When he saw Ananzi coming, he caught hold of the tail, pretending to tug at it as if he were pulling the ox out of the hole. Ananzi seeing this, ran up as fast as he could, and tugging at the tail with all his might, fell over into the river, but he still had hold of the tail, and contrived to get across the water, when he called out to Quanqua, 'You idle fellow, you couldn't take care of the ox, so you shan't have a bit of the tail', and then on he went. When he was gone quite out of sight, Quanqua took the ox home, and made a very good dinner.

Next day he went to Ananzi's house, and said, Ananzi must give him some of the tail, for he had got plenty of yams, but he had no meat. Then they agreed to cook their pot together. Quanqua was to put in white yams, and Ananzi the tail, and red yams. When they came to put the yams in, Quanqua put in a great many white yams, but Ananzi only put in one little red cush-cush yam. Quanqua asked him if that little yam would be enough, he said, 'Oh! plenty', for I don't eat much.

When the pot boiled, they uncovered it, and sat down to eat their shares, but they couldn't find any white yams at all; the little red one had turned them all red. So Ananzi claimed them all, and Quanqua was glad to take what Ananzi would give him.

Now, when they had done eating, they said they would try which could bear heat best, so they heated two irons, and Ananzi was to try first on Quanqua, but he made so many attempts, that the iron got cold before he got near him; then it was Quanqua's turn, and he pulled the iron out of the fire, and poked it right down Ananzi's throat.

THE EAR OF CORN AND THE TWELVE MEN

[This tale is imperfect at the beginning.]

Ananzi said to the King, that if he would give him an ear of corn, he would bring him twelve strong men. The King gave him the ear of corn, and he went away. At last he got to a house, where he asked for a night's lodging which was given him; the next morning he got up very early, and threw the ear of corn out of the door to the fowls, and went back to bed. When he got up in the morning, he looked for his ear of corn, and could not find it anywhere, so he told them he was sure the fowls had eaten it, and he would not be satisfied unless they gave him the best cock they had. So they were obliged to give him the cock, and he went away with it, all day, until night, when he came to another house, and asked again for a night's lodging, which he got; but when they wanted to put the cock into the fowl-house, he said no, the cock must sleep in the pen with the sheep, so they put the cock with the sheep. At midnight he got up, killed the cock, threw it back into the pen, and went back to bed. Next morning when it was time for him to go away, his cock was dead, and he would not take anything for it but one of the best sheep, so they gave it to him, and he went off with it all that day, until night-fall, when he got to a village, where he again asked for a night's lodging, which was given to him, and when they wanted to put his sheep with the other sheep, he said, no, the sheep must sleep with the cattle; so they put the sheep with the cattle. In the middle of the night he got up and killed the sheep, and went back to bed. Next morning he went for his sheep, which was dead, so he told them they must give him the best heifer for his sheep, and if they would not do so, he would go back and tell the King, who would come and make war on them.

So to get rid of him, they were glad to give him the heifer, and let him go; and away he went, and walked nearly all day with the heifer. Towards evening he met a funeral, and asked whose it was? one of the men said, it was his sister, so he asked the men if they would let him have her; they said no, but after a while, he begged so hard, saying he would give them the heifer, that they consented, and he took the dead body and walked away, carrying it until it was dark, when he came to a large town, where he went to a house and begged hard for a night's lodging for himself and his sister, who was so tired he was obliged to carry her, and they would be thankful if they would let them rest there that night. So they let them in, and he asked them to let them sit in the dark, as his sister could not bear the light. So they took them into a room, and left them in the dark; and when they were alone, he seated himself on a bench near the table, and put his sister close by his side, with his arm round her to keep her up. Presently they brought them in some supper; one plate he set before his sister, and put her hand in it, and the other plate for himself, but he ate out of both plates. When it was time to go to bed, he asked if they would allow his sister to sleep in a room where there were twelve strong men sleeping, for she had fits, and if she had one in the night, they would be able to hold her, and would not disturb the rest of the house. So they agreed to this, and he carried her in his arms, because, he said she was so tired, she was asleep, and laid her in a bed; he charged the men not to disturb her, and went himself to sleep in the next room. In the middle of the night he heard the men calling out, for they smelt a horrid smell, and tried to wake the woman-first one man gave her a blow, and then another, until all the men had struck her, but Ananzi took no notice of the noise. In the morning when he went in for his sister and found her dead, he declared they had killed her, and that he must have the twelve men; to this the townsmen said no, not supposing that all the men had killed her, but the men confessed that they had each given her a blow-so he would not be satisfied with less than the twelve, and he carried them off to the King, and delivered them up.

THE KING AND THE ANT'S TREE

There was a King who had a very beautiful daughter, and he said, whoever would cut down an Ant's tree, which he had in his kingdom, without brushing off the ants, should marry his daughter. Now a great many came and tried, but no one could do it, for the ants fell out upon them and stung them, and they were forced to brush them off. There was always someone watching to see if they brushed the ants off.

Then Ananzi went, and the King's son was set to watch him. When they showed him the tree, he said, 'Why, that's nothing, I know I can do that.' So they gave him the axe, and he began to hew, but each blow he gave the tree, he shook himself and brushed himself, saying all the while, 'Did you see me do that? I suppose you think I'm brushing myself, but I am not.' And so he went, on until he had cut down the tree. But the boy thought he was only pretending to brush himself all the time, and the King was obliged to give him his daughter.

THE LITTLE CHILD AND THE PUMPKIN TREE

There was once a poor widow who had six children. One day when she was going out to look for something to eat, for she was very poor, she met an old man sitting by the river side. He said to her 'Good morning.'

And she answered, 'Good morning, father.'

He said to her, 'Will you wash my head?'

She said she would, so she washed it, and when she was going away, he gave her a 'stampee'[A small coin], and told her to go a certain distance, and she would see a large tree full of pumpkins; she was then to dig a hole at the root of the tree and bury the money, and when she had done so, she was to call for as many pumpkins as she liked, and she should have them.

So the woman went, and did as she was told, and she called for six pumpkins, one for each child, and six came down, and she carried them home; and now they always had pumpkins enough to eat, for whenever they wanted any, the woman had only to go to the tree and call, and they had as many as they liked. One morning when she got up, she found a little baby before the door, so she took it up and carried it in, and took care of it. Every day she went out, but in the morning she boiled enough pumpkins to serve the children all day. One day when she came back she found the food was all gone, so she scolded her children, and beat them for eating it all up. They told her they had not taken any--that it was the baby--but she would not believe them, and said, 'How could a little baby get up and help itself'; but the children still persisted it was the baby. So one day when she was going out, she put some pumpkin in a calabash, and set a trap over it. When she was gone the baby got up as usual to eat the food, and got its head fastened in the trap, so that it could not get out, and began knocking its head about and crying out, 'Oh! do loose me, for that woman will kill me when she comes back.' When the woman came in, she found the baby fastened in the trap, so she beat it well, and turned it out of doors, and begged her children's pardon for having wronged them.

Then after she turned the baby out, he changed into a great big man, and went to the river, where he saw the old man sitting by the river side, who asked him to wash his head, as he had asked the poor woman, but the man said:

'No, he would not wash his dirty head', and so he wished the old man 'good bye'.

Then the old man asked him if he would like to have a pumpkin, to which he said 'yes', and the old man told him to go on till he saw a large tree with plenty of pumpkins on it, and then he must ask for one. So he went on till he got to the tree, and the pumpkins looked so nice he could not be satisfied with one, so he called out, 'Ten pumpkins come down', and the ten pumpkins fell and crushed him.

THE BROTHER AND HIS SISTERS

There were once upon a time three sisters and a brother. The sisters were all proud, and one was very beautiful, and she did not like her little brother, 'because', she said, 'he was dirty'. Now, this beautiful sister was to be married, and the brother begged their mother not to let her marry, as he was sure the man would kill her, for he knew his house was full of bones. So the mother told her daughter, but she would not believe it, and said, 'she wouldn't listen to anything that such a dirty little scrub said', and so she was married.

Now, it was agreed that one sister was to remain with their mother and the other was to go with the bride, and so they set out on their way. When they got to the beach, the husband picked up a beautiful tortoise-shell comb, which he gave to his bride. Then they got into his boat and rowed away over the sea, and when they reached their home, they were so surprised to see their little brother, for the comb had turned into their brother. They were not at all glad to see him, and the husband thought to himself he would kill him without telling his wife. When night came the boy told the husband that at home his mother always put him to sleep in the blacksmith's shop, and so the husband said he should sleep in the smithy.

In the middle of the night the man got up, intending to kill them all, and went to his shop to get his irons ready, but the boy jumped up as soon as he went in, and he said, 'Boy, what is the matter with you?' So the boy said, when he was at home his mother always gave him two bags of gold to put his head on. Then the man said, he should have them, and went and fetched him two bags of gold, and told him to go to sleep.

But the boy said, 'Now mind, when you hear me snore I'm not asleep, but when I am not snoring, then I'm asleep.' Then the boy went to sleep and began to snore, and as long as the man heard the snoring, he blew his bellows; but as soon as the snoring stopped, the man took his irons out of the fire, and the boy jumped up.

Then the man said, 'Why, what's the matter? why, can't you sleep?'

The boy said 'No; for at home my mother always gave me four bags of money to lie upon.

Well, the man said he should have them, and brought him four bags of money. Then the boy told him again the same thing about his snoring and the man bade him go to sleep, and he began to snore, and the man to blow his bellows until the snoring stopped. Then the man took out his irons again, and the boy jumped up, and the man dropped the irons, saying, 'Why, what's the matter now that you can't sleep?'

The boy said, 'At home my mother always gave me two bushels of corn.'

So the man said he should have the corn, and went and brought it, and told him to go to sleep. Then the boy snored, and the man blew his bellows till the snoring stopped, when he again took out his irons, and the boy jumped up, and the man said, 'Why, what's it now?'

The boy said, 'At home my mother always goes to the river with a sieve to bring me some water.'

So the man said 'Very well, I will go, but I have a cock here, and before I go, I must speak to it.'

Then the man told the cock if he saw any one moving in the house, he must crow; that the cock promised to do, and the man set off.

Now when the boy thought the man was gone far away, he got up, and gave the cock some of the corn; then he woke up his sisters and showed them all the bones the man had in the house, and they were very frightened. Then he took the two bags of gold on his shoulders, and told his sisters to follow him. He took them to the bay, and put them into the boat with the bags of gold, and left them whilst he went back for the four bags of money. When he was leaving the house he emptied the bags of corn to the cock, who was so busy eating, he forget to crow, until they had got quite away.

When the man returned home and could not find them in the house, he went to the river, where he found his boat gone, and so he had no way of going after them. When they landed at their own place, the boy turned the boat over and stove it in, so that it was of no use any more; and he took his sisters home, and told their mother all that had happened, and his sisters loved him, and they lived very happily together ever afterwards, and do so still if they are not dead.

THE GIRL AND THE FISH

There was once a girl who used to go to the river to fetch water, but when she went she was never in a hurry to come back, but staid so long, that they made up their minds to watch her. So one day they followed her to the river, and found when she got there, she said something (the reciter forgets the words), and a fish came up and talked to her; and she did not like to leave it, for it was her sweetheart. So next day they went to the river to see if the fish would come up, for they remembered what the girl said and used the same words. Then up came the fish immediately, and they caught it, and took it home, and cooked it for dinner--and a part they set by, and gave to the girl when she came in. Whilst she was eating, a voice said, 'Do you know what you are eating? I am he you have so often talked with. If you look in the pig's tub, you will see my heart.' Then the voice told her to take the heart, and wrap it up in a handkerchief, and carry it to the river. When she got to the river she would see three stones in the water, she was to stand on the middle stone, and dip the handkerchief three times into the water. All this she did, and then she sank suddenly, and was carried down to a beautiful place, where she found her lover changed from a fish into his proper form, and there she lived happily with him for ever. And this is the reason why there are mermaids in the water.

THE LION, THE GOAT, AND THE BABOON

A Lion had a Goat for his wife. One day Goat went out to market, and while she was gone, Lion went out in the wood, where he met with Baboon, who made friends with Lion, for fear he would eat him, and asked him to go home with him; but the Lion thought it would be a good chance, so he asked the Baboon to go home with him and see his little ones. When they got home, the Baboon said to the Lion.

'Why, you have got plenty of little goats here.'

The Lion said, 'Yes, they are my children.'

So the Baboon said, 'If they are, they are little goats, and they are very good meat.'

So the Lion said, 'Don't make a noise; their mother will come presently, and we will see.'

So these little goats took no notice, but went out to meet their mother, and told her what had passed.

Their mother said to them, 'Go back, take no notice, and I shall come home presently, and shall do for him.'

So she went and bought some molasses, and took it home with her. The Lion said, 'Are you come; what news?'

'Oh!' she said, 'good news, taste here.' He tasted, and said, 'It's very good, it's honey.'

And she said, 'It's baboon's blood; they have been killing one to- day, the blood is running in the street, and every one is carrying it away.'

The Lion said, 'Hush, there's one in the house, and we shall have him.'

At this the Baboon rushed off, and when they looked for him, he was gone, and never came near them again, which saved the little goats' lives.

ANANZI AND BABOON

Ananzi and Baboon were disputing one day which was fattest. Ananzi said he was sure he was fat, but Baboon declared he was fatter. Then Ananzi proposed that they should prove it; so they made a fire, and agreed that they should hang up before it, and see which would drop most fat.

Then Baboon hung up Ananzi first, but no fat dropped.

Then Ananzi hung up Baboon, and very soon the fat began to drop, which smelt so good that Ananzi cut a slice out of Baboon, and said,

'Oh! brother Baboon, you're fat for true.'

But Baboon didn't speak.

So Ananzi said, 'Well, speak or not speak, I'll eat you every bit to- day', which he really did. But when he had eaten up all Baboon, the bits joined themselves together in his stomach, and began to pull him about so much that he had no rest, and was obliged to go to a doctor.

The doctor told him not to eat anything for some days, then he was to get a ripe banana, and hold it to his mouth; when the Baboon, who would be hungry, smelt the banana, he would be sure to run up to eat it, and so he would run out of his mouth.

So Ananzi starved himself, and got the banana, and did as the doctor told him; but when he put the banana to his mouth, he was so hungry he couldn't help eating it. So he didn't get rid of the Baboon, which went on pulling him about till he was obliged to go back to the doctor, who told him he would soon cure him; and he took the banana, and held it to Ananzi's mouth, and very soon the Baboon jumped up to catch it, and ran out of his mouth; and Ananzi was very glad to get rid of him. And Baboons to this very day like bananas.

THE MAN AND THE DOUKANA TREE

There was once a man and his wife, who were very poor, and they had a great many children. The man was very lazy, and would do nothing to help his family. The poor mother did all she could. In the wood close by grew a Doukana Tree, which was full of fruit. Every day the man went and ate some of the fruit, but never took any home, so he ate and he ate, until there were only two Doukanas left on the Tree. One he ate, and left the other. Next day, when he went for that one, he was obliged to climb up the tree to reach it; but when he got up, the Doukana fell down; when he got down the Doukana jumped up; and so it went on until he was quite tired.

Then he asked all the animals that passed by to help him, but they all made some excuse. They all had something to do. The horse had his work to do, or he would have no grass to eat. The donkey brayed. Last came a dog, and the man begged him hard to help him; so the dog said he would. Then the man climbed up the tree, and the Doukana jumped to the ground again, when the dog picked it up and ran off with it The man was very vexed, and ran after the dog, but it ran all the faster, so that the man could not overtake him. The dog, seeing the man after him, ran to the sea shore, and scratching a hole in the ground, buried himself all but his nose, which he left sticking out.

Soon after the man came up, and seeing the nose, cried out that he had 'never seen ground have nose'; and catching hold of it he tugged till he pulled out the dog, when he squeezed him with all his might to make him give up the Doukana. And that's why dogs are so small in their bodies to this very day.

NANCY FAIRY

There was once an old woman called 'Nancy Fairy'. She was a witch, and used to steal all the little babies as soon as they were born, and eat them. One day she stole a little baby, who was so beautiful that she had not the heart to eat her; but she took her home and brought her up. She called her 'daughter', named her 'Nancy Fairy', after herself, and the girl called the old woman 'Granny'.

So the girl grew up, and the more she grew the more beautiful she got.

The old woman never let her daughter know of her doings; but one day when she had brought a baby home, and had locked herself in a room, her daughter peeped through a chink to see what she was about, and the old woman saw her shadow, and thought her daughter had seen what she was doing, and the daughter thought her granny had seen her, and was very much afraid.

So the old woman asked her, 'Nancy Fairy, did you see what I was doing?'

'No, Granny.'

She asked the girl several times, 'Nancy Fairy, did you see what I was doing?' and the girl always said, 'No, Granny.'

So the old woman took her up to a hut in a wood, and left her there as a punishment; and she took her food every day.

One day it happened that the king's servant, going that way, saw the beautiful girl come out of the hut. Next day he went again and saw the same beautiful girl again. So he went home and told the prince that he could show him in the wood a girl more beautiful than he had ever seen. The prince went and saw the girl, and then sent a band of soldiers to fetch her home, and took her for his bride.

A year after she had a baby. Soldiers were set to keep guard at the gate, and the room was full of nurses; but in the middle of the night the old woman came in a whirlwind and put them all to sleep. She stole the child, and on going away gave the mother a slap on the mouth which made her dumb.

Next morning there was a great stir, and they said the mother had eaten the child. There was a trial, but the mother was let off that time.

Next year she had another baby, and the same thing happened again. The old woman came in the middle of the night in a whirlwind, and put them all to sleep. She stole the child, and struck the mother on the mouth, which made it bleed.

In the morning there was a stir; and the servant maid, who was jealous, said the mother had eaten the child. All believed it, as her mouth was covered with blood; and, besides, what would be expected of a girl brought out of the wood? So she was tried again, and condemned to be hanged.

Invitations were sent out to all the grand folk to come and see her hanged; so many fine carriages came driving up. At last, just before the time, there came a very grand carriage, all of gold, which glistened in the sun. In it were the old woman and two children, dressed in fine clothes, with the king's star on them. When the queen saw this grand carriage she got her speech and sung,

'Do spare me till I see that grand carriage.'

The old woman came into the courtyard, and asked the people if they saw any likeness to any one in the children. They said, 'they were like the prince', and asked her how she came by them, and told her she had stolen them. She said she had not stolen them; she had taken them, for they were her own; the prince had taken away her daughter without her leave, and so she had taken his children; but she was willing to give them back, if they would allow that she was right.

So they consented, and the old woman made the prince and his queen a present of the grand carriage, and so they lived happily. The old woman was allowed to come and see the children whenever she liked. But the servant girl, who said the queen had eaten her babies, was hanged.

'THE DANCING GANG'

A water carrier once went to the river to fetch water. She dipped in her calabash, and brought out a cray-fish. The cray-fish began beating his claws on the calabash, and played such a beautiful tune, that the girl began dancing, and could not stop.

The driver of the gang wondered why she did not come, and sent another to see after her. When she came, she too began to dance. So the driver sent another, who also began to dance when she heard the music and the cray-fish singing:

Vaitsi, Vaitsi, O sulli Van.   Stay for us, stay for us, how long will you stay for us?

Then the driver sent another and another, till he had sent the whole gang.

At last he went himself, and when he found the whole gang dancing, he too began to dance; and they all danced till night, when the cray- fish went back into the water; and if they haven't done dancing, they are dancing still.

NOTES

[1]

How strange is the terror of Natural Science, which seems to possess, with a religious possession, so many good and pious people! How rigidly do they bind themselves hand and foot with the mere letter of the law, forgetting Him who came to teach us, that 'the letter killeth, but the Spirit giveth life!' What are we to say of those who, when the old crust which clogs and hampers human knowledge is cracking and breaking all around them, when the shell is too narrow an abode for the life within it, which is preparing to cast it off, still cling to the crust and shell, looking, like the disciples by the sepulchre, at the linen clothes lying, and know not that He has risen in glory? These are they who obstinately refuse to believe in the 'Testimony of the Rocks', who deny Geology the thousands, nay millions, of years which she requires to make her deposits in Nature's great saving-bank. These are they for whom the Nile, as he brings down year by year his tribute to the sea from Central Africa, lays down in vain layer after layer of alluvial deposit, which can be measured to an inch for tens of thousands of years. These are they to whom the comparatively younger growth of trees, the dragon tree of Orotava, and the cedars of California, plead in vain when they show, year after year, ring on ring of wood for thousands of years. 'No; the world is only five or six thousands of years old, or thereabouts. The Old Testament'--the dates in which have been confessedly tampered with, and in some cases forged and fabricated by Hebrew scribes-- 'says so. We believe in it--we will believe in nothing else, not even in our senses. We will believe literally in the first chapter of Genesis, in working days and nights of twenty-four hours, even before the sun and moon were made, on the fourth day, "to divide the day from the night", and to be "for signs and for seasons, and for days and years". We will not hear of ages or periods, but "days", because the "letter" says so'. This is what our Western Brahmins say; but if they remembered that He who set sun and moon also planted the eye and ear, that he gave sense, and speech, and mind; if they considered that faith is a lively thing, elastic and expansive; that it embraces a thousand or a million years as easily as a moment of time; that bonds cannot fetter it, nor distance darken and dismay it; that it is given to man to grow with his growth and strengthen with his strength; that it rises at doubts and difficulties, and surmounts them; they would cease to condemn all the world to wear their own strait-waistcoat, cut and sewn by rabbis and doctors some thousand years ago; a garment which the human intellect has altogether outgrown, which it is ridiculous to wear, which careless and impious men laugh at when it is seen in the streets; and might begin to see that spirit is spirit, and flesh is flesh; that while one lives for ever, the other is corruptible and passes away; that there are developments in faith as in every thing else; that as man's intellect and human knowledge have grown and expanded, so his faith must grow and expand too; that it really matters nothing at all, as an act of faith, whether the world is six thousand or six million years old; that it must have had a beginning; that there must be one great first cause, God. Surely there is no better way to bring His goodness into question, to throw doubt on His revelation, and to make it the laughing stock of the irreligious, than thus to clip the wings of faith, to throw her into a dungeon, to keep her from the light of day, to make her read through. Hebrew spectacles, and to force her to be a laggard and dullard, instead of a bright and volatile spirit, forward and foremost in the race of life.

[2]

But if the first heir of my invention prove deformed, I shall be sorry it had so noble a godfather, and never after *ear* so barren a land, for fear it yield me still so bad a harvest'-- SHAKESPEARE, *Dedication to Venus and Adonis*.

[3]

As a specimen of their thoughtful turn of mind, even in the *Vedas*, at a time before the monstrous avatars of the Hindoo Pantheon were imagined, and when their system of philosophy, properly so called, had no existence, the following metrical translation of the 129th hymn of the 10th book of the *Rig-Veda* may be quoted, which Professor Mueller assures us is of a very early date:

> Nor aught nor naught existed; yon bright sky
> Was not, nor Heaven's broad woof outstretched above.
> What covered all? what sheltered? what concealed?
> Was it the water's fathomless abyss?
> There was not death--yet was there nought immortal.

There was no confine betwixt day and night;
The only One breathed breathless by itself,
Other than It there nothing since has been.
Darkness there was, and all at first was veiled
In gloom profound--an ocean without light--
The germ that still lay covered in the husk
Burst forth, one nature, from the fervent heat.
Then first came love upon it, the new spring
Of mind--yea, poets in their hearts discerned,
Pondering, this bond between created things
And uncreated. Comes this spark from earth,
Piercing and all pervading, or from Heaven?
Then seeds were sown, and mighty powers arose--
Nature below, and power and will above--
Who knows the secret? who proclaimed it here,
Whence, whence this manifold creation sprang?
The Gods themselves came later into being--
Who knows from whence this great creation sprang?
He from whom all this great creation came,
Whether His will created or was mute,
The Most High Seer that is in highest heaven,
He knows it--or perchance even he knows not.

If we reflect that this hymn was composed centuries before the time of Hesiod, we shall be better able to appreciate the speculative character of the Indian mind in its earliest stage.

[4]

'A Brahmin, who had vowed a sacrifice, went to the market to buy a goat. Three thieves saw him, and wanted to get hold of the goat. They stationed themselves at intervals on the high road. When the Brahmin, who carried the goat on his back, approached the first thief, the thief said, "Brahmin, why do you carry a dog on your back?" The Brahmin replied: "It is not a dog, it is a goat." A little while after, he was accosted by the second thief, who said, "Brahmin, why do you carry a dog on your back?" The Brahmin felt perplexed, put the goat down, examined it, and walked on.

Soon after he was stopped by the third thief, who said, "Brahmin, why do you carry a dog on your back?" Then the Brahmin was frightened, threw down the goat, and walked home to perform his ablutions for having touched an unclean animal. The thieves took the goat and ate it.' See the notice of the Norse Tales in *The Saturday Review*, January 15. In Max Mueller's translation of the *Hitopadesa*, the story has a different ending. See also *Le Piacevoli Notti*, di M. Giovan Francesco Straparola da Caravaggio (Venice, 1567), Notte Prima, Favola III: 'Pre Scarpacifico da tre malandrini una sol volta gabbato, tre fiate gabba loro, finalmente vittorioso con la sua Nina lietamente rimane'. In which tale the beginning is a parallel to the first part of 'The Master Thief', while the end answers exactly to the Norse tale added in this edition, and called Big Peter and Little Peter'.

[5]

The following are translations from Saxo, the *Wilkina Saga*, and the *Malleus Maleficarum*. The question is completely set at rest by Grimm, *D. M.* p. 353 fol. and p. 1214.

'Nor is the following story to be wrapped in silence. A certain Palnatoki, for some time among King Harold's bodyguard, had made his bravery odious to very many of his fellow-soldiers by the zeal with which he surpassed them in the discharge of his duty. This man once, when talking tipsily over his cups, had boasted that he was so skilled an archer, that he could hit the smallest apple placed a long way off on a wand at the first shot; which talk, caught up at first by the ears of backbiters, soon came to the hearing of the king. Now, mark how the wickedness of the king turned the confidence of the sire to the peril of the son, by commanding that this dearest pledge of his life should be placed instead of the wand, with a threat that, unless the author of this promise could strike off the apple at the first flight of the arrow, he should pay the penalty of his empty boasting by the loss of his head. The king's command forced the soldier to perform more than he had promised, and what he *had* said, reported by the tongues of slanderers, bound him to accomplish what he had *not* said'...'Nor did his sterling courage, though caught in the snare of slander, suffer him to lay aside his firmness of heart; nay, he accepted the trial the more readily because it was hard. So Palnatoki warned the boy urgently when he took his stand to await the coming of the hurtling arrow with calm ears and unbent head, lest by a slight turn of his body he should defeat the practised skill of the bowman; and, taking further counsel to prevent his fear, he turned away his face lest he should be scared at the sight of the weapon. Then taking three arrows from the quiver, he struck the mark given him with the first he fitted to the string. But, if chance had brought the head of the boy before the shaft, no doubt the penalty of the son would have recoiled to the peril of the father, and the swerving of the shaft that struck the boy would have linked them both in common ruin. I am in doubt, then, whether to admire most the courage of the father or the temper of the son, of whom the one by skill in his art avoided being the slayer of his child, while the other by patience of mind and quietness of body saved himself alive, and spared the natural affection of his father. Nay, the youthful frame strengthened the aged heart, and showed as much courage in awaiting the arrow as the father, skill in launching it. But Palnatoki, when asked by the king why he had taken more arrows from the quiver, when it had been settled that he should only try the fortune of the bow *once*, made answer "That I might avenge on thee the swerving of the first by the points of the rest, lest perchance my innocence might have been punished, while your violence escaped scot-free'".-- ***Saxo Gram.***, Book X, (p. 166, ed. Frankf.)

'About that time the young Egill, Wayland's brother, came to the court of King Nidung, because Wayland (Smith) had sent him word. Egill was the fairest of men and one thing he had before all other men--he shot better with the bow than any other man. The king took to him well, and Egill was there a long time. Now, the king wished to try whether Egill shot so well as was said or not, so he let Egill's son, a boy of three years old, be taken, and made them put an apple on his head, and bade Egill shoot so that the shaft struck neither above the head nor to the left nor to the right; the apple only was he to split. But it was not forbidden him to shoot the boy, for the king thought it certain that he would do that on no account if he could at all help it. And he was to shoot one arrow only, no more. So Egill takes three, and strokes their feathers smooth, and fits one to his string, and shoots and hits the apple in the middle, so that the arrow took along with it half the apple, and then fell to the ground. This master-shot has long been talked about, and the king made much of him, and he was the most famous of men. Now, King Nidung asked Egill why he took out *three* arrows, when it was settled that one only was to be shot with. Then Egill answered "Lord", said he, "I will not lie to you; had I stricken the lad with that one arrow, then I had meant these two for you." But the king took that well from him, and all thought it was boldly spoken'.-- *Wilkina Saga*, ch. 27 (ed. Pering).

'It is related of him (Puncher) that a certain lord, who wished to obtain a sure trial of his skill, set up his little son as a butt, and for a mark a shilling on the boy's cap, commanding him to carry off the shilling without the cap with his arrow. But when the wizard said he could do it, though he would rather abstain, lest the Devil should decoy him to destruction; still, being led on by the words of the chief, he thrust one arrow through his collar, and, fitting the other to his crossbow, struck off the coin from the boy's cap without doing him any harm; seeing which, when the lord asked the wizard why he had placed the arrow in his collar? he answered "If by the Devil's deceit I had slain the boy, when I needs must die, I would have transfixed you suddenly with the other arrow, that even so I might have avenged my death."'-- *Malleus Malef.*, p. ii, ch. 16.

[6]

See *Pantcha-Tantra*, v. ii of Wilson's *Analysis*, quoted by Loiseleur Deslong-champs, *Essai sur les Fables Indiennes* (Paris, Techener, 1838, p. 54), where the animal that protects the child is a mangouste (Viverra Mungo). See also *Hitopade-sa*, (Max Mueller's Translation, Leipzig, Brockhaus, p. 178) where the guardian is an otter. In both the foe is a snake. [7]

The account in the *Nibelungen* respecting the *Tarnhut* is confused, and the text probably corrupt; but so much is plain, that Siegfried got it from Elberich in the struggle which ensued with Schilbung and Niblung, after he had shared the Hoard.

[8]

Thus we find it in the originals or the parallels of Grendel in *Beowulf*, of Rumpelstiltskin, of the recovery of the Bride by the ring dropped into the cup, as related in 'Soria Moria Castle,' and other tales; of the 'wishing ram', which in the Indian story becomes a 'wishing cow', and thus reminds us of the bull in one of these Norse Tales, out of whose ear came a 'wishing cloth'; of the lucky child, who finds a purse of gold under his pillow every morning; and of the red lappet sown on the sleeping lover, as on Siegfried in the *Nibelungen*. The devices of Upakosa, the faithful wife, remind us at once of 'the Master-maid', and the whole of the stories of Saktideva and the Golden City, and of Viduschaka, King Adityasena's daughter, are the same in groundwork and in many of their incidents as 'East o' the Sun, and West o' the Moon', 'the Three Princesses of Whiteland', and 'Soria Moria Castle'.

[9]

Koelle, ***Kanuri Proverbs and Fables*** (London Church Missionary House, 1854), a book of great philological interest, and one which reflects great credit on the religious society by which it was published.

[10]

Notte Duodecima. Favola terza. 'Pederigo da Pozzuolo che intendeva il linguaggio de gli animali, astretto dalla moglie dirle un segreto, quella stranamente batte.'

[11]

The story of the Two Brothers Anesou and Satou, from the ***D'Orbiney Papyrus***, by De Ronge, Paris, 1852.

[12]

See the Ananzi Stories in the Appendix, which have been taken down from the mouth of a West Indian nurse.

[13]

See ***Anecd. and Trad.***, Camd. Soc. 1839, pp. 92 fol. See also the passages from Anglo-Saxon laws against 'well-waking', which Grimm has collected: ***D. M.***, p. 550.

[14]

One of Odin's names, when on these adventures, was Gangradr, or Gangleri. Both mean 'the ***Ganger***, or way-farer'. We have the latter epithet in the ' ***Gangrel*** carle', and ' ***Gangrel loon***', of the early Scotch ballads.

[15]

So also Orion's Belt was called by the Norsemen, Frigga's spindle or ***rock, Friggjar rock***. In modern Swedish, ***Friggerock***, where the old goddess holds her own; but in Danish, ***Mariaerock***, Our Lady's rock or spindle. Thus, too, ***Karlavagn***, the 'car of men', or heroes, who rode with Odin, which we call 'Charles' Wain', thus keeping something, at least, of the old name, though none of its meaning, became in Scotland 'Peter's-pleugh', from the Christian saint, just as Orion's sword became 'Peter's-staff'. But what do 'Lady Landers' and 'Lady Ellison' mean, as applied to the

'Lady-Bird' in Scotland?

[16]

Here are a few of these passages which might be much extended: Burchard of Worms, p. 194, a. 'credidisti ut aliqua femina sit quae hoc facere possit quod quaedam a diabolo deceptae se affirmant necessario et ex praecepto facere debere; id est cum daemonum turba in similitudinem mulierum transformata, quam vulgaris stultitia **Holdam** vocat, certis noctibus equitare debere super quasdam bestias, et in eorum se consortio annumeratam esse.'

'Illud etiam non omittendum, quod quasdam sceleratae mulieres retro post Sathanam conversae, daemonum illusionibus et phantasmatibus seductae credunt se et profitentur nocturnis horis cum **Diana** paganorum dea, vel cum **Herodiade** et innumera multitudine mulierum equitare super quasdam bestias, et multa terrarum spatia intempestae noctis silentio pertransire, ejusque jussionibus velut **Dominae** obedire et certis noctibus ad ejus servitium evocari.' --Burchard of Worms, 10, I.

'Quale est, quod noctilucam quandam, vel **Herodiadem**, vel praesidem noctis Dominam concilia et conventus de nocte asserunt convocare, varia celebrari convivia, etc.'--Joh. Sarisberiensis Polycrat. 2, 17 (died 1182).

'**Herodiam** illam baptistae Christi interfectricem, quasi reginam, immo deam proponant, asserentes tertiam totius mundi partem illi traditam.'--Rather. Cambrens. (died 974).

'Sic et daemon qui praetextu mulieris cum aliis de nocte, domos et cellaria dicitur frequentare, et vocant eam **Satiam** a satietate, et **Dominam Abundiam** pro abundantia, quam eam praestare dicunt domibus quas frequentaverit; hujusmodi etiam daemones quas **dominas vocant**, vetulae penes quas error iste remansit et a quibus solis creditur et somniatur.'--Guilielmus Alvernus, 1, 1036 (died 1248).

So also the Roman de la Rose (Meon line 18, 622.)

Qui les cinc sens ainsinc decoit

Par les fantosmes, qu'il recoit,

Don maintes gens par lor folie

Cuident estre par nuit estries,

Errans aveques **Dame Habonde**:

Et dient, que par tout le monde

Li tiers enfant de nacion   *S*
unt de ceste condicion.
And again, line 18,686:
Dautre part, *que li tiers du monde*
Aille ainsinc *eavec Dame Habonde*.
[17]
See the derivation of *pagan* from paganus, one who lived in the country, as opposed to urbanus, a townsman.
[18]
Keisersberg Omeiss, 46 b., quoted by Grimm, *D.M.* pp. 991, says:
   Wen man em man verbrent,   so brent man wol zehen frauen.
[19]
See the passage from Vincent, *Bellov. Spec. Mor.*, iii, 2, 27, quoted in Grimm, *D. M.* pp. 1,012-3.
[20]
The following passage from *The Fortalice of Faith* of Alphonso Spina, written about the year 1458, will suffice to show how disgustingly the Devil, in the form of a goat, had supplanted the 'Good Lady': Quia nimium abundant tales perversae mulieres ine Delphinatu et Guasconia, ubi se asserunt concurrere de nocte in quadam planitie deserta ubi est *caper quidam in rupe*, qui vulgariter dicitur *el boch de Biterne* et clued ibi *conveniunt cum candelis accensis et adorant illum caprum osculpntes eum in ano suo*. Ideo captae plures earum, ab inquisitoribus fidei et convictae comburuntur.'

About the same time, too, began to spread the notion of formal written agreements between the Fiend and men who were to be his after a certain time, during which he was to help them to all earthly goods. This, too, came with Christianity from the East. The first instance was Theophilus, vicedominus of the Bishop of Adana, whose fall and conversion form the original of all the Faust Legends. See Grimm, D. M. 969, and 'Theophilus in Icelandic, Low German, and other tongues, by G. W. Dasent, Stockholm, 1845.' There a complete account of the literature of the legend may be found. In almost all these early cases the Fiend is outwitted by the help of the Virgin or some other saint, and in this way the reader is reminded of the Norse Devil, the successor of the Giants, who always makes bad bargains. When the story was applied to Faust in the sixteenth century, the terrible Middle Age Devil was paramount, and knew how to exact his due.

[21]

How strangely full of common sense sounds the following article from the Capitularies of Charlemagne, *De part. Sax.*, 5:

Si quis a diabolo deceptus crediderit secundum morem. Paganorum, virum aliquem aut faeminam strigam esse et homines comedere, et propter hoc ipsum incenderit, vel carnem eius ad comedendum dederit, capitis sententia punietur.' And this of Rotharius, Lex. Roth., 379: 'Nullus praesumat aldiam alienam aut ancillam quasi strigam occidere, quod Christianis mentibus nullatenus est credendum nec possible est, ut hominem mulier vivum intrinsecus possit comedere.'

Here the law warns the common people from believing in witches, and from taking its functions into their own hands, and reasons with them against the absurdity of such delusions. So, too, that reasonable parish priest who thrashed the witch, though earlier in time, was far in advance of Gregory and his inquisitors, and even of our wise King James.

[22]

The following is the title of this strange tract, *Newes from Scotland, declaring the damnable life of Doctor Fian, a notable Sorcerer, who was burned at Edenbrough, in Januarie last 1591, which Doctor was register to the devil, that sundrie times preached at North Baricke Kirke to a number of notorious Witches. With the true examinations of the said Doctor and witches, as they uttered them in the presence of the Scottish king. Discovering how they pretended to bewitch and drowne his Majestic in the sea, comming from Denmarke, with such other wonderfull matters as the like, hath not bin heard at anie time*. Published according to the Scottish copie. Printed for William Wright. It was reprinted in 1816 for the Roxburghe Club by Mr H. Freeling, and is very scarce even in the reprint, which, all things considered, is perhaps just as well.

[23]

The following specimens of the tortures and confessions may suffice; but most of the crimes and confessions are unutterable. One Geillis Duncane was tortured by her master, David Seaton, dwelling within the town of Tranent, who, 'with the help of others, did torment her with the torture of the Pilliwinkes (thumbscrews), upon her fingers, and binding and wrinching her head with a cord or roape, which is a most cruel torment also.' So also Agnes Sampson, 'the eldest witch of them all, dwelling in Haddington, being brought to Haleriud House before the kinge's majestie and sundry other of the nobilitie of Scotland, had her head thrawne with a rope according to the custom of that countrie, beeing a payne most greevous.' After the Devil's mark is found on her she confesses that she went to sea with two hundred others in sieves to the kirk of North Berwick in East Lothian, and after they had landed they 'took handes on the lande and daunted, this reill or short daunce, saying all with one voice:

Commer goe ye before, Commer goe ye,

Gif ye will not goe before, Commer let me.

'At which time she confessed that this Geillis Duncane did goe before them playing this reill or daunce upon a small trumpe called a Jew's trump, until they entered into the kirk of North Barrick.' 'As touching the aforesaid Doctor Fian', he 'was taken and imprisoned, and used with the accustomed paine provided for these offences, inflicted upon the rest, as is aforesaid. First by thrawing of his head with a rope, whereat he would confesse nothing! Secondly, he was persuaded by faire means to confesse his follies, but that would prevaile as little. Lastly, he was put to the most severe and cruell paine in the world, called the Bootes, who, after he had received three strokes, being inquired if he would confesse his damnable actes and wicked life, his toong would not serve him to spaake.' This inability, produced no doubt by pain, the other witches explain by saying that the Devil's mark had not been found, which, being found, 'the charm' was 'stinted', and the Doctor, in dread probably of a fourth stroke, confessed unutterably shameful things. Having escaped from prison, of course by the aid of the Devil, he was pursued, and brought back and re-examined before the king. 'But this Doctor, notwithstanding that his own confession appeareth remaining in recorde, under his owne handewriting, and the same thereunto fixed in the presence of the King's majestie and sundrie of his councell, yet did he utterly deny the same, whereupon the King's majestie, perceiving his stubborne wilfulness...he was commanded to have a most strange torment, which was done in this manner following: His nailes upon all his fingers were riven and pulled off with an instrument called in Scottish a Turkas, which in England wee call a payre of pincars, and under everie nayle there was thrust in two needels over even up to the heads. At all which torments, notwithstanding the Doctor never shronke anie whit; neither would he then confesse it the sooner for all the tortures inflicted upon him.

'Then was he with all convenient speed, by commandement convaied againe to the torment of the Bootes, wherein hee continued a long time, and did abide so many blowes in them, that his legges were crusht and beaten together as small as might bee, and the bones and flesh so brused that the blond and marrow spouted forth in great abundance, wherby they were made unserviceable for ever. And notwithstanding all these grievous panes and cruel torments, he would not confesse aniething, so deeply had the Devil entered into his heart, that hee utterly denied all that which he had before avouched, and would saie nothing thereunto but this, that what he had done and sayde before, was onely done and saide for fear of paynes which he had endured.' Thereupon as 'a due execution of justice' 'and 'for example sake', he was tried, sentenced, put into a cart, strangled and immediately put into a great fire, being readie provided for that purpose, and there burned in the Castle Hill of Edenbrough on a saterdaie, in the ende of Januaire last past, 1591.' The tract ends significantly: 'The rest of the witches which are not yet executed remayne in prison till further triall and knowledge of his majestie's pleasure.'

[24]

Ecl., viii, 97:

His ego saepe lupum fieri
et se condere silvis Maerin--vidi.

[25]

See Grimm's **D.M.**, 1,047 fol.; and for this translation from Petronius, a very interesting letter prefixed to Madden's Ed. of the old English Romance of **William and the Werewolf**, 1832, one of the Roxburghe Club Publications. This letter, which was by the hand of Mr Herbert of Petworth, contains all that was known on this subject before Grimm; but when Grimm came he was, compared with all who had treated the subject, as a sober man amongst drunkards.

[26]

Bisclavaret in the **Lais** of Marie de France, 1, 178 seems to be a corruption of Bleizgarou, as the Norman **garwal** is of **garwolf**. See also Jamieson Dict., under *warwolf*.

[27]

Troldham, at kaste ham paa. Comp. the old Norse *hamr, hamfoer, hammadr, hamrammr*, which occur repeatedly in the same sense.

[28]

Comp. Vict. Hugo, *Notre-Dame de Paris*, where he tells us that the gipsies called the wolf *piedgris*. See also Grimm, *D. M.*, 633 and *Reinhart*, lv, ccvii, and 446.

[29]

Thus from the earliest times 'dog', 'hound', has been a term of reproach. Great instances of fidelity, such as 'Gellert' or the 'Dog of Montargis', both of which are Eastern and primeval, have scarcely redeemed the cringing currish nature of the race in general from disgrace. M. Francisque Michel, in his *Histoire des Races Maudites de da France et de l'Espagne*, thinks it probable that *Cagot*, the nickname by which the heretical Goths who fled into Aquitaine in the time of Charles Martel, and received protection from that king and his successors, were called by the Franks, was derived from the term *Canis Gothicus* or *Canes Gothi*. In modern French the word means hypocrite, and this would come from the notion of the outward conformity to the Catholic formularies imposed on the Arian Goths by their orthodox protectors. Etymologically, the derivation is good enough, according to Diez, *Romanisches Woerterbuch*; Provencal *ca*, dog; *Get*, Gothic. Before quitting *Cagot*, we may observe that the derivation of *bigot*, our bigot, another word of the same kind, is not so clear. Michel says it comes from *Vizigothus, Bizigothus*. Diez says this is too far-fetched, especially as 'Bigot', 'Bigod', was a term applied to the Normans, and not to the population of the South of France. There is, besides another derivation given by Ducange from a Latin chronicle of the twelfth century. In speaking of the homage done by Rollo, the first Duke of Normandy, to the King of France, he says:

Hic non dignatus pedem Caroli osculari nisi ad os suum levaret, cumque sui comites illum admonerent ut pedem Regis in acceptione tanti muneris, Neustriae provinciae, oscularetur, Anglica lingua respondit '*ne se bi got*', quod interpretatur 'ne per deum'. Rex vero et sui illum deridentes, et sermonem ejus corrupte referentes, illum vocaverunt Bigottum; unde Normanni adhuc Bigothi vocantur.

Wace, too, says, in the **Roman de Rou**, that the French had abused the Normans in many ways, calling them Bigos. It is also termed, in a French record of the year 1429, '**un mot tres injurieux**'. Diez says it was not used in its present sense before the sixteenth century.

[30]

The most common word for a giant in the Eddas was Joetunn (A. S. **coten**), which, strange to say, survives in the Scotch Etin. In one or two places the word **ogre** has been used, which is properly a Romance word, and comes from the French **ogre**, Ital. **orco**, Lat. **orcus**. Here, too, we have an old Roman god of the nether world degraded.

[31]

These paroxysms were called in Old Norse **Joetunmodr**, the **Etin mood**, as opposed to **Asmodr, the mood of the Aesir**, that diviner wrath which, though burning hot, was still under the control of reason.

[32]

It may be worth while here to shew how old and widespread this custom or notion of the 'naked sword' was. In the North, besides being told of Sigurd and Brynhildr, we hear it of Hrolf and Ingigerd, who took rest at night in a hut of leaves in the wood, and lay together, 'but laid a naked sword between them'. So also Saxo Grammaticus says of King Gorm, 'Caeterum ne inconcessum virginis amorem libidinoso complexu praeripere videretur, vicina latera non solum alterius complexibus exult, sed etiam **districto mucrone** secrevit. Lib. 9, p.179. So also Tristan and Isolt in Gottfried of Strasburg's poem, line 17,407-17.

Hierue ber vant Tristan einen sin,
Si giengen an ir bette wider,
Und leiten sich da wider nider,
Von einander wol pin dan,
Reht als man and man,
Niht als man and wip;
Da lac lip and lip,
In fremder gelegenheit,

Ouch hat Tristan geleit Sin ***swert bar*** enzwischen si.

And the old French Tristan in the same way:

Et qant il vit la nue espee

Qui entre eus deus les deseurout.

So the old English Tristrem, line 2,002-3:

His sword he drough titly

And laid it hem bitvene.

And the old German ballad in ***Des Knaben Wunderhorn***, 2, 276:

Der Herzog zog aus sein goldiges schwert,

Er leit es zwischen beide hert

Das schwert soll weder hauen noch schneiden,

Das Annelein soll ein megedli bleiben.

So Fonzo and Fenizia in the ***Pentamerone***, I, 9:

Ma segnenno havere fatto vuto a Diana, de non toccare la mogliere la notte, mese la spata arranata comme staccione 'miezo ad isso ed a Fenizia.

And in Grimm's story of 'The Two Brothers' where the second brother lays 'a double-edged sword' at night between himself and his brother's wife, who has mistaken him for his twin brother. In fact the custom as William Wackernagel has shewn in ***Haupt's Zeitschrift fuer Deutsches Alterthum*** was one recognized by the law; and so late as 1477, when Lewis, County Palatine of Veldenz represented Maximilian of Austria as his proxy at the betrothal of Mary of Burgundy, he got into the bed of state, booted and spurred, and laid a naked sword between him and the bride. Comp. Birkens Ehrenspiegel, p. 885. See also as a proof that the custom was known in England as late as the seventeenth century, ***The Jovial Crew***, a comedy first acted in 1641, and quoted by Sir W. Scott in his ***Tristrem***, p. 345, where it is said (Act V, sc. 2): 'He told him that he would be his proxy, and marry her for him, and lie with her the first night with a naked cudgel betwixt them.' And see for the whole subject, J. Grimm's ***Deutsche Rechts-Alterthuemer***, Goettingen, 1828, p. 168-70.

[33]

M. Moe, ***Introd. Norsk. Event*** (Christiania, 1851, 2d Ed.), to which the writer is largely indebted.

[34]

Note: The following list, which only selects the more prominent collections, will suffice to show that Popular Tales have a literature of their own:--Sanscrit. The *Pantcha Tantra*, 'The Five Books', a collection of fables of which only extracts have as yet been published, but of which Professor Wilson has given an analysis in the Transactions of the Asiatic Society, vol. I, sect. 2. The *Hitopadesa*, or 'Wholesome Instruction', a selection of tales and fables from the Pantcha Tantra, first edited by Carey at Serampore in 1804; again by Hamilton in London in 1810; again in Germany by A. W. von Schlegel in 1829, an edition which was followed in 1831 by a critical commentary by Lassen; and again in 1830 at Calcutta with a Bengali and English translation. The work had been translated into English by Wilkins so early as 1787, when it was published in London, and again by Sir William Jones, whose rendering, which is not so good as that by Wilkins, appeared after his death in the collected edition of his works. Into German it has been translated in a masterly way by Max Mueller, Leipzig, Brockhaus, 1844. Versions of these Sanscrit collections, the date of the latter of which is ascribed to the end of the second century of the Christian era, varying in many respects, but all possessing sufficient resemblance to identify them with their Sanscrit originals, are found in almost every Indian dialect, and in Zend, Arabic, Persian, Hebrew, Greek and Turkish. We are happy to be able to state here that the eminent Sanscrit scholar, Professor Benfey of Goettingen, is now publishing a German translation of the *Pantcha Tantra*, which will be accompanied by translations of numerous compositions of the same kind, drawn from unpublished Sanscrit works, and from the legends current amongst the Mongolian tribes. The work will be preceded by an introduction embracing the whole question of the origin and diffusion of fables and popular tales. The following will be the title of Prof. Benfey's work: '*Pantcha Tantra. Erster Theil, Fuenf Buecher Indischer Fabeln, Maerchen, and Erzaehlungen*. Aus dem Sanskrit uebersetzt, mit Anmerkungen and Einleitung ueber das Indische Grundwerk und dessen Ausfluesse, so wie ueber die Quellen und Verbreitung des Inhalts derselben. Zweiter Theil, Uebersetzungen und Anmerkungen.' Most interesting of all for our purpose is the collection of Sanscrit Tales, collected in the twelfth century of our era, by Somadeva Bhatta of Cashmere. This has been published in Sanscrit, and translated into German by Hermann Brockhaus, and the nature of its contents has already been sufficiently indicated. We may add, however, that Somadeva's collection exhibits the Hindoo mind in the twelfth century in a condition, as regards popular tales, which the mind of Europe has not yet reached. How old these stories and fables must have been in the East, we see both from the ***Pantcha Tantra*** and the ***Hitopadesa***, which are strictly didactic works, and only employ tales and fables to illustrate and inculcate a moral lesson. We in the West have got beyond fables and apologues, but we are only now collecting our popular tales. In Somadeva's time the simple tale no longer sufficed; it had to be fitted into and arranged with others, with an art and dexterity which is really marvellous; and so cleverly is this done, that it requires a mind of no little cultivation, and a head of more than ordinary clearness, to carry without confusion all the wheels within wheels, and fables within fables, which spring out of the original story as it proceeds. In other respects the popular tale loses in simplicity what it gains in intricacy by this artificial arrangement; and it is evident that in the twelfth century the Hindoo tales had been long since collected out of the mouths of the people, and reduced to writing; in a word, that the popular element had disappeared, and that they had passed into the written literature of the race. We may take this opportunity, too, to mention that a most curious collection of tales and fables, translated from Sanscrit, has recently been discovered in Chinese. They are on the eve of publication by M. Stanislas Julien, the first of Chinese scholars; and from the information on the matter which Professor Max Mueller has kindly furnished to the translator, it appears that they passed with Buddhism from India into China. The work from which M. Julien has taken these fables, which are all the more precious because the Sanscrit originals have in all probability perished,--is called ***Yu-lin***, or 'The Forest of Comparisons'. It was the work of Youen-thai, a great Chinese scholar, who was President of the Ministry of justice at Pekin in the year 1565 of our era. He collected in twenty-four volumes, after the labour of twenty years, during which he read upwards of four hundred works, all the fables and comparisons he could find in ancient books. Of those works, two hundred were translations from the Sanscrit made by Buddhist monks, and it is from eleven of these that M. Julien has translated his Chinese Fables. We need hardly say that this work is most anxiously expected by all who take an interest in such matters. Let it be allowed to add here, that it was through no want of respect towards the memory of M. de Sacy that the translator has given so much prominence to the views and labours of the Brothers Grimm in this Introduction.

To M. de Sacy belongs all the merit of exploring what may be called the old written world of fable. He, and Warton, and Dunlop, and Price, too, did the day's work of Giants, in tracing out and classifying those tales and fables which had passed into the literature of the Aryan race. But, besides this old region, there is another new hemisphere of fiction which lies in the mouths and in the minds of the people. This new world of fable the Grimms discovered, and to them belongs the glory of having brought all its fruits and flowers to the light of day. This is why their names must ever be foremost in a work on Popular Tales, shining, as their names must ever shine, a bright double star in that new hemisphere. In more modern times, the earliest collection of popular tales is to be found in the ***Piacevoli Notte*** of John Francis Straparola of Caravaggio, near Milan, the first edition of which appeared at Venice in 1550. The book, which is shamefully indecent, even for that age, and which at last, in 1606, was placed in the ***Index Expurgatorius***, contains stories from all sources, and amongst them nineteen genuine popular tales, which are not disfigured by the filth with which the rest of the volume is full. Straparola's work has been twice translated into German, once at Vienna, 1791, and again by Schmidt in a more complete form, ***Maerchen-Saal***, Berlin, 1817. But a much more interesting Italian collection appeared at Naples in the next century. This was the ***Pentamerone*** of Giambattista Basile, who wrote in the Neapolitan dialect, and whose book appeared in 1637. This collection contains forty-eight tales, and is in tone, and keeping, and diction, one of the best that has ever appeared in any language. It has been repeatedly reprinted at Naples. It has been translated into German, and a portion of it, a year or two back, by Mr. Taylor, into English. In France the first collection of this kind was made by Charles Perrault, who, in 1697, published eight tales, under a title taken from an old ***Fabliau***, ***Contes de ma mere L'Oye***, whence comes our 'Mother Goose'. To these eight, three more tales were added in later editions. Perrault was shortly followed by Madame D'Aulnoy (born in 1650, died 1705), whose manner of treating her tales is far less true to nature than Perrault's, and who inserts at will, verses, alterations, additions, and moral reflections. Her style is sentimental and over-refined; the courtly airs of the age of Louis XIV predominate, and nature suffers by the change from the cottage to the palace. Madame d'Aulnoy was followed by a host of imitators; the Countess Muerat, who died in 1710; Countess d'Auneuil, who died in 1700; M. de Preschac, born 1676, who composed tales of utter worthlessness, which may be read as examples of what popular tales are not, in the collection called *Le Cabinet des Fees*, which was published in Paris in 1785. Not much better are the attempts of Count Hamilton, who died in 1720; of M. de Moncrif, who died in 1770; of Mademoiselle de la Force, died 1724; of Mademoiselle l'Heritier died 1737; of Count Caylus, who wrote his *Feeries Nouvelles* in the first half of the 18th century, for the popular element fails almost entirely in their works. Such as they are, they may also be read in the *Cabinet des Fees*, a collection which ran to no fewer than forty-one volumes, and with which no lover of popular tradition need trouble himself much. To the playwright and the story- teller it has been a great repository, which has supplied the lack of original invention. In Germany we need trouble ourselves with none of the collections before the time of the Grimms, except to say that they are nearly worthless. In 1812-14 the two brothers, Jacob and William, brought out the first edition of their *Kinder-und Haus- Maerchen*, which was followed by a second and more complete one in 1822: 3 vols., Berlin, Reimer. The two first volumes have been repeatedly republished, but few readers in England are aware of the existence of the third, a third edition of which appeared in 1856 at Goettingen, which contains the literature of these traditions, and is a monument of the care and pains with which the brothers, or rather William, for it is his work, even so far back as 1820, had traced out parallel traditions in other tribes and lands. This work formed an era in popular literature, and has been adopted as a model by all true collectors ever since. It proceeded on the principle of faithfully collecting these traditions from the mouths of the people, without adding one jot or tittle, or in any way interfering with them, except to select this or that variation as most apt or beautiful. To the adoption of this principle we owe the excellent Swedish collection of George Stephens and Hylten Cavallius, *Svenska Folk-Sagor og Aefventyr*, 2 vols. Stockholm 1844, and following years; and also this beautiful Norse one, to which Jacob Grimm awards the palm over all collections, except perhaps the Scottish, of MM. Asbjoernsen and Moe. To it also we owe many most excellent collections in Germany, over nearly the whole of which an active band of the Grimm's pupils have gone gathering up as gleaners the ears which their great masters had let fall or let lie. In Denmark the collection of M. Winther, *Danske Folkeeventyr*, Copenhagen, 1823, is a praiseworthy attempt in the same direction; nor does it at all detract from the merit of H. C. Andersen as an original writer, to observe how often his creative mind has fastened on one of these national stories, and worked out of that piece of native rock a finished work of art. Though last not least, are to be reckoned the Scottish stories collected by Mr. Robert Chambers, of the merit of which we have already expressed our opinion in the text.

[35]

After all, there is, it seems, a Scottish word which answers to *Askepot* to a hair. See Jamieson's *Dictionary*, where the reader will find *Ashiepattle* as used in Shetland for a 'neglected child'; and not in Shetland alone, but in Ayrshire, *Ashypet*, an adjective, or rather a substantive degraded to do the dirty work of an adjective, 'one employed in the lowest kitchen work'. See too the quotation, 'when I reached Mrs. Damask's house she was gone to bed, and nobody to let me in, dripping wet as I was, but an *ashypet* lassy, that helps her for a servant.'-- *Steamboat*, p. 259. So again *Assiepet*, substantive 'a dirty little creature, one that is constantly soiled with *ass* or ashes'.

[36]

The Sagas contain many instances of Norsemen who sat thus idly over the fire, and were thence called *Kolbitr*, *coalbiters*, but who afterwards became mighty men.

www.bookjungle.com *email: sales@bookjungle.com fax: 630-214-0564 mail: Book Jungle PO Box 2226 Champaign, IL 61825*

The Codes Of Hammurabi And Moses
W. W. Davies

QTY

The discovery of the Hammurabi Code is one of the greatest achievements of archaeology, and is of paramount interest, not only to the student of the Bible, but also to all those interested in ancient history...

Religion   **ISBN:** *1-59462-338-4*   **Pages:132**
MSRP $12.95

The Theory of Moral Sentiments
Adam Smith

QTY

This work from 1749. contains original theories of conscience amd moral judgment and it is the foundation for systemof morals.

Philosophy **ISBN:** *1-59462-777-0*   **Pages:536**
MSRP $19.95

Jessica's First Prayer
Hesba Stretton

QTY

In a screened and secluded corner of one of the many railway-bridges which span the streets of London there could be seen a few years ago, from five o'clock every morning until half past eight, a tidily set-out coffee-stall, consisting of a trestle and board, upon which stood two large tin cans, with a small fire of charcoal burning under each so as to keep the coffee boiling during the early hours of the morning when the work-people were thronging into the city on their way to their daily toil...

Childrens   **ISBN:** *1-59462-373-2*   **Pages:84**
MSRP $9.95

My Life and Work
Henry Ford

QTY

Henry Ford revolutionized the world with his implementation of mass production for the Model T automobile. Gain valuable business insight into his life and work with his own auto-biography... "We have only started on our development of our country we have not as yet, with all our talk of wonderful progress, done more than scratch the surface. The progress has been wonderful enough but..."

Biographies/   **ISBN:** *1-59462-198-5*   **Pages:300**
MSRP $21.95